DEVIL'S
PITCHFORK

FORTHCOMING BY MARK TERRY

The Serpent's Kiss

ALSO BY MARK TERRY

Dirty Deeds
Catfish Guru

A DEREK STILLWATER NOVEL

THE

DEVIL'S
PITCHFORK

MARK TERRY

MIDNIGHT INK
WOODBURY, MINNESOTA

FIRST EDITION
First Printing, 2006

Book design by Donna Burch
Cover design by Kevin R. Brown
Cover U.S. capitol image © Digital Stock

Midnight Ink, an imprint of Llewellyn Publications

Library of Congress Cataloging-in-Publication Data
Terry, Mark, 1964–
    The devil's pitchfork : a Derek Stillwater novel / Mark Terry. — 1st ed.
    p. cm.
    ISBN-13: 978-0-7387-0883-6
    ISBN-10: 0-7387-0883-6
        1. Special forces (Military science)—Fiction. 2. Terrorism—Prevention—Fiction.
    I. Title.

    PS3620.E769D48 2006
    813'.6—dc22   2006048180

Midnight Ink
Llewellyn Publications
2143 Wooddale Drive, Dept. 0-7387-0883-6
Woodbury, MN 55125-2989, U.S.A.
www.midnightinkbooks.com

Printed in the United States of America

For my brother Pete.
Love ya, bro.

PROLOGUE

Descent

PROLOGUE

Iraq—1991

Derek Stillwater and Richard Coffee crouched on a desert ridge, peering across the expanse of sand toward an Iraqi ammunition depot. Dressed in biological containment suits camouflaged for night work with black face paint and tight black gloves, they watched the target site through night-vision goggles. They hated the suits. They were clumsy, bulky, and hot. Sweat soaked their skin and rolled down their backs and sides. Both men were thankful they didn't have to wear the gas masks unless all hell broke loose. They were both Special Forces. Above them the desert night was overcast, cloud cover at a maximum, no stars or moon visible. A Special Forces kind of night.

Coffee went about setting up a laser targeting system. Somewhere overhead flew an F-117A Stealth fighter. Once the ammunition depot was targeted and Stillwater gave an okay, the fighter would take out the depot, leaving a massive gaping hole in the Iraqi supply line.

Twenty miles away coalition troops were ready and waiting to break through the Iraqi defense.

Stillwater didn't like it. Through his night-vision goggles the desert glowed green. Two miles north he could see the shapes of men guarding the depot. Off to his left, much closer, was an Iraqi patrol. They were noisy and used flashlights; he found it hard to believe they would be so careless. But so far everything about the Iraqi army had surprised him. It had been amazingly easy to slip through its patrols in a specially equipped dune buggy, driving in the dark while wearing night-vision goggles.

Quickly Stillwater went about laying out his equipment. He was a specialist in biological and chemical weapons. The first thing he set up was a miniature weather station. Whether the Iraqis knew it or not, they had picked a good spot for their ammunition stores; the weather conditions here were unpredictable, particularly the wind, which shifted and veered and swirled around a series of low and high ridges on three sides of the depot.

The anemometer began to spin. Wind speed: 15 knots. Direction: unstable. Mostly a north or northwest wind. Stillwater grimaced. *Bad, bad, bad*, he thought. The Iraqis were known to have large stores of biological and chemical weapons. Saddam Hussein was a big fan of sarin and cyclosarin gas. If the bomber nailed the depot and the wind was blowing toward the U.S. and coalition troops, even at a distance of twenty miles there was likely to be fallout with unpredictable results.

In a briefing regarding the mission, Stillwater had recommended that allied troops stay even farther back. The answer: greater distance was not tactically efficient. Meaning when the depot was blown, the troops would advance quickly.

So now, on the front line, Stillwater had to make a decision. Were the weather conditions going to allow this bombing? Derek felt sand peppering the back of his neck. That was fine. If it began to hit his face, they were in trouble.

Suddenly, behind them appeared two Iraqi soldiers, also wearing night-vision goggles. They began to shout at Coffee and Stillwater in hoarse Farsi and point their guns.

"Dast kasidan! Payin! Payin!"

Not seeming to pay attention, Coffee clicked one more switch and gave Stillwater a thumbs-up.

Shit, thought Stillwater, and he hit a preprogrammed sequence on his radio, giving the all-ahead. His mission was clear. The targeting laser took priority over the safety of the troops.

The wind direction suddenly shifted from the west. If only it would hold. He watched the vane shift: north, west, north, north, west, south, west . . .

The soldiers barked orders, clearly wanting the two Americans to surrender. Slowly, eyes on the vane, Stillwater placed his hands on top of his head.

In a rough voice Coffee snarled, *"Madhar eta coon mae kun um!"*

The Iraqis began to scream at them.

"Offering to buy the beer?" Stillwater asked.

"I was suggesting that I would like to have anal sex with their mothers," Coffee said.

"Oh, good. I was worried you'd say something that might make matters worse." Stillwater didn't take his eyes off the weathervane.

West, west, west.

"Just buying time."

"I would prefer they didn't kill us—"

4

They didn't hear the F-117A fly overhead or see its batlike shadow blot out the sky. But Stillwater had a sense of the five-hundred-pound bombs coming down just prior to impact. The roar, even from two miles away, was deafening, setting off other bombs, a chain reaction of explosions. The ground shook, seemed to undulate like a writhing snake. For a moment it felt like the end of the world. Dust rose like flies from a corpse.

Stillwater, thrown to the ground with Coffee, kept his eyes on the weathervane.

An alarm went off in his ear, the small earphone connected to a chemical agent monitor, the second piece of equipment that was his responsibility. It was rigged for audio alarm only. The display that would indicate intensity and type of gas was blacked out for covert night action.

"Gas!" he shouted at Coffee.

But Coffee was rolling on the hard desert floor, handgun pulled, firing at the Iraqi soldiers, who had also been flung to the ground by the force of the shockwaves.

In the distance the depot continued to explode, armaments going off from the compression caused by the U.S. bombs. In comparison, Coffee's .45 seemed like a popgun.

Stillwater pulled his gas hood over his head and ran to Coffee, staggering as the ground shook beneath his feet. Coffee was gasping for air, scrabbling for his own hood. Snatching it from his hands, Stillwater yanked it over his head. *Antidote, antidote*, he thought, quickly grabbing for the kit attached to his belt.

With practiced hands he slammed together the ampule of atropine and injected it into Coffee's thigh. Coffee slumped to the ground, chest heaving. Turning, Stillwater saw that the Iraqis were on the ground, gasping for breath, clawing with bleeding fingers at their throats, dying for air. They would soon be dead.

Stillwater's gaze returned to the weathervane.

A gust of wind struck the helmet of his gas mask, sand making skittering sounds against the shield.

North, north, north.

The wind had shifted. It was blowing the poison gas and whatever else Saddam Hussein had in that depot. It was blowing the fallout toward the waiting troops.

He glanced at the Iraqi soldiers. Both were still, skin blistered, faces swollen, lying in pools of vomit and blood and shit.

Lugging Coffee onto his shoulders, Stillwater carried him to their dune buggy and dropped him into the passenger seat. Stillwater felt for a pulse beneath the hood.

Weak. But steady.

He'd live.

It took Stillwater only minutes to load their equipment into the dune buggy and haul ass out of there, back to the troops. As he drove, he radioed a warning of the cloud of toxic waste that was coming their way.

He hoped he wasn't too late.

PART I

The Gates of Hell

1

Baltimore, Maryland—Present

LIZ VARGAS LEANED AGAINST the wall outside the locker room on the second floor of U.S. Immunological Research. Just off her left shoulder, a sign read:

HOT LEVEL 4
HIGHEST LEVEL BIOCONTAINMENT
AUTHORIZED PERSONNEL ONLY

Beneath the sign, in blood red paint, was the spider-like biohazard symbol.

Liz tapped her foot and glanced at her watch. Michael was late. So what else was new? She didn't like working with Michael Ballard in Hot Level 4, but her usual partner, Jim Scully, had called in sick.

No one was allowed to work HL4 alone. No one. And since there were only five authorized people to work HL4, only five people whose ID badges would open the door to the locker room, she had needed to make arrangements. The two other people authorized had been unable to partner with her today. Frank Halloran, the head of the division, was in meetings all day and couldn't get out of them. Nancy Latrelle had turned her down. Liz was pretty sure Nancy would no longer be working HL4, the hot zone. They worked with the most dangerous and lethal infectious agents on the planet in HL4. Some people—most people with any degree of sanity—began to worry about working there. Any normal, intelligent human being began to worry about what one mistake, one slip of a glass pipette or a scalpel, might mean. Working with Ebola and Hantaviruses, Marburg, and others—the engineered nightmares—was not work for the squeamish. Nor was it work for the crazy. Crazy people weren't afraid. Sane people . . . well, sane people feared the demons inside HL4.

But Nancy probably hadn't developed that sort of problem. What Nancy seemed to have developed was far more common in hot zones: claustrophobia. In order to work in a hot zone like HL4, you had to wear a biohazard suit—a spacesuit—and some people couldn't handle it at all. And some who *could* handle it, like Nancy, started to lose their grip on it and began to sweat and panic inside the suit. It had happened the last three times Nancy had suited up.

Liz was pretty sure Nancy was done with Hot Level 4. So that left Michael. Who was chronically late.

She was just about ready to drop down to his office when the elevator door opened and a short, bustling man race-walked toward her down the fluorescent-lit corridor. He flung his arms up in the air when he saw her standing there. It was exactly his fast movements and nervous energy that made Michael Ballard a liability in a hot zone.

"Sorry, sorry," he said. "Angie called me, and we got into it. . . ."

Angie. The soon-to-be ex-wife. Yet another reason Liz didn't like to work with Michael. All the emotional agitation was not meant for Hot Level 4. In a hot zone you needed a cool head.

"She's starting to quibble over the boat. The boat! She didn't want me to buy it, she didn't want to go out on it, and now she wants to—"

"Michael! Are you ready for this?"

"Hey, sure, no—"

She came off the wall and stood squarely in front of him, tapping him on the chest, making sure she had his full attention.

"We have to do this," she said. "But I'm not going in there with you if you've got your undies in a bunch. Don't spend time thinking about Angie or your lawyer fees or your goddamned boat. Think about getting in and out of there without any mistakes. Pay attention."

"Hey, no problem."

Liz was an inch or two taller than Michael's five-five. She gazed into his blue eyes and saw him take a deep breath, relaxing. Centering himself. He became visibly calmer.

"Okay, sorry," he said. "You go in, get changed. I'll be ready in a few minutes."

The locker room for HL4 was unisex. With so few people qualified to work the space, there had been no sense putting in separate locker rooms.

"You're sure?"

He nodded and ran his left hand through his wiry brown hair. She noticed that he wasn't wearing his wedding band. She wondered if this was because he had taken it off in anticipation of the impending divorce or because no jewelry was allowed in the hot zone. "Yeah," he said. "I'm sure. I'll be fine. Go on."

She nodded and pressed her ID badge to the reader. A green light clicked on, and she pushed her way into the locker room.

Five miles away from the two-story building housing U.S. Immunological Research, three white panel vans traveled down I-695. Inside each van were four men, one driving and three in the back, waiting. They were all in contact with one another via scrambled radios. All but the drivers wore white Tyvek biohazard suits. Hanging around their necks were rubber North respirator masks with Lexan faceplates and two purple virus filters jutting out like insect mandibles. They were seven minutes out.

The locker room was tiny. It contained half a dozen metal lockers, a bench to sit on, a mirror, and shelves. Liz opened a locker and stripped naked. She took off her Timex Indiglo, her earrings, and the gold chain she wore around her neck and placed them on the top shelf of the locker. She twisted her diamond ring and wedding band. The diamond definitely had to go. It was impossible to wear a diamond ring under rubber gloves, and the risk of the diamond cutting the thick rubber was too great. She took off both rings, her heart thudding in her chest. Her husband, Alan, had died two years before in a motorcycle accident, and she still wore the rings. She hated to take off the wedding band. Usually she did, just like the rules said. But she also knew that most everybody took some sort of good-luck charm into the hot zone. Level 4 pathogens did that to seemingly rock-steady people. She put the diamond ring on the shelf but slipped the simple gold wedding band back on her finger.

Quickly she pulled on a set of green surgical scrubs. Underwear was not allowed into the hot zone. She donned a cloth surgical cap. She wore her blond hair short, partly to make this work easier, and partly because she thought she looked pretty good with it short. She worked hard at keeping in shape, was still two years shy of forty, and knew she could pass for younger thirties—not in her twenties, that wasn't possible. But thirty-two, maybe.

She took a calm, steadying look at herself in the mirror, then walked to the door and knocked on it so Michael would know he could come in. She crossed the room to the opposite door and pushed it open, feeling pressure sucking at the door. Everything beyond the locker room was under negative air pressure, designed to keep nasty germs—bugs—from floating out on the air currents. The room beyond, Level 2, was filled with blue ultraviolet light. UV light destroyed viruses and bacteria. Level 2 was a staging area into HL4.

A mile from U.S. Immunological Research, the three vans sped off the expressway onto an exit ramp, then split up, one van heading for the rear entrance, two for the main entrance. The two-story U.S. Immunological Research building was a long, low-slung concrete box with few windows. The second floor contained no windows at all. It looked industrial and uninteresting except for an unusually large number of air vents and stacks on the roof. It was surrounded by a largely empty parking lot, narrow grass borders populated with mature ash, oak, and pine trees, and a six-foot-tall chain-link fence. The gates—one in the front and one in the rear—weren't designed to keep serious intruders out, but rather to provide a psychological barrier to the randomly curious. When asked, employees of U.S. Immunological Research told people they were a small biotech company trying to create new vaccines, which was essentially true. A uniformed security guard manned a booth at both entrances, and employees were required to display ID and sign in with the guard before a barrier arm was raised.

The three vans were two minutes out.

Liz walked through Level 2, which consisted of a shower stall lit by UV light. There was soap and shampoo. She grabbed a pair of socks off a shelf as she passed and slipped them on, then moved into the staging area that contained a desk, sink, and chair. On the desk was a roll of duct tape, which she used to tape the base of her pants to her socks, creating a seal. Then she slipped on a pair of latex gloves and proceeded to tape the shirtsleeve to the gloves. It was a pain in the neck to use tape while wearing rubber gloves, but she managed it without tearing the gloves.

In an overgrown closet next to the desk, her spacesuit hung with four others. It was the newest out from Chemturion, a prototype, bright blue and bulky. She laid it out on the concrete floor and slithered into it. She was staggering to her feet when Michael appeared, his wrists and ankles taped. She shouldered her way into the sleeves, then pulled the facemask over her head, zipping up the zipper. Her faceplate immediately fogged up. Coiled on the wall were plastic air hoses. She unhooked one and plugged it into the suit, which instantly inflated with pressurized air. Her faceplate cleared, but she could barely hear through the roar of the air. She watched as Michael donned his own spacesuit and hooked up to the hoses. They took turns examining each other's fittings and connections, taking extra time to make sure there weren't any

13

breaches in the suits. They each gave the other a thumbs-up, un-hooked their air hoses, and proceeded to the passage leading into Hot Level 4.

It was a stainless steel airlock with nozzles built into the ceiling and walls that could spray water and bleach or Lysol for decon-tamination. It was called the decon room on the technical specs, though everyone who worked HL4 called it Styx. Liz didn't know who had called it Styx first, but the name of the mythological river one crossed into the afterlife had stuck for the decon room. Black humor, to be sure.

At the far end was another heavy metal door. Liz unlatched the door, thinking, *Welcome to Hades*, and stepped into the hot zone.

The vans' attacks were so closely coordinated that two of the ve-hicles hit the front gate at almost exactly the same time the solo van hit the rear gate. Pulling up to the gates, the vans' side doors slid open, and fully geared men fired their Colt XM-177s into the guardhouses, the 45mm rounds immediately shredding the secu-rity guards. Roaring forward, splintering the gate arms, the vans raced to the entrances. The two vans in the front pulled to the front door, and five armed men dressed in white biohazard suits exploded through the main doors. They fired their machine guns at the shocked guards at the main entrance, racing through the main corridor at a dead run, hitting the elevator in seconds. Two white-suited men stayed outside the elevator and fired at anyone who stuck a head out of an office as their three companions rode the elevator to the second floor.

The rear van took a similar approach: only two men went in through the loading dock, emptying their weapons at anyone they saw, breaching the main building and setting up perimeters at two crossways so no one could get to the elevator.

Hot Level 4 opened into a small concrete-block room, about ten feet by sixteen. The walls were covered with metal cabinets that contained a variety of laboratory materials and were lit by UV lights. Everywhere was the red biohazard symbol. At the opposite end of the room was a long concrete corridor with rooms jutting off it. Some of those rooms contained laboratories with microscopes and hoods and centrifuges, while others contained animals—caged monkeys in three of the rooms—and yet others were autopsy suites.

Momentarily unhooked from the air supply, Liz shouted, "We need to feed the monkeys, then check the Marburg cultures. Frank said—"

Above their heads a yellow light began to strobe. There were two lights, one yellow, one red. The yellow one indicated someone was entering HL4. That was unexpected, but they had just a moment to be glad it wasn't the red strobe light. The red light indicated that the negative pressure air system had been compromised and any bugs in the area might be able to get to the outside world.

Their relief was short-lived as two figures in white Tyvek biohazard suits burst into the hot zone. Both carried machine guns. One had a bulky bag slung over his shoulder.

"What the hell?" Michael stepped forward, hands held out in a "stop" gesture. "Who the hell—"

The machine guns chattered. Michael flew backward, blood spattering his blue suit. Clumsy in her spacesuit, Liz spun and began to sprint down the hallway, hoping to dive into one of the rooms. She could lock herself in. She was into the corridor when a massive impact struck her back and, slamming into the concrete-block walls, she was flung to the ground.

She heard the two men shouting to each other in a foreign language. She didn't move. Didn't want to bring their attention to the fact she was alive.

Alive!

She didn't know why she was alive. Her back hurt like she'd been hit with a sledgehammer, but she otherwise seemed uninjured. Her heart thundered in her chest, her breathing fogging her faceplate. *Oh God!* she thought. *Don't let them see the mist on the faceplate.*

Out of the corner of her eye, she saw the two figures disappear into the first room on the left, the storage room for the frozen samples of all the Level 4 pathogens. It contained refrigerators, freezers, and liquid nitrogen containers.

Who were they?

She heard one of the men say something. It sounded . . . Asian? She didn't know. Foreign. She tried to focus on the words. Tried to remember, but her brain wasn't working right. Her usually nimble mind seemed to be stuck in a pit of thick tar. There was a dim rumble and clatter, then a hissing sound. A moment later she heard the sound of footsteps as the figures left Hot Level 4.

She tried to take a deep breath but found she couldn't. When she tried to inhale, a blistering shot of pain seared across her back and shoulder blades. She was getting sleepy, her eyes barely able to open. *God*, she thought. *Maybe I am dying.* And then she realized that without an air hose hooked up, she was rapidly depleting the remaining oxygen in her suit. Staggering cautiously to her feet, she noted that the yellow strobe light had stopped, but she could hear klaxons going all throughout the building. Reaching over, she snagged an air hose and hooked it up to her spacesuit. Her suit inflated again, the roar in her ears almost a comfort. She looked down at Michael, lying still in a puddle of blood, and began to shake. Then it hit her, hit her hard, the shock, the fear . . . and she crumpled again to the hard floor.

2

Chesapeake Bay, Maryland

DEREK STILLWATER LEANED FORWARD and dug his paddle into the flat surface of Chesapeake Bay. He was far out in the bay on his ocean-going kayak, the afternoon sun beating down hard, spangles of reflected light like silver fish darting along the waves. Only three miles into a fifteen-mile workout, the tank top beneath his life vest was already soaked with sweat. In the distance he heard the beat of helicopter rotors, not unusual in this very busy body of water. He knew from living on the bay that Coast Guard helicopters routinely flew overhead, as well as military, private, and tourist choppers.

He aimed the prow of the kayak toward the Chesapeake Bay Bridge and paddled hard. He was only starting to warm up, the muscles in his shoulders and back starting to loosen as the blood and oxygen flowed. Sucking in the salt air, Derek felt good. Life was good. A beautiful day, gorgeous water, the sun on his face, skimming across the waves like a dolphin.

The sound of the helicopter grew louder. Turning his head, he saw a red, white, and blue Coast Guard chopper sweep around him, very low.

Jesus, he thought. The prop was kicking up so many waves he was afraid he might capsize.

The helicopter's loudspeaker boomed, "Are you Dr. Derek Still-water?"

He gave a thumbs-up.

The voice from the helicopter: "We're dropping someone down to help you up."

Stillwater sighed. This was not good news. So much for the beautiful day. From the open door of the helicopter, a figure in a black wetsuit began to descend on a rope. When the officer hit the water, he swam over to Stillwater, rope towed behind him.

"Secretary Johnston ordered us to find you ASAP and deliver you to an investigation site, sir. There are cops at your boat and cutters cruising the bay. We got to you first. You're going to need to take off your vest and put this harness on."

The Coast Guard officer had a deep voice with a Texas twang.

"This is a three-thousand-dollar kayak," Stillwater said, slouching out of his life vest. "I'm not going to just abandon it." He paused, squinting up into the down-blast of the chopper rotor. "Any experience with kayaks?"

The Texan broke into a broad grin. "Yes, sir."

Derek nodded and slipped into the harness. He handed over the paddle and shouted, "Slip 112, Bayman's Marina, the *Salacious Sally*. Just leave the kayak on the rear deck."

"Don't worry, sir. I'll take care of her."

"Yeah, and have fun."

The Texan laughed. "Yes, sir. You too."

Stillwater shook his head. "Un-fucking-likely." The Texan gave a thumbs-up to the chopper, and they reeled Derek Stillwater skyward.

The pilot of the helicopter was a young woman with black hair cut in a wedge. She had flashing green eyes and an oval face, and Stillwater thought she was pretty cute, though entirely too young to be behind the controls of a helicopter. He kept both observations to himself. There was another coastguardsman on the flight deck, manning the winch. He helped Stillwater in.

Derek shouted, "Can you land at the marina? I need some things."

"We're to take you directly to the—"

"I have two Go Packs on my boat. I have to have them!" The wind roaring into the chopper was so loud they could hardly hear each other. "Can you stop there?"

"Yes, sir. We'll call ahead and have the local cops clear the lot. Will you be long?"

"No."

The guardsman was a lean redhead with freckles. *I'm getting old*, Derek thought, darting another glance at the pilot. *Well, maybe not too old . . .*

The chopper ascended in a hurry, arcing toward land. Through the open cockpit Derek watched the Texan in his kayak diminish in size. *Going, going, gone,* he thought.

In about four minutes the chopper landed in the marina parking lot. On each end two cop cars, lights flashing, were keeping people at bay. Jumping out, Stillwater dashed to the docks, aiming for slip 112, his boat and home, a fifty-two-foot Chris Craft Constellation. It was a large marina, heavy on sailboats rather than cabin cruisers. Derek didn't know why that was the case, but it was, the marina looking like a denuded forest with hundreds of masts jutting skyward. He jumped aboard, unlocked the cabin door, quickly snatched a fax from the machine, snagged a blue nylon frame backpack and a military-issue duffel bag, and sprinted back to the helicopter. He threw his Go Packs into the chopper and clambered in after.

He gave an okay and they lifted off. Derek glanced at the fax.

To: Dr. Derek Stillwater, PhD
From: James Johnston, Secretary
      Department of Homeland Security

CODE RED
Immediately evaluate, coordinate and investigate assault on U.S. Immunological Research in Baltimore, MD. Preliminary reports indicate possible theft of a Level 4 bio-engineered infectious agent by unknown subjects. FBI on scene. Inform ASAP.

Below the typed message was a handwritten note. It said:

Why aren't you wearing your goddamned phone?
Godspeed and take care. JJ

Derek tore the message into pieces and let them flutter out the open cockpit door. Then he dug through his nylon pack and drew out a pair of jeans, a T-shirt, socks, underwear, and a pair of shoes. Stripping, he noticed the cute pilot taking a glance over her shoulder. Buck naked, he grinned, made a turn-around gesture with his finger, and shouted, "Not on the first date."

The copilot grinned, then looked startled. "What are you doing?"

Having pulled on his clothing, Derek was holding his swimsuit and tank top out the hatch. "Drying my clothes," he said.

From the marina it was a short hop over Baltimore to the incident site. The chopper set down in the parking lot of U.S. Immunological Research. Before climbing out, Derek scrambled up next to the pilot. "Thanks for the lift. What's your name?"

"Cynthia Black."

"Cindy?" He offered his hand. "Derek Stillwater. Mind if I call you when this is over?"

"When what's over?" she said, shaking his hand.

He shrugged. "If I get called in, it usually means the end of the world."

She considered him for a moment. "Well," she said, "if it doesn't end, sure, give me a call." She picked up a pen Velcroed to the dashboard. "Got some paper?"

Stillwater held up his hand. "Write it here."

Cynthia Black cocked an eyebrow, then scribbled her cell phone number on the palm of Stillwater's hand. "Good luck."

He grinned, clutched a chain around his neck for a moment, then tipped a salute to the other guardsman and jumped out of the chopper, Go Packs over each shoulder.

3

THE COAST GUARD HELICOPTER lifted off into the azure sky, and Derek ran about thirty yards before he was surrounded by tense, armed men. Three of them wore suits, but four were decked out in military fatigues. All of them were aiming their weapons—a variety of rifles and handguns—directly down his throat.

He froze. "Whoa! I'm not moving! I. Am. *Not*. Moving!"

One of the suits said, "Identify yourself!"

Still unmoving, he said, "Derek Stillwater. Department of Homeland Security. My wallet and ID are in my right rear pocket."

Some sort of silent communication spun around the circle, then one of the Army guys lowered his M-16, stepped over, and plucked Derek's ID from his pocket.

He flipped it open and read. "Okay. He's legit. Says you're a troubleshooter."

The men lowered their weapons. "That's the job title," Derek said. "Who's running things?"

The head suit, a slender blond guy wearing wire-rimmed glasses, said, "Spigotta. Hang on. I'll let him know you're coming."

Two of the suits led Derek to the building's entrance. It didn't take a trained eye to see that it had been shot to pieces. Derek paused to take in the destruction. His gaze lingered on the human-shaped mounds beneath blood-soaked white sheets. The odor of death and blood and cordite lingered in the air. He flinched. Images of war zones flashed in his head. Iraq. Panama. Bodies rotting in the sun, flies buzzing in swarms. For a moment he swayed, then took a deep breath, returning to the present, which wasn't much better. He'd come after the photographs and triage, but before they could move the bodies out. He felt something clench in his stomach, thought, *Good God, what do we have here?*

Blond Suit, who hadn't bothered to ID himself, described what they thought had happened: the three vans, the automatic weapons, the penetration of the building. "We've got guys going over the security tapes now."

"How many casualties?"

"Looks like twenty-three dead, eighteen wounded. Let's go."

Before following, Derek turned around and scanned past the chain-link fence. There were mobs of TV crews, onlookers, and cop cars. He realized he'd probably make the news with his dramatic entrance and hoped everyone had the sense to keep their mouths shut about him.

Blond Suit was looking at him impatiently. "Spigotta's debriefing a couple of the scientists. Hope we can figure out what this is all about."

24

I'm afraid I already know exactly what this is all about, Derek thought, and followed the agent into the facility. He processed the sight of all the vent stacks on top of the building. He knew that meant heavy-duty air filtering and treatment. Usually it meant negative air pressure and infectious agents and chemicals that God should never have invented, that human beings should never have discovered.

"What time did this go down?" Derek asked.

"11:43."

It was 1:30. Derek reflected that the response time had been pretty good overall. He was led down a tiled corridor that seemed too utilitarian to fit a for-profit company. The place was swarming with crime-scene people who looked federal, maybe military. He'd already figured some sort of military involvement from the soldiers outside, but he had never heard of this place.

Blond Suit knocked on a door and pushed it open. Three people were inside what appeared to be a conference room. There was a projection screen, three tables pushed together to form a large conference area, and a mishmash of chairs. Low budget, he guessed.

Two people were seated, a man and a woman. The man was in a white shirt and dark tie and khaki slacks. His hair was gray and short, almost military in style. There was something about his bearing that shouted military—the stiff back, the square shoulders. He looked tired, impatient, his big hands tapping on his chair's armrests.

The woman was blond and looked like she was in shock. Her blue eyes had that deer-in-the-headlights look, and her complexion was gray. But she seemed to focus on him with interest. The other guy didn't. He just looked impatient.

The guy standing looked big and muscular, like he lifted weights. Maybe in his fifties, his face was craggy, jaw square, accustomed to being in charge. He snapped, "You from Homeland?"

Derek set his gear down and proffered first his ID, then his hand.

"Huh." The guy took his hand. "Agent Rick Spigotta, FBI." He pointed to the two others. "Dr. Frank Halloran, head of this facility, and Dr. Elizabeth Vargas. We were just going over some things. Here's what we got so far. Three white vans merged on the facility right around 11:45, give or take. Two went through the front gate, using automatic weapons to take out the guard. At the same time a van took out the rear entrance. Looks nicely coordinated. Two guys went in the back way—the loading dock—taking out everyone they saw. ATF and the Bureau people are working the scenes now."

"What is this place?" Derek interrupted.

Spigotta glared at him. "Why don't you sit down, Dr. Stillwater. We've got a lot of ground to cover, and it'd be best if you saved your questions for the end. Or am I going to have trouble with you?"

Derek slid into a seat at an angle from Halloran and Vargas. "No, no trouble. Sorry."

Liz Vargas said, "We're a biological-warfare think tank. Kind of a practical one. We try to come up with vaccines and cures for typical biowarfare agents. Our funding is largely through the Pentagon."

"Any relationship with USAMRIID?" The United States Army Medical Research Institute of Infectious Diseases at Fort Detrick in Frederick, Maryland, was the heart of the U.S. Army's research into biowarfare.

"We consult with—"

Spigotta spat out, "Later, dammit." To Derek: "There are people from Detrick on the way. We'll get to that."

"Go on," Derek said.

Spigotta described how the commandos entered the building, rode up in the elevator, and penetrated Hot Level 4. Which is when he let Liz Vargas talk.

Liz didn't think she had been out for very long when she regained consciousness. For a few disoriented seconds, she didn't know where she was. Then she realized with horror that she was in the hot zone, and the last few minutes flooded in on her. Sitting up abruptly—too abruptly in a spacesuit—she looked over at Michael, then scuttled over to him. Dead. Without a shadow of a doubt, dead. Not only had the bullets stitched a bloody zipper from waistline to collar, Michael's plastic faceplate had been shattered.

She looked away, panting, knowing that to vomit in the spacesuit would be a major problem. Slowly her gorge receded and she felt herself edge back under control.

The intruders had been in the storage room. What had they taken? Walking slowly toward the room, booted feet kicking aside spent shell casings, she stepped into the bare cinder-block space. The walls had been covered with thick white goop, as had all the walls and floors in the hot zone, to prevent pathogens from seeping through the concrete. There were three chest freezers capable of −70 degrees Celsius. But it was the waist-high liquid-nitrogen tanks that drew her attention. All three were plastered with biohazard warnings and the blood red biohazard petal symbol. This was the heart of Hot Level 4, where the worst bugs on the planet were stored. But how to inventory?

And then she saw it.

A black binder, pages encased in acetate. It lay open on the counter. Normally it would be on a shelf, one of seven such books documenting the contents of each nitrogen tank and freezer.

She stared at the open page. Beads of sweat began to roll down her forehead, into her eyes, burning. She blinked, unable to wipe the moisture away or to rub her eyes. She blinked again, eyes tearing even more. She shook her head, tasted bitter bile as her guts twisted. "Oh dear God," she prayed. "Don't let it be."

With trembling hands she punched the four-digit code to allow entry into the tank, and following the coding in the book, removed a stack of triangular storage boxes. Liquid nitrogen fog curled around the edges of the tank, reminding her of playing with dry ice as a child. Box 6. Tubes 6 through 25. She pulled thick insulated gloves over the three layers of gloves she already wore—the new gloves to protect from the liquid nitrogen—and opened the box. Empty.

Tears trickled down her cheeks.

During her recitation Derek climbed to his feet and began to pace the conference room. He stopped and stood staring out the room's sole window. The media crowd had grown. Helicopters circled like turkey vultures.

"What did they steal?" Spigotta demanded.

"It's a . . . an entirely bioengineered organism," Liz said.

"What's that mean?" Spigotta said. "What's that mean? 'Entirely bioengineered'?"

Without turning from the window, Derek said, "You ever work a bioterror case before, Agent Spigotta?" His voice was mild, just curious, it said. Nonconfrontational.

"I worked the anthrax mail case."

"Ah," Derek said. "Well, that makes me feel better."

"You got a problem?" Spigotta snapped.

"We've all got a problem," Derek said. Glancing over his shoulder, he said, "Go on. What's it called?"

"Chimera M13. Like I said, it's completely bioengineered."

"Virus, bacteria, or prion?" Derek said.

"What?" Spigotta said, his face turning red.

"Not knowing the difference in a case like this is like not knowing the difference between a revolver and a semiautomatic," Derek said. "You need to get up to speed on the vocabulary."

"It's a virus," Liz said.

"You *made* a virus?" Spigotta asked.

Liz Vargas nodded.

Halloran cleared his throat. "Dr. Eckard Wimmer from the State University of New York at Stony Brook constructed a poliovirus completely from scratch in 2002. The military funded the project. They did it solely from data found on the Internet and chemicals and genetic components available from commercial medical supply houses. Using $300,000 of military funding, they created a poliovirus entirely in the lab, injected it into animals, and proved that it worked. That's the level of genetic engineering we're capable of. We can literally create life. It was possible. So we wanted to know if it was a practical possibility to manufacture a completely new pathogen in the lab. If we could do it, terrorists could do it. So we brainstormed, decided to see if we could create a virus with the toughness of hepatitis, the immunosuppression qualities of *Yersinia pestis*—"

"Bubonic plague," Derek said. "A bacterium." He didn't turn from the window.

"Yes," Halloran said. "We decided it should have the infectious properties of Ebola—and the hemorrhagic qualities, as well—yet still be transmissible as an aerosol. Weaponizable, in other words."

"And you succeeded?" Spigotta asked, dropping into a chair. He looked as if they had hit him in the forehead with a ball-peen hammer.

"Yes. We succeeded."

"Do you have an antidote for it? Antibiotics?"

Derek spoke up. "We're back to basic vocabulary again. It's a virus. It doesn't respond to antibiotics. Does it respond to protease inhibitors or any of the antivirals?"

"No," Halloran said. "As far as we know, it doesn't respond to anything. Bleach can kill it. That's it. It's highly infectious, can be transmitted through the air, in water, on food, by touch. It remains alive and active on plain surfaces like a countertop for as long as six days. From infection to first symptoms, it's twelve hours, sometimes less. Around twelve hours the subjects develop internal bleeding, usually bloody noses, which rapidly progresses to bleeding from the ears and the rectum. Within another six hours the internal organs are so compromised that soft tissues—eyes, mouth, gums, penis, vagina, and bruised skin—are bleeding uncontrollably. Eventually even the skin deteriorates, but by that time most hosts are essentially dead."

"Death occurs within twenty-four hours?" Derek asked.

"As early as eighteen hours, depending on where the infection site is," Liz Vargas said.

"And this is what a bunch of terrorists stole?" Spigotta's voice had risen in anger and disbelief. "You invented this—this Chimera—just to prove it could be done, then you kept it? Why in God's name didn't you destroy it? Whatever possessed you to put it in cold storage?! Why in hell did you *save* it?!"

Still looking out the window, Derek muttered, "The devil's pitchfork."

Halloran looked startled. Spigotta snarled, "What did you say?"

Derek turned from the window, his expression grim. "When human beings steal the devil's pitchfork, they don't destroy it. They think by stealing it they've stopped the devil." His gaze rested on Frank Halloran. "Instead, you've become the devil." He swallowed, his Adam's apple bobbing. "Congratulations."

4

THE MAN THEY CALLED Fallen stepped out of the white van, looked around, and took in the surroundings. They had parked the three vans on the second level of the Frederick Municipal Airport parking garage. He spotted the security cameras and turned, acting as if he did not notice; acting as if he were just an average businessman heading out of town. He and the rest of his people had rid themselves of their white Tyvek suits and their biological hazard masks after Lee had transferred the transport container into another double-lined, completely sealable container. They now wore nondescript slacks and shirts, their Colt XM-177s stowed in gym bags and suitcases.

A private jet, a Lear, Fallen thought, roared down the runway and leapt into the sky. Once the decibels diminished, he looked to Lee and asked him in Korean if the samples were safe.

Lee, who had gone into the hot zone with him, just nodded.

His men all looked at him, waiting for direction. Fallen had recruited them from various countries. They were specialists in a wide assortment of military and espionage skills—all warriors of one sort or another—who had fallen from their government's graces. Fallen had offered them money first. Then he had offered them a sense of belonging. Finally, he had offered them a sense of mission. They were fanatically loyal to him, to his vision.

Fallen's face split into a wicked grin. "Comrades," he said. "That went perfectly. On to the next stage of the operation."

They dispersed, all except one of the men, a short, wiry man with curly hair the color of weak tea cut close to his scalp.

"Dieter?" Fallen said, slipping into German. "*Was machst du da?*" (What are you doing there?)

Dieter stepped out of one of the vans and carefully shut the panel door, then turned to Fallen. He described the presents he had left in the vans.

Fallen was impressed. Dieter had special skills. He had simply told him to sabotage the vans for when the authorities had found them. But Dieter, like so many of his people, had surpassed his expectations.

"Dieter, *du bist ein Klugscheißer!*" (You are a clever shit.)

Dieter crawled into the second van, his thick voice wafting out of the door. "*Ich bin ein tödlich Scheißer.*" (I am a deadly shit.)

"*Gut,*" Fallen said. "*Das ist gut.*"

Once Dieter was done with all three vans, he followed Fallen from the second level to the first, where the rest of his people waited. As he walked Fallen pulled out a cellular phone and placed a call. It was answered by a woman.

"Nadia," Fallen said, and spoke in Russian. "*Dushka*, the operation has gone perfectly."

"You are safe?"

"We all are. Have you been tracking the enemy?"

"*Da*. The FBI, led by a Richard Spigotta. And the Department of Homeland Security, a Dr. Derek Stillwater."

Fallen's hand gripped the cell phone. "Who?"

"Dr. Derek Stillwater."

Fallen's eyes flashed, and for a moment he felt a rage that threatened to engulf him. He whispered, a harsh voice, "I was promised. *I was promised!*"

"Fallen—"

"No," Fallen whispered into the phone. "No. I need you for this. You and only you. You must track this Derek Stillwater. Where is he now?"

"Probably at U.S. Immunological Research."

"Pick him up there if you can. Then get back to me immediately. Have them pull his records so you can identify him. Follow him."

"Yes. Be careful."

"You, too, *Dushka*. You too." *Dushka*. Darling.

Fallen clicked off the telephone, the anger clear on his face. His men watched him carefully. He took a deep breath, thinking of empty promises and of betrayal. He thought of things that might go wrong, the uncontrollable elements of any operation.

Einstein had said that God did not play dice with the universe.

Fallen was certain that Einstein had been wrong. God routinely played dice with the universe and took great pleasure in unexpected turns of chance.

Derek Stillwater was an unexpected problem.

He paused, thinking, then climbed into one of the waiting vehicles, a black Mercedes sport utility vehicle.

Derek Stillwater could be an asset. Or Derek Stillwater could be a major problem.

Thinking of divine powers and plans, Fallen wondered which Derek Stillwater would turn out to be. He wondered if he would be forced to kill Derek Stillwater.

He wondered *when* he would be forced to kill Derek Stillwater.

And he imagined dice rolling across the sky and knew that he was the one who was flinging them.

5

U.S. Immunological Research

DEREK STOOD FRONT AND center. "Okay. I'm going into HL4. Who's qualified to go in with me?" He let his gaze settle on Halloran and Vargas.

"I will," Liz said. She swallowed hard, looking ill.

"Now wait a minute," Halloran said. "Who are you? Nobody goes in the hot zone unless they're—"

Derek said, "I was trained in the Level 4 facility at USAMRIID. I spent the Gulf War on the front lines as a bio and chem warfare specialist, then I spent a year or two afterward defusing biowarheads in Iraq. Then I joined UNSCOM as a weapons inspector until Saddam Hussein kicked us out in '98." He paused. "I'm qualified. I'm going in. And with all due respect, Doctor, you don't really have all that much say about it right at the moment."

He turned to Spigotta. "I've got an underwater camera in my Go Pack. I'll get pics so you can see things. Send in the Detrick people when they get here. In the meantime there are a few things

36

you might consider." Derek held up a finger. "One, I want to see the local security cameras." He added a finger, counting off his points. "Two, I suggest you start a team of as many as you can getting every traffic cam, ATM camera, or security tape in a five-mile radius of this facility. See if we can get a look at the people in these vans." Another finger. "Three, somebody with an ID badge and somebody who knew or had access to the entrance codes to HL4 is involved. Better find out—"

"We know that," Spigotta growled. "James Scully. It was his ID. He called in sick today. I've sent a couple agents to his house."

"He's not involved in this," Halloran said. "Jim and I came here together from USAMRIID. He's completely trustworthy."

"He's sure as hell involved, Doctor," Spigotta snarled. "It was his ID badge that gave them access." Ignoring Halloran further, Spigotta turned to Derek, his face twisted in skepticism. "Anything else, Stillwater?"

Derek turned to Liz Vargas. "The language the two men spoke to each other. Can you repeat any of it?"

Liz sighed. "I . . . I don't know. It sounded Asian."

Derek sat in the chair next to her. "Close your eyes. Think back. Listen."

Liz did as he said. A flurry of emotions flitted across her heart-shaped face. Then, recognition. "'Polly' . . . kind of . . . 'Pah-lee,'" she said. "And the other said something like, 'Yee ruin . . . something, something . . . see duh rule.' Or something like that."

Derek looked up at Spigotta. The FBI agent shrugged. Halloran shrugged too. Derek, thinking for a moment, said, "How about 'Pa-Li' and, hmm . . . 'Yi-Ru-Han Kyoung-Wu-Ee-Neun Seo-Du-Reul Su-Ga Up-Seum-Ni-Da'? How's that?"

Slowly, Liz nodded. "Yes. Yeah, I think so." She tried out the words. "Yes, that sounds about right, I guess."

"Okay, Stillwater. Spill it." Spigotta looked, if possible, even crankier than before.

"Korean," Derek said. "The first guy said, 'Hurry,' and the other guy said, 'You can't hurry this.'"

"You speak Korean," Spigotta said. Not really a question, more a statement of disbelief. Or suspicion.

"Not much. But I spent some time in Korea along the DMZ when I was in Special Forces. I'm good with languages and picked up a few words and phrases." Derek cocked an eyebrow at Spigotta. "Korean."

Liz Vargas, Frank Halloran, and Agent Spigotta led Derek Stillwater to the second-floor staging area to HL4. An armed soldier stood guard at the locker room door. Derek thought, *Barn door—locked; horse—gone; Halloran's career—over.*

Halloran said, "I still think this is a bad idea. What do you expect to find in there?"

Derek shrugged. "If I knew, I wouldn't have to go in."

Spigotta said, "Take pictures. Don't mess around."

Derek frowned. "Is the HMRU on their way?" The HMRU was the FBI's Hazardous Materials Recovery Unit.

"Yes."

"Good. They can deal with this crime scene. USAMRIID can deal with this crime scene. But aside from that, I'm the only one here who can deal with this crime scene. You'll have to live with it."

"Don't fuck it up."

"I'll go in," Derek said, "look around, take pictures. When the USAMRIID and HMRU people get here, they'll be able to use my pics to make a plan for clearing the evidence and retrieving Michael Ballard's body. That's going to present quite a logistical problem all in itself." He looked pointedly at Halloran. "You might want to start thinking about that."

Liz let herself into the locker room first. The guard remained stoic, but Spigotta whipped out his cell phone and started punching keys, demanding updates from whoever he talked to. Within five minutes Liz knocked on the door and Halloran used his badge to let Derek in. Derek was glad to leave Halloran's numb shock and Spigotta's frenzied organizing behind. Liz's face, however, was the same color as chalk dust. She bit her lip. "You and Jim Scully are about the same size. You can use his suit. Ever wear a Chemturion?"

"Yes," Derek said. "I also have a field suit in my duffel, but it'd be better if I didn't have to use it. By the way . . . why aren't you dead?"

Liz sighed. "Are you familiar with the latest model Chemturion?"

"Not really. They make a new model?" Derek crossed over to a bench and dropped his gear. "Scrubs?"

She found him a pair and turned her back, giving him a modicum of privacy.

"No peeking now," he said, and began to change into the green scrubs.

Not responding to the lightness of his tone, she said, "The new Chemturion was designed to be multipurpose—air hoses *or* a portable air supply. So they reinforced the back and shoulders with Kevlar to prevent the air tank or straps from cutting the suit."

"You're lucky." Derek walked over to her so he was right behind her. "I want to see your back."

"*What?*"

"Your back," he repeated. "Please raise your shirt so I can—"

She spun to glare at him. "Are you nuts?"

Derek shook his head. "Does your back hurt?"

"Yes, of course!"

"Getting shot at, even with Kevlar, leaves a hell of a bruise. I want to document it."

She stared at him, her barely controlled composure beginning to crumble. "You don't believe me?"

He gripped her shoulder. "Dr. Vargas, I wouldn't be going into a hot zone with you if I didn't believe you. But when Spigotta gets his priorities straightened out, he's going to wonder whether you were an insider on this assault. He'll want some sort of proof that they actually shot at you and that you just got lucky. Let's give him the proof before he comes looking for it."

Tears slowly rolled down her cheeks. Reluctantly she turned away from him and raised her scrub shirt. Derek whistled at the discoloration—black and blue and orange and yellow and purple—that ran from about mid-back up to the nape of her neck. "You've got a lovely back, but that's got to hurt like hell."

She laughed ruefully. "It does. Believe me."

"You should get into a hot tub as soon as you can, or you won't be able to move tomorrow. You got a Jacuzzi at home? Hold still, I'm going to shoot a couple pictures."

She stood still. "No, no Jacuzzi. You?"

"No. I live on a boat. No bath, just a shower."

He snapped a couple pictures. "Okay," he said. "Onward."

She turned and saw that his own composure seemed to be slipping. The skin on his face seemed stretched over his cheekbones, and his forehead was damp with sweat. She pointed to his neck. "No jewelry."

Derek pulled back his shirt so she could see. Around his neck were two necklaces. One was a string of dark-colored beads; the other was a heavy chain from which dangled a gold four-leaf clover and a St. Sebastian's medallion.

"It's not jewelry," he said. "And I'm not taking them off."

She stared at him. His color seemed to be getting worse, taking on a grayish-green tinge. "What are the beads? Is that a St. Christopher's medallion?" she said.

"Juju beads. Got them from a friend who spent some time in Somalia. It's a St. Sebastian's medallion. He was believed to fend off plague."

"You're superstitious!"

"I believe in luck, good and bad. Now, you got a john in here? I've got to go throw up." His tone was flat, matter-of-fact.

Liz's eyes widened. "I don't think you're up to this!"

"I'm up to it," he said in a strangled voice. Without pausing, he rushed past her. "This is just stage fright." He found the sink and vomited into it.

A moment later, clear-eyed, he splashed water on his face, closed his eyes, and tried to center and calm himself. He could feel his pulse slow, his respiration even out. *Just stage fright*, he thought.

Liz said, "Aren't we a pair. Neither of us should go in."

"Yeah," Derek said. "We should both be on a beach somewhere, drinking rum drinks and thinking about our sex lives. Unfortunately, I've never been that lucky. Let's go."

They donned their spacesuits and progressed through Styx and into Hades.

Inside HL4, spacesuit filled with pressurized air, Derek paused to take it all in. Using the underwater camera, he snapped pictures from several angles, including a careful shot of the empty shell casings on the floor. It seemed to him that the physical evidence supported Liz Vargas's version of events. That was good, because he had been suspicious of how she had survived the encounter. The bruises were even more convincing.

Careful of where he put his feet, Derek moved through the facility, peering in each door. Autopsy tables, laboratories, cages occupied by monkeys, rats, mice, and guinea pigs. All appeared unchanged. Moving from room to room, switching air hoses as he went, he snapped pictures. Finally he stood at the entrance to the storage room. More photographs. Liz stood silently next to him.

"I assume you've got all the usual suspects in here. Ebola, Marburg, Hanta . . ."

"Plus anthrax, Tularemia, and cholera."

"Great." He didn't proceed into the room. His breathing sounded loud in the suit, despite the roar of air from the hose. *A room full of demons*, he thought.

What Derek had not shared with Spigotta, Halloran, and Vargas was that he had attempted to retire after being booted from Iraq. He had spent several months under the care of a psychiatrist, who had finally told him, "You've spent most of your professional life peering through the gates of hell. You're handling the stress better than most. Go take a vacation somewhere warm. Drink some margaritas, get laid, have some fun. Remind yourself why you do this kind of work. Then make the decision whether or not to quit."

Remind yourself why you do this kind of work.

Because I can.

The vacation had lasted until September 11, 2001. When President Bush later created the Department of Homeland Security, one of the first people called had been Colonel Derek Stillwater, PhD (Retired).

The secretary of Homeland Security wanted people skilled in various aspects of terrorism—organization, nuclear, financial, biological, logistical, chemical—who could be dropped into any situation and provide advice, offer investigative and preemptive skills, and be able and willing to work within and without the established law enforcement channels.

Derek shook his head to clear his thoughts and took a deep breath of air that smelled suspiciously of the previous occupant's body odor. Jim Scully must have had a serious case of nervous perspiration when working HL4. Derek stepped into the storage room and took a picture of the liquid-nitrogen tank, which, except for the punch-button code lock and the biohazard warnings, resembled a beer keg.

Leaning over the black binder, Derek took a series of photographs, then called for Liz to open the tank and display Box 6, the now-empty container of Chimera M13. With nitrogen fog curling from the mouth of the container, Derek snapped more pictures. Finally he had Liz put it away.

He wasn't sure what to look for. It would make sense to do a thorough inventory of all the freezers, but that would take hours, and he didn't have hours.

Everything was just as Liz had described it. He turned slowly, scanning the room, shifting the air hose as he went, his peripheral vision severely impaired by the plastic faceplate.

He tried to think it through. A highly trained, coordinated assault. Twelve men. He assumed men, though it wasn't a given. The drivers and a guard stayed with the vans. Two men from each vehicle entered the building. Four of the men set up perimeter posts to guard the intersecting hallways and the elevator doors. Two men entered HL4. They knew exactly where to go, had an ID badge, and knew the entrance security codes to Styx and to the freezer containing the bug.

Inside, they had wasted no time. Lucky for Liz Vargas they hadn't checked on her. "Hurry," one of them had said in Korean. "You can't hurry this sort of thing," the other had probably said, the one opening the freezer and stealing the bugs. That implied that the guy doing the hands-on work had experience with high-level infectious agents. If he was Korean, that put him in a very small group worldwide.

Then they left. They didn't put the binder away or check on Liz or go to any other part of HL4. They did close the nitrogen container—thank God for small favors. That didn't require more than dropping the top in the hole so it clicked shut, but they could have kicked the damn thing over, which would have made the room damned near impossible to clean up. Perhaps they hadn't wanted to risk infecting the outside of their own suits, which would be a problem back in the vans or wherever their headquarters or staging area was. It wouldn't do to wipe out your own guys.

With clumsy gloved fingers Derek flipped pages in the binder. Probably fifty pages of acetate-covered paper.

He picked up the binder.

He stared. Liz said, "What the hell?"

Beneath the binder was a playing card. On the back of the card was a leering devil with cloven hooves, spiked tail, and jutting horns. In one long-fingered hand, the devil held a pitchfork.

6

WHEN DEREK AND LIZ got out of HL4, the spacesuits hanging bathed in purple UV light and the underwater camera soaking in a bucket of Lysol, Spigotta was swearing into a cellular phone and Frank Halloran was gone.

"Tell the fucking press it was some sort of crazed employee or something!"

Spigotta listened, the cellular mashed up against his ear. "Hey, *you* do the media, *I* handle the investigation. But you can't tell the fucking press that some Army assholes let some man-made super-germ loose on the world. So use your goddamned imagination." He clicked off and glared at Derek.

"Well?" He spat out the word like a bullet.

"Camera's soaking, but there is a—"

Liz broke in and described the playing card. Spigotta stared at her, then shifted his gaze to Derek. "What the fuck?"

"Under the binder," Derek said. "I shot it. There'll be pictures."

"The devil and his goddamned pitchfork? That's what you said before! You!" Spigotta jabbed Derek in the chest with a thick finger. "You got an explanation, Stillwater?"

"No." Derek shook his head.

Spigotta squinted suspiciously. "What card is it? Please tell me it's not a tarot."

"No, regular deck. It's a joker."

"So? C'mon. Feed me up some bullshit explanation of the devil card and your statement about the devil's pitchfork. Nice coincidence. Or would you like to try at Bureau headquarters?"

Derek rolled his eyes. "I've been calling superbugs 'the devil's pitchfork' since before the Gulf War. I've written position papers analyzing the U.S. and military and worldwide risk from biological warfare and bioterrorism. The president, the joint chiefs, the secretary general of the UN—they've all read my reports."

"Swell." Spigotta scowled. "Fuck. What a mess. Any brilliant suggestions?"

"Brilliant? No. Fresh out of brilliant. But I do have a few suggestions that I imagine you've already thought of."

Spigotta's gaze lingered on Derek. "Aren't you the diplomat. Okay. Hit me with your less-than-brilliant ideas."

"We need to notify the CDC and have them keep an eye out for anyone showing internal bleeding. USAMRIID can coordinate. Has the Bureau's Hazardous Materials Response Unit gotten here yet?"

"On their way."

"Good. They can work with Rid," Derek said, meaning USAMRIID. "We've got to figure out who knew about Chimera M13." He turned to Liz. "Was it ever published?"

She shook her head. "No, but there are black patents on it."

Black patents. Patents on top-secret government products. The paperwork existed somewhere in a government archive. Access was severely restricted.

"And," she added, "we wrote a lengthy report on it. The Pentagon got it. Probably the National Security Council did, too."

"Shit," Spigotta said.

"We also need to figure out who had plans to this building," Derek said. "These guys knew just where to go."

Spigotta was already punching the buttons on his phone. "I'll get somebody on it."

Derek knew three of the USAMRIID people and all of the HMRU people. Liz had gotten the film out of the camera and was developing it. Derek told them what he'd seen and what he thought the problems were going to be. He asked if the facility had a portable embalming machine in the hot zone. Frank Halloran said no. They would have been able to embalm Michael Ballard right in HL4; the formaldehyde would've killed the bugs, and they would have been able to transfer his body out of the biocontainment area.

Dr. Sharon Jaxon, from USAMRIID, suggested they just incinerate the body and quit screwing around. No autopsy was necessary, because they knew what killed him. "My vote," she said, "is dump Ballard's body, suit and all, in the incinerator. Goodbye safety issue."

Derek grinned. Jaxon was a hard-edged blond with broad shoulders, blunt fingers, and a take-no-prisoners attitude. He personally knew her to like fast motorcycles and spicy Mexican and Thai food and knew that after making love she liked to sit up in bed with the sheets pooled around her waist and channel-surf on the TV. He and

Sharon had trained together at Fort Detrick. She had stayed in research. He had headed off to join UNSCOM to play hide-and-seek with Saddam Hussein. It had been a long time between meetings. He said, "Do you have a strong desire to spend the next decade in congressional hearings or civil courts being sued by his family?"

"This is a national security issue," she said. "Sometimes we have to put aside tact."

"Let's try not to put aside our humanity," Derek said. Actually, he thought her suggestion was a good one, political repercussions be damned. It wasn't his job to worry about public image. It was his job to make sure this man-made germ didn't get loose. He glanced at his watch. "Sorry, but this really isn't my problem. You guys figure it out."

She looked like she was going to punch him, but Spigotta stomped into the room before she could.

"Stillwater!" He jerked his thumb over his shoulder. "Out here. Now."

Derek followed the FBI agent into the hallway. He thought Spigotta's ruddy complexion had gone a little pale. Spigotta had stuck an unlit cigar in his mouth and was chewing on it, acting like he was going to break a no-smoking rule at any moment. Derek knew the feeling.

This stretch of corridor was body bag free, painted an industrial pale green and lit by harsh fluorescent lights. The tile floor was a dingy speckled white. Everything about the facility, especially security, seemed to have been done on the cheap.

Spigotta, voice hoarse, said, "I think you need to get over to Scully's house. I can't leave here, but I'm going to have my second-in-command, Aaron Pilcher, drive you there."

Derek cocked his head. "What's at Scully's house?"

Spigotta swallowed. "The team I sent over there says it looks like a massacre."

7

AARON PILCHER WAS THE blond suit who had originally delivered Derek to Spigotta. He shook hands with Derek and led him to a waiting Ford Taurus. Pilcher had pale blue eyes and bony cheeks. His teeth were small and even and reminded Derek of some undersized scavenger, like a ferret or raccoon. Where Spigotta seemed like a G-man, a leftover from J. Edgar Hoover's FBI, Pilcher was definitely one of the newer breed of agents—intelligent, articulate, and curious. The man wanted information, a lot of it. Good or bad, he would make the evaluation himself, thank you very much. Just answer the questions, do it now, give me your opinions, I'll decide what they're worth.

Derek tossed his Go Packs in the trunk of the Taurus and climbed into the passenger seat. Pilcher gunned the engine and headed for the front gate. "If you don't want to end up on the evening news, I suggest you slouch or something."

Derek settled with resting an elbow on the windowsill and seeming to prop his head with his hand, managing to cover part of his face.

"Any idea where to go with this?" Pilcher asked after the armed soldiers had cleared the press and gawkers out of the way. Within minutes they were speeding east on I-695.

"The Korean angle's a possibility," Derek said. "Get on your computers and see what comes up for Korean foreign nationals with experience in biology, especially high-end ID experience."

"ID?"

"Infectious disease."

"We can do that. See what immigration and the CIA have to say."

"I'd run all your terrorism files, too."

"Sure. Makes sense."

Pilcher pulled off I-695 and headed north into wooded suburbs. "What's your take on this?" he asked. "This is your specialty, right?"

"Right." Derek watched the urban landscape slide into semirural suburbia. Still plenty of strip malls, chain stores, and fast-food restaurants, but there were also more trees and farms, and the residential lots were larger. He was starting to feel impatient. Starting to feel that every second that went by was a step closer to disaster. The feeling was like having a rat gnawing at your stomach from the inside. It was a feeling he had often, and he didn't care for it. He could feel the rat, the panic rat, start to nibble. "My take?" he said, trying to concentrate on the agent's questions.

"What're they after?"

"Political blackmail is a possibility. If so, we'll be hearing from them soon."

"Like, U.S. out of South Korea now or we let this bug loose at McDonald's?"

"Right. Or release our prisoners out of wherever."

"Camp X-Ray." The al-Qaeda prisoners at Guantanamo Bay, Cuba.

"Sure," Derek said. "Or they want to develop it as their own strategic weapon system."

"Strategic?" Pilcher said.

"Versus tactical." Derek wasn't sure Pilcher understood. He said, "Anthrax is a tactical weapon. You drop it on troops, it kills them in a finite way. Smallpox or Chimera, as weapons they're not tactical. You can't control them. They're too infectious, they take off and kill everybody. If you have your own troops vaccinated against small-pox, or your own genetically enhanced version of smallpox, it's still not really tactical. You use it as a threat. Like having seventy-five hundred nuclear warheads. Nobody needs that many. But it's stra-tegic. You bargain with it. We've got them, so we're tougher than you. It's fucking stupid, but that's how the world works. Smallpox or Chimera as strategic weapons—it's suicidal."

"Huh," Pilcher said. "You've thought a lot about it."

"I've thought a lot about it. Yeah."

"What else?"

Derek turned to look at him. "Give us fifty million bucks in a Swiss bank account or else. Or, here Syria, fifty million in a num-bered account. Nice doing business with you."

"Greed," Pilcher said with a nod. He seemed comfortable with greed.

"Then there's Basic Terrorism 101."

"Being?"

"The point of terrorism is to terrorize. Most people agree that the anthrax letters weren't very effective at killing people, but psychologically they were just terrific. Even bin Laden's lunatics could understand that. Their airplanes killed about thirty-five hundred people, but hell, they shut down U.S. air traffic for a day and turned New York City upside-down. The economic fallout lasted for years. Of course, this bug's too dangerous for traditional terrorism."

"Think they know that?" Pilcher turned off the main road down a two-lane highway. The houses, which all seemed large, were on five- and ten-acre lots, isolated from each other by distance and copses of trees. Pines and hardwoods—ash, oak, and maple. Green leaves still untouched by the oncoming fall.

Derek glanced at his watch again. He felt the panic rat gnawing. He wondered what he was missing, what he should be doing. "It's not my biggest concern," Derek said. "We almost there yet?"

"Almost. Just over the hill, if the map's any good. What's your biggest concern?"

"A suicide group. What is technically known as the apocalyptic terrorist."

Pilcher stared at him, then readjusted his steering as the Taurus began to drift over the yellow line. "Like al-Qaeda."

"No," Derek said. "I was thinking Aum Shinrikyo, the Japanese suicide cult that let sarin gas out on the Tokyo subway. I hope that's not what we're dealing with here, a group of suicidal nuts who want to bring about the end of the world."

Pilcher didn't comment. Once over the hill he pulled the car into a long, paved driveway. There were already a handful of cars—more sedans that seemed to scream Federal Government and two local police cars, lights flashing. Derek and Pilcher climbed out and displayed their IDs to the approaching cops.

Above them, two helicopters did a midair dance, circling, circling. Derek figured the choppers had probably followed them from U.S. Immuno. Pilcher looked around. "Pretty isolated spot."

"Uh-huh." Derek gestured for Pilcher to open the trunk. He rummaged through his backpack and came up with a disposable camera, a cell phone, a notepad and pen, and a 9mm semiautomatic in a belt clip. He attached the phone and gun to his belt and said, "Ready?"

Pilcher looked thoughtfully at him. "Suicidal maniacs?"

Derek said, "Hope we get a ransom call soon," and strode toward the sprawling two-story colonial.

It happened in the family room at the rear of the house. The front of the house, where Derek and Aaron Pilcher entered, was a formal sitting room with plush crushed-velvet furniture and crystal lamps. Very formal. Derek had the sense the room was rarely if ever used. He stopped to examine a large, formal family photograph on one wall: a man, Mike Scully; his wife, an attractive woman about forty years old or so with blond hair; two kids, a boy and a girl. With a shake of his head, he followed Pilcher.

The kitchen was roomy with oak cabinets, shiny appliances, and a blue-tile-topped serving island. It was teeming with FBI Evidence Recovery Team members. It looked, based on an oak dining-room table set for four, minus two chairs, that dinner preparation had been interrupted.

Derek cautiously sniffed. Pilcher said, "Something burned."

"Spaghetti sauce, I think."

One of the ERTs, a short, stocky woman with dark hair and red plastic-framed glasses, said, "Water in the pot boiled off, and the pasta burned. Sauce simmered into a lump. Garlic bread in the oven got turned into briquettes. The rest of the smell . . ." She made a gesture past them. "Go on in. But I may never eat Italian again."

Even more ERTs were in the family room, a cozy, low-ceilinged space with a fireplace, sliding glass doors overlooking a redwood deck, a big-screen TV, and a sofa, love seat, and lounge chair. A comfortable room, one that looked well used. A nice place for the family to sprawl out and watch TV, catch a movie, eat popcorn.

In the center of the room were the two missing dining-room chairs. In one, a man sat, tied with rope and duct tape. Liz had been right, Derek thought. Scully had been about his size. Slightly over six feet, athletic but not bulky. He had brown hair cut short and a lean, handsome face. His throat had been slit, and his gray "ARMY" sweatshirt and blue jeans were crusted with dried blood.

Sitting tied and taped to the second chair so they were facing each other was the woman. Unlike her husband, she was nude, her legs splayed obscenely. Like her husband, her throat had been cut, but for her it had probably been a relief.

Her breasts and face and pubic region had been burned with what had probably been a match or cigarette lighter. There had been mutilations—a little finger, one ear, a nipple. Her left eye appeared to have been carved out.

Derek drew in a ragged breath and felt acid rise up into his throat. He took deep breaths to regain control, biting back the bile.

One of the ERTs, a grizzly-sized bald guy in his fifties, said, "If you're gonna barf, use the john. I already processed it. You wouldn't be the first one in there today."

Derek shook his head, turned to Pilcher. "Kids?"

"Upstairs," the bald guy said. "Throats slit . . . bastards."

Derek took it in, eyes wide, trying to process it analytically, to keep his emotions in check. Finally, "They told him what they'd do to her if he didn't answer their questions. And they used the burns probably to soften him up, make him believe them. And they did it anyway, cut her, to make him tell more. To confirm."

"Or he didn't tell them because . . ."—Pilcher hesitated—"he knew what they wanted. He knew what was at stake."

"They got what they wanted," Derek said. "They might have threatened to do this to the kids as confirmation. He spilled. Who wouldn't have?"

They did it because they liked it, he thought. *Berzerkers.*

They lapsed into silence. The techs took photos, vacuumed for trace evidence, dusted for fingerprints. From upstairs they could hear similar activity.

Derek pointed to a doorway. "What's in there?"

"Kelly's just started in there. Give her a few minutes to finish the trace collection."

Pilcher went off to discuss things with the original agents who'd been sent to the house. Derek found the stairs and checked out the second floor—four bedrooms, a bathroom off the master suite, another bathroom off the hall.

He found the children in one of the bedrooms. A boy of about seven and a girl about nine or ten. Blindfolds over their eyes, hands and feet duct-taped. Gaping slashes at their throats. Both lying together on a bed with a Star Wars comforter, posters of dinosaurs, jets, Harry Potter, and spaceships on the wall.

Derek wondered if they had heard their mother's torture downstairs or if they had been killed before. But he knew the answer.

They had saved the children for last, just in case Scully had needed more persuading. Scully would have seen what they were doing to his wife and known where it was heading. But maybe, just maybe, he had prayed, they would spare the children if he kept cooperating.

Derek no longer felt nauseous. He felt murderous. A coldness was settling in that brought with it an awful kind of clarity. It pushed him into a world of black and white, good and evil, where there was very little faith in the goodness of human beings or hope for humanity. This, he knew, was how it was all over the world. The world was filled with people who could do this to other people without a blink of an eye. Monsters. Devils. Evil incarnate. The case was no longer an abstraction, no longer about the theft of something no one had ever seen. It was now about the unnecessary cold-blooded murder of two children and their parents.

He turned on his heels and went downstairs. He asked Kelly, a willowy redhead with flashing green eyes, if he could come into the office.

"You the Homeland guy?" Her voice had a trace of Georgia in it.

"Yeah." He introduced himself.

She was concentrating on the desk. It was a large, elegant maple table strewn with papers. A laptop computer was parked on one corner. Off to the right, next to a half-full bottle of Budweiser, was a Dictaphone.

Kelly said, "The tape's at the end. I wonder . . ." With a latex-gloved finger, she rewound the tape and pushed Play. A flat, soft male voice said, ". . . work is progressing on the experiments with ribaviran and monkey pox with IL-4—"

"Do you understand that?" Kelly asked.

"Unfortunately, yes." They had been testing an antiviral drug on monkeys infected with a genetically engineered form of monkeypox, a disease similar to smallpox that only infected monkeys. The monkeypox had been modified with a molecule that seemed to make the virus work on monkeys vaccinated against monkeypox—in effect, neutralizing the vaccine.

Suddenly, in the background, there was a crack, and then screams, followed by voices. A confusion of voices, the television on in the next room. Then Scully's voice, clear because he was so close to the microphone. *"What the fuck?"* followed by what was probably the pounding of feet.

As suddenly as it began, it ended. The TV, which had been playing what sounded like a cartoon, was clicked off.

And then a voice. Clear. Male. *"Take the kids upstairs. Dr. Scully, sit down. We have a lot to talk about."*

"What do—"

"Sit. Now." There was a sharp, female cry. *"Do it."*

Rustling.

"Get her clothes off."

"Hey!"

"Not another word until I tell you to speak. Do it."

More rustling. Sobs.

It went on and on. Pilcher and the three other agents had crowded into the office, listening intently. Kelly, the ERT, said, "Dear God," almost a moan.

On the tape, they questioned James Scully about where Chimera M13 was located at U.S. Immuno. He refused to talk. At first. They threatened to cut off his wife's little finger and then burned her to convince him they were serious. Scully tried to be vague, to tell them it was in a secure area of the facility. They cut off his wife's finger, and he told them it was on the second floor in the front storage room of the Hot Level 4 biocontainment area. They asked more questions. Even when he was clearly being honest and straightforward, they burned his wife and threatened to cut her again, and when he answered they cut her anyway.

Scully talked. Begged them to stop. He would tell them everything. Everything. If only they would stop.

A half hour later, after the killers cut off his wife's ear but before they cut off a nipple or gouged out an eye, the tape came to a merciful end with a final click.

Everyone in the room looked stunned.

Derek looked worse, if that was possible. His face had grown pale and gray, and sweat once again had begun to trickle down his forehead and armpits. He felt the back of his shirt clinging to his spine.

That voice. It couldn't be. It wasn't possible.

He wondered if he was going crazy. If the stress had gotten to him. He was hallucinating. Had to be.

He recognized the voice of the interrogator.

But . . .

The owner of the voice was dead.

8

—

"GET THAT TAPE INTO evidence," Derek snapped. He glared at the tape machine. "Go back. Let's see, it was around 0183 on the meter."

Kelly obliged, rewinding. She hit Play.

Pilcher said, "What're you listening for?"

Derek held up his hand to shush the agent. That voice came on again.

"Okay, Doctor. Which freezer is Chimera M13 in? Think about your answer. . . ."

There was a pause that was filled by an indistinct sound in the background.

"There," Derek said. "Play it again and jack up the volume."

Kelly did. There was a lot of tape hiss, but the sound was better. They all held their breath, straining to hear.

Pilcher said, "Somebody said, 'Fallon.' I'm pretty sure that's it. 'Fallon,' to get this motherfucker's attention. Then something like, 'the kids are . . .' something."

"'Secure,'" Kelly said. "'Fallon . . . Hey, Fallon. The kids are se-cure.' That's it." She turned the tape off. "Sounded like he had an accent. German?"

Derek nodded, his mind spinning. *Fallon?* He blinked, not pro-cessing his surroundings, trying to remember. *Fallon?*

Without warning Derek turned and strode out of the room, heading for the front door. Outside, leaning against the Taurus, he punched out a number on his cell phone. It was picked up on the first ring.

"Sam Dalton." Dalton was the second-in-command of the De-partment of Homeland Security.

"Sam, it's Derek Stillwater. I'm not on a secure phone."

"Get to one. We need an update ASAP."

Derek told him where he was. "I need a ride to the Pentagon. I can get on a secure phone there and fill you in, but I need to get to the Pentagon. The HMRU is at the facility, they've got Hueys—"

"They're already on their way to Detrick. Can you drive?"

"During rush hour? Clock's ticking. What about the Coast Guard?" Derek glanced at his watch. He clenched his jaw and tried to ignore the panic rat.

"Okay," Dalton said. "They're on the way."

Pilcher appeared a few minutes later. He held his own cellular in his hand and stared curiously at Stillwater. Derek had retrieved a portable CD player from his pack and was sitting on the hood of the Taurus, sipping from a bottle of water.

"What're you listening to?" Pilcher asked.

"*Chant II.*"

Pilcher stared in disbelief. "*What?*"

"Benedictine monks singing Gregorian chants. They were really popular in the '90s. Put out a bunch of CDs, but the public sort of lost interest after the first two or three."

Pilcher squinted his eyes. "Jesus Christ!"

"That's the idea."

"Who the hell *are* you? Didn't you see what happened in there?" He moved toward Derek, head bobbing like a fighting cock.

From the south came the approaching beat of helicopter rotors. Derek stood up and said, "I'm going to head out back. That should be my ride."

He grabbed up the backpack and the duffel and started to walk around Pilcher. Pilcher grabbed his arm and spun him around, saying, "What the hell are you—"

Derek caught Pilcher's wrist in one hand, twisted it at a sharp angle, and torqued the arm behind the agent's back, applying pressure and using the man's weight against him. For just a moment Derek applied more pressure, then suddenly let go.

"You've got things under control," he said. "I've got to get over to the Pentagon, make a report on a secure phone."

"Who's Fallon?" Pilcher said. He followed after Derek, snapping at his heels like a cocker spaniel. "The look on your face. You know something. This isn't the time to withhold information, Stillwater. What do you know? Who's Fallon?"

The helicopter arced toward them, flying in fast.

Derek turned. "I don't know anybody named Fallon. I thought I recognized the voice. But you tell me, Pilcher. Am I crazy? Am I losing it? Is the stress too much for me?" Derek took an aggressive step toward the FBI agent, who stood his ground. "I thought I recognized the voice, but the guy it belongs to has been dead for over a decade. Still want to know his name? It isn't Fallon. But you tell me. Does the FBI want to waste time chasing after a phantom that could be a figment of my imagination?"

Pilcher stepped back. "You're bullshitting me."

"No, I'm not."

The two men locked eyes. Pilcher finally said, "What else? What does Fallon mean to you?"

Derek shook his head. "I wonder if we misunderstood. The guy who said that had what sounded like a German accent. Or Russian. Maybe Czech. Something Slavic, at least as much as we can tell with the shitty sound reproduction. Maybe the FBI lab can clear it up. They're good at that sort of thing."

The red, white, and blue helicopter, an Agusta MH-68A, nicknamed the Mako, was settling down in the Scully's backyard, fifty yards from where they stood.

Shouting to be heard over the roar of the chopper, Pilcher said, "Who's Fallon?"

Derek leaned closer. "I thought he said, 'Fallen.'"

Pilcher looked puzzled.

"You know," Derek shouted, "like Fallen Angel."

Pilcher's expression changed to that of a man who had taken a step off a tall cliff.

He thinks I'm crazy for sure now, Derek thought.

"Fallen Angel?" Pilcher said. "You're insane!"

"Fallen Angel," Derek repeated. "Weren't you ever in Sunday School? You know. Lucifer. The Devil."

It was the same Coast Guard crew who had picked him up on the Chesapeake Bay. The Texan grabbed the backpack and helped Derek in. Derek settled into one of the seats.

Cynthia Black, the pilot, said, "How's the end of the world coming?"

Derek gave her a thumbs-up. "Let's go."

The chopper rose quickly into the air. The Texan said, "Your kayak's back on your boat. Sweet, both the *Salacious Sally* and the kayak."

"Glad you like it." He ignored them and put the earphones back over his ears.

"Doctor."

He looked at the Texan. "Yeah?"

"Can you tell us what's going on? This is . . . pretty irregular."

He shook his head. "I wish I could, but . . ." He shrugged, considering the three. "It's bad. Really bad."

Derek settled back in the seat, buckled up, and closed his eyes. A career in the military had taught him how to catch a nap when the opportunity appeared, and he decided to take it. With Gregorian chants in his ears, he quickly dozed off for the short flight from Baltimore to Washington, D.C. He woke up as they were coming in toward the Pentagon. He noted that the roads were clogged with cars. He glanced around, as he almost always did when flying into D.C., looking for the Washington Monument and the Capitol, the usual suspects.

The chopper descended toward the Pentagon helicopter pad.

Derek was met by a young and efficient Army officer in dress whites. He grabbed the duffel bag and led Derek at a crouching run toward the Pentagon entrance. "Staff Sergeant Stanley O'Reilly, sir. I'm to get you to a secure communication room and then provide you with everything you need."

"Good. I could use a bite to eat, a Mountain Dew, and the complete file of a Special Forces officer I served with in the Gulf War. Captain Richard Coffee."

"Serial number, sir?"

"I don't know. But the time frame should narrow it down."

"Yes, sir. This way, sir."

The security guards confiscated his sidearm and went through his bags, but he was quickly led to a secure communications room, a small, bland office probably wrapped in copper to eliminate the possibility of radio eavesdropping. It contained a desk on which was an STU, or secure telephone unit. Everybody who used them called them "stew phones." O'Reilly said, "I'll be back soon. Any food preference, sir?"

"Some sort of sandwich. Turkey, preferably, on rye with lettuce, no tomato. And an apple. Yeah, an apple. Thanks."

"Yes, sir. And a Mountain Dew."

"Yeah, better make it two. I'm going to need the caffeine."

O'Reilly supplied a key for the phone's encryption lock and left, closing the door behind him.

The stew phone looked like any other phone except for the lock and an LCD panel. Derek unlocked the phone and called Dalton. When Dalton answered, Derek told him he was ready to go. He pushed a button and the LCD screen read: GOING SECURE.

Silence for maybe thirty seconds. Then the LCD read: US GOVERNMENT SECRET, and Dalton said, "O-kay—Der-ek—Fill—us—in."

The scrambler on the stew phones, even the newer models, distorted voices, especially if the callers talked too fast. Dalton and

Derek were old hands at stew phones and knew from experience to talk slowly and deliberately.

Derek filled in his boss, knowing that General James Johnston, the secretary of the Department of Homeland Security, was also listening in.

"Your recommendation?" Dalton said.

"The FBI's already on it in a major way," Derek told him. "Pilcher and Spigotta. They've got different styles, but they both seem sharp, especially Pilcher. HMRU's already on the facility, and Rid's involved. Get with them, they'll know what to do. Bring in the CDC if you can get it through their heads that this is a possible major incident in biowarfare, not a public health emergency. They can be a little slow about that, though maybe they've learned something from the anthrax attacks and SARS."

"Good. Stay on top of things. Continue to coordinate."

Derek hesitated. "Sir. I'm going to pursue what is possibly a tangent." He explained about recognizing the voice on the tape recording.

There was a long silence on the stew phone. Dalton said, "Are you feeling all right, Derek?"

"I'm standing on the edge of Armageddon here, Sam. How the fuck am I supposed to be feeling?"

Suddenly the voice on the phone was that of James Johnston, the Homeland Security secretary. "Do you think the FBI and USAMRIID can handle both the routine investigation and any containment procedures?"

"Yes, sir. They know their job and, I believe, especially now that Rid's involved, are aware of the potential problems."

"Fine, then. You investigate this hunch you have, but keep in touch with the Bureau and the institute. I've been at war with you, son, and I trust your instincts."

There was a knock at the door, and Derek opened it to reveal Sergeant O'Reilly standing there with a plastic tray bearing a turkey sandwich, an apple, and two cans of Mountain Dew. "If you're done with your phone call, sir, we've got an empty office for you to use. Someone will be bringing you the file in a few minutes."

"Great." Derek took the tray and followed O'Reilly through what seemed to be a mile of corridors. He had spent a year at the Pentagon writing position papers on biological warfare. He hadn't cared for the environment, although he'd enjoyed the almost academic nature of brainstorming BW scenarios and creating war-game simulations for the military to test out. But in all his time there he had never gotten the hang of the Pentagon floor plan.

O'Reilly led him into another bare office, this one without a secure phone. It smelled of fresh paint and contained only a desk, two chairs, a regular telephone, and a bank of filing cabinets that Derek assumed were empty.

"Enjoy your food, sir, and if you need anything, please contact me." Before leaving, he handed Derek a card with his pager, telephone, and fax numbers and his e-mail address on it. Derek put his earphones back on and ate his dinner, glancing at his watch repeatedly, wondering when the file on Richard Coffee was going to arrive. He was halfway through his apple when there was a knock on the door.

"Come in," he called.

Into the room strode a tall, thin man in his fifties with a gray crewcut and elegant, slim features. He wore gold wire-rimmed glasses, and the insignia on his uniform indicated he was a lieutenant colonel—Lieutenant Colonel Jerome Tallifer specifically, according to his ID badge. Tallifer carried a briefcase secured with two combination locks.

"Dr. Derek Stillwater?"

"Yes, sir."

"I'm Lieutenant Colonel Jerome Tallifer, Military Intelligence. May I see some ID, please?"

Derek provided it. Tallifer, his voice hinting at a childhood in the hills of Kentucky or maybe Mississippi, said, "Retired Army, I understand."

"Yes, sir. Colonel, Special Forces. Retired, sir."

"But a professor."

"Yes."

"I believe I've read your papers. Might even have caught a talk or two you gave."

"Possibly, sir." Derek remained in his seat despite the temptation to stand at attention. Though the years of service and conditioning had been deeply ingrained and the inclination to salute never went away, he had found that his ability to ignore the response had grown stronger every day he was out of the military.

"Yes, well, we would like to know why you're interested in a dead soldier, Doctor."

Derek leaned back in his chair and studied the standing lieutenant colonel. He gestured to the other chair. "Have a seat. I'll make it quick because, quite frankly, the clock's ticking."

To his surprise, Tallifer sat.

Derek laid it out for him. The stolen infectious agent, the murder of the family, the tape, and his recognition of a voice he thought was Captain Richard Coffee's.

Tallifer considered him for a few minutes. "If I may say so myself, Doctor, that doesn't make any sense whatsoever. Captain Coffee died in Iraq."

"I'm aware of that. I was there."

"But you want to read his file."

"Yes, sir."

"And you suspect what, exactly?"

Derek said, "I suspect that I have precious little to go on and know that the FBI has the manpower to pursue a more conventional route of investigation, but my mandate as a Homeland troubleshooter is to evaluate, coordinate, and investigate. It is my determination that all conventional avenues are currently being covered. However, I am pursuing a long shot, what some might call a WAG, or 'wild-assed guess.' I am pursuing it because everyone else is busy. And I'm pursuing it because I think it needs to be pursued, especially since some terrorist lunatics have stolen a BW organism that could wipe out most of the population of the planet in less than a month. Now," he said, an edge to his voice, "are you going to let me see the file, or shall I have the request put to the joint chief by Secretary Johnston, who I just spoke to on the telephone less than twenty minutes ago?"

Tallifer shrugged. He picked up the briefcase and let it rest on his lap. He turned the dials on the combination locks, opened the lid, pulled out a file, and dropped it on the desk. He closed the briefcase and spun the dials. "Good luck, Doctor." Tallifer stood up and headed for the door. Turning, he said, "Good luck with your wild-assed guess."

"Colonel," Derek said. He hadn't touched the file.

"Yes, Doctor?"

"How many files were there in your briefcase?"

Lieutenant Colonel Tallifer's cool blue gaze lingered on Derek for a moment, then without a word he left the office.

Derek nodded, thinking that a lieutenant colonel from Military Intelligence was a rather unusual delivery boy. He picked up the file and began to read.

9

The White House

In the White House secure communications center, Sam Dalton hung up the stew phone and whirled to look at Secretary James Johnston, who raised an eyebrow. "You have a problem?"

Dalton was tall, his physique as taut as a bowstring. He could have been a recruiting poster for the Army, a sandy-haired, square-jawed man in his forties, his gaze steady and hard. He leaned back in the chair, which creaked beneath him. "You never should have assigned Stillwater to this case."

Johnston crossed his arms. He was older, closing on sixty, his shoulders broad, his thick chest swelling the tailored shirt beneath his dark blue suit. "I understand that you're not Derek's biggest fan. I have confidence in him, though."

"I don't," Dalton said. He tapped a finger on the chair's armrest. "The man is a cowboy. Or a nutcase. You figure it out. I think he's unreliable. You remember his last trip out to Kansas City?"

Johnston nodded. It had been memorable. One of the truths of working antiterror, especially bioterror, was that luckily it was filled with false alarms. Every time the FBI's HMRU was called out to investigate an envelope filled with white powder, or a food poisoning case that occurred in some government cafeteria, or water contamination, Derek or one of his colleagues for the Department of Homeland Security was sent with them to evaluate. Two months ago, in Kansas City, the HMRU had been called because someone thought their Cheerios box had been contaminated with anthrax. By the time they got there, it had been determined that the family's kids had filled a bowl with Cheerios, added sugar, then decided they wanted toast instead and threw the bowl's contents back in the box. Had the mother of the children not been a semihysteric with a job in a state senator's office, it would never have even come to the attention of the FBI, or anyone else, for that matter.

But she had freaked out and gone to her boss, who had called in the Bureau. Derek and the HMRU had flown in, and Derek had taken one look at the box of cereal and flung it in the woman's face, turning and storming out of the house. Johnston hadn't known whether to laugh or reprimand Stillwater. Derek had offered to resign and buy the lady a new box of cereal, but Johnston had talked him into an apology. It was a legendary story within DHS. For that matter, Derek's offers to resign were legendary—and weekly.

Johnston shrugged. "Derek has an instinct for bullshit. And he's right this time. If the FBI and USAMRIID have things under control, let him chase the long shots."

Dalton scowled. "I wanted to assign Swanson. Why did you assign Stillwater? Next time he offers to resign, let him."

Johnston sighed, craned his neck, and looked at the ceiling. "You know, Sam, I've got to go and talk to the entire administration tonight about this. They're going to want to know what we're doing that the FBI and USAMRIID aren't doing. It's very useful for me to have an answer for the president besides, 'Dogging the FBI.' Besides, Stillwater's much better than Swanson."

"Swanson is by the book."

"Swanson hasn't had an original thought in his head in twenty years. He just likes being on the government payroll. He's strictly an academic. His experience with terrorism and bioterrorism comes from books and made-for-TV movies."

Dalton looked disgusted. "He gives us clear and articulate reports on time and doesn't have panic attacks before every assignment."

Johnston headed for the door. "Derek Stillwater's reports are clear and articulate, too."

Dalton flung himself out of the chair. "Oh, right. Let me see, do you remember this one: '*The substance in the fucking envelope was fucking talcum powder.*'"

Johnston suppressed a smile. That report had been memorable as well. Derek's entire incident report: one sentence, two epithets. And completely accurate. Johnston put on his official face and turned to Sam Dalton. "Sam," he said. "I still think Derek Stillwater's my best troubleshooter. He stays on the case."

Johnston opened the door, but Dalton tried one more thing. "He's a psychiatric case. You know that. He has panic attacks in the field. It's well documented."

Johnston nodded. He met Dalton's gaze. "Derek knows better than most that what he's investigating could kill him. It's a valuable bit of knowledge. He stays, Sam. Meanwhile, I want you to start nagging all our intelligence people to see if we can find out about Fallen Angels and this Richard Coffee. I'll want a report before nine tonight. Consider it an order."

10

U.S. Immunological Research

Liz Vargas leaned back in one of the mismatched conference room chairs and felt waves of exhaustion wash over her. What a day! She hadn't experienced anything resembling this kind of stress since, well, never. The closest had been the death of her husband.

She rotated her neck, hoping to shake off the thought and relieve some tension. That was not a good place to go, and this was not a good time to go visiting the worst period in her life. In her current condition she might start crying and not be able to stop for days.

Toughen up, Vargas! We've got a problem to solve.

Sipping coffee from a Styrofoam cup, she looked at Frank Halloran. Frank had sunk into a kind of dazed depression, head down, staring at his hands. He looked somehow diminished. She knew he was a fine scientist and a good administrator. Something had gone wrong—wrong in the worst way—and she didn't blame Frank. But she got the feeling that the FBI and these Army guys did. And maybe blamed her as well.

Frank and Jim Scully had left the Army to start a more speculative biowarfare research center than what had been practiced at USAMRIID. From rumors she had heard, part of it may have been the pay. The Army paid their doctors and veterinarians and PhDs only a fraction of what they could make in the outside world. Their new think tank had succeeded beyond their wildest dreams, if pay was the only issue. It had turned out to be easier than they had thought to find government funding, and there had been a few successful gene products and potential vaccines that had provided ongoing commercial income.

But this disaster would probably ruin Frank's career.

For the first time it occurred to her that she was likely to be painted with the same career-ruining tone of paint.

She closed her eyes again, trying not to think of what had happened to Mike Ballard and Jim Scully . . . and Scully's family. She tried to push aside selfish thoughts of career and think about all the people she had worked with who were dead or in the hospital. She tried *not* to think about the ramifications of a terrorist group getting their hands on Chimera M13. An involuntary shudder shook her.

Her thoughts were interrupted by the gentle but commanding voice of Colonel Benjamin Zataki. Zataki was head of the science division—the scientific head of USAMRIID. A fit and aggressive career military man, he had been involved with biowarfare development in the '60s before Nixon put an end to it in 1969.

"Okay, everyone. Let me summarize our progress. The HMRU has moved Dr. Ballard's body and all the physical evidence to Detrick for processing.

"All of today's casualties have been moved to the local medical examiner's office. Agent Spigotta has moved the investigation center to the Strategic Information and Operations Center at the Hoover Building in D.C. We've brought in a team of MPs to secure the perimeter here."

He cleared his throat. "I've had a chance to read up on Chimera M13." Zataki paused. He had a thin, craggy face that looked as if he'd spent a lot of time on the water squinting into the sun. It was lean and weatherbeaten, tanned dark and leathery. It was hard to tell exactly how old he was, but Liz figured he had to be in his early sixties, at least. Despite the rank of colonel, he was not currently in uniform, instead wearing a pair of green surgical scrubs.

"Frank," Zataki said. "I understand that M13 stands for 'Manufactured number 13.'"

Frank Halloran looked up, expression bleak. "Right," he said slowly, as if coming awake from a deep sleep. "It was the thirteenth version. It did everything we planned for it to do, then we shut down the program."

"Had you tried to develop a vaccine to M13?"

"No," Halloran said, shaking his head. "The project was purely speculative. Could we develop a biowarfare weapon to our specifications entirely in the laboratory? Once we accomplished our goals, we closed it down."

There was silence. Nobody said what they all must have been thinking: You should have destroyed it, not tucked it away in a freezer.

Zataki picked his words carefully. "Do you have more samples of M13?"

Halloran looked up again. "Well . . . yes. We had an A and B tank. As far as I can tell, they only stole from tank A. Why?"

Zataki nodded, his blue eyes seeming to gleam. "And Chimera M1 through M12. Are they similar to M13?"

Halloran narrowed his eyes. "Yes. We think of some of them as failures, but each additional iteration was built on the previous."

"Why a failure?" Zataki asked.

"Well . . ." Halloran trailed off.

Liz said, "They didn't kill their host."

All eyes turned her way. Zataki's expression seemed to intensify, if that was possible. "Which ones?"

"M1, M2, M3, and M4. The test subjects got sick—in the cases of 3 and 4, very sick—but they recovered."

Captain Sharon Jaxon said, "What about M5 through M12?"

Liz looked at her, recognizing in the athletic blond someone that, under different circumstances, she could have been friends with. "They all killed their hosts. They didn't always do it in a way we expected or in a time frame that would have been considered practical for biological warfare. Everything after M4 was really just refinement."

"What would happen," Zataki asked, "if someone were inoculated with M1, 2, 3, or 4, then later inoculated with M13? Would the subject have developed an immunity to M13 from the early versions of the bug?"

Halloran was sitting up now, a little color and energy returning to his face. "We never tested that. We never even really discussed it. Chimera was a theoretical exercise, not a full-range research project."

"It might work," Liz said thoughtfully. "M1, 2, 3, or 4 just might work as a Chimera vaccine."

Traditionally, there are two types of vaccines against viruses. The first is to find a similar but weaker type of virus to infect the host. Dr. Edward Jenner, in 1796, noticed that milkmaids infected with cowpox, a disease similar to but weaker than smallpox, were immune to smallpox. He intentionally infected a boy with cowpox, then infected him a few days later with smallpox. The boy did not get smallpox. It worked—luckily for the kid—and the first vaccine was created.

A hundred and fifty years later, Dr. Jonas Salk developed a vaccine against polio. Unable to find a similar virus, he eventually was able to "kill" the poliovirus by using formaldehyde, which he then filtered out.

A form of genetic engineering is now used to identify, modify, and kill viruses for vaccines, the most common being the yearly flu vaccination. It is, essentially, a variation on the Salk vaccine. It is effective, safe, and time-consuming.

What Dr. Zataki was proposing was a version of the smallpox vaccine. His plan was to see if one of the earlier versions of Chimera M13 could make an effective emergency vaccine if the stolen Chimera M13 was let loose on the world.

Nobody much wanted to talk about what would happen if this plan didn't work and the terrorists used Chimera.

It was decided to split up the operation between U.S. Immuno and USAMRIID. The reason for this was availability of disease-free monkeys. Sharon Jaxon suggested they get the CDC in Atlanta involved. Zataki said he would inform them of what was going on as soon as possible. In the meantime, the clock was ticking. They had to get started.

Three of the USAMRIID biologists were going to stay at U.S. Immuno. The rest would work at Fort Detrick. As Zataki set up the logistics, Liz realized with dismay that she was not being included in the plans.

"Hey! Wait a minute! I'm one of only two remaining people on the planet who've worked with Chimera. What's going on?"

Halloran said, "You've been through enough—"

"Fuck you, Frank. I'm not going home to rest. I helped create this mess. I'll help fix it."

An awkward silence settled over the room. She didn't know if it was just her paranoia creeping in, but she thought they were all looking at her accusingly.

A wiry man from USAMRIID, Captain Jay Beckenstein, said, "I personally feel that there are a number of questions concerning your presence in HL4 during the actual theft—not to mention the question of your survival—that haven't been answered." He had a thick New England accent that reminded Liz of Bobby Kennedy.

Liz glared at him. "What are you saying? You're saying you don't trust me? That you think I was in on it?"

Beckenstein, who had curly black hair and a lethal five o'clock shadow, nodded his head. "Yeah. That's what I'm saying." His dark eyes met hers unflinchingly.

Liz saw that a number of the others were nodding their heads in agreement. She felt her stomach churn and thought she would be sick.

Sharon Jaxon said, "I'll work with you."

Liz looked at her in relief and surprise. "Thank you."

Jaxon nodded. "Okay, Ben?"

Zataki nodded. "Frank will be working with my people here. Why don't you come to Rid with the rest of us. We can use your help. Whatever you're up for."

"I'm up for anything," Liz said.

Zataki nodded. "That's it, then. Let's get going."

Within an hour Liz found herself strapped into the seat of a Huey flying above Interstate 270 toward Fort Detrick, the Catoctin Mountain ridge glimmering in the haze ahead.

11

—

The Pentagon

DEREK SAT BACK IN the office chair, thinking over the file he had just read on Richard Coffee.

Education: A dual degree in linguistics and Slavic languages from the University of Colorado.

Special language abilities: Fluent in Russian, Lithuanian, Czech, Yugoslavian, German, and Italian. In addition to his startling abilities in Slavic languages, Richard Coffee had been proficient, though probably not fluent, in French, Spanish, and Greek.

And probably Sanskrit, Latin, and Esperanto, Derek thought.

Derek remembered being stationed in Korea with Richard and how quickly Coffee had picked up the language. Fast enough to get around, talk to the natives, barter in the stores, and order at the restaurants. They had only been in Korea for six months.

According to his file, Coffee had been at the very top of his training group and was considered to have "significant leadership potential." His marksmanship was rated as "excellent," which was above "sharpshooter."

He had, like Derek, served in Panama and been stationed throughout the world: Korea, Japan, Germany, England, Italy, Cuba. With his language skills he had been shifted back and forth between liaison and training positions with the locals and what was probably translating materials used in Psychological Operations, or PsyOps.

After Coffee had been exposed to an unidentified mix of chemical and biological agents, Derek had rushed him to the nearest medivac chopper, where he had been whisked away to the 807th MASH. Derek had been ordered to move with the advancing troops to evaluate the ongoing risk of biological and chemical weapon attacks.

He had not been able to check on his friend until the end of the war. He was informed that *"Captain Richard Coffee died of unexplained lung and neurological damage caused by an unspecified and unidentified combination of biological and chemical agents believed to have been stored at the arms depot at An Nasiriyah."*

His body, Derek had been informed, had been shipped home to Boulder, Colorado, for burial.

It was all in the file.

Well, Derek thought, flipping to the end again, *not quite all.* Under the circumstances he would have expected a complete medical file, including an autopsy report. Coffee's death had been unusual, an anomaly in a war with relatively few casualties. On the other hand, medical records in a war zone were something of a luxury, and thousands had been mislaid during the Gulf War. Perhaps that had happened in Coffee's case.

Given the later controversy over Gulf War syndrome, the unexplained mix of health syndromes many veterans had complained of, it was slightly odd that the one certifiable American death by Iraqi biowarfare weapons wasn't more thoroughly documented.

Or was that why it wasn't?

Gulf War syndrome had never been satisfactorily explained. Many in the military believed it was all nonsense, just veterans trying to get more money or insurance benefits out of Uncle Sam. The latest "official" explanation was that the wide and varied mix of simultaneous vaccines given to such a large group of people in preparation for desert warfare against a country with a penchant for using bio and chem weapons had overloaded many GIs' immune systems, leading to the odd mix of health problems.

Derek had always assumed the reason Coffee's death had never reached the media was because it would have given ammunition to the Gulf War syndrome argument.

But now he wondered.

He flipped through the file again, trying to pinpoint what he was missing. What wasn't there that should have been?

Leaning back in the chair, he closed his eyes and let his mind drift. There was something there, he knew, some odd little factoid that he was trying to remember.

Yi-Ru-Han Kyoung-Wu-Ee-Neun Seo-Du-Reul Su-Ga Up-Seum-Ni-Da.

You can't hurry this.

He sat up. Opened his eyes. Flipped through the file again.

When he and Coffee had been stationed in Korea, playing tag with North Koreans along the DMZ, evaluating land mines and North Korea's biological and chemical weapons potential, they had shared more than a few beers in Seoul bars.

He remembered Coffee, tilting his bottle of Hite, a popular Korean brand, and saying he had plans to leave the Army.

"Don't we all," Derek had said. "You're out of your mind, though. We're lifers. Where else are you going to get your regular adrenaline fix? I tell you, Java, you're not going to get the same buzz playing golf."

"CIA," Coffee had said.

Derek had rolled his eyes. "What? With your background in languages? They'll stuff you in an office the size of a telephone booth in Langley, probably in a fucking sub-sub-sub-basement somewhere, and you'll be translating grocery lists and bureaucratic memos twelve hours a day. Fuck it. I don't believe you."

"Nah. I applied, man. I'd make a great field agent."

"Bullshiiiiit."

But now, Derek couldn't find it. Had it been bullshit? Would it have made it into military records if Coffee had officially applied to the Central Intelligence Agency?

He tried to remember the look on Coffee's face when he had told him. Had he been serious? With Coffee—or Java, as he was called by everyone—it was hard to tell. The man had been a world-class poker player and one hell of a liar.

"Fucking CIA cash cow," Derek said, his voice sounding slightly strained in the empty room. He glanced at his watch. He had to make up his mind soon. Was this a chase of the wild-goose variety, or a long shot worth pursuing?

His gaze settled on the chair where Lieutenant Colonel Tallifer, the Military Intelligence spook, had sat.

What would I do if I were MI and somebody official came around trying to dig up something they'd buried a long time ago?

He came around the desk and took a look at the other chair in the room.

He found it attached to the right metal leg with a magnet. What appeared to be a bug—of the electronic kind.

Holding the tiny transmitter between his two fingers, Derek dropped the listening device into his second, half-finished can of Mountain Dew. He rattled the can good and hard. "Half full or half empty, Lieutenant Colonel? What do you say?"

Derek called O'Reilly with a simple request: the current location and phone number of Captain Simona Ebbotts and a lift to a rental-car facility.

"What is that noise, sir?"

Derek had been shaking the Mountain Dew can during their brief telephone conversation. "Sorry. Nervous habit."

"Yes, sir. We can supply a vehicle. Secretary Johnston has expressed his desire for full cooperation."

"I'm sure he has. Thank you. That will be fine. The phone number, though?"

"I'll get it for you, sir."

"Good. And Sergeant? This request is confidential."

"Yes, sir."

The military vehicle O'Reilly came up with was a forest green Ford Explorer. Derek loaded his gear into the back, took the slip of paper with Simona Ebbots's contact information on it, thanked O'Reilly, and sped away. He didn't want to use his cellular phone for this. It took a mile of driving before he found a pay phone in front of a 7-Eleven.

The number was in San Antonio, Texas. Glancing at his watch, he decided to try the work number first. It was late, but it was an hour earlier in Texas.

Using a phone card, he dialed the number. After four rings, a female voice said, "Brooke Community Army Hospital, Medical Surgical Floor."

"Dr. Simona Ebbotts, please."

"Hmm. I think she's with a patient."

"Please tell her it's Derek Stillwater and that it's an emergency."

"Well . . ."

"Tell her," he said, voice short.

"Just a moment, please."

He waited. And waited. He glanced at his watch again. He wondered how the investigation was going. What was Pilcher up to now? Spigotta? More important, what was . . . what was Richard Coffee and his band of merry men doing?

Because, whether true or not, he had begun to think of the terrorists as being linked to Richard Coffee.

He thought about the woman he was trying to get hold of. His ex-wife. A military marriage that had lasted two years, until their separate careers had forced them apart more than they were together.

"Derek, what do you want?"

"Hi, Simona. Look—"

"No, Derek. We're very busy here. I'm doing follow-ups on surgical patients. And we've gone to Code Red, but nobody knows why. What do you want?"

"I know why you've gone Code Red," he said.

There was silence on the line. "I thought you were retired."

"I'm with Homeland. A troubleshooter."

More silence. "This news in Baltimore . . ."

"Yes."

"What is it?"

She knew. *She is so smart,* he thought. She knew.

"Bioengineered," he said. "Nothing like it. Pretend it's smallpox without a vaccine."

"Dear God. What do you need from me?"

"I need the names of some nurses and doctors who worked at the 807th MASH in February and March of 1991. Iraq. People with good memories."

"I can do that, honey," she said. "I can get you a list of names in ten minutes."

Derek's mind locked on "honey." He remembered Simona's long dark hair, which she usually wore in a braid. Remembered braiding that hair for her a time or two, both of them naked, fresh out of the shower, pink and clean, her fine straight back in front of him, her long silky hair in his fingers. So long ago.

"E-mail it to me," he said, and gave her his address. "Thanks, Simona."

"Derek . . ." Her voice broke. "Take care of yourself."

He smiled. "What a concept. Bye, love. And thanks."

He sat in the Explorer in the 7-Eleven parking lot, watching what looked like three gang members shoulder through the front door. Baggy jeans hanging off their asses, Baltimore Ravens jerseys, red doo-rags on their heads. He hoped they weren't knocking the place off. He didn't have time for crap like that. He made his next call on his cell phone.

"Pilcher here."

Derek ID'ed himself.

"Where the hell are you?" the FBI agent demanded. "Find what you wanted at the Pentagon?"

"Maybe. I've got to talk to one more person. Let's just say I've found a set of extremely suspicious circumstances."

"Give me a name, Stillwater."

"It's too early."

Pilcher's exasperated sigh burst through a clutter of static. "I don't have to remind you the clock is ticking here."

"No, you don't. I understand what's at stake. What's going on at your end?"

"Spigotta's moved to SIOC. Everybody's on high alert. You tell me, how long would it take to make Chimera usable?"

"Depends on their plan. You only need to infect a couple people to get it going, if that's their intention. Hell, infect a handful of your own people and send them out on the subway or take in an Orioles game. Sneeze on a salad bar somewhere. If that's the plan, they could already be on the move."

Pilcher was silent a moment. Then, "But if they need to grow more?"

"Anywhere from a few hours to a couple days. Not long."

"That's what I thought. Okay, Stillwater. End of briefing unless you share what you're working on. I want the name."

Derek grimaced. "I don't want to send you on a wild-goose chase."

"It's what we do," Pilcher snapped. "Name a name, or we're through. And I've got info you want."

Derek sighed. "Richard Coffee," he said. "U.S. Special Forces." He told Pilcher what he knew so far.

"Huh," Pilcher said. "Bears some follow-up."

"If I can do it fast. I should have a list of names of medical personnel in a couple minutes. Now . . . what's going on?"

"We recovered the vans."

Derek sat straighter. "Where?"

"The Frederick Municipal Airport, second level of a parking garage. We got the license plates and makes from U.S. Immuno's security cams and put out a BOLO. Local cops regularly cruise parking garages. Looks like they flew out of here. ERTs are going over the vans, and we've got people checking over the airport manifests and questioning everybody we can find."

"And the security tapes?"

"Spigotta informed me they've got about a hundred. He's put as many people on them as they can find. Still, it's going to take time. Plus he's got a team doing background on all the personnel at U.S. Immuno. Somebody spilled details besides Scully."

"Okay. Anything else?"

"No," Pilcher said. "How about you?"

"Nothing. Just MI's odd behavior."

"Let's not use the C word, okay?"

"The C word?" Derek asked.

"Yeah. Conspiracy. I hate those."

"I won't if you won't," Derek said.

"Good, then don't. Keep in touch." He clicked off.

Derek pulled out his cell phone and checked his e-mail. Simona had sent him eight names, all scattered around the world, except one: Dr. Austin Davis, an ER doc at Walter Reed. Right here in town.

Derek dialed Davis's number. The man answered on the second ring. Derek told him he was an agent for Homeland Security and needed to talk to him about a patient he might have had in Iraq. Davis, his voice sounding very Kentucky, or maybe Tennessee, said, "Iraq. Iraq now or Iraq back in '91?"

"'91."

"Sure. I'm wrapping up here, can't talk. But I can meet you at Jimmy's on 19th in half an hour. I'll be the tall, good-looking blond at the bar." He laughed and hung up.

Derek checked his watch. *Yeah, that might work.*

Jimmy's was two blocks down from the Walter Reed complex. Derek had expected a yuppie bar with ferns, but got instead an old-fashioned dark hole filled with wall-to-wall medical types more intent on drinking than socializing. He glanced at the bar and zeroed in on the guy he thought was Austin Davis. He was right. The tall, good-looking blond at the bar. Austin Davis had gone antimilitary. He wore his dirty blond hair long past his shoulders and had a thick beard, reddish with gray making inroads. Tall and lithe with concert-pianist fingers that tapped nervously on the tin bar, he wore a green scrub shirt and faded jeans. Derek verified who he was and showed him ID.

"You're Simona's ex, right?"

"Yes."

Davis eyed him suspiciously. "Hey, I guess it can happen to anybody, but from my angle, you must have lost your mind to let her go."

Derek silently agreed with him, but his response was, "Can I buy you a drink?"

"Sure. Gin and tonic."

Derek placed the order with the bartender, adding a coffee for himself.

"Teetotaler?" Davis said, a question whose subtext Derek assumed was actually, *Are you an alcoholic?*

"I expect to be up all night," Derek said, and explained what he wanted. He was halfway through his explanation when Davis said, "Richard Coffee."

Derek turned away from the bar to stare at Davis. "You remember."

"Hell yes, I remember. I've always wondered when something about this guy was going to come up. Now it has."

"Why do you remember?"

"Huh. Well, for one, he was the only one I've ever run into. It's not every day you get a patient exposed to biological and chemical warfare agents. The others I saw in Iraq were in a morgue, and they were usually Iraqi. Dead from being caught near their own shit when we dropped a five-hundred-pound bomb on their heads. So do I remember Coffee? Yeah, you bet." He nodded to someone who walked by.

"Is that why you thought the subject would come up someday?"

"Huh? Oh, the BCW exposure? No. Just that there was some serious weirdness there. I mean, I was off-shift when he died, but I wasn't familiar with the name of the doctor who signed the death certificate. I asked who he was, was told he was a specialist in that kind of treatment, but I'd never heard of him. Never met him, either. Supposedly he flew in special from Saudi or some such bullshit. The rumor was he was somebody from USAMRIID or something, but I think that was just a crock. I don't think the guy existed."

Derek waited. When Davis didn't continue, Derek prompted him. "Meaning?"

"Meaning I didn't think Coffee was that bad. He had burns on his face from whatever the gas was, and there seemed to be some minor lung involvement and maybe some nerve trauma, but someone gave him a shot of atropine immediately and got him out of there. I thought Coffee would get some treatment for the chemical burns, spend some time breathing oxygen for the lungs, have a little therapy, and he'd be okay. Next thing I know some doc I've never heard of signs off on his death certificate and the body is out of there."

The bartender brought them their drinks. Derek took a sip of his coffee and set it down on the tin bar. It tasted like it had been made with lawn clippings. "Do you remember the name of the doctor?"

"No," Davis said.

"Do the names Frank Halloran or James Scully ring a bell?"

"Nope."

"How about Benjamin Zataki?"

"Yeah, rings a bell. He's at USAMRIID now. But that wasn't the name. I'm sorry, I just don't remember."

"Sure." Derek thought for a moment. "Well, what do you think happened?"

"No idea."

"Guess."

"What's this about, Mr. Stillwater?"

"I can't say, but it's important. It's of national security proportions."

"I see. Well, if I had to guess, I'd say for some reason they wanted people to think Coffee was dead. Like they were going to reposition him somewhere with a new identity."

"Sounds . . . I don't know, Doctor. That sounds a little far-fetched."

Davis laughed. "You been in the military long? Were you *ever* in the military? Far-fetched covers a lot of it. But you want to know what my bottom line is?"

"Sure."

"Richard Coffee, to the best of my medical knowledge, was nowhere near death. Now, that isn't to say I haven't had seemingly healthy patients drop dead without warning. Maybe that's what happened. But Coffee just seemed too healthy. He'd been exposed to some serious shit, but he got lucky. He seemed strong, clear, wasn't having problems with his lungs or anything else. My biggest concern was long term."

"Long term?"

"Yeah. You've been exposed to a mix of weird chemicals. You recover. Good for you. Then ten years later you get cancer. Or something else. I've heard neurologists speculate that some of this stuff could lead to mental problems, schizophrenia, bipolar disorders, stuff like that. Cancer's the easy shot, long term. But we know, from a history of organophosphate case histories of pesticide research, that there's more to it. And most chemical warfare stuff got their beginnings in the pesticide business. That stuff affects the nervous system, big time. Expose somebody to low levels of some BW weapon and ten years later you might get a raving paranoid schizophrenic with delusions of grandeur."

"Swell," Derek said. "Well, Doctor. Thank you for taking the time to talk to me."

"Hey, no problem. Can I ask what this is about?"

"Oh, I just thought I had run into Richard Coffee."

"Yeah? He seem okay to you?"

"No, Doctor. I wouldn't say that at all. Thanks again."

Davis knocked back his gin and tonic. "No problem. I'll walk out with you. Got to go work out before I go home."

Derek tossed a bill on the bar and followed the doctor outside. They began to walk down 19th Street. Derek handed him a card. "If the name of that doctor comes back to you, give me a call."

Davis took it. "Sure, no—"

Davis staggered backward, slamming against the red brick wall of Jimmy's before sliding to the ground. A blossom of scarlet appeared on his green scrub shirt. Derek glanced around and then started to reach for Davis when another bullet whined past him, tugging at his collar, chunking into the wall. He dived to the concrete, rolled, came up running. Another bullet ricocheted off a parking meter in front of him.

He slid behind a minivan. Glass exploded above his head. The tire, only inches from his hand, sagged with a hiss. He was being bracketed.

He held his breath. Glancing back, he saw that Davis was dead, blood everywhere. Somewhere somebody screamed. Another bullet whocked into the fiberglass body of the minivan just inches from his head.

He sprang to his feet and sprinted down the sidewalk, bullets peppering the walls behind him.

To his left he saw motion, a Chevy Blazer. The woman at the wheel shouted, "Get in! Hurry!"

Another bullet ripped past him. He dived into the Blazer and it peeled away before he could get the door shut.

12

Frederick Municipal Airport

AGENT AARON PILCHER SNAPPED his phone off and stared out at the three white vans parked against the far wall. Beyond the vans was the main airstrip. As he watched, a small jet, probably a Lear, roared down the runway and lifted into the hazy dusk. Night was coming on.

Frederick Municipal Airport was about six hundred acres and catered mostly to private jets and the military, Ford Detrick being nearby. He didn't like that this airport was so close to Detrick, home of USAMRIID. Didn't like it at all. Maybe it was just a coincidence. Frederick was small and relatively near U.S. Immuno and dominated by small private aircraft. If he were a terrorist trying to make a hasty exit from the country, he might have preferred to charter a private jet out of a small airport rather than fly commercial out of Dulles or Ronald Reagan.

Three flatbed trucks appeared one after the other at the mouth of the second level of the parking garage. From where he was standing on the other side of the garage, Pilcher saw Rodriguez wave them over. The ERTs had processed everything they could in situ, and wanted to move the vans to their lab before opening them up. They hadn't even cracked the doors.

When Tres Rodriguez had told him that, Pilcher had raised his eyebrows. "Tres, we're in a hurry with this. We can't treat it like a typical criminal case."

Tres Rodriguez was short, but short like a pit bull. He was as tenacious as a pit bull, too. He wore his curly dark hair close to his skull, his dark eyes slanting upward so he appeared vaguely Asian, though he insisted he was Mexican through and through. Tres and Pilcher had gone through Quantico together, sharing a dorm room. Their families got together a couple times a year, Pilcher and his wife and two daughters, Rodriguez with his wife and three sons.

"Aaron, my man," Tres had said, putting on his jive-ass Latino act like he did when he was about to insist on having things his way. "I am a fo-ren-sic ge-ni-us, certified by the effa-bee-eye of the U-nited States of A-mer-i-ca. I"—he placed both hands on his meaty chest—"am an ex-pert heah, mah man. I am not some Jew-boy field agent who doesn't understand the intricacies—no, mah man, the *mysteries*—of the fo-ren-sic sciences! I am the Magician of the Microscope, the Wizard of the—"

Pilcher waved his hand. "Jesus, Tres. If you'll just shut up, you can do what you want."

Tres grinned. "In the long run, it's faster my way. We don't screw around transporting evidence and risk contamination. Trust me."

"Yeah, yeah. Just get on it."

Pilcher didn't think there *was* any long run. He hoped these terrorists and their stolen Chimera M13 took the first private jet to

Korea or Iraq or Pakistan. That would be just fine with him. Did he really think those countries would use those things if they got hold of them? He hoped not, but you never knew. He knew that those miserable twits couldn't feed their own people, but they were perfectly capable of building atomic bombs and bioengineered superviruses.

What he did *not* want, what he was afraid they had here, was exactly what Stillwater had been afraid of. A bunch of suicidal loons with a big, bad bug to let loose in his jurisdiction. He wondered what he would do, what he would say to his wife and daughters if it happened. He prayed it didn't. Prayed he wouldn't be forced into that situation. That nobody would.

Now, trying to get hold of Spigotta, he was standing on the opposite side of the garage, because the reception was better. Must be a cell antenna nearby somewhere. And also because Rodriguez could be a real prima donna and didn't want field agents breathing down his neck while his team processed a scene. *Pit bull,* Pilcher thought with a grin. *Only all bark and no bite.* He flipped open his phone and called Spigotta at SIOC on the fifth floor of the J. Edgar Hoover Building.

"Yeah?" Spigotta snarled into the phone.

"I just got off the phone with Stillwater. He gave me a name," Pilcher said.

"What name?" Spigotta sounded on the verge of a heart attack. On a good day he sounded like he might be having chest pains; today was not a good day.

"Richard Coffee. Apparently an old Army buddy of Stillwater's. Thinks he might have disappeared into the CIA or something at the end of the Gulf War." He filled in his boss on Military Intelligence's odd behavior and the state of Coffee's military records.

"You believe him?" Spigotta asked.

"No reason not to."

"The USAMRIID people knew him. They say he's good," Spigotta said. "But a couple of them also said he's a burnout. Seen too much."

Pilcher shrugged, a gesture whose effect was lost on the telephone. "What do you want to do?"

"We'll process the name. I need you here by eight o'clock. The director needs a full brief before he heads to the White House. Full staff meeting at the White House at nine, everybody's going to be there to update the president."

"Yes, sir." Pilcher swallowed and turned to watch the flatbed trucks maneuver into position. The drivers were on their backs, hooking chains to the first van's frame. "I've got agents going over parking-lot surveillance tapes here to see if we can get a look at these guys. And see if they're still around."

"Good. Keep me informed." Spigotta clicked off.

Tucking his cell phone into his pocket, Pilcher headed toward the vans and the ERTs. He could hear the motor of the winch kick into action and begin to pull the first of the three vans onto the flatbed. Rodriguez was standing by the vehicle, supervising.

At the precise instant the van hit 33 degrees off-level, there was a massive *ker-whump*, and the van exploded into a flaming ball of flying metal, fabric, and plastic.

Seconds later the other two vans erupted into flame.

13

Washington, D.C.

THE WOMAN RACED THE Blazer through the D.C. streets, taking
seemingly random turns whenever she could, glancing in the rearview mirrors often to check for someone following. In the passenger seat Derek clutched the chain around his neck and tried not to
think about bullets pinning him down, about the petals of blood
exploding on Dr. Davis's chest. Trying to keep his voice even, he
said, "Where are we going?"

"Somewhere safe."

He didn't comment. His mind was spinning. It was like flying
through a hurricane, looking for the eye. And then he found it, a
center of calm surrounded by a whirlwind. He looked at her, taking in the shoulder-length dark hair, strong features made up of
sharp nose, high cheekbones, and square jaw. Her blunt fingers
gripped the steering wheel. She seemed tough, maybe the set of
that square jaw or the way her attention was focused on the road.
In leather hiking boots, black jeans, and a white button-down shirt

under a leather bomber jacket, she projected an image of someone who could handle almost anything.

He reached over and tugged at the leather jacket. Her right hand shot out and brushed his hand aside, but not before he saw the grip of a matte-black semiautomatic in a shoulder rig.

"Who are you?" Derek repeated.

"Irina Khournikova."

He thought she had a trace of an accent. The name and the accent pointed toward Russian.

"Okay," he said. "I'm—"

"Dr. Derek Stillwater. Or do you prefer Professor?"

Derek lapsed into silence. His brain spun. The Blazer was still racing through the streets, never stopping or slowing. Irina Khournikova, or whoever she was, had perfected the rolling stop, never slowing under twenty miles per hour, even at stop signs. "Let me out here," he said. "I'll be fine."

"It is not safe."

"Who are you?"

She brushed hair impatiently away from her face. Derek noticed a small, C-shaped scar, very faint, on her right cheek. "You need to be briefed," she said. "I didn't imagine they'd go after you."

"They?"

The Blazer zigged and zagged through city streets. Not comfortable in D.C. on a good day, Derek had lost all sense of direction except for the reddish glow of the setting sun to the west. The only comfort he felt was that his Colt was still on his hip under his jacket. It was his ace in the hole, and he didn't want to misplay his hand.

"Your own people," Khournikova said. "The shooter back there."

Derek settled his gaze on her. "You're saying somebody from Homeland Security shot Dr. Davis?"

"No, no." Her accent intensified. She shook her head. "Not *your* people like that. Others. Probably CIA. Maybe your Military Intelligence. State Department. My guess is CIA."

Derek said nothing, but thought of FBI agent Aaron Pilcher. *Let's not use the C word.*

His creeping feeling of dread had caught up to him. Confusion or fear or paranoia, he couldn't be sure which, but he was feeling it. The panic rat was back, chewing on his intestines. He struggled to stay calm, to focus on what was happening and not shift into analytical mode. There would hopefully be time for that later. Now he had to find out as much as he could and stay on top of the risk factor. He shoved aside his confusion.

"Who are you with?" he asked.

She shook her head again. "When we get to the safe house. Then I'll answer your questions. We're almost there."

There turned out to be a five-story apartment building made of dirty gray brick. It wasn't inviting. To Derek it looked like an upscale tenement, if there was such a thing. He suspected that in Washington, D.C., there were. On the street, people were out and about, but not many, and he had the sense that most of them were beginning their evening prowl, looking for trouble. The neighborhood projected that feeling. She found a spot to park the Blazer on the street and told him to follow her.

Evaluate, coordinate, investigate, he thought.

Derek followed her. A block away somebody shouted in Spanish. Farther off he heard music, a heavy bass beat. Even farther away, a siren. The sounds of the nation's capital. There was nobody at the door of the building, just a buzzer console Khournikova ignored, letting herself in with a key. She headed for the stairwell. He followed, keeping his hand near the Colt on his belt, senses highly attuned to the environment. There were the background sounds of TVs and radios and muttered conversations. The stairs were bare concrete, the metal handrail showing peeling white paint. It smelled of dampness and insect repellent.

She stopped at the third floor and led him down a long hallway with poor lighting, every fourth bulb burned out. The carpet was a worn blue, the walls a dingy white. *Fading lower-middle-class,* he thought. *Welcome to the American Dream.*

She stopped at apartment 302, jabbed another key into the door, and walked in, flicking on a light.

He followed, pulling the Colt as he stepped into the entryway. When she turned he had it aimed directly at her face. She did not seem surprised.

"Who are you?" Derek demanded.

"Lieutenant Irina Khournikova, Directorate T, Russian Federal Security Service."

"Directorate T?" He did not lower the gun.

"Antiterrorism. We need to talk about Richard Coffee. If you put the gun away, we can." Her hazel eyes met his gaze, not flinching.

Yeah, tough, he thought, confirming his initial assessment. He lowered the gun but didn't put it away.

"Turn around," he said.

She continued to stare up at him, then slowly turned.

"Take your gun out—two fingers—very slowly and drop it gently on the floor."

For a second he didn't think she'd comply. Then she reached gingerly into her jacket and removed the gun, holding it with two fingers. She bent over and dropped it on the floor.

"Kick it back to me."

She did without comment. He crouched, gun still aimed at her, and picked up her weapon.

"Go on in. Slowly. Hands on head."

She did. He followed her. It was a two-bedroom apartment, the living room off to the right, the kitchen/dining area to the left. Straight ahead were three doors: the bathroom and two bedrooms. The carpet was the color of a rotten avocado, the walls a single coat of eggshell. There was battered furniture that looked like it came with the apartment: a TV in the living room, two chairs, and a threadbare sofa. The kitchen table appeared to be forty or fifty years old, steel tubing and Formica, the chairs a mismatched set of red and blue vinyl and chrome.

Derek jammed the gun in her back and pushed her through the apartment. One of the bedrooms had a double bed with two pillows and a gray blanket and a thick blue comforter. The second bedroom had a desk with a computer on it.

He examined every room, shoving her ahead of him. Finally they were back in the kitchen. "Hands on the table, wide apart. Lean forward."

She assumed the awkward position without comment. Derek patted her down, retrieved a man's wallet from her jacket pocket.

"Do you carry a purse?"

"When I need to."

He flipped through the wallet. She started to stand up, but he said, "Eh, eh, eh. Stay right there until I tell you differently." The wallet contained an unfamiliar ID written in Russian and another ID that appeared to provide her access to the Russian embassy.

"Have a seat," he said, and poked around in the kitchen, finding it to be reasonably well stocked. Otherwise the apartment looked barely lived in. In fact, the toiletries in the bathroom appeared non-descript, as if from an inexpensive hotel. The whole place appeared to be exactly what the Russian claimed it to be: a safe house, a bolt hole.

Derek sat at the table, dumped the ammunition from Khournikova's gun, and slid the weapon across the table to her, keeping the full magazine. He holstered his Colt.

"Okay," Derek said. "Talk."

"Satisfied?" She slipped her gun into her shoulder holster and shot him an irritated look.

"Not hardly, lady. I'm very pressed for time today. You have exactly five minutes to convince me you're not wasting my time, so start talking."

"I need your help."

"If the Russian government wants help from the United States, there are proper channels to use. I'm not one of them."

She shrugged. "You are looking for a man called Richard Coffee."

"What makes you think that?"

"My people have ways of knowing certain things. One of those things is when and if someone is checking Richard Coffee's records on computer."

"Then I'll recommend the Pentagon double-check their computer security. Okay. I might be looking for information about Richard. So what?"

"Why are you looking for him?" She sat perfectly still, forearms resting on the table in front of her. She seemed to be working very hard to appear nonthreatening.

"What? *Your people don't have ways of knowing that?*" He imitated her accent, sarcasm dripping off every word.

"Are my five minutes about up, Dr. Stillwater? Do you wish to play games, or do you wish to obtain information?"

Derek closed his eyes. He opened them and glared at her. "Why does Russia's antiterrorism unit want to keep tabs on a dead U.S. soldier?"

"Richard Coffee is not dead."

Derek felt his heart thud harder in his chest. Confirmation.

"U.S. military records indicate he is," he said. "As you know."

Khournikova smiled a hard, tight smile. "Richard Coffee 'died' in Iraq in 1991. He was reborn a short time later as Surkho Andarbek. The name, by the way, is Chechen for 'strong warrior.' This was shortly after Chechnya declared their independence. We did not become aware of his presence for some time."

Derek thought the timing and the Russian language skills would have been perfect. He said, "The military doesn't run spies like that."

She snorted in derision. "Really, Doctor? How interesting. Let us not argue that point. As you said, you are pressed for time. We are convinced that Coffee was working for your Central Intelligence Agency at the time."

"Okay," Derek said. "Let's say I go along with your premise."

"It is not a *premise*. It is a fact." Her voice carried a harsh, bitter tone. She leaned forward, fingers stabbing the Formica tabletop. "Richard Coffee was inside Chechnya for the CIA."

"Whatever you say. That's nice. So?" Derek glanced at his watch.

"Richard Coffee's mission," she snarled, "was to foment revolution on the part of the Chechen rebels, to filter money and military weapons—U.S. money and weapons—to the Chechens. It was the express policy of the CIA to increase Russia's internal problems by supporting a known domestic terrorist group on Russian soil."

Derek thought it over. He could believe it. The U.S. had a long history of doing very similar things. Having an ear inside Chechnya would have been considered a very good thing by U.S. foreign-policy makers. Russian leadership insisted the Chechens were terrorists, not a separatist movement caused by Russian heavy-handedness. The U.S. was reluctantly willing to go along with this as long as Russia supported the United States' war on terrorism. It put the U.S. in an awkward position, calling the Palestinians terrorists and supporting Israel while supporting Russia and calling the Chechens an internal problem.

"Okay," he said. "So what makes you think Richard Coffee—assuming that he didn't die in Iraq—is now in the United States? And what makes you think—" He paused. "You were following me."

"I was, yes."

"For how long?"

"Since you left the Pentagon."

He looked at her. She brushed her hair away from her face. "And you knew I was at the Pentagon because . . ."

"I already told you. We were informed that you were showing an interest in Richard Coffee. I was to follow you and see if you could lead me to his whereabouts."

"That was rather quick. I was only at the Pentagon for about two hours."

"Yes," she said. "Richard Coffee is something of a priority to my government."

"Because?"

"Because, Dr. Stillwater, he is, as you might say, public enemy number one. He stopped working for your government five years ago." She waited for his inevitable question.

"What happened five years ago?"

"He died."

Derek broke into a grin and slapped the table. "Well, hell, Irina! Then I guess he's nobody's problem. The man's dead. Twice over." His grin faded and he said, "Just tell me."

It was believed that Richard Coffee died during a major Russian offensive into Chechnya. A man Chechen captives called Surkho Andarbek had been caught by a mortar. They wrote it off as good news, and later the FSB picked up some signal intelligence indicating that the CIA had lost contact with their man in Chechnya. With the shifting tides of U.S.-Russian relations, Coffee's active role in inciting Chechen separatism and covert U.S. financial support to the rebels was a major embarrassment to the U.S. and a major bargaining chip for the Russians.

Then there started to be rumors of some other group working on the Russian-Georgian border. A group of multinational terrorists who could supply any kind of military weapon you could ask for. They were led by a man who called himself the Fallen.

"The Fallen," Derek said.

"Yes. That's what the group called themselves. The Fallen, or the Fallen Angels."

They were believed to have belonged to various military, espionage, and antiterror agencies around the world. Disaffected by their own countries, they pledged their allegiance to their leader, known as Fallen, or the Fallen. He was considered to be charismatic, a great warrior, and a master of many languages. His mission was to bring about chaos to the world through terrorist acts. Only by destroying the current world government infrastructure could a better world be reborn from the ashes.

"Proof," Derek said. "I need more than your word."

"In the office. I have files."

"Get them."

It was a thick file filled with documents—all written in Russian, unfortunately—and a series of photographs. Derek stared at the first photograph. It was among what seemed to be a destroyed city, burned-out buildings bombed to charred ruins. A half-dozen men were firing rifles over a brick wall. The man nearest to the camera wore camouflage fatigues and a black watch cap. He had a heavy beard and was sighting down an AK-47. It could have been Richard Coffee, but the angle was wrong and the beard made it difficult to see his face.

Derek flipped to the next photograph.

The man had turned and snarled at the photographer. The photograph caught the man head on, mouth open, eyes blazing from an inner fire.

Derek couldn't take his eyes off the photograph. It was Richard Coffee. Definitely, without a doubt, the Richard Coffee he had worked with in Panama, Korea, and Iraq. He shuffled through the photographs. Many were taken in Chechnya, all during battles and what appeared to be guerilla actions. Long-range photographs.

Then there were a series of what appeared to be surveillance photographs. An older Richard Coffee, now minus the beard, wearing boots and jeans and sweaters, or in business suits, meeting with various men of various nationalities in what appeared to be cities in different countries around the world. Derek stared at one. Coffee was in a restaurant that appeared Asian. He wore an off-white linen suit. He was talking to a man who appeared to be Korean.

Khournikova said, "North Korea."

He looked up at her.

"We had the other man under surveillance. Kim Pak Lee. One of Korea's top biowarfare specialists."

Derek looked back at the photograph.

Khournikova said, "Lee disappeared shortly after that meeting."

"Disappeared."

"Yes. Or perhaps a more appropriate thing to say is, he fell."

"Fell."

"Yes. Kim Pak Lee joined the Fallen Angels, Dr. Stillwater."

14

Frederick Municipal Airport

THE FIRST EXPLOSION KNOCKED Pilcher flat on his ass. He had fast reflexes and scrambled to his feet and was sprinting toward the explosion site when the second and third vans exploded. This time the blasts slammed him against the side of a red Jeep Cherokee, stunning him. As he tried to fill his lungs, a pressure wave of hot air like dragon's breath engulfed him. He dropped to the pavement and rolled under the Cherokee as flaming debris fell around him. His chest felt like it was on fire, and he squeezed his eyes shut to protect them from the heat.

Beneath the Jeep, Pilcher thought the fallout lasted forever as sizzling plastic and metal clattered to the concrete, but it was probably only seconds.

Far off, muffled, he heard sirens. Good.

He crawled out from under the Jeep and surveyed the garage. The lights had been blown out by the explosions, but the scene was lit by the flaming vehicles and dozens of smaller fires caused by the incendiary debris. Squinting through the acrid, billowing smoke, he picked his way toward the vans.

He stepped on something, nearly twisting his ankle as he caught his balance. Glancing down he saw with horror that he had stepped on the severed torso of one of the ERTs. Vomit rose up in his throat, but he clamped down on his emotions. This was not the time to lose his cool.

He knelt next to the remains and peered at it. Not enough light. Fishing in his pocket, he came up with his key chain and a small flashlight attached to the ring. Pushing his thumb down on the switch, a narrow beam of yellow light cascaded over the body. The tag on the tattered coveralls said RODRIGUEZ, T. *Oh God.* Pilcher hung his head, eyes stinging from emotion and smoke. *Oh Tres*, he thought. *How am I going to face your family? Oh dear God!*

Using the flash to illuminate his route, he stepped over and around dismembered limbs and scraps of scorched meat, the stink of the burning vans and flesh driving deep into his sinuses. It was like standing at the gates of hell. Finally, he was as close as he could get, heat roaring off the burning vehicles. He circled the perimeter, searching for survivors. He didn't find any.

He turned back to see an ambulance race through the entrance to the second level. Within moments airport security guards and fire crews were swarming the site. He sifted through the growing throng, looking for a familiar face, trying to identify the guy who would take over the scene.

He saw a smooth-faced man in fire gear shouting into a radio. The fireman had clean, angular features, a strong cleft jaw, and dark, snapping eyes. He was good looking enough to be the poster boy for firefighters, or a male model. Pilcher thought he looked too young to be in charge of airport fire control, but he was clearly the one in charge here.

Holding his ID badge in front of him, Pilcher approached, coughing into his hand. The fireman turned when he saw Pilcher and quickly waved over an EMT, who came at a dead run.

"Take care of this man."

"I'm FBI," Pilcher shouted. His voice sounded like it was coming from a great distance, his ears affected by the blasts. The fireman's voice sounded like a whisper. Pilcher coughed again and spat black phlegm onto the ground.

"Sir—"

"I'll brief you," Pilcher shouted. "This is a national security issue."

The fireman waved him to follow. Pilcher leaned against a fire truck. He forced himself to be calm, to tell the man what had happened in a logical, chronological order. As he talked, a crew of firefighters began to spray foam on the vans. He stared, not speaking, thinking, *We'll never get useful evidence off those things.*

The next time Pilcher checked his watch, he realized it was dead, the crystal a spiderweb of cracks. He must have hit it on the ground when he fell.

The EMT insisted he sit for a few minutes, gave him a water bottle to drink from and a canister of oxygen. He daubed gingerly at Pilcher's face with a damp rag. "How close were you, sir? You're burned. Looks like a sunburn. Not too bad. If it gets worse or you start to feel a lot of pain, get to a doctor. Don't want an infection."

No, Pilcher thought. *Wouldn't want an infection.*

"And your eyebrows are singed."

"I'm alive." Pilcher greedily sucked on the oxygen, thinking that he wanted to go home and turn this mess over to someone else. But he knew he couldn't. He felt a responsibility to the original investigation, tracking down the people who stole the virus. And now these monsters had murdered his friend and a whole team of FBI agents. Now it was personal. He thanked the EMT for his care, kept the water, and asked him for his watch.

"What?"

"I need a watch. Mine's busted. How much for yours?"

The EMT had curly black hair and a thick black mustache. He was built like a marathoner, thin and lanky. Pilcher put him in his early twenties. The guy didn't understand what he wanted.

Pilcher held up his badge. "FBI. I'm commandeering your wrist watch. Give it to me."

Slowly, the EMT figured out what Pilcher was getting at. He unhooked his cheap Swatch sports watch from his wrist and handed it over.

Pilcher strapped it on. He handed the kid his card. "Call me when this is over. I'll get it back to you with a check for a hundred bucks. Thanks."

He strode past the ambulance, looking for his people—those who survived.

He found three of his agents near the stairwell. They seemed surprised to see him.

"What happened?" Agent Sara Magnusson asked. Red hair, blocky build, dark suit. Pilcher had worked with her before. She was like a moray eel—once she clamped on she wouldn't let go of a case.

"Booby trapped. I'm betting explosives with a mercury switch. When the van was tilted enough, it set it off. The explosion set off the other two. Anybody done a head count?"

Magnusson nodded. "Four ERTs, three truck drivers, and two agents. Three airport security guys. We thought you were dead."

Twelve, Pilcher thought. Plus the four at the Scully's house and twenty-eight at U.S. Immuno. A total, so far, of forty-four. If that didn't indicate these terrorists' intentions, nothing did.

"Media here?"

John Yenor nodded. Middle-aged and chunky, Yenor was slow and steady. He was a veteran agent with no apparent ambitions beyond being a good field agent. "We decided they have to wait. We needed to know what the situation up here was."

"You're the agent-in-charge," said the third agent, Benjamin Sanchez. Aggressively handsome, dark and Latino, Sanchez was a Harvard Law School grad. He clearly *did* have ambitions beyond being a field agent.

Pilcher wanted to take a deep breath, but started to cough when he did. When he got it under control, he pointed at Magnusson. "What's that?" She was clutching an evidence bag under one arm.

"Oh. Security tapes. We got 'em."

They all stared at her. Pilcher was the first to find his voice. "What? Explain."

Magnusson couldn't contain her grin. "Parking garage security tapes. I was watching the one from this level when the vans blew up. I made sure I collected them before I ran up here."

Pilcher nodded. "Good. What've we got?"

She seemed to nearly vibrate from excitement. "I watched the three vans come in and what looked like twelve men get out. They didn't head for the stairs or the elevators. I think they were going to different vehicles already parked here."

"That was on the tape?" Sanchez asked, dark eyebrows raised.

"Not this one. But I've got all of them. We can even see faces."

Pilcher nodded, also excited. "Okay." He took another deep breath and was again racked with harsh coughing. He hawked up phlegm and spat. Gray now, not black. He guessed that was an improvement. "Sorry. Magnusson, get those tapes to SIOC. I'll call Spigotta and tell him you're coming. He'll have a lab guy waiting. Good job."

She just stood there. "Go," he snapped. She nodded and took off at a run.

"Sanchez, call Newman. He's coordinating the media. You'll handle the press here."

Sanchez clearly liked his assignment. His lean face split into a wide grin. "Yes, sir."

"Go."

Sanchez went, phone already pressed to his ear.

Pilcher turned to John Yenor. "Get on the phone and get an ERT team out here to get the vans. Get people picking up the security and road cameras in a five-mile radius of this airport. We need to figure what direction these bastards headed. Also, call ATF—I want this parking garage swept for more bombs."

"Yes, sir." Yenor didn't need more prompting. He headed off toward the stairs, punching numbers on his phone.

Pilcher leaned against the doorway to the elevators, heart piledriving in his chest. A wave of nausea swept over him and again he bit it back. No time. Turning, he strode over to where he could get a clean signal and, leaning over the concrete wall looking out at the city lights, he called Spigotta at SIOC.

"I'm glad you called. I've got—"

Pilcher interrupted and described the situation. He waited patiently through the senior agent's cursing. When he wound down, Spigotta said, "It's a diversion."

"Yes," Pilcher agreed. "I think so, too. We may gets leads off it, though. Magnusson's on her way with the tapes."

"I'll have the lab on standby."

Pilcher filled in Spigotta on his other actions.

"Good," Spigotta said. "Good. Very good, Aaron. Okay. I've got something I need you to do. Turn over the reins to . . . Sanchez is busy with the press?"

"Yes."

"Yenor, then. I need you to track down Frank Halloran. We've got some questions for him that came up during the background checks. If he's not at U.S. Immuno, track him down ASAP."

"I'm in Frederick. There should be agents closer to Baltimore."

"I've got a feeling about this, Aaron. I want *you* to talk to him. You up to it?"

That was the question of the day. Pilcher thought of his friend Tres Rodriguez, blown to pieces. "Yes, sir."

Spigotta told Pilcher what had come up on the background checks. Pilcher nodded and clicked off. With a deep breath of night air that didn't make him cough, he went looking for Agent Yenor.

15

USAMRIID, Fort Detrick, Maryland

LIZ VARGAS FELT ENERGIZED. She didn't know why. Maybe it was the helicopter ride, something she'd never done before. Maybe it was simply relief at being alive, at having survived a massacre. Maybe it was the light supper and an hour lying on a cot, dozing. Whatever the reason, she felt up to whatever happened and just wanted to get on with things.

She tapped her fingers on Sharon Jaxon's desk, a cluttered, gray-steel government issue in a cramped, windowless office at the United States Army Military Research Institute for Infectious Diseases, or USAMRIID. Jaxon smiled at her. She was on the phone with some guy, a boyfriend. Liz had offered to leave, give her some privacy, but Sharon waved her off, saying she just wanted to tell him they had a "situation" and she wouldn't be over tonight.

Liz's impatient gaze took in the office. Some of the clutter was paperwork, but a lot of it was memorabilia from parts of the world where Lieutenant Sharon Jaxon had been stationed: Asian dolls from Korea and Japan, odd bits of sculptured rock from Kosovo shaped like men with packs on their backs, aerial photographs of the Panama Canal.

"Okay. Sure. If the timing's right, I'll swing by for breakfast. Yeah, that too." Jaxon laughed. "Naughty, naughty. Don't count on it, though. I expect to be here a couple days. Yeah. Love you, too."

She hung up, her face flushing a little pink with embarrassment. "Guys," she said.

Liz smiled, but it was a little strained. "Good friend?"

Sharon nodded. "I'm thinking of moving in. Barring disaster, I'll be here at Rid for the rest of my career. Dave's a good guy. He's a freelance copywriter, pulls in three times what I do working out of his back bedroom. Marketing materials mostly. Some ad copy. Not a scientist or in the Army, thank God. You have someone?"

Liz shook her head quickly. "No."

Sharon reached out and touched her hand. "Hey, it's all right. I didn't mean to hit a nerve. I'm sorry."

Liz sighed, some of her energy seeping away. "It's just been a bad day. I was married for three years. Mitch was an oncologist at Hopkins. He died in a motorcycle accident two years ago."

"I'm so sorry."

Liz shrugged. "Thanks. The only reason I'm being bothered by it is because of . . . you know. Surviving a terrorist attack." Tears welled up in her eyes, but she wiped them away. She wouldn't allow herself to think of all of the dead. So many of her friends, colleagues, people she talked to daily, ate lunch with. All gone.

Sharon turned serious. "If you're not up to this, no one will think less of you."

"If that's possible," Liz said bitterly. "You're the only one who trusts me."

Sharon leaned back in her chair, which let out a high-pitched creak. "That's because Derek trusted you. If he went into a hot zone with you, that's good enough for me."

"Jeez, that guy. I didn't know what to make of him. He got all freaked out before going into HL4, even . . . even barfed, but he told me it was just stage fright. I mean, all those good-luck charms!"

Sharon smiled tightly and steepled her fingers. "How was he inside?"

"No problem. Better than me. He knew just what to do, and the only time he acted even mildly rattled was when he found that playing card."

Sharon nodded. "Let me tell you a little bit about Derek Still-water. When it comes to hot zones—in the lab or the field—Derek is the most realistic person I've ever met. He knows in a way most of us don't that one mistake can mean his death. He knows it." Something troubling crossed her face, a combination of worry and stress. Sharon paused for a moment, then shrugged. "Derek can probably take care of himself. We have something else to worry about. Just . . . you can trust Derek. In a pinch, you can trust him."

There was something in Sharon Jaxon's voice when she talked about Derek Stillwater that suggested they had been more than friends, but she didn't pursue it.

"What's taking so long?" she asked.

Sharon smiled. "Ben's very cautious. Consider what he's doing. You would be, right?"

Ben Zataki had taken the cultures of Chimera M13 and the cultures of Chimera M1, M2, M3, and M4 into the Level 4 suite and was inoculating them into cultures, preparing them to be injected into a batch of monkeys. He decided to do the preparations himself, then would organize the teams when dealing with the monkeys.

"Well, yes. But why didn't he want my help?"

"You looked like you needed the rest."

Liz sighed. Despite her second wind, her body ached, and she knew exhaustion, both physical and emotional, was just around the corner. There was a knock at Jaxon's door. "Come in."

Ben Zataki stuck his head in. He looked as neat and put-together as before. "Ladies, I've scheduled a meeting for everybody in fifteen minutes. I've got to make a couple quick phone calls to Atlanta and D.C., and then we'll be on our way." His gaze met Liz's. "You okay?"

"I'm fine. Ready to go."

"Good. See you there."

The team met in a second-floor conference room with no windows. The room was full, and it was the first time Liz got a sense of unseen machinery at work, that the theft of Chimera M13 had set in motion forces that she could not stop.

Zataki gestured for everyone to sit, but he remained standing. Even in green surgical scrubs he held a kind of dignified authority.

"Okay, everyone. I've prepared our cultures, including extras. I've set up an experimental procedure and assigned teams. Similar tests are currently being started at the U.S. Immunological Research facility, and samples are being flown to the CDC. All of you will be assigned to monkeys, and all but two will be inoculated with a high dose of Chimera M13. Four will be injected first with one of the weaker strains. The rest will receive doses at different intervals."

Liz studied the schedule that was handed around the room. She was paired with Sharon Jaxon. They were to assist in injecting the four monkeys with Chimera M1, M2, M3, and M4 and in injecting the rest of the animals with Chimera M13. Then, four hours later, they were to inject four of the monkeys with M1, 2, 3, and 4. Other scientists were assigned similar procedures with other monkeys at later increments: eight hours, twelve hours, and twenty-four hours.

Liz wondered if they would have twenty-four hours. She wondered if the terrorists, whoever they were, would unleash Chimera on the public before twenty-four hours passed.

Everyone listened carefully as Zataki outlined their objectives, reminding everyone of safety issues. Liz saw that some of the people present seemed confused. Two of them were older men in military uniforms—Army, she thought. Two more were in navy blue three-piece suits. They looked like government agents of some sort, or lobbyists or politicians. Rigid, clean-cut, serious. They, in particular, seemed confused.

One of them said, "Will this work?"

Zataki shrugged. "Mr. O'Brien, right?"

O'Brien nodded.

Zataki said, "We don't know. That's what we're trying to determine."

"But you think it will?" O'Brien fidgeted with a gold pen, tapping it nervously on a leather-bound folder in his lap.

Zataki gazed at him. "If it doesn't, Mr. O'Brien, we're in serious trouble."

"But what should I advise the president?"

Zataki said, "There isn't much to advise, Mr. O'Brien. I've spoken with Anthony Pfeiffer at the CDC, and he'll be at the meeting. We won't have anything useful or definitive before tomorrow night."

"That's not good enough," O'Brien said, unable to keep a petulant whine out of his voice.

"Without a doubt," Zataki said. "But it is, nonetheless, the best we can do. The best *anybody* can do."

The second suit said, "If this works, and if these terrorists let this germ loose, will we have enough of the vaccine available to use on the public?" He was heavier set than his lean, younger partner and spoke more slowly with fewer fidgets.

Zataki peered at him over his half-moon reading glasses. "Samples of all four of the weaker strains—"

"M1, M2, M3, and M4?"

"Yes, as well as a sample of M13—have been turned over to Sidney Alloway. She is the head of Geiger Pharmaceuticals. She runs a vaccine-manufacturing facility in New Jersey and has the means to mass-produce a virus or bacterial agent. They will begin growing large amounts of M1, M2, M3, and M4 as soon as possible in case we're able to use them as a vaccine."

Liz's stomach did a slow flip-flop.

Zataki continued. "They will also be growing M13 and attempting to develop a Salk vaccine for Chimera." A Salk vaccine was a dead virus, treated with formaldehyde.

All the color drained out of Liz's face, and she thought she was going to vomit. Sharon glanced at her, then grabbed her arm. "Are you okay?" she whispered.

"You're going to grow industrial lots of Chimera?" Liz burst out.

Zataki turned. "Yes, Dr. Vargas."

"That's . . . Chimera's too dangerous. That's crazy! It's the most dangerous virus on the—"

"We're well aware of the danger," Zataki said, voice even. "But we don't have a choice." He paused, gaze piercing her. "Do we?"

She shook her head and collapsed back in her chair, realizing fully the Pandora's box they had opened. She remembered Derek Stillwater saying, "When you steal the devil's pitchfork, you become the devil."

O'Brien said, "And if these don't work? What are we going to do if none of these versions of Chimera work? What will we do if we don't have a workable vaccine and the terrorists release M13 somewhere on the public?"

Zataki frowned. "The standard procedure is rings of containment. In the case of a virus like Chimera, victims will be transported to isolation facilities—here at USAMRIID or at the CDC or various hospitals—and anybody who has come into contact with the victims will also be isolated, thus setting up rings of containment around the victims."

"And if someone gets through the rings of containment?" O'Brien demanded. "If you miss somebody?"

Zataki said, "If the virus spreads faster than we can contain it? If the public panics and runs? If the public is noncompliant? That's simple, Mr. O'Brien. Hundreds, thousands, maybe even millions of people will die."

In time the meeting was wrapped. The White House representatives headed back to Washington, D.C., to tell their boss that the only thing being done to deal with a possible biological attack was a risky long shot that most of the scientists thought wouldn't work.

The military was preparing its troops and, more importantly, setting up armed perimeters around U.S. Immuno and Geiger Pharmaceuticals.

Somewhere out there, Liz thought as she changed into scrubs, was a lone troubleshooter and an FBI team trying to track down the terrorists before they unleashed Chimera. She made a silent prayer to a god she didn't really believe in that they would be successful.

Once dressed, the two women proceeded into the next level to tape rubber gloves to their scrubs and socks, then don their spacesuits.

"Looks like Frank and . . ." Acid flooded Liz's throat. She swallowed it back, breath coming hard. ". . . and Jim based our hot level facility on yours."

"There are only so many ways to do it," Jaxon acknowledged. She took a close look at Liz. "You up to this? You look a little strained."

"Yes. I'm up to this."

"Good. There will be a bunch of observers this round. In the middle of the night, it ought to thin out, but don't get freaked by the number of spacesuits you see."

"Sure."

They moved into the spacesuit area and donned their blue suits. The one Liz Vargas wore was brand new and crinkled as she unfolded it. It had the distinctive "new suit" smell. She didn't like the smell. For some reason it reminded her of her husband's death, of the medical examiner's office, of the funeral home. It reminded her of saying goodbye. They suited up and checked each other's suits for cracks or leaks, then proceeded into USAMRIID's Biological Safety Level 4 facility.

Jaxon had been right. There were eight or nine people already in there, trying not to bump into each other. She didn't like the crowd. They would be working with hypodermic needles contaminated with Chimera M13. One pinprick would mean certain death.

Chimera M13, within the limits of their testing, was fatal 100 percent of the time. Marburg and Ebola were fatal about 25 to 35 percent of the time. That was largely because they were simian viruses that made the leap to *Homo sapiens*. They were not well-adapted to human beings.

Smallpox, which was perfectly adapted by nature to infect and kill human beings, was also fatal about a third of the time.

U.S. Immuno had improved on nature, if any sane person would consider it an improvement. Chimera M13 killed every subject it had been tested on. They believed, from a population point of view, that the real number would be somewhere in the 90 to 95 percentile range, that in a large human population there would be a small percentage of human beings with immune systems resistant to this disease.

Of course, Chimera had never actually been tested on human beings. It had been tested on cultures of human cells with spectacular success, and on monkeys as well. They had run it on a barrage of mice, rats, guinea pigs, and rabbits. Fatal, fatal, fatal. On laboratory animals it was 100 percent fatal. No human being had ever actually been infected.

The monkey room was at the far end of the hot zone, a large rectangular space. On top of countertops were wall-to-wall monkey cages, each draped with plastic sheeting to prevent the spread of airborne disease. Liz and Sharon gestured for the crowd to stay along the walls, which they did, more or less. Like any crowd, it had a life of its own, shifting and drifting, people gesturing to each other with sign language, barely able to hear each other through their spacesuits, even when shouting.

Jaxon picked up a metal tray containing syringes of M1, M2, M3, and M4. Together they proceeded to the four monkeys on the far left. At the first cage Jaxon used a lever to bring the false rear wall of the cage forward until the monkey was pressed and immobile against the front of the cage. Jaxon took a syringe from a second tray and injected the monkey with the tranquilizer Telazol. She stepped back and waited. Within moments the monkey became unconscious.

With smooth, deliberate motions, Liz took the syringe labeled M1 and injected it into the first monkey.

Turning, she saw that the crowd of blue suits was pressing in toward her. They recoiled as a group at the sight of the syringe, moving back toward the far wall. She shuffled over to a red "sharps" container on the wall and dropped the syringe into it. She squirmed as a muscle spasm rippled along her back. Grimacing, she adjusted her posture. Her back ached from where the bullets had struck the Kevlar in the spacesuit. After a moment, the spasm passed.

Jaxon repeated her tranquilizing procedure with the second monkey, and Liz injected it with M2. This proceeded through the first four monkeys. Each time she turned, the crowd had moved a little bit closer. Inside her suit she sighed, reflecting on Derek Stillwater's comment about stage fright. No kidding. She felt like she was performing.

The next stage was trickier. They were going to inject all twenty monkeys with M13.

She stood back, sweat beading on her forehead, the blower loud in her ears. Another spasm assaulted her back. She gasped, twisted a bit, and it went away. Jaxon stood close to her, face shields touching. "Ready?"

"Ready."

It was time-consuming and exhausting. The trick was to not rush. To work slowly and deliberately. To concentrate on what she was doing, not get into an automatic sequence.

But it was hard. It had been a long, exhausting day. Every few minutes her back seized up and she had to twist inside her spacesuit to relieve the pain. She knew she was tiring, knew that maybe she should take a break or turn this over to someone else. But she had something to prove. She had started this mess, had actually been one of the creators of Chimera, and she wanted to be one of the people to fix it.

By the time they hit monkey number twenty, a large, thirty-pound male with gray tufted ears and yellowish brown fur, she just wanted to finish. The tidal ebb and flow of the crowd was getting to her. She wanted to get away from them. She wanted to get off her feet, out of the spacesuit, and around a cup of coffee. Her back was complaining constantly now, a deep, uncomfortable ache split by the occasional spasm.

She moved in toward the twentieth monkey. The blue suits moved toward her, circling. Everyone wanting to mark this moment. As she stepped forward, the syringe in her hand, a jagged, searing pain raced through her back like an electrical current. With a cry she bent forward, the syringe jolting out of her grasp. Involuntarily she clutched at it, trying to catch it. She felt the jab of pain immediately, saw the tear in three layers of gloves, saw the drops of blood ooze through the hole.

She had been injected with Chimera M13.

16

Washington, D.C.

Detective Lou Matthews double-parked the Crown Victoria and followed his partner, Detective Chris Flemming, over to the crime scene. Flemming, who stood six-three and weighed nearly three hundred pounds, his coal-black shaved skull standing out like a beacon, headed over to talk to the patrol officers who had cordoned off the area near Jimmy's Saloon. Matthews, who wasn't as tall as his partner and whose skin was more chocolate in tone, moved toward where the crime scene squad was doing their thing. Dressed in a navy blue pinstripe three-piece suit, Matthews brushed back his suit coat and stuffed his hands into his pockets.

"What've we got?"

The CSI was a skinny guy with fuzzy brown hair, his complexion red, making his high rounded cheekbones seem rouged. Matthews had worked with him a couple times before. Todd Fawkes, he remembered. Yeah. That was his name. Annoying little shit, but seemed to know his business.

"Large-caliber bullet to the heart," Fawkes said, not looking up from taking evidence. "Looks like a handful of shots. One or two hit the wall here, haven't got them yet. Couple hit vehicles. Winston's working on them."

"Sniper?"

"Maybe."

Matthews crouched down and took a hard look at the victim. Long blond hair. Reddish beard. He took in the green scrub shirt now caked with drying blood, the jeans, and tennis shoes. "Got an ID?"

"Got gloves?"

Matthews took a pair of latex gloves from his pocket and tugged them on. Fawkes handed him a bagged wallet from his evidence kit. Matthews took it out of the bag and examined it. Maryland driver's license. Austin Davis. Age: 49. Matthews took another look at the victim. Davis looked younger than 49. There was a doctor tag on the license. He flipped through more of the information, jotting notes in his notebook. AMA card. Walter Reed ID. The usual collection of credit cards and identification. No photographs. Shifting to the two pockets, he noted that Davis carried a fair amount of cash: six twenties, two tens, one five, three ones. In the other pocket of the wallet was a collection of receipts and what appeared to be notes. The receipts looked straightforward, one from a Starbucks this morning, one from the Walter Reed cafeteria at noon. The man kept track of his expenses. A little anal-retentive, but so what? He was a doctor, right? Attention to detail would be a pretty good quality in a doctor.

The notes seemed to be a collection of to-do lists, all on folded yellow Post-It notes. There was one with a list of things labeled one through five, number one being "Pick up dry-cleaning" and number five being "Staff mtg @ 3:30." The staff meeting was crossed out, but none of the others were.

There was a yellow note that said, simply: "Derek Stillwater @ Jimmy's, 7:00."

He wanted to say, *Aha!*, his gaze shifting thirty yards to the entrance to Jimmy's. Nothing like a real clue to make you feel like a real detective.

He went through the rest of the wallet, angling it to the light from several patrol cars, their headlights cutting brilliant swaths through the dark night. Finally he handed it back to Fawkes. "Anything else?"

"Not so far."

Matthews thanked the CSI and headed over to where his partner was deep in discussion with a female patrol officer. She was built like a weightlifter, with broad shoulders stretching the tight uniform blouse, and had the bad complexion of a steroid freak. She adjusted her hat and brushed a flyaway strand of brown hair out of her face when he approached. He introduced himself and she identified herself as Officer Sheila Broadway.

"I was just telling your partner here what we've been doing."

"Got a wit," Flemming said. He pointed to a patrol car. "Supposed to be a good one, too."

"Good. So, what's going on here?" Matthews asked Broadway.

"Witness reports that the victim was walking down the street with another man. The victim was shot and the other man ran. There were other shots. Then the second man jumped into a vehicle and drove off."

"Huh," Matthews said. "The witnesses think the second man shot the first man?"

Broadway shrugged. "Conflicting accounts. Some do, some don't. Some think it was a sniper and the shots were coming from across the street, maybe from a vehicle. Some people think the second man was the shooter. At least two people were sure he had a gun."

"They describe the second man?"

"Tall, muscular, jeans and a T-shirt, dark red windbreaker. Curly brown hair. Age is anywhere from twenty-five to fifty."

They asked her more questions, and she consulted her notes and answered them as best she could. "And the wit in the patrol?" Flemming asked.

"Got a good description of the vehicle the man jumped into. Plus a license plate."

"Quite an eagle eye."

"Yes, sir. He scribbled it on his hand. He was lying in the street, hoping not to get shot. I've already run the plate. Belongs to a D.C. address, a Dolores Smithson."

Flemming said, "Call dispatch, have a patrol sent to that address, and have them pick up Ms. Smithson and bring her in for questioning."

Broadway grinned. "Yes, sir."

"Let's talk to this eagle-eye witness," Matthews said.

The wit's name was Andy Rosenbaum. He was thin, average height, with long dark hair and a scraggly beard. They invited him to step out of the car, and he did, stretching, arching his back.

They questioned him back and forth and inside-out. Officer Broadway had been right. Rosenbaum was the best witness. They got his contact information and let him go. Matthews walked back over to Fawkes. "Any idea on the angle of those bullets? Or caliber?"

"No, but large."

"Handgun?"

Fawkes shrugged. "If it was, it was a cannon. And not point blank. There's no burn on this guy's shirt. We'll be able to work out trajectories later. Winston's measuring everything. My guess— and that's all it is, a guess—is that the shooter was across the street, shooting from a vehicle using a rifle."

They were headed for Jimmy's when Officer Broadway caught their attention. She hurried over. "Cops went to look for that address for Dolores Smithson. The address doesn't exist. It's not anywhere in the computer."

Matthews and Flemming looked at each other. Then they called in a "be on the lookout" on the Chevy Blazer. And they wanted a check run on somebody called Derek Stillwater.

17

U.S. Immunological Research

". . . THE DEPARTMENT OF HOMELAND Security has declared a Level Red Alert, indicating an active threat of a terrorist attack. In a press conference a short time ago, Secretary James Johnston said that the government was on high alert after a group of unidentified commandos made an armed assault on a government-funded biological research facility in—"

Aaron Pilcher reluctantly clicked off the radio as he pulled up to the first checkpoint outside the U.S. Immuno facility. The Army had set up a double perimeter of Humvees and armed, uniformed soldiers. Portable floodlights cast a harsh, uncompromising glare across the parking lot. It looked as desolate and barren as a lunar landscape. The press was out in force, and Pilcher knew it would make good, though frightening, images for TV.

A soldier asked him to step out of his vehicle. Pilcher did and handed over his FBI credentials and showed them his gun. The soldier made a phone call, then nodded and hung up. "You're expected. Please get back in your vehicle and follow the route ahead to the main gate."

"Sure."

Pilcher saw that an entry road wide enough for two vehicles to pass had been formed out of concrete barriers. He drove along it, noting the regularly posted sentries. At the main gate the way was blocked by more concrete barriers and guarded by heavily armored vehicles with machine guns mounted in the backs. His skin prickled as he thought of unseen snipers with high-powered rifles and night-vision scopes, of fingers on triggers.

The front gate double-checked his ID, checked his gun, searched the car, then gave him an armed escort in a Humvee to the front entrance. In the hours since Pilcher had been there, U.S. Immuno had transformed from a research facility into a military command post. He was led to a command center and met by a Captain Theresa Kavalevski, who demanded to see his ID once again. Kavalevski looked about forty years old and had a youthful, oval face. She wore dark hair cut short and round, wire-rimmed glasses that flashed in the unforgiving fluorescent lights.

She took his ID, compared it to something on a computer screen in front of her, and returned it to him with a brisk nod. "I received a lengthy fax for you from SIOC." She handed him a folder marked TOP SECRET, AARON PILCHER ONLY, FBI.

"What happened to your face?" she asked.

He involuntarily put a hand to his cheek, felt heat radiating off his skin. "A little too close to an explosion."

"The one at the municipal airport?"

He nodded.

"You were lucky. I heard we lost a lot of people today."

135

"Good people. My people." He didn't like to think about it. Thinking about it enraged him, and being pissed off didn't help him be· analytical. He needed to think, not freak out. He compartmentalized and hoped he'd still be able to open the door to the compartment when the time to examine those emotions came.

Kavalevski nodded. "Dr. Frank Halloran is changing now. He should be down any minute." She gestured to a soldier who hurried over.

"Adam, please take—"

"I need a few minutes to go through this file," he said, lifting it. He pointed to an empty desk. "That okay?"

"Certainly."

He sat down and adjusted the lamp. Besides a computer there was a photograph of a family: a man, a woman, and three children. They were at Disney World, hamming it up with Minnie Mouse. They were happy. He wondered which of them was dead. Had the terrorists killed the mother or the father? Had they been told? What were they thinking now? What were they feeling?

Shaking it off, he continued through the file. It contained a summary, which he read carefully before proceeding on to the next twelve pages of documentation. He was a very fast reader with an excellent memory. He put the file aside and reviewed the information in his head. The Bureau had done their usual fine and fast job of background checks. It was what they did best, gather information. But he understood that the FBI wasn't good at preemption. Preemption required more than information gathering, it required a willingness to break away from a standard mindset and imagine what the terrorists might do. Intuitively, Pilcher understood that Derek Stillwater was trying to do that, to think outside the box.

"Do you have a shredder?" he asked Kavalesky.

She looked startled. "Yes, right here."

He shredded the contents of the file and then shredded the file itself. "Ready," he said.

She called the soldier back over. "Adam, please take Mr. Pilcher to Dr. Halloran's office. Thank you."

The U.S. Immuno facility had become a ghost town. Private Adam Nabreau led Pilcher silently down empty corridors, walls pocked with bullet holes, tiled floors looking freshly clean—the refuse of violent death having been mopped up.

Halloran's office must have been one of the few in the building to actually have a window. Considering he was the head of the place, it was pretty spartan. There was a large burled-walnut table for a desk, cluttered with paperwork. A computer dominated one corner. A wall of bookshelves were crammed with textbooks and bound technical journals. Gray utilitarian filing cabinets stood sentry, doors shut. On one wall hung photographs and memorabilia from when Halloran was in the military. Pilcher recognized Scully in one of the photographs.

Pilcher welcomed the few minutes in Halloran's office alone, a chance to get a feel for the man, a chance to get into character. He had three distinct characters he preferred to use for interrogations, with varying degrees of range between each three. With his white-blond hair, though thinning, and his square jaw and lean build, he was able to pull off what he referred to as Icy Bastard. By bringing forth a more fussy nature, and generally by working as second fiddle to Spigotta's Raging Bastard, he could do a very effective Officious Prick. Then, when needed, he was able to totally mellow out and be Surfer Buddy. Somewhere between Officious

Prick and Surfer Buddy was the good cop he needed when Spigotta toned down Raging Bastard to his own version of Seriously Bad Cop. With Halloran's military background, Pilcher thought that Icy Bastard was the way to go.

When Halloran walked into his own office in khaki slacks and a green scrub shirt, Pilcher was sitting behind Halloran's burled-walnut desk, hands clasped in front of him, a hard frown on his face.

"Who are you?"

"Sit down, Doctor."

When Halloran didn't sit, Pilcher reached inside his jacket, making sure that Halloran saw his gun in its holster, and retrieved his ID. He held it up. "Special Agent Aaron Pilcher. Federal Bureau of Investigation. Sit down."

Halloran reluctantly sat. To his credit, he didn't ask what this was about.

Pilcher stared at him for a long moment. He said, "The Bureau has some questions."

"I thought I answered all of them earlier."

"We have more. Are you happily married, Dr. Halloran?"

Halloran raised an eyebrow. "Excuse me?"

"Are you happily married, Dr. Halloran?"

"Why are you asking that? What does that have to do with anything?"

"Answer the question!" Pilcher shouted.

Halloran jumped. "Jesus Christ! Yes. What's your—"

"Do you love your children?"

"What? Now look—"

"Answer the question!"

"Yes."

"Who are you having an affair with?"

Halloran squinted and leaned forward in his chair. "What?"

Voice cold, colder than ice, Pilcher said, "I asked you a question, Dr. Halloran. In the interest of national security, I want you to answer it."

"National security?"

Pilcher stared at him. "Every Wednesday night for the last two months, you have eaten dinner at a number of restaurants in the Baltimore area. After eating at those restaurants, you have checked into a variety of hotels nearby."

"How—"

"Since this occurred two months prior to a terrorist assault on your facility, resulting in the theft of a bioengineered germ that could cause a pandemic, it amazes me that you would be so stupid to think there's no connection."

Halloran's face drained of color. His voice shook as he protested, "There isn't."

"Who is she?"

"A . . . just a friend. She's not involved in this."

Pilcher thought Halloran was an idiot. Voice dripping with ice, he said, "The Bureau will decide whether or not she is involved in this. We want a name. We want a telephone number. We want an address. If you have pictures, we want them. If you do not give us this information—immediately—I am authorized to take you into custody. We will be forced to ask your wife and your children questions—in the interest of national security—concerning your relationships. Do I make myself clear, Dr. Halloran?"

Obviously he was making himself crystal clear, because Halloran's hands were shaking in his lap. He clutched the arms of the chair and shook his head. "No. No, my life . . . this . . . you . . . you're ruining my life."

"Name," Pilcher intoned.

Halloran leaned forward and pressed his face into his hands. "Oh God. I can't believe . . ." He fell silent, fingers pressing into his closed eyes. Finally: "She's just a friend."

"Phone number."

"She's married. I never called her. She called me."

"Phone number."

Halloran looked up. "I don't have one."

"Where does she live?"

Halloran shook his head. "Somewhere in D.C., but I don't really know."

"How did you meet her?"

Halloran sighed. "Dear God. She's . . . she's just a friend."

Aaron Pilcher thought of the Scully family, of what had been done to them. He wondered if there was a connection. There probably was. "More than a friend. How did you meet her?"

"A talk I gave at . . . Georgetown University. She was in the audience. She's adjunct faculty there. You know, she teaches but isn't a member of the faculty. She taught microbiology. She has a master's degree in microbiology, taught a lot of laboratory courses."

"How old?"

He shrugged. "Thirties, I guess."

"Her name?" Pilcher waited.

Halloran said, "Look, she's not involved in this. It was a—"

"When you met her for the first time, what did she say?"

"Well, uh, she said she liked my talk, thought it was really interesting, she'd like to know more about my work and the research we do."

"And?"

"And what?" Halloran, the poor fool, looked utterly confused.

"And what? You offered to buy her a drink somewhere and talk about your work?"

"Well . . ." Halloran's face grew red. "Yes. Exactly."

"Or did she offer to buy you a drink and let you talk about your work?"

He shook his head. "I think . . . no, I . . . I don't remember."

Pilcher stared. "What's her name?"

"Look—"

Pilcher reached under his jacket and retrieved his handcuffs. "I'm really quite through with you, Doctor."

Sweat beaded on Halloran's forehead. "No, really. Her name . . . her name is Irina Khournikova."

"Sounds Russian," Pilcher said.

"It is. Her English is excellent. She's been here in the U.S. for years, but she's originally from Russia."

"Adjunct faculty at Georgetown?"

"Yes."

"Do you have any photographs?"

"N-no."

"Describe her."

"Well, mid-thirties, athletic, shoulder-length brown hair. Attractive. Very intelligent."

She played you like a goddamned piano, Pilcher thought. He stood up. "I wouldn't be surprised if someone comes back to discuss this with you again."

He walked past Halloran and was halfway out the door when Halloran said, "You . . . you think she's involved in this, don't you? In the theft of Chimera."

Pilcher nodded and walked out of Halloran's office. He was immediately on his cell phone, calling Spigotta, giving him the name and the information. Spigotta said, "Have you been in touch with Stillwater?"

"No."

"Get hold of him. I want an update. Brief him on what we know."

Pilcher clicked off and called Stillwater's cell phone. Stillwater sounded cagey. "I need an update. What have you got?" Pilcher asked.

"I've confirmed my theory," Stillwater said. He sounded like someone was in the room with him.

"Are you alone?"

"No."

"Is Richard Coffee behind this like you think?"

"Yes. And others."

"Okay. I've got a lead on somebody we can check on. A microbiology instructor at Georgetown U. Irina Khournikova—"

"Say that again."

Pilcher did, wondering at Stillwater's interruption.

"I'll call you back," Stillwater said, and clicked off.

"Wonder what that was about," Pilcher said out loud. He turned to leave and was just walking around the corner when he heard a gunshot fired from behind him. He froze, then slowly turned back, heading toward Halloran's office. The shot must have been heard throughout the building, because two soldiers swept past him at a dead run. He followed, reluctant to witness what he knew he was going to see.

Halloran had taken the time to get up from his chair and retrieve a Colt .45 service weapon from a desk drawer. Then he had sat down behind his desk and written on a piece of stationary merely the words, *I'm sorry. I'm so sorry.* Then Halloran had put the barrel of the gun in his mouth and pulled the trigger.

18

Washington, D.C.

DEREK STILLWATER STARED AT the photograph of Richard Coffee and Kim Pak Lee, the Korean bioweapons expert. Then he slid it aside.

"How many in this organization?"

Irina Khournikova shrugged. "Estimates say as small as ten, as large as fifty. It may be that its size is fluid. I don't have dossiers on all the members. Just a few confirmed cases."

"Let's see them."

He followed her into the bedroom that apparently served as a makeshift office. She retrieved a handful of files and turned, seeing him standing close behind her. She moved around him without comment, but her expression said, *You don't trust me.* That was okay by Derek. He didn't trust her.

He followed her back to the kitchen and joined her at the table. She opened a folder. In it was a head-and-shoulders shot of a scowling woman with dark hair. She appeared to be in her fifties and had a fleshy face and dark, unhappy eyes. "Masha Khattan. An Israeli expert in nuclear weapons." Irina tapped the photograph. "Mossad would very much like to find her."

She opened four more folders, describing the nationalities and expertise of the people inside. Japanese, Korean, Italian, German. Expertise in biological and chemical warfare, nuclear physics, computers, intelligence.

"What's their goal?"

Irina met his gaze. "Money, Dr. Stillwater. The Fallen Angels buy or steal weapons—any kind—or the materials to build weapons of mass destruction and sell them. Sometimes they auction them. Sometimes they fill an order."

Derek said, "For instance, Syria is willing to pay ten million dollars, U.S., for fifteen pounds of enriched plutonium."

"Exactly."

He flipped through the files again and felt his heart sink. He would not ever have thought Richard Coffee would go bad for money. In the years he had worked with the man, he had known him to be a professional, a patriot, a man who was unusually knowledgeable about geopolitics and was concerned, legitimately concerned, about the growing threats of terrorist organizations and their access to weapons of mass destruction.

A part of him refused to believe that Richard could be behind this.

And yet . . .

If it had been ideological, maybe Derek could believe that Richard had had a breakdown over ideology. The man had been passionate about his beliefs.

Soldiers were trained to support their commander in chief, to fulfill the commands and obey orders without question. Yet at the same time, both Richard and Derek had been in branches of the military requiring a great deal of independent thought. Derek, as a bioweapons specialist, had been required to give his honest opinion on a course of action. He gave it. Richard had been like that, too. But, like Derek, he had also questioned orders and decisions made by politicians and commanders with motives other than success, or questioned orders that required too large or senseless a sacrifice of men.

What had Richard seen in Chechnya? What had happened to him there?

Derek's phone chirped. He saw Irina tense. He got up from the table and turned sideways to her. "Yes?"

"Stillwater! It's Pilcher. I need an update. What have you got?"

"I've confirmed my theory."

"Are you alone?"

"No."

"Is Richard Coffee behind this like you think?"

"Yes. And others." Out of the corner of his eye, he saw Irina watching him, sitting still, hands in her lap, out of sight.

"Okay," Pilcher continued. "I've got a lead on somebody we can check on. A microbiology instructor at Georgetown U. Irina Khournikova—"

Derek stiffened, then forced himself to relax. He turned farther away from the Russian so she couldn't see his face. "Say that again."

"A Russian microbiology instructor at Georgetown. Her name is Irina Khournikova. She was having an affair with Halloran at U.S. Immuno, the simpleton."

"I'll call you back."

Derek clicked off the cell phone at the same time he heard a ripping sound. He was already in motion as Khournikova pulled out a handgun that had been duct-taped to the underside of the kitchen table. He flung the cell phone in her face and dived to the floor as the air filled with bullets.

He rolled and came up under her, shoulder into her chest, slamming her back against the kitchen cabinets. She kneed him. He turned, catching it on his hip. Caught her gun hand with his own, twisting. She clawed at him with her free hand.

He twisted again. Her gun went flying.

She spun, booted foot catching him in the ribs. He stepped back and she moved in fast with flying arms and legs. He shuffled back, shuffled again, like fencing, slapping her blows away, on the defensive. He caught a blow to the shoulder. His arm went numb.

He scrambled back before her attack, back, hit the wall. Turning sideways to her, he got his gun out of its clip, only to have her kick it away.

"Fuck this," he snarled, and dived after it.

She went after it, too, just as he had expected.

Derek shifted his weight and caught her on the side of the head with his closed fist, followed up with an elbow strike to the jaw. She staggered and he kicked her in the stomach.

It knocked her off her feet. She stumbled over a chair and crashed to the floor. She lay on the cheap linoleum, struggling for air, dazed.

He picked up the guns and quickly ripped the cords out of the two living-room lamps. Before she could completely recover, he grabbed her by the hair and lifted her into one of the kitchen chairs. Using the cord he tied her securely to the chair.

Derek stepped back and took a deep breath. Her eyes were half open, breathing ragged. He didn't trust it. She could be faking.

He looked for his cellular phone and found it in pieces on the floor. He searched for a phone, but found none. The computer was hooked to a cable line—no help there. She didn't carry a cell phone. Maybe it was in the SUV.

When he returned to the kitchen, she was fully conscious, eyes lit with rage. Derek leaned close to her. He was overly conscious of the time ticking away, aware that everything she had told him so far could be an outright lie.

"Is your real name Irina Khournikova?"

"Fuck you."

He nodded. "Now listen carefully, Irina. I'm going to ask you some questions. You're going to answer them. Here's what I want to know. One, what does your group—"

"The Fallen Angels! I told you!"

"Fine. What do the Fallen Angels plan to do with Chimera M13? That's number one. Number two—"

"We are going to release it," she hissed. "We are going to start over. Eliminate nations, politics, war. We're going to wipe out most of the human race and start over again."

"Where and when?"

She turned her head away from him, chin raised in defiance.

"Where are the Fallen Angels?" he asked.

She did not answer.

"Where will they start?"

Again, silence.

"Well," he said, standing up, "so much for the easy way." He stepped behind her and began to rummage in the kitchen drawers.

"Oh, Derek," she said. "Going to torture me?" She clucked her tongue. "Richard doesn't think you have the will for such an action. He said you're too nice a guy. He wanted you delayed. I was to find out what you knew, then detain you. Richard could have killed you back on 19th Street. But he wanted to pick your brain. He wanted me to try and recruit you. It's too bad you didn't let me—you might have liked it."

"Sorry. I'm not much of a joiner."

"So now you will torture me?" She laughed. "I don't think so."

"Were you at the Scully house, Irina?"

She laughed again, goading him. "Oh yes. I enjoyed her screams. Is that what you're getting back there, Derek? Looking for a sharp knife? Going to threaten to cut off my ear if I don't tell you what you want to know? Going to threaten to cut off a nipple? Ha! You do not have the—"

Derek brought a plastic freezer bag over her head and pulled it tight. She struggled, gasping for breath. In her ear he whispered, "Knives really aren't my style." He waited, then pulled the bag away.

Face red, Irina gasped for air, struggling to pull oxygen into her lungs.

"Where can I find the Fallen Angels?" Derek said.

In a gasp she said, "Never."

He yanked the bag back over her head. Held it there, watching her twist against her bindings, sucking the plastic against her open mouth. He pulled it off.

"Where . . . are they?"

"Fuck—"

Back went the bag. Again and again he took her to the edge of unconsciousness and asked her where the Fallen Angels were, asked her what their plan was, where and how were they going to release Chimera.

She did not tell him. Her voice, hurling epithets in his face, grew weaker. He felt frantic. If he went hunting for a phone to call Pilcher and waited for an FBI team to show up, then waited for her to be officially processed, for paperwork to be filled out, for lawyers to be consulted, hours would pass. He didn't have hours. The world didn't have hours. She wouldn't tell them anything. She would not deal.

Derek pulled the bag over her head and held it tight. He held it, held it. . . . She passed out. He removed the bag and checked her pulse. He couldn't tell if it was his imagination, but her pulse seemed erratic. It was there, however, beneath his finger. She was still breathing, still alive.

He took the time to search the apartment again, going through closets, looking under the bed, through every drawer. Nothing. When he returned Irina was conscious, a line of spittle oozing down her chin. She looked up and glared at him. He didn't like her color. She looked gray. And despite the hatred in her eyes, he thought they had lost their brightness.

"Hello," he said conversationally. "Ready to go again?"

"I won't tell you anything."

He sighed and deliberately pulled the bag over her head, pulling it taut. "I know," he said in her ear. "But I'm going to keep going, just in case. I'm a thorough professional. And the stakes are just too damned high. I'm very sorry. I guess Richard never told you that, nice guy or not, I would do what I had to do."

She struggled, her energy dissipating fast.

"I know you'd rather die than betray the Fallen Angels, and that's too bad. What I'm wondering is, which will come first? Irreparable brain damage? Or death?"

She twisted her head, groaning. Then abruptly slumped. He removed the bag and checked her pulse. With a growing sense of unease, he shifted his touch, trying to locate her heartbeat.

"Goddammit!" He peeled back an eyelid, saw a fixed pupil. No pulse.

Heart racing, he untied her, pulled her onto the floor, and started CPR. Compression, one, two, three . . .

Breathe, breathe . . .

But he knew it was too late. He'd screwed up. Caused a fatal heart arrhythmia. He had killed the only lead he had.

Derek left the apartment after going through Irina's pockets and finding the keys to the Blazer. The neighborhood hadn't improved with the descent of night. The people who drove by seemed to belong to the darkness, to be on errands and business that fell on the wrong side of the law. *Like me,* he thought.

He quickly searched the Blazer and came up with a cell phone. He called Pilcher.

"Stillwater, where the—"

"Shut up. Send an evidence team to this address." He reeled it off. "They'll find Irina Khournikova. She needs to be printed. Send a computer guy. She claimed she was with Russia's Directorate T, but I don't know if what she said was true or not. Now—"

Two cops were bracketing the Blazer. Derek hadn't noticed them approach.

"Shit."

"Stillwater, what's going on?"

"Cops are here."

Derek clicked off and dropped the phone into his pocket. "Hello," he said.

"Step out of the vehicle, sir. Keep your hands visible at all times."

Derek, right hand up, opened the driver's side door slowly and stepped out. If they hauled him in for questioning, he'd be out of business for hours. He couldn't allow that.

"I've got a gun on my right hip," he said. "I'm with the Department of Homeland Security. We're on—"

The cop on his side of the Blazer leaned forward to remove Derek's gun from the holster. It was a mistake.

Derek slammed his elbow into the cop's face, grabbed his arm, and spun him around so his bulk was between him and the second cop.

"Freeze!" The second cop started to move around the Blazer, gun drawn.

Derek pressed the first cop's own gun against his head. "Stay where you are. Put your gun down."

The second cop, a young, frightened rookie, didn't put down his gun.

"Put the gun down," the cop repeated.

The last thing in the world Derek needed was a standoff. "Look," he said. "I'm an agent with Homeland Security—"

The cop Derek was holding slammed his head back into Derek's jaw, jerking away. The young cop on the other side of the Blazer fired his weapon. Derek felt a searing pain rip through his side. Instinctively, Derek tucked and rolled, moving in toward the truck, automatically returning fire, then leapt up over the hood of the truck and kicked the cop in the head, sprinting away into the darkness. He ducked into the nearest alley, the sound of pounding feet behind him.

At the end of the alley was a wooden fence, six feet tall. Jived on adrenaline, Derek vaulted it in one smooth motion, dropped to the other side and immediately hit a crossroads. Behind him one of the cops was clambering awkwardly over the fence. Derek didn't have much time.

He raced to the right, then right again, into another alley, doubling back. And saw it. A rusty fire escape, its ladder eight feet off the ground. But a barred window ledge was within reach.

He monkeyed onto the window ledge and caught the ladder. It rocked under his weight. Ignoring the sudden exploding pain in his side, he climbed up the ladder, up, up, up, then over the lip of the building, where he collapsed, gasping for breath.

Sirens filled the air. He touched his side and brought his fingers away wet. He had been shot and he couldn't tell how bad it was. He shrugged out of his windbreaker, peeled off his shirt and balled it up, and pressed it against the wound. His skin broke out in goose flesh, the night air chilly on his bare skin. He tugged the windbreaker back on, feeling ill. For a moment he saw lights flashing before his eyes and felt like he might pass out.

Below him somewhere he heard voices, the approach of cars. Somebody said, "He just fucking disappeared. When I came around the corner, he was gone."

Gulping air, Derek tried to think, tried to get his head on straight. *The cell phone!*

He reached into his jacket pocket. It was gone. Frantic, he searched the windbreaker, then crawled around on the ground in the dark trying to find it. Nothing. Panic. He was starting to panic, he knew, his heart racing, his lungs kicking in. He had to get it together. If the panic rat started chewing on your guts, it was all over. Everything. Everything would be all over.

Not only had he lost his lifeline to Aaron Pilcher and the FBI and the Homeland Security director, the phone's memory and any numbers Irina Khournikova might have called were gone. Derek slumped back against the ledge and buried his face in his hands.

19

Washington, D.C.

THE MAN THEY CALLED the Fallen waited in a green and tan Subaru Outback. He checked his watch, frowning. Nadia was supposed to signal him when she made her decision. Would Derek come or would he go? Would he fall, become one of his angels? Or would he have to be sacrificed? Or could he be let loose to spread disinformation among the world, to further the Fallen Angels' goals and increase the inevitable confusion and panic that was going to roll over the country and the planet in a very short time?

Fallen rubbed his forehead and closed his eyes against the stabbing pain. Starbursts and neon worms flashed before his interior vision. He smelled smoke and tasted blood; for a moment he was back in Chechnya, but he fought the fragmentation inside his head, the odd fugue states he sometimes fell into during moments of stress. He dragged himself back to the present.

Nadia was late, and this worried him. He waited in the Subaru a block from the Washington hovel, that miserable apartment that reminded him of Grozny, Chechnya, before the Russian army destroyed the city.

The door to the building opened, and he watched as Derek Stillwater stepped outside, looking up and down the street, then crossed over to the Blazer. Derek did not seem to notice the police cruiser, but Fallen did. He noticed and watched as they moved in on Derek.

Bad field craft, Derek, he thought. *You're distracted or you've lost your touch. What's happened to you during our time apart? Gone soft?*

Fallen watched as the two cops struggled with Derek, who overpowered them and disappeared down an alley, the cops giving chase. Fallen's fingers twitched on his cell phone, the desire to call Nadia strong. But the police were coming back, and he could hear sirens drawing near. He looked toward the third-floor window, waiting. Nothing.

What did you do, Derek?

Fallen winced at the stabbing pain behind his forehead. Again he smelled smoke and tasted blood. This time he slipped back in time.

Once, long ago, he had been known as Richard Coffee. He had been reborn twice. Derek Stillwater had been present at his death in Iraq, an unwitting witness to his first transformation, a ridiculous bit of subterfuge by the geniuses in Langley. They had flown him from the MASH unit in Iraq and sped him through their training school in Virginia, then inserted him into Chechnya with a new name: Surkho Andarbek.

The Chechens had just declared their independence, and Moscow had treated them like it was just another internal rebellion, not the beginning of a civil war that would threaten to tear Russia apart. The CIA wanted someone inside, providing information to be bartered with. Surkho Andarbek appeared in the city, arriving from the outskirts of the republic, a laborer. With money coming from the CIA, Surkho was able to open a small restaurant, a place where men came to meet and talk. And Surkho got to know them, gathered information, became a part of their plans, a part of their rebellion.

He moved up in their ranks. Surkho's handlers back in Langley were pleased because of the information he gave them and because he could help the rebels organize. Surkho was a warrior and a natural-born leader, and his fellow Chechens would follow him into hell and back.

Surkho outstripped his American mandate. Richard Coffee had died in Iraq, and Surkho Andarbek was the rebirth—a leader, a warrior, the man who would lead the Chechens to freedom. He took the American money and bought weapons to fight the Russians, and when America's priorities changed, as they always seemed to do, Surkho Andarbek was told to stop fighting the Russians, to work to bring peace. But Surkho Andarbek laughed, because there was no negotiating, there was only the chaos of war, and hatred, and men who would follow him. There was no going back. The CIA agent named Richard Coffee had ceased to exist.

And then there appeared a man from Canada. Or so he claimed. One of a group of independent relief workers, traveling in a beat-up station wagon filled with medical supplies and food. Surkho, with his tentacles reaching throughout the republic, heard that this Canadian was looking for Surkho Andarbek and showing around a photograph of him.

Not an aid worker.

Surkho debated whether to bring the Canadian to him or to await his arrival. Chechnya was a dangerous place, even for aid workers. It was always possible the man would die trying to find him. Let him come.

One day he did come. Surkho knew he had been found and he knew that this man who was not a Canadian was there to kill him, to stop what he was doing.

Surkho was alone, as he had planned, sitting in the shade of a half-destroyed building, what, ironically, had been his place of business before Russian missiles had turned it to rubble. It was a hot day, Grozny's skyline a fractured, tortured tableau of twisted metal and bombed-out hulks. Smoke from burning buildings hung over everything like a shroud. The man came on foot. He was muscular, his face weathered, a grizzled beard on his face.

"Surkho?" he asked, approaching. "Surkho Andarbek?"

Surkho pretended to be dazed. "Who're you?" he rumbled in Chechen.

"Anthony. From . . . Canada. Are you Surkho Andarbek?"

"Maybe," he said in Chechen.

Anthony looked flustered. He stepped closer. "Speak English?"

Surkho glared at him. "Anthony who?" he asked in English.

"Coffee? Richard Coffee?"

Surkho glared at him. "Did you come to kill me?" In English.

"Time to come home," the man named Anthony said. "You've been here too long, Richard. Time to come home."

Surkho stood up and faced the American assassin. "We both know better. They don't like me any more, do they?"

Anthony blinked. "Times change. Priorities change. You've fallen out of . . ." The CIA assassin trailed off. Richard Coffee was holding a hand grenade in front of him. He grinned, his teeth flashing white in his dark face.

158

"Fallen, have I? Where's your gun? Or are you a blade man? Garotte? Poison?"

"None of that," Anthony said. "Nothing like that. Just time to come—"

But Anthony was on the move, lightning fast, fist coming around with a gun in it, firing. Surkho Andarbek tossed the grenade as bullets tore along his ribs. He kept moving, away from the grenade, away from the explosion that killed the CIA assassin sent to clean up the mess.

The wounds had been worse than Surkho Andarbek initially thought, and he made it into the shelter of an abandoned basement before he passed out. When he came to, he was being cared for by a woman named Tatiana, who had treated his wounds and brought him back to life. Tatiana was now dead, murdered by Russians. When she asked him who he was, he had known that Surkho Andarbek was dead, that he and Richard Coffee had fallen. The Fallen Angel. And this new being, whose mind was now aflame with hatred for the world, had said, "My name is Fallen."

Now, years later in a different time and a different place, Fallen looked at his watch, then back to the apartment where Nadia might be. The police were close and the clock was ticking, ticking. The next stage of the operation was about to begin, and he couldn't be here when it happened.

Dropping the Subaru into gear, he drove away, calling up his angels on his cell phone and telling them that finding Derek Stillwater was now a priority.

With a final look at the apartment receding in the distance, the entrance lit up with flashing indigo and scarlet lights, Fallen whispered, "Nadia."

20

Liz Vargas watched in horror as a drop of blood—her blood—gathered on her finger, gained weight, and fell—*plop!*—on the countertop. Her heart skittered, a roar crescendoing in her ears. *I've been infected*, a distant, rational voice in her head said, as if commenting on a knickknack in a maiden aunt's house: *Oh, how pretty.*

I've been infected.

The tidal wave of blue spacesuited scientists surged forward. Liz raised her hand in warning: she still held the syringe.

She turned her head to look at Sharon Jaxon. Through her helmet's faceplate she could see Jaxon's expression—grim, concerned, sympathetic, horrified. Jaxon held up a metal tray. Hesitating, Liz dropped the syringe into it. Then she stepped back, away from the monkey cages.

As hands gripped her and began to lead her toward decon, she saw Jaxon inject the final monkey with Chimera M13.

But that oddly detached voice, the one that undercut the panicked, frightened Greek chorus of voices in her head, said: *Oh no, Dr. Vargas—you're the last monkey.*

She spent the required seven minutes under the decontamination shower, yellow Lysol jetting out of the showerhead, raining down the faceplate of her suit, obscuring the view of her companions.

Seven minutes.

Seven long, lonely minutes in which to consider her death. She thought of everything she knew about Chimera M13, of how fast it killed, how thoroughly it destroyed its host, of what an ugly death it created—hemorrhaging, bleeding from the eyes, the ears, the mouth, nose, vagina, and rectum. Blindness came early, the eyes affected first, the whites turning scarlet as they suffused with blood before rupturing. Of the excruciatingly painful disintegration of the internal organs. But that, at least, didn't last long. Usually, the patients—victims—drowned in their own fluids, gasping for air as their lungs ruptured and filled with blood.

She realized the shower had stopped and two people were waiting for her. She shook herself and moved into the next level, Level 3, a gray zone between the hot zone and the safer locker rooms. Awkwardly she stripped out of her borrowed spacesuit. Her finger had stopped bleeding, but it throbbed painfully in time to her heartbeat. Every heartbeat, every stroke of that tireless muscle, shot racing particles of Chimera M13 through her bloodstream to infiltrate every cell of her body.

In a matter of minutes, the antigen molecules on the exterior of the virus would match up with the receptors on her body's cells, like putting a key in a lock. They would convince the cells to throw open their doors to the virus, which would enter the nucleus of those cells, intercalate itself into the DNA, and take over the genetic machinery of those cells. Chimera would turn her cells into Chimera-manufacturing facilities that would churn out more and more virus, which would infect more and more cells. . . .

She began to hyperventilate, her head light, blood roaring in her ears. Two of the scientists led her out of the Biosafety Level 4 facility, down another corridor, then back through another airlock.

It looked like a motel room. She realized she was in the Biosafety Level 4 hospital suite, dubbed the Slammer. She was going to be isolated, cared for—what a joke!—by nurses and doctors wearing spacesuits and rubber gloves. She would never again feel the touch of a human hand. In the remaining hours before her painful death, blind, bleeding, paralyzed when her brain suffered a series of debilitating strokes as the arteries in her brain ruptured, she would die alone.

And this time, she did pass out.

PART II

Fire and Brimstone

21

Washington, D.C.

ON TOP OF THE building, Derek shook himself awake, "No" on his lips. He moved stiffly, ruefully thinking that he should have kept moving, not taken a break here out in the night air. He willed away his memories of his recruitment, of the complexities of the anthrax case, of his own frustration with the lack of communication between the investigating agencies and his vocal complaints to General Johnston that what Homeland Security needed were troubleshooters who could work inside or outside the existing bureaucracies. Someone, he had written in a now-famous memo, "to evaluate, coordinate, and investigate" in a fluid, nonbureaucratic fashion. And how he had calmly, unthinkingly, braided the noose into which he would shove his own neck.

Derek tested his side and struggled to his feet. He moved cautiously across the roof to the room containing the elevator housing for the building. The steel door was locked. *Of course,* he thought, leaning against the concrete block of the squat outcropping. *Anything else would be just too damned easy.*

The door was designed to give access to the roof. He crouched by the door and examined the lock in the poor light. He could hear sirens below him. He wished he had his Go Packs with him. One of the tools he carried was a power rake, a noisy but effective electric lock pick.

He pulled off his belt, which was a money belt. He unzipped the compartment. Along with several hundred dollars in cash, he kept the basics of a set of lock picks, a tiny flashlight, a steel match to start a fire if need be, and a narrow piece of steel that could be used to either 'loid a lock in lieu of wrecking a credit card or, in a pinch, be used as a tiny knife or screwdriver. He took out the picks and went to work on the lock. Within ten minutes he was inside the building and looking for an empty apartment.

The first four apartments were occupied. He muttered, "Hey, is this Jimmy Ray's place," to irritated residents. God only knew what they thought of him. It didn't matter, because they never opened their doors, just hollered through them.

When there was no response at the fifth door, he went after the lock with the picks and was inside within two minutes. He did a quick recon to assure himself nobody was home, then made for the telephone in the kitchen. He dialed James Johnston's office and got the voice mail. He left a message and tried Sam Dalton's number. Voice mail again.

Puzzled, he couldn't imagine that either man had just gone home during this crisis. He had Dalton's cell phone, and was again transferred to voice mail. He left a tense message indicating he'd be out of touch for a while, and hung up.

Now what?

The apartment was similar to the one belonging to Irina Khournikova. Two tiny bedrooms, a bath, a kitchen/dining room combination. Based on the photographs on the wall, the residents were an older couple.

He ran through a list of people who might be able to help him, thought of Aaron Pilcher and tried that number again. Busy. His gaze fell on his hand. There was a phone number scrawled on the palm. He grinned. *Well . . . why not?*

Twenty minutes later the Coast Guard helicopter was hovering over the roof of the building. A rope dropped about twenty feet from the hatch. Derek had spent the time lurking in the shadows, waiting for the Tylenol he'd stolen from the apartment to take effect. He sprinted out from hiding and strapped the harness around his chest. In moments he was being helped into the chopper by the Texan. "This is a little bit irregular," he said.

"But much appreciated."

"There are a couple TV choppers heading in," said Cynthia Black, the pilot. "Let's get out of here."

Derek gave a thumbs-up and the chopper roared away. He wondered what the local cops were thinking. Through the helicopter's windows Derek looked at the Washington Monument jutting upward from the base of the Mall.

Black said, "It would probably be a good idea if you tell us what's going on. We're going to have to eventually justify using the chopper as a taxi."

Derek leaned forward and groaned. "You got a first-aid kit here, by any chance?"

The Texan nodded. Derek pulled off his windbreaker and gingerly peeled the blood-soaked shirt away from his ribs, grimacing. "I need some help here."

"You need a doctor."

"Later . . . but . . . you could set me down at Walter Reed. My truck and gear's hopefully still over there."

Cynthia Black repeated herself. "We need to know what's going on."

As the Texan cleaned and bandaged Derek's wound, Derek considered her request, if that's what it was. "I can't tell you everything, because your security clearance isn't high enough."

That got their attention.

"But let's put it this way," he continued. "I'm tracking a terrorist organization. I'm part of Homeland Security. You're part of Homeland Security. I answer directly to Secretary Johnston. Therefore, I outrank you in every way. As of right now, you work for me. My military rank was colonel. So I outrank you in that way as well. Are there any questions?"

Cindy Black met his gaze and shook her head. "No, sir. But I will need to notify my commander."

"Fine. Tell them you're working directly for Secretary Johnston. We've got a mission. Suffice it to say, it's probably one of the most important missions you'll ever undertake. Take it seriously."

22

Washington, D.C.

IT TOOK AGENT AARON Pilcher almost an hour to race from the U.S. Immuno facility to Washington, D.C., spending most of it on his cell phone shouting orders. When he finally reached the address Derek Stillwater had given him, he realized instantly that something had gone wrong. Although there were FBI vehicles, most importantly an ERT van, there were also half a dozen D.C. police vehicles. *Shit,* he thought. *How did they get involved?*

He climbed out of his Ford Taurus, badge hung on a lanyard around his neck. Simultaneously, he was approached by a uniformed D.C. cop and an FBI agent in a three-piece suit.

"Sir," the cop began, "this is a crime scene—"

"He's with us," the agent said, identifying himself as Agent Ron Tittaglia. "Agent Pilcher, your line's been busy. We've got a situation here."

Pilcher sighed. He glanced at the cop. "I'll get with you in a minute."

The cop, a middle-aged guy with flinty gray eyes and gray side-burns, hesitated. Pilcher raised his badge. "FBI. National security. Shoo!"

With a sneeze that sounded an awful lot like a muffled "fuck you," the cop went off to inform his superiors that another federal pain-in-the-ass was here to muck things up.

Pilcher turned back to Tittaglia. "What's going on?"

"When the ERT team and my group showed up, this place was swarming with local cops. Seems some doctor from Walter Reed got shot a couple hours ago."

"Here?"

"No, over on 19th, by Reed. Name was Austin Davis." Tittaglia took a deep breath, organizing his thoughts. He was short and wiry, with curly graying hair and a bristly mustache.

"So—"

"They got witnesses who saw the shooting. Saw some guy they think might be a Derek Stillwater jump into a Chevy Blazer during or after the shooting and disappear. He was supposedly meeting Davis at a local pub, Jimmy's. One of the wits got the plate number on the Blazer."

"Do they think Stillwater shot this doctor?" Pilcher asked, glancing around at the cops. He saw a couple he thought were detectives talking earnestly to the uniform he had blown off. It was only a matter of time before he got hauled into this, and he wanted to see the scene first.

"Not as far as the D.C. cops can tell," Tittaglia said.

"Good. Tell me as we go to the scene."

Tittaglia led him toward the entrance. "The D.C. cops would gladly pin Davis's death on Stillwater right now, but they claim he's just a witness. They got a real reliable witness who said it looked like Stillwater was being bracketed after the doc got popped."

"Jesus, what did he grab hold of?"

"Who?"

"Stillwater. He's with Homeland Security. One of those troubleshooters."

Tittaglia led him up the stairs. "No shit?"

"No shit. He called in the scene here. So why do the cops—"

"The two patrol guys found Stillwater in that Chevy Blazer. They had a BOLO on the plates. When they tried to take him in for questioning, he resisted arrest. One of the patrols has a sprained wrist and a broken jaw from where Stillwater kicked him when he jumped over the truck."

Pilcher stopped on the second-floor landing and focused his gaze on Tittaglia. "He jumped over the Blazer?"

"Well," Tittaglia said with a shrug, "over the hood of the Blazer. To listen to these cops talk, Stillwater was Superman or something. One drew down on him and the other was trying to take Stillwater's gun when he overpowered them and ran. One chased him, but he went over a fence and disappeared. They shot at him and it looks like they hit him. There's a blood trail, but it disappears."

"They think somebody picked him up?"

They continued climbing the stairs. Tittaglia shrugged again. "Either somebody picked him up or he ducked into a phone booth and used his cape to fly away. They sent out a bunch of cops looking, but he's gone."

"Okay. I'll think about that later. What about the scene, the apartment. Is it secure?"

Tittaglia gestured to the third-floor doorway. "Yeah, secure. This is our terrorist hit, right? It got a name yet?"

"Nobody's told me. It'll be something like Project Bloodstream or something."

"Sure," Tittaglia said. "Anyway, the ERTs headed up here right away while the rest of us screwed around with the D.C. cops, pissing over turf. They didn't come up here. Good thing, too. This is a major clusterfuck. Even knowing what's going on—well, sort of knowing what's going on—I gotta say this looks bad. If the locals tied this apartment to Stillwater, they'd turn it into a massive manhunt. He *is* Homeland, right?"

Pilcher and Tittaglia stopped outside the doorway to apartment 302. Pilcher squinted, cocking his head at the agent. "He is. An expert on biowarfare. He told me there's a witness whose fingerprints we—"

"We got 'em. Had 'em rushed over to the lab ASAP. They're running them now."

"Fine. What did she—"

He stepped into the room and froze, his heart sinking. He should have put it together. Tittaglia had all but shouted it in his face.

"Your witness is dead," Tittaglia said. "And it looks like Stillwater tortured her to death."

Pilcher stared at the mess in apartment 302, trying to get a handle on what he was seeing, wondering, even more strongly than he had before, what the deal was with Derek Stillwater. At U.S. Immuno and later at the Scully house, he hadn't acted much like an investigator. He had acted like a man seeing his worst nightmares come to life. Pilcher frowned over Spigotta's comment that the USAMRIID people who knew Stillwater thought he had seen too much, that he was flaky.

Flaky, Pilcher thought.

The table and chairs had been overturned as if during a fight. Three living-room lamps had been dumped on the floor, their cords torn out of the bases. A dead woman lay neatly on the kitchen floor. Too neatly. She lay on her back, arms by her side. There were marks on her wrists that suggested they had been bound with the lamp cords. Probably the legs, too, though the cords were now tossed carelessly in the corner. A clear plastic freezer bag was crumpled next to the cords and a cellular phone that appeared to be broken in three pieces. Pilcher thought the phone would be Stillwater's.

What happened here?!

The person in charge of this ERT team was a no-nonsense woman with black hair cut so short she was almost bald. She stood eye to eye with Pilcher and said, "We'll have to get the local ME to do a post—that's not our deal, as you know. My guess is she was tied to one of those chairs with the light cords. Somebody used the plastic bag to suffocate her, torture her, maybe, into talking."

"You think she did?"

The tech stared at him. "I don't know. But she died from it. And I can't be sure, but I've got to wonder why if she died and her killer planned it that way, why he untied her and laid her out like this, unless it's positioning, you know, like some sexual serial killers do? Posing their victims' bodies? But this doesn't feel like that to me. I may be reading too much into it. This is our terrorist thing, you said."

"Yeah. The guy here was following a lead of some sort."

"Yeah. The files, I bet." She pointed to a series of manila folders now in clear evidence bags.

"Can I look?"

"Wear gloves."

Pilcher took the files, donned rubber gloves, and flipped through the evidence, frowning. Lots of photographs, but he didn't like them. Something about the files, the excellent photographs but sketchy documentation in Russian. It struck him as being wrong. Too much of one type of information, not enough of another. He wasn't sure what or why, but they made him suspicious. He wondered if they had made Stillwater suspicious.

Another tech walked past him, carrying a computer. "We'll tear it apart in the lab."

"Good," the head tech said. "Notice anything weird?"

"Yeah," the tech said. "No phones."

Pilcher looked up from the file. "What?"

"There's no telephone in this apartment. The computer had a cable modem, the TV has cable. There's almost no clothes in the closets, just a bed, the desk, computer, a few files—the ones you've got. Bathroom's got a few toiletries and the kitchen's pretty well stocked. But no phones."

"She have a phone on her?"

"No."

Pilcher turned his gaze to the broken cell phone on the floor. Stillwater had called him. From where?

He took out his own phone and started clicking on the menu, checking his calling history, remembering the order of the calls he had made after receiving Stillwater's two phone calls: the one about the apartment, when Stillwater had told him about Irina Khournikova, and the one a while later that had been interrupted by the cops. The first call had been from Stillwater's cell phone. The second call, though, had been placed from a different number. He jotted the number in his notebook, then dialed it from his cell phone.

The number rang and rang, but no one answered. *Dammit, Stillwater! Where the hell are you?*

Pilcher left the building and stood at the entryway, feeling the weight of the last nine hours on his shoulders. The night was warm with a light breeze, only a hint of smog. A pleasant night, not the type of night one would associate with such evil. Above him circled three or four helicopters—TV news, he assumed.

"You the head FBI guy?"

Pilcher turned to face a broad-shouldered man in a trench coat. He displayed his badge, identifying himself as Detective Christopher Flemming. Pilcher's own ID still hung around his neck.

"I'm not in charge of this particular scene," Pilcher said carefully.

"That would be Tittaglia," Flemming said. "But you're his boss."

Pilcher nodded. "Sort of. What can I do for you, Detective?"

"You can tell me what this is all about." Flemming kept his hands in his pockets, but his expression was watchful.

Pilcher came off the steps and locked eyes with the detective. "You're familiar with the attack in Baltimore?"

"Sure. We get Homeland's bulletins, too. Code Red. Might even mean something for a change. This Stillwater one of them?"

Pilcher shook his head. "No. He's a special investigator for the Department of Homeland Security. He's at least a step or two closer to these bad guys—"

"He *is* a bad guy, Pilcher. He busted the jaw of a cop. He resisted arrest. He's a material witness and a possible suspect in a homicide. We want him. He's ours."

Pilcher started to protest, but stopped. He changed tack. "Who was Austin Davis?"

"You tell me. He a terrorist?"

Pilcher shrugged. He needed information, not this crap. "I was told Austin Davis was a physician at Walter Reed. Is he military?"

Flemming scowled. "Was. Served in the Army in the Gulf War. He's been a civilian since '92."

There's the connection, Pilcher thought. His gaze took in the remaining onlookers. Overhead, at least two helicopters continued to circle.

Flemming said, "What's going on upstairs?"

"Nothing to concern you."

"If it's a murder up there, it's our jurisdiction. If it's in any way related to this Derek Stillwater, it's our jurisdiction."

Pilcher gave Flemming a flat stare. "It's not going to happen, so don't bother asking. File the paper if you have to, but that apartment is ours, end of story."

Flemming opened his mouth to argue but apparently decided to save his breath. "This Stillwater, what can you tell me about him?"

Pilcher said, "Nothing. I can't tell you shit. And you're wasting my time. When Superman Stillwater took his amazing leap over the truck, managing to overpower two armed cops at the same time, which way did he go before he disappeared?"

Flemming glared at him. "What's Stillwater do for Homeland? Some kind of spook?"

"Which way did he go, Detective?"

Flemming shook his head. "You tell me something and I'll tell you something."

Pilcher wanted to scream. "Fine," he said through clenched teeth. "He's an expert on biological and chemical warfare."

Flemming's eyes grew wide. "So this attack in Baltimore—"

"Hey, you're catching on. Which way did he go?"

Flemming pointed.

Leaving the detective behind, Pilcher retrieved a big Maglite from the Ford Taurus and headed into the alleyway. The far end was blocked by a tall wooden gate. He aimed the flash toward the ground, saw what might have been dots of drying blood. He followed them to the fence. Impatient, he pulled out his cellular and punched in the number of Stillwater's last known phone. He listened. Nothing. He shut off the phone and, with a sigh, pulled himself over the fence and dropped down on the other side. Pilcher, bending to the ground, found more of the blood trail, drips maybe six, seven feet apart. Stillwater hadn't been bleeding in a way that seemed fatal, and he had probably been moving fast. Did he have a vehicle around here? After he'd been picked up by the Coast Guard at the Scully house, Pilcher had no idea how the troubleshooter had been getting around.

Pilcher followed the blood but lost it after twenty or thirty yards. Stillwater might have stopped bleeding or might have jumped into a car and sped away. He couldn't tell.

He tried the cell phone number again, straining his ears to hear the ring. He raised his eyebrows. Was that . . . ?

He followed the faint sound of the cellular phone vibrating, growing louder as he approached another alley about one building down from the dead woman's apartment. Slowly, he stepped into the dark corridor. The sound of the phone was loud. He scanned the flashlight beam around. There was movement in the debris, and a large black rat scuttled out, eyes glittering in the light before moving farther into the shadows.

There!

Pilcher shut off his phone and the electronic buzzing stopped. There was no sign of Stillwater except a black cell phone in a pile of debris next to the gray stone wall of the building. He picked up the phone and carefully dropped it into his jacket pocket.

He felt conflicted. He had the phone. The phone was evidence. The phone was a direct link to the terrorists. He needed to get it to the lab as fast as possible and start a team of agents tracking down any calls that had gone out or come in to the phone.

But what about Stillwater? Despite the fact the two men were from different agencies, Pilcher had recognized something in the man, a kindred spirit, someone who wasn't interested in climbing the political or corporate ladder, in currying favor or kissing ass. Stillwater just wanted to get the job done.

Pilcher thought of his daughters. Whenever his energy flagged on the job, he thought about his children and his wife, reminded himself that he was protecting them, creating a country, a world even, for them to live in safely. America . . . Americans . . . was too big a concept. Too ephemeral, too abstract. But he would fight for his children.

He decided to give the search for Stillwater ten more minutes, then rush the phone back to the lab.

So . . .

Where had Stillwater gone?

The alley was dark, dirty, the pavement slick with grime and grease and God-knows-what. There was an odor of rotting food that seemed to rise up from the pavement. A rusted green Dumpster halfway down the alley spewed garbage—the rat's home, no doubt. He flashed his light in the Dumpster, just in case, but saw only garbage. He was sure the cops would have, too.

He gazed upward, taking in the lit windows. Rooms with a view, windows looking nowhere. The lower windows were barred, not uncommon in a major city, but something that made Pilcher feel like a failure as a law enforcement officer. The bad guys should be behind bars, not the good guys.

His eyes lingered on the rungs of the fire-escape ladder dangling a good four or five feet above his head. There was no way Stillwater, injured or not, could have jumped and snagged the ladder. Unless . . .

He stepped close to the nearest window and shined his light on the bars and the recessed concrete sill they were set into.

There. A smear of blood.

Glad for his regular workouts, Pilcher clambered up on the windowsill, looking over to realize the bottom rung of the fire escape ladder was now neck level. He reached out, caught the bars and pulled himself up. *To the top,* he thought. *That's where Stillwater is. On top of the damned building.*

He began the long climb up the fire escape.

He was coming to the end of his ten minutes when he pulled himself over the ledge and onto the roof of the building. He shined the flash around and quickly recognized a small puddle of blood on the tarred roof. No drops. A puddle. It was hard to evaluate from blood, but Stillwater's wound had been more than a scratch.

Blood, but no Stillwater.

He paced around, looking for him, but he wasn't on the roof. Pilcher approached the elevator housing, a concrete and steel box in the center of the roof. There was a steel door, and it was open. He let himself in. No Stillwater. Had he been here? Had he let himself into the building and walked out the front door while the cops were searching for him?

Pilcher checked his watch and decided he had to get going. He reminded himself as he entered the building and descended to the main floor to not underestimate Stillwater. The man would get hold of him when he could.

But right now Pilcher had to get this dead woman's cell phone to the lab.

23

Liz Vargas opened her eyes, then promptly closed them. She waited, eyes shut, listening. *This is a nightmare,* she thought. *A very bad dream of the worst sort. I am going to wake up. I am in my own bed. I will get out of bed, take a shower, have a bagel and coffee, then drive to work.*

She opened her eyes.

On a chair next to the bed she was lying on sat a figure in a blue spacesuit. Through the faceplate Liz recognized Sharon Jaxon.

The room looked remarkably similar to a hospital room. There was a TV on the wall, a hospital bed, a couch, a chair, and one of those wheeled tray tables that only exist in hospitals.

A curtain hung over the window, but Liz was certain the window looked out over some observation area of the Slammer. The outer walls of the Slammer, she knew, would be like those of the hot zone, designed to keep lethal microorganisms inside.

Sharon Jaxon reached out and pinched off her oxygen hose to stop the roaring inside her suit. "How are you feeling?"

Propped on a pillow, Liz had to think about it. She was tired. That was understandable. It had been a totally hellish day. Long and stressful did not even begin to describe it. But aside from the fatigue? Well . . .

"I'm scared," she said.

Jaxon's helmet bobbed as she nodded. She reached out and patted Liz's arm. "We're going to make a decision in five hours whether to inoculate you with one of the early Chimeras. We're running hourly antibody screens on the monkeys. In the meantime, we want to give you some antivirals, but we wanted your opinion on which ones are the best bet."

Liz struggled to a sitting position. "How long? How long have I been unconscious?"

"About fifteen minutes. Not long."

Liz felt herself calm slightly. She had Chimera M13 in her system. Chimera was an astonishingly fast-acting virus, closer in reaction time to the effects of salmonella or botulism than a typical virus. It wasn't something they had specifically designed for when they'd created the bug. There were arguments against a fast biological weapon. Some epidemiologists felt that bugs with rapid spread—and that killed their hosts—tended to burn themselves out. The spread of the infection, in other words, was faster than the travel velocity of the host. These scientists argued that this was why Ebola hadn't run completely amuck and killed off Africa during the last two outbreaks in Zaire and Cameroon.

It was why smallpox, with a ten- to fourteen-day incubation period, was so lethal. During the infectious period the patient, not knowing he was infected, exposed a potentially higher number of people. Same thing with HIV, only worse.

The counterargument was that a bug like Chimera could wipe out a vast population exactly *because* it acted so quickly.

Nobody knew which was true. Until Chimera hit the population, scientists could only guess.

"We didn't try any antivirals on Chimera," Liz said, feeling hope flood her body like a warm drink.

"Colonel Zataki's in Washington," Jaxon said. "I got him on the phone just before he went into the briefing, and he suggested we try Acyclovir, Ritonavir, Ribaviran, and Pleconaril. Or any combination. What's your opinion?"

"Briefing?" Liz realized she was distracted, that she should be concentrating on her treatment, but her brain, like a three-year-old's, was looking for distraction. She was thinking, *There is no cure, don't you understand? I'm going to die and I'm going to die soon and it is going to be horrible.*

Jaxon said, "He's briefing the White House personally. He decided the aides they'd sent over weren't smart enough to get it right. Plus the president called and told him to be there."

"That would probably be a factor."

Jaxon smiled. "Yeah. Liz . . . the antivirals."

"Why not all four?"

"I'll check to see what the cross-reactions are. I'll be back."

"Did you ask Frank Halloran? He'd probably have an opinion."

Sharon Jaxon shuffled out of the room without answering, the door closing behind her with a sucking sound. Liz sighed, trying to think, but couldn't. Her brain would not work. All she could think was, *I am going to die.*

24

Washington, D.C.

DEREK STILLWATER APPROACHED THE location on 17th Street where he had left the Explorer. He came in circuitously, on the opposite side of the street, circling the block on foot. The chopper crew had informed him that the D.C. cops were probably looking for him for the shooting of Austin Davis. It was also possible, he thought, that the FBI might want to pull him in after they saw the carnage at Irina Khournikova's apartment.

He didn't know if the cops had any idea how he had gotten to Walter Reed. The Explorer had been supplied by the Pentagon, so it was possible nobody knew anything about it. Still, for the same reason he hadn't wanted to be pulled in back at the apartment, he was making every effort to continue the investigation.

It was dark and late and traffic was light. There were only a handful of pedestrians, late-night barflies and people coming and going to social events, though in light of the day's news, social events were few and far between.

He walked casually toward the Explorer. The one good thing to happen so far was he still had the keys.

Without any kind of warning, he popped the lock, got into the driver's side, fired up the engine, and pulled into the street. He began a complicated, random route, heading roughly in the direction of the Pentagon.

He found an open parking spot within shouting distance of the Pentagon and hunted through his Go Packs. There was a spare cellular phone and charged batteries. He sat in the driver's seat, thinking it over. Should he call in, check with Dalton or Johnston? With a shake of his head he decided to do a little more work.

He rummaged through his wallet and came up with the contact information for Staff Sergeant Stanley O'Reilly, the military officer who had acted as his host at the Pentagon. The phone to O'Reilly's office rang exactly once before it was picked up.

"O'Reilly, this is Derek Stillwater."

"Yes, sir. How can I help you, sir?"

Perky little hotel clerk, Stillwater thought. He said, "You're on duty rather late tonight."

"Yes, sir. We are at a heightened alert, sir."

"Don't I know it. Well, I would like contact information for Lieutenant Colonel Tallifer. Could you get hold of him for me?"

"Yes, sir. Will you hold?"

"No. Here's my number. Have him call me." Derek rattled off his new cell's number and clicked off. While he waited he rummaged through his Go Packs, looking for the nice little bag of amphetamines he kept there for exactly these types of occasions. He swallowed two hits of the speed with lukewarm bottled water from one of his packs. Cars drove by. In the night sky he saw helicopters, lots of them. He imagined there was a regular shuttle service between the Pentagon, USAMRIID, the White House, and points unknown. He wondered if the president was on Air Force One. He hoped so. He hoped everybody was taking this seriously.

His phone rang. It was O'Reilly again. "Sir, Lieutenant Colonel Tallifer isn't on the premises. His office indicates he is out."

"What time did he leave?"

"I don't know, sir."

"Can you find out?"

"Yes, sir. Will you hold?"

"Yes."

He held. After a minute of dead air, O'Reilly was back. "Shortly after you left, sir." Something in the man's voice communicated concern.

"Does that strike you as unusual, O'Reilly?"

Silence.

"O'Reilly?"

"Unexpected, sir. I'm not sure if it's unusual. Since going to Code Red, most of us have stayed on duty. We will be on duty through the night, possibly longer, until emergency rotations are in place. The attack at U.S. Immunological Research is being taken seriously by the Pentagon, sir."

"I see," Derek said, mind racing. "Do you have cellular information or a home telephone number for Tallifer?"

"Yes, sir. Here it is, sir." O'Reilly rattled it off. Derek scrawled it down in a notebook.

"Thank you, Sergeant."

"Are you making progress, sir?"

"On?"

"You're working on that U.S. Immuno thing, aren't you, sir? You are an expert on biological warfare."

"Yes, I'm working on it," Derek conceded.

"Are you making progress?"

"I hope so, Sergeant. I surely hope so."

Above Stillwater's Explorer, the Coast Guard helicopter circled. Cynthia Black, the pilot, said, "Still in sight?"

"You bet," said Tex. He was using the chopper's night-vision capabilities to track the Ford Explorer. It was easier said than done, but this crew had been together for a number of years, beginning with search and rescue and moving to drug interdiction and then, post–September 11, 2001, into antiterrorism activities.

They had officially become part of Derek Stillwater's team, although "official" probably wasn't the correct word. Since the Coast Guard was now part of the Department of Homeland Security, and Derek needed them, they were now working with—or for—the Homeland Security troubleshooter.

Sid Kerkowski, their third crewmate and gunner, said, "How're we doing on fuel?"

"Fine for now," said Black. She looked at Sid, whose youthful face was filled with anticipation.

"We're rockin' and rollin'," he said.

Black rolled her eyes but had to admit to a surge of adrenaline. She had been philosophical about their taxi services today. Although Stillwater had declined to give specifics, they had been following the news related to the U.S. Immuno attack and had a pretty good idea what the man was up to. When Stillwater finished justifying his commandeering their helicopter, she had said, "Whatever you need, sir, we can give you."

"Well, thanks. I'm not sure—"

"Sir," Black had said. "I'm not sure you understand. This helicopter . . ." She waved around her. "It was originally commissioned for drug interdiction, but its mandate has been broadened for antiterrorism activity."

"I see," Stillwater said, but clearly he didn't.

"No, sir," she said. "You need to know a little bit about this helicopter."

Derek had sighed. "I'm not sure I have time for a sales pitch—"

"This is an MK-68 Mako," she said. "It has a maximum speed of 168 knots and a cruising speed of 137 knots. Its range is 363 nautical miles."

"That's nice, but—"

"Shut up!"

Derek raised his eyebrows.

Tex spoke up. "Maybe Sid can explain."

Stillwater turned to the third crewman. "What?"

Sid grinned. "We're armed with an M-240 machine gun, a Robar .50-caliber sniper rifle—"

"He's a sharpshooter, too," Black added.

"Yes, sir," Kerkowski said.

"And," Black said, "we're equipped with night-vision goggles, FLIR—that's forward-looking infrared—Light Eye and NightSun searchlight, and a GPS moving map."

"In other words," Tex said, "we're one well-armed, well-trained group of motherfuckers."

Derek glanced around at the three Coast Guard officers. "Then I think we need to make a plan." He paused, listening to the thunder of the helicopter rotor. "I think we need to set a trap."

"A trap, sir?" Black asked.

"Yes."

Tex brushed his mustache. "And what, exactly, are we going to use for bait?"

Derek smiled. "Me."

Now, above the Explorer, Black's radio crackled. "TS-One, receiving. This is Black." The Coast Guard pilot had supplied Stillwater with a handheld radio to communicate with them.

"Any tail?"

"Sid?"

"Negative."

"Negative," she relayed to Derek.

"Okay. I'll be back to you in ten."

Derek phoned the number for Lieutenant Colonel Tallifer's cellular phone. It was answered on the second ring with an abrupt, "Yes?"

"Colonel, this is Derek Stillwater, with Homeland Security."

"Yes, Doctor. What can I do for you?"

"I need to meet ASAP to discuss Richard Coffee further."

"I'm not sure there's anything else to discuss, Doctor. You've read the file."

"Yes, I have. And that's exactly why we need to discuss it further."

"Just a moment."

There was silence on the line. Then Tallifer came back on. "I can meet you in about an hour. How about—"

"I'll meet you at Rock Creek Park," Derek said, and supplied a detailed description of the parking lot in the huge park where he wanted to rendezvous. "In one hour. I'll be in the green Explorer."

Before Tallifer could argue or negotiate, Derek clicked off. Then he radioed the helicopter to tell them the plan.

25

FBI Headquarters, Washington, D.C.

Aaron Pilcher passed through security into SIOC, the Strategic Information and Operations Center on the fifth floor of the J. Edgar Hoover Building. There was a constant flow of agents and support staff in and out of the wedge-shaped room. There were a dozen huge screens connected to computers on the walls, dozens of agents working computers and telephones. The Bureau, Pilcher thought, was doing what it did best: marshaling information.

Agent Spigotta, his jaw muscles bunched like he had walnuts tucked in his cheeks, was glaring at one of the huge VDTs on the wall. "How many total?" he growled.

Two agents, one at a computer terminal that controlled the VDT, started counting the figures on the screen.

Pilcher stepped up. Spigotta glanced over and nodded brusquely. "You look like shit, but I'm glad you're alive."

"Glad to be alive." He gestured at the screen. "The parking garage?"

"Three vans, four each," said the agent doing the counting. She was a willowy redhead with pale blue eyes.

"I want them isolated, and start working on IDs," Spigotta growled.

Pilcher held up the stack of file folders retrieved from the D.C. apartment. "Hang on. I've got faces. Let's see if we can tie them together now."

Spigotta's head snapped around. "What've you got?"

Pilcher opened the file and held up the clearest photograph of Richard Coffee. "Quite possibly the leader. Ray?"

The agent at the keyboard took a close look at the photograph and started isolating images on the screen. He was a heavyset bald man with a fringe of gray hair and wire-rimmed bifocals. His pudgy fingers flashed on the computer keys.

"There." The redhead pointed.

"Enhance," Spigotta barked.

The image dissolved, resolved, closed in, dissolved and resolved again. The four FBI agents stared. "Bingo," Pilcher said. "Meet the Fallen, formerly known as Richard Coffee, a U.S. citizen, former Special Forces—"

"Domestic?" Spigotta's face burned red.

"Not really," Pilcher said. He supplied the sketchy information Derek Stillwater had acquired.

Spigotta raised his hands. "Everybody, listen up. We've got a backstory. Aaron, you've got the floor."

Taking a deep breath, Pilcher described what they knew so far. When he was done Spigotta pointed at a slight, scholarly-looking man. "Adams, you're our terrorism guy. Ever heard of the Fallen Angels?"

"No, sir."

"Get on it."

"I'd like the photographs you've got."

Spigotta nodded and Pilcher turned them over.

Pilcher said, "Um, Rick . . . these could all be bullshit. As far as Coffee goes, I'm a believer. Everything else though . . . pretty suspect."

"Got it. Thanks."

Agent Jonathan Adams took the files and rushed out of the SIOC.

"Unrau." Spigotta pointed at a stout woman with brassy brown hair and thick eyeglasses. "Who at the Russian embassy would know about this group?"

"Yuri Arkady Rostovitch," she said without hesitation.

"Please arrange an invitation for Mr. Rostovitch to join us here."

"Yes, sir." She turned to leave.

"Bridgette?"

Agent Unrau turned back.

"If he declines, send out a team of agents to deliver him here ASAP."

She paused, no doubt thinking of the consequences of kidnapping a Russian embassy official, then shrugged and smiled. "I'm on it, sir."

Spigotta continued to direct his troops. Pilcher took a moment to slip into a chair. Waves of exhaustion washed over him. He leaned back and glanced up at the VDT displaying the vans. To Ray O'Brien, manning the keyboard, he said, "Is the explosion on there?"

Ray looked over, his face flushed. "Yes. You're lucky."

"Yeah. Let's make sure the media doesn't get hold of that until we want them to."

"Yes, sir."

Spigotta was in conference with another agent, a serious-minded female agent who Pilcher recognized as one of the senior domestic terrorism people. He didn't, right off hand, remember her name. His cell phone buzzed. He clicked it on and identified himself.

"Pilcher, this is Zerbe, in the lab."

"Sure. What's up?"

"I've been tearing that phone to pieces that you found? I've brought up the call history and will be uploading it to the system for you to access in just a minute. I've put a team on analyzing the calls. We should have most of that nailed down in less than an hour."

"Good. See if you can speed them up."

"Yes, but . . ." Zerbe's voice dropped to a low tone, almost a whisper.

"What is it?" Pilcher said, sitting up straight.

"Sir, one of the last numbers called? It's Sam Dalton's private number."

It took a second for Pilcher to focus on the name. "Sam—"

"The deputy director of Homeland Security, sir."

Pilcher's brain raced. "Okay," he said. "No big deal. These Homeland troubleshooters have direct access to the directors during a crisis. Do you have a—"

"The call was about three-thirty this afternoon," Zerbe said.

Pilcher blinked. He had been thinking that after killing the Russian, Derek Stillwater had used her phone to call his bosses because his own was busted. But in the middle of the afternoon . . .

"Hey, Zerbe," he said, voice low. "Keep a lid on this, understand?"

"Does this mean what I think it means?" Zerbe responded.

"I hope not. But we'll work it. Thanks." Pilcher clicked off and stared over to where Spigotta was directing agents. Spigotta must have sensed the focus of Pilcher's gaze, because he turned to look at him. Pilcher waved him over.

"What?" Spigotta said.

"We need privacy for this," he said, getting to his feet.

Spigotta narrowed his eyes. "You look even more like shit than you did before."

"Private," Pilcher said.

Spigotta led him over to a quiet corner, his back to the walls so he could glare off anyone approaching. "Okay, Aaron. I don't know how you could possibly have more bad news."

"This Russian woman phoned Sam Dalton this afternoon, less than two hours after they stole Chimera. It's in her cellular records."

Spigotta raised his eyebrows. "Meaning . . . ?"

"I don't know. But it could mean that Dalton was in on this. Don't forget, he's former Military Intelligence. Richard Coffee is former Military Intelligence. Stillwater claims he's getting the run-around from Military Intelligence."

"Fuck," Spigotta said. He glared around SIOC. "Fuck," he repeated. "What're we going to do?"

"We should probably get somebody to talk to Dalton," Aaron said.

Spigotta looked at him. "Dalton's where, at the White House?"

"Yes. I think they're out of the West Wing."

"You're up, Aaron. But wash your face first, whaddaya say?"

26

The White House

SECRETARY JAMES JOHNSTON SETTLED into his chair at the long conference table and took a long sip from the water glass by his spot, using the drink as an opportunity to inspect the people who had already arrived. The president wasn't there yet, no surprise. The attorney general was—she would be chairing things—as were the joint chiefs, the director of the Centers for Disease Control and Prevention, and the director of Health and Human Services. He recognized Dr. Daniel Zataki from USAMRIID and was surprised. He had been under the impression Zataki wouldn't be there. He hoped his presence didn't indicate an even uglier turn of events.

There were a dozen representatives from various emergency response units, the director of FEMA, and a handful of civilians he suspected were from the National Science Board. He wasn't wild about that. In his years in the military, he'd hated dealing with scientists. Ask five scientists the same question, you were likely to get five different answers. He remembered during the Gulf War asking his scientific advisors what the most dangerous biological or chemical agent Iraq might use on the coalition troops.

One had said anthrax.

Another confidently claimed botulin toxin.

Yet another said VX gas.

The fourth asserted smallpox.

Exasperated, Johnston had turned to Derek Stillwater, who, at that time a captain, had not offered an opinion.

"Well, Captain?"

Derek had said, "Whichever one they use, General. The one they use, that's the most dangerous one to the coalition troops."

Johnston had decided on the spot that this captain was worth keeping around.

In the White House conference room, Johnston glanced at his watch and wondered how things were going for Stillwater. He also wondered why he hadn't heard from Sam Dalton, his deputy director.

After Stillwater's last contact and the information regarding Richard Coffee, Dalton had made a few calls to the CIA and the Pentagon to try to shake loose a few more hard facts. None had been immediately forthcoming, so Johnston, exasperated, had suggested Dalton head over to the Pentagon or to Langley and do the shaking in person. "Put the full weight of the White House behind it, goddammit."

He hadn't heard from Dalton since. Or Stillwater.

The door opened, and everyone in the room rose to their feet as the president of the United States entered, followed by the national security advisor, the director of the FBI, and the director of the CIA. This was, thought Johnston, as top-level a meeting as you could get. Except, he added with a frown, the director of the Department of

Homeland Security had not been included in this tête-à-tête. His and the president's meeting had been face to face an hour ago, and it had been as frank and politics-free as it was possible to get. He hoped the president had listened to him. If he did, he thought, it would be the first time. He had told the president that he shouldn't wait for this bug to get loose, that he should act as if it already were. Don't worry about a panic, he had counseled. Act as if there's a possibility that a lethal virus with a twelve-hour incubation period has been let loose on the American public. Then act accordingly.

Johnston did not think President Langston would listen. His appointment to the post of secretary of the Department of Homeland Security had been a political maneuver to appease members of the Republican Party who feared that Langston's emphasis on the economy and on downsizing the military made him look weak. They had encouraged Langston to place an experienced military man in the domestic position to give the appearance of a strong stance on thwarting domestic terrorism while relegating the outspoken general to a relatively innocuous political posting.

Even though his office was currently in the West Wing, Johnston was acutely aware that he was not in the inner circle. And furthermore, Langston did not like him personally and went out of his way to neutralize whatever clout he might have.

The president, a sandy-haired man in his late fifties, sat. Everyone followed suit.

"As you know," President Langston began, "our country has come under attack by a terrorist organization. I'll let Director Boardman fill you in on the details. Fred, you have the floor."

FBI Director Frederick Boardman was a round-faced, chubby man in his early sixties. He looked like a guy who ate chocolate-chip cookies and milk before bed, doted on his grandchildren, and listened to easy-listening stations on the radio. All of which were true. He was also a former attorney general with a cutthroat grasp of Beltway politics who had spent much of his career locating and identifying the closeted skeletons of the nation's elite. He also, Johnston reflected, had only a nodding acquaintance with civil liberties. Under the circumstances that might be a good thing, but only if he could let his ruthlessness win out over his political tendencies.

Johnston remembered something Derek Stillwater had said during a lecture on pandemics. "Politicians don't understand infectious disease. From the earliest history, politicians were slow to react to epidemics. Whether it was bubonic plague in the 10th or 16th centuries, flu in the 1920s, or HIV in the 1980s. They always, without exception, wait too long to act."

Boardman said, "At 11:43 a.m. today, an organized assault by three vehicles containing four men each breached the security of a Pentagon-funded biological-warfare research facility, U.S. Immunological Research. A team of highly trained commandos penetrated the facility, entered a Level 4 biohazard containment area, and stole approximately a dozen vials containing a genetically engineered virus." The FBI director went on with his talk, describing what almost everyone in the room already knew. After ten minutes he paused, took a sip of water, and continued.

"Our investigation so far points toward a Russian-based terrorist group known as the Fallen Angels. They are not, as far as we've been able to tell, usually more than illegal-weapons merchants. They acquire weapons, from small arms to missiles to weapons of mass destruction, and sell them to whoever can afford them."

"So you don't think this group's intention is to immediately use this . . . this Chimera?" The speaker was Admiral Steven Lancaster, one of the joint chiefs.

Director Boardman hesitated. "We're still developing a profile. We don't have very much information on this group."

"Why is that?" asked one of the blue suits Johnston assumed were science advisers.

Richard White, the director of the CIA, spoke up. His diction was clean and careful, a reflection of his East Coast, moneyed background and two years at Oxford on a Rhodes Scholarship. Tall and angular, his thick hair had the unnatural blackness of dye. He tended to tilt his head back and peer along his long aristocratic nose through the gold-rimmed glasses perched there. "Because," he said, "they have not fallen into our sphere of activity. By and large, they have been an internal Russian problem, believed to be associated with the Chechen rebels."

General Johnston stared at Richard White, wondering whether the CIA had ever heard of the Fallen Angels. *He* hadn't. He was supposedly privy to all intelligence relating to homeland security, though the CIA, NSA, DIA, and the other dozen intelligence-gathering agencies had a tendency to define that in varying ways. It was possible that because the Fallen Angels were, in fact, an internal Russian problem, the CIA hadn't seen any reason to provide anything about them to the Department of Homeland Security. Or, equally possible, the CIA had once again been caught with their pants down around their ankles, butt firmly planted on the potty while the world's bad guys came knocking at their door.

White and Boardman batted information back and forth for a while before President Langston asked Colonel Zataki what USAMRIID was doing about Chimera.

In his soft voice, Zataki said, "There were earlier versions of Chimera, some of them nonlethal, that we're testing on monkeys to see if they can be used as vaccines. We should know by morning if any of them are effective that way. If they are, we've put in place ways to manufacture it in massive quantities for emergency use, should Chimera be let loose on the public."

"And if they aren't?" asked President Langston.

Colonel Zataki said, "The CDC has been alerted to be on the lookout for any signs of the illness. They are on a full alert. I also suggest that the National Guard and the military be put on full alert. Hospital emergency rooms are already being informed. Any patients coming in with the symptoms of Chimera will need to be placed in isolation immediately, and concentric rings of isolation created around the subject. I'm sure that Fred Richards can fill you in more."

Voices started to babble, raised in a chorus of responses to these emergency actions. President Langston cleared his throat, and the hubbub subsided. "Colonel Zataki, thank you. Do you and Dr. Richards feel that this Chimera presents a clear and present danger to the American public? Should we, in fact, treat this as a national health care crisis?"

"Mr. President," Colonel Zataki said, "we should treat this as the start of Armageddon."

There was a rise in the volume of background conversation, broken by the national security advisor, who snapped, "Colonel Zataki, this is not a forum in which melodrama is appreciated."

Colonel Zataki eyed Taylor James calmly. "Ms. James, no melodrama was intended."

"I agree with Colonel Zataki," said Dr. Richards, the director of the CDC.

"So do I," Secretary Johnston said. "You need to take this seriously."

"Seriously?" said Taylor. "You're talking Armageddon. How seriously can we take it when you insist on referring to it as if it were a movie? We don't want overstatement or melodrama. We want scientific fact. We want—"

"We're talking a bioengineered virus," Zataki interrupted in his cool voice, "with an apparent 100 percent fatality rate within twelve hours. It is 100 percent infectious, as far as we know, can be communicated via air, touch, or in food or liquids. Imagine, if you will, that one person is infected with Chimera. If that person has minimal contact with people, he or she will probably infect twenty or thirty people in one day. Also, if the subject coughs or spits or bleeds onto a surface, that surface will become infectious. It's not known how long Chimera can survive outside its host. We'll test for it, but we don't have time. None of us has time to make assumptions, especially *conservative* assumptions, about the danger of this virus. Meanwhile, those twenty infected individuals, the second ring of infection, are infecting anywhere from twenty to hundreds of people. This isn't smallpox, with an incubation period of two weeks. This germ is fast, Ms. James. It will burn through the population like wildfire."

"More drama," James said. She was a tall, elegant African-American woman with a brain like a razor. As far as Secretary Johnston was concerned, though, she was far too political an animal for this particular crisis. She said, "Mr. President—"

Taylor James broke off speaking, her eyes wide and staring. At the rear of the room, one of the people sitting there had snapped his head back against the wall with a bang. A young, clean-cut man in a three-piece suit, possibly a senator's aide or somebody from HHS, he started to convulse, a foam of saliva pouring from his mouth as he arched his back and fell from the chair. Suddenly the people on both sides of the man began to twitch, drooling, convulsing, vomiting.

Secretary Johnston reacted instantly, leaping across the table, grabbing the president's arm and hauling him from his chair. "Evacuate!" he bellowed, rushing for the door. "Evacuate!"

Colonel Zataki was right behind him, reaching for the director of the FBI, who had started to convulse. Zataki, a small man, but strong, hefted him over his shoulder and ran through the now-open door.

With horror they saw that the hallway outside the conference room was littered with bodies.

"Outside," gasped Johnston. "Outside."

They raced through the hallways, heading for any room with a window, an exit, anything. There were dozens of bodies in the hallways, convulsing.

Johnston felt the president lag and snarled, "Keep moving, goddammit!"

Zataki was struggling, gasping for air, feeling the effects. He panted out, "Atropine injectors! We need—"

Johnston rushed down a flight of steps, dragging the president, and slammed shoulder-first into a fire exit and out onto the south lawn. The president fell to the ground, gasping. Johnston turned, saw Zataki stumble to his knees, dropping the director of the FBI. Zataki, struggling for air, pressed his fingers against the man's neck, shaking his head.

"Dammit! VX gas! Somehow the White House was attacked with VX gas!"

27

Captain Jaxon approached Liz Vargas with a tray of needles and tubes and pouches of saline and drugs. The faceplate of her space-suit had fogged up before she could make it to one of the air hoses, and she shouted to be heard. "These are the antivirals. We're going to try a cocktail of Acyclovir, Ritonavir, and Pleconavil." Jaxon set the tray down and reached for an air hose, connecting it to her suit. It immediately puffed up, and her faceplate began to clear.

Liz sat up in her bed in the Slammer and turned so her stock-inged feet hung off. "Take a break, Sharon," she said.

"You just lie down and—"

Liz jumped to her feet, a fierce expression on her face. "I'm the only living expert on this virus. I'm not going to roll over and . . . I'm fighting. Understand? I'm fighting. And there's no reason for you to risk a needle stick when I'm perfectly capable of doing it myself."

"You need rest," Jaxon insisted.

"Stop it! Just stop it!" Liz pulled the IV pole close to the bed. "You're acting like a doctor. This isn't a doctor-patient relationship. It's not! I'm a guinea pig." She hooked the saline bag into the stand and sorted out the clear plastic lines. From the tray she laid out the needle and rubber tourniquet. "I'm a goddamned laboratory animal, and you'd better figure that out fast because there's not a lot of time."

Perching on the edge of the bed, Liz strapped on the tourniquet, flicked at the bulging vein in the crook of her left elbow, then deftly inserted the needle. With considerably less dexterity she tore off a piece of surgical tape and taped down the needle.

Standing, she hung the bags of the antiviral medicines and manipulated the lines and needles until they were feeding into the IV lines. "Dosage?"

Jaxon said, "Set the drip rate. . . . Here. I can do that." With her clumsy gloved hands, she adjusted the drip rate of the IVs. She turned to Liz. "We can get you a phone so you can call your parents."

"Later," Liz said. "Here's what I need. I need a computer with an Internet connection. I'm going to connect to U.S. Immuno's database. I need full access to all our work on Chimera. I'm one of the few alive with security clearance."

Jaxon crossed her hands over her chest. It was a comical posture in the blue spacesuit. Her voice was muffled. "We can do that."

"And I need one more thing," Liz said. "I need you to get hold of Dr. Lester Hingemann. He's at Michigan State University, in the Life Sciences Department, Microbiology and Public Health. I want him either on the phone with me ASAP or, even better, some sort of video conference call. And do it quick. Track him down."

"Who is he?" Jaxon asked.

"He's a bacteriologist and an expert on immune responses to bacteria. He's the leading expert on *Yersinia pestis*."

"Chimera is a virus," Jaxon countered. "You know that. What good is—"

"Do it! I have an idea. It might be a long shot, but . . ." Her eyes welled up with tears and she brushed them aside with both hands, the lines to the IV jiggling and bouncing. "It's time to make the long shots."

Jaxon nodded. "I'll get right on it."

28

Rock Creek Park, Washington, D.C.

DEREK PARKED THE EXPLORER in the funnel of illumination cast by an overhead light in one of the many parking lots along the huge Rock Creek Park. The park was over 21,000 acres and ran for more than five miles. Situated in the heart of Washington, D.C., it was a huge, dark wilderness in which to ambush or be ambushed. It was also a popular body-dumping site for the D.C. area. Only fools or bad guys ventured there after dark. Derek knew he wasn't a bad guy. . . .

He sat in silence for a moment, taking in the tall trees and tumbles of boulders. Less than twenty-four hours ago, he had been paddling his kayak on the Chesapeake Bay, living aboard his boat, occasionally traveling to other countries to discuss bioterrorism with military experts. Sometimes he taught classes at Georgetown or lectured at one of the military academies. Life had been relatively simple.

Times change. Yet all he craved was to reset his life back a day.

He sighed and tried to concentrate on the problems at hand. Rock Creek Park was not safe at night. Just ask Chandra Levy, the Senate intern who disappeared prior to September 11th. Linked by an affair to Senator Gary Condit, her disappearance had struck a national chord—the investigation covered on the nightly news, on CNN, her picture on the cover of *People* magazine.

Then nineteen of Osama bin Laden's martyrs had slammed four planes into the World Trade towers, the Pentagon, and a Pennsylvania cornfield. Nobody except Chandra's friends and family spent much time thinking about her after that until some guy found her skeleton in the park while he was looking for turtles in one of the creeks.

Right around here, Derek thought.

He retrieved his Rigel 3250 night-vision goggles and double-checked his Colt to make sure it was loaded with a full magazine, the safety was off, and he had a round in the chamber. Strapping the goggles on his head, gun in hand, he left the Explorer and melted into the woods. This was strictly recon. Derek didn't think Tollifer or anybody else would have gotten here ahead of him. Still, he crept silently from tree to tree and shrub to shrub, slipping behind rocky outcroppings and over boulders, making sure the perimeter was secure. The world was lit up in a ghostly green glow.

Finally he slung the goggles over his shoulder and moved away from the light, standing just inside the tree line, motionless.

Right on time, a Jeep Cherokee pulled into the lot.

Through a whisper mic clipped to his collar, Derek said, "See anyone?"

"Negative, sir. Not in the immediate area," Cynthia Black's voice spoke in his ear.

"Check."

The Cherokee stopped, motor running. From the trees Derek inspected the driver. It was Tollifer. Keeping to the cover of the woods, Derek moved to a flanking position. Into his mic he said, "Anything?"

"Not nearby. There's a van at the next lot up, and some traffic on the road. Light tonight."

Slipping from shadow to shadow, Stillwater approached the Cherokee. Finally, heart thudding in his chest, Stillwater crept around to the driver's side, gun pointing toward Tollifer.

"I saw you in the rearview," Tollifer said through the open window.

"I was more interested in your rear seats."

"I'm alone."

"Shut it down and get out. Keep your hands where I can see them."

Tollifer followed directions, standing opposite Derek, hands out to his sides. He was no longer in uniform, now wearing khaki Dockers and a dark polo shirt.

"My sidearm's in the Jeep," Tollifer said.

"Forgive me for not just taking your word. Assume the position."

Tollifer leaned against the Jeep, legs spread, arms wide. Quickly, keeping his gun pressed against the back of the Military Intelligence man, Derek frisked him. "Okay," he said, moving back two steps.

Tollifer stood up and turned to look at him. "Satisfied?"

"Hardly. Let's walk."

Tollifer shrugged and fell into step, crossing the parking lot.

"Tell me about Richard Coffee," Derek said.

"You read the file."

"The file's bullshit."

"Not as far as I know, it isn't." Tollifer stopped and turned. "Do you know something different?"

"Keep walking."

Tollifer stepped away. "As far as we know, Coffee died in Chechnya working for the CIA."

"Why bug me at the Pentagon?" Derek asked.

Tollifer hesitated.

"Tollifer," Derek said, waving the gun to get the man's attention, "I'm not having a good night. I'm pressed for time. Talk to me."

Tollifer considered him for a long moment. Then, "Is he alive?"

Derek was perplexed. "You tell me."

"I think so. Yes. Is he?"

"Yes. I think he's the head of this group—"

"The Fallen Angels," Tollifer said.

"You know of them?"

Tollifer nodded slightly. "Yes. They're . . . sort of a hobby of mine."

They moved across the lot, in and out of lights, keeping to the edge of the illumination, savoring the shadows. Derek noted bats flitting among the trees, their agitated flight paths unmistakable.

"Hobby?" Derek said. "Why?"

Tollifer stopped and turned. Derek adjusted the aim of his Colt. Tollifer held his hands out. "Hey, I'm unarmed. I think we can help each other."

"So talk." He didn't lower his gun.

"If Coffee's alive," Tollifer said. "I want him."

"Why?"

They locked eyes. Tollifer finally said, "Anthony Tollifer."

"A relative?"

"My brother."

"Okay. I'm listening."

"This is off the record. Let's call it a rumor."

"I'm not a congressional hearing, Tollifer. Talk. Tell me a story. I'm all ears."

"Tony worked for . . . a certain government agency in Virginia."

The CIA, Derek thought.

Tollifer went on. "Tony had a certain kind of training. A special skill set that this government agency doesn't like to admit that it employs."

An assassin, Derek thought.

"This government agency sent Tony into Russia—Chechnya to be exact—to bring in a rogue agent."

"Coffee."

"You bet. Coffee was off the reservation. Way off. He went from intelligence provider to infiltration to leading a fucking civil war. A war that the powers that be decided was no longer prudent policy. Coffee was a loose cannon rolling around the deck, and Tony was sent over there to tie him down. But Tony disappeared. At the same time, Coffee disappeared. But there was a new group, independent of the Chechens, called the Fallen Angels, made up of a bunch of disenfranchised agents from all over the world, committed to making money and causing trouble. I've spent years putting this together from sources I have in the DIA, CIA, NSA, all over the world. These Fallen Angels, they're like ghosts. Phantoms. But they exist, and I'm convinced Richard Coffee killed my brother and is now leading this terrorist group. And I want him, Stillwater. I want to put a bullet in his—"

Tollifer's head exploded, his brains and blood and bits of skull splattering over Derek, the shot ringing out a moment later. Derek dived, rolled, and was on his feet, sprinting into the shadows, heading for the relative safety of the trees. More gunfire exploded into the silence. He returned fire in the general direction of his assailants, emptying his gun. He didn't have an extra magazine on him. He raced through the trees, unable to stop long enough to pull on the night-vision goggles, running blind, branches scratching at his face. He tumbled behind a tall granite outcropping and lay still, silently donning the goggles. The world lit up in a sea of green.

In his ear Cynthia Black said, "Derek?"

He tapped once at the whisper mic, but didn't speak. There were hunters in the woods. They were well armed, they probably had night-vision goggles as well, and they were hunting him.

In his ear Cynthia said, "We're picking up four bogeys on IR. One's about fifteen yards south of you. The other three are moving off to the west."

He tapped the mic. Slowly, making every effort not to make a sound, he pulled a knife from a hasp on his belt. It had a nine-inch blade and was as sharp as a razor.

"He's moving in your direction, ten yards."

Black continued to feed him information. Abruptly she stopped, and he knew it was because the bogey was close. He couldn't hear anything except the sound of his own heartbeat. There was the soft whisper of a footstep, and through his night-vision goggles Derek saw a figure move carefully past the boulder. The approaching bogey probably had his own night-vision goggles. Infrared, too? Would he be tracking his heat signature? That was bad enough; movement would only draw his attention.

The bogey moved in silence, slow and stealthy.

Derek lunged. Crack! He stepped on a branch, which snapped under his weight. The bogey was alerted and spun, raising his weapon as Derek drove in hard. There was the sharp rattle of semiautomatic fire, the dazzle of the muzzle momentarily lighting up the woods. Derek hit him with his shoulder, driving up under the rifle, slamming it away.

The terrorist grunted and swung the butt of the weapon, making contact with Derek's head. The night-vision goggles went flying. Blinded, stunned, Derek fell backward to the leaf-strewn ground, rolling as he fell, kicking out and sweeping the killer's legs from beneath him.

In his ear: "Three bogeys heading for your position."

The two men crashed into each other, fingers grappling for throats, trying to gouge at eyes. "Air . . . support," Derek gasped.

He stayed in close, fighting to keep the rifle between them. If the terrorist could create space between them and bring up the weapon, he would cut Derek to ribbons.

There was the growing thunder of the helicopter, followed by the *pok! pok! pok!* of the Coast Guard .50-caliber sniper rifle and the returning chatter of the bogey's automatics.

The terrorist got his hands around Derek's throat, squeezing.

Derek, gagging, didn't bother to attack the killer's arms. Tightening his fist, he smashed his knuckles directly onto the protruding snout of his attacker's night-vision goggles.

His attacker groaned and loosened his grip on Derek's throat.

In his ear: "Two down . . ."

"I need . . . light," Derek sputtered.

The terrorist leaped back from Derek and was swinging his assault rifle up when the helicopter flooded the woods with the harsh glare of the floodlight.

Derek's attacker involuntarily raised his hands to his eyes. Night-vision goggles magnify existing light. Sudden illumination creates a brilliant white flash in the wearer's vision before the circuit breaker can cut in. Light, magnified by a thousand, exploded in his attacker's eyes, searing his retinas.

Ducking in low Derek slammed his foot against the man's knee, grabbed the rifle from his grip, and turned it on him.

In his ear: "Fourth bogey closing . . ."

Derek spun as another camo-garbed assailant raced toward him. There was a loud *pok! pok! pok!* from above, and the man collapsed to the ground.

Derek's attacker was crumpled on the ground, clutching his leg. The helicopter hovered, then lit up the area again with light.

Raising the weapon, a Colt XM-177 assault rifle, Derek said, "Goggles off. Slowly."

The man raised his arms and lifted off the night-vision goggles, tossing them to the forest floor.

Derek's jaw clenched and a tremor of disbelief rocked him. His attacker was Sam Dalton, deputy director of the Department of Homeland Security.

29

FBI Headquarters

Aaron Pilcher was taking a quick shower in the locker room when an agent he didn't know dashed in and stuttered, "You—you're needed in SIOC immediately."

Aaron nodded. "Something—"

"Full alert," the agent said. "It's the White House."

Hair still wet, back in his begrimed suit, Pilcher arrived in SIOC to find the command center a buzzing swarm of high-tension activity. He'd noticed the difference immediately upon leaving the locker room anyway. Nobody walked, they ran as they moved down the corridors. Voices were either raised in harsh, rushed dialogue or urgent, confidential whispers. Eyes were wide, faces drawn tight, the sudden tension palpable.

Someone raised the stakes, he thought. *But how?*

In SIOC, Spigotta was deep in conversation with someone Pilcher recognized as Terrance McIvoy, the deputy director of the Bureau.

Then his attention turned to one of the many TV monitors lining the walls. This one was tuned to CNN, and it was a live feed at the White House, which was lit by the red and blue flashing lights of civilian and military emergency vehicles.

Spigotta saw him and waved him over. "We've got a situation," he said. "A gas attack—maybe VX, maybe sarin—on the White House."

Pilcher felt sucker-punched. He wanted to sit down. He wanted to wake up and find this to be a nightmare. A really bad nightmare.

"Is—"

"So far the only known survivors are Colonel Zataki from Detrick, Secretary Johnston from DHS, and the president."

McIvoy said, "Director Boardman is believed dead. As are the joint chiefs, the directors of the CIA, FEMA, the CDC, the national security advisor, and most of the White House staff." McIvoy ran a hand through his thick dark hair. "We also believe the first lady and the two children are dead."

Pilcher blinked, speechless.

Spigotta said, "The Army and our Hazardous Materials Recovery Unit are going to treat the White House as a crime scene. The liaising agent there is Simon Berra. I want you over there to see if there are any leads."

"Where's the president?"

"President Langston, Zataki, and Johnston are at Walter Reed. The president's location from this point on is going to be classified. As is the vice president's."

Pilcher ran a hand through his own thinning blond hair and blew out a lungful of air. "Okay," he said. "What—"

"You'll go where you're needed," Spigotta said. "So first, go to 1600 and talk to Berra, see what the inside teams are seeing."

"You want me to go in?"

Spigotta frowned. "Do I? No. But if you think it's necessary to see with your own eyes, yeah, suit up and go in."

"Yes, sir."

Spigotta was going to suggest something when Agent Unrau, the agent Spigotta had sent to the Russian embassy, entered SIOC, escorting two people over to where they stood.

Agent Unrau brushed red hair off her forehead and pushed up her glasses. "Director McIvoy . . . Agent Spigotta. This is Ivan Sergeyevitch Tetchin, with the Russian embassy."

Before Unrau could introduce the woman with them, Tetchin stepped forward and offered a big, meaty hand. In his fifties, he was a large, bulky figure with a shaved scalp and ruddy complexion. "I am the security attaché at the Russian embassy. We understand you believe there is some sort of Russian connection to today's terrorist activity."

McIvoy took the offered hand. "Yes, we have information indicating this group, the Fallen Angels, is responsible for today's attack. We understand further that they are based in Russia."

The woman spoke for the first time. "The Fallen Angels are not Russian. They are multi-ethnic, believed to be led by a Chechen named Surkho Andarbek."

"Yes," Aaron said, jumping in before Spigotta or McIvoy could speak. "That's our information, too. Just a moment. May I have a word with you two for a moment?" he said to Spigotta and McIvoy. They moved out of earshot of the Russians.

"Surkho Andarbek might be Richard Coffee," said Pilcher. "At least, if anything Stillwater got from Irina Khournikova is accurate."

"So it would be best," McIvoy said with a nod, "if we didn't let the Russians know the Chechen group was actually being led by an American rogue CIA agent."

Pilcher nodded.

"Excellent advice. Okay."

They returned to the Russians. The woman, who was tall and wore her short, reddish brown hair in an elegant shag cut, focused her brown eyes on Pilcher. "We understand you have the body of a Russian national."

Spigotta said, "She's at the morgue in D.C."

"Who is she?" Tetchin said.

"She was identified to us as Irina Khournikova. She claimed she was with your Directorate T, but we believe she was actually working with the Fallen Angels."

The Russian woman, her English excellent with only a slight accent that could have been mistaken for German or Serbian, said, "She is not who she claimed to be. I wish to see her body."

"Fine," McIvoy said. "That can be arranged. But how do you know she isn't Irina Khournikova?"

"Because," she said, "I am Irina Khournikova."

30

Rock Creek Park

DEREK MARCHED SAM DALTON at gunpoint, night-vision goggles again perched on his own face. Dalton's hands were on top of his head as he walked, and Derek didn't bother telling him when low-hanging branches were going to smack him in the face. Derek was having enough problems controlling the urge to empty the assault rifle into Dalton's back.

"He wants you alive," Dalton said.

"He being . . . ?"

"Fallen."

"Ah," Derek said. When Dalton stopped walking, confused by a wall of shrubbery in the darkness, Derek nudged him to his left. "The mysterious Fallon. Or is it Fallen? What's his real name?"

Dalton laughed. "Your pal and mine, Richard Coffee."

"The Lazarus of the terrorist set. Okay, I'll bite. Why does Richard want me alive?"

"Maybe he feels he owes you." Dalton stumbled on a patch of rough ground, flinging his arms out for balance. Derek adjusted his grip on the rifle, sure Dalton was going to try something, but Dalton regained his footing and placed his hands back on his head.

"Feels he owes me for what?" Derek said.

"For saving his life, man! What do you think?"

"A thank-you note would have been sufficient. I'm touched. Really. How about you, Sam? Why are you involved in this?"

Dalton stopped and turned. He was taller than Derek, with broad shoulders and chiseled features. He still kept his light-colored hair military-short, and his square jaw belonged on a recruiting poster. Derek knew Dalton was in his early fifties, but he didn't look it. Derek raised the XM-177, ready to shoot if necessary.

"In a word? Money."

"Let me guess," Derek said. "The Fallen Angels sell whatever they can beg, borrow, or steal to the highest bidder."

"Bingo."

"And with your military and government contacts, you can get it or show where it is. For a fee."

"Right. And don't forget, Derek, I worked Delta antiterrorism intelligence for a decade. I have contacts with the *buyers*. Just like you do."

Derek grew cold and still. "Do I?" he said.

"Sure, man. You've consulted with most of the legitimate governments that manufacture CBW, you've made contact with some of the people who want them. You're a gold mine. Between the two of us, we could bring in half a billion a year just hooking up the right people."

Tiring of the direction of the conversation, Derek ordered Dalton to turn around and keep walking. Their feet crunched softly on the leaves and pine needles, the wind rustling the branches of the trees. Even in the eerie green light of the night scope, he saw Dalton smile. Derek didn't like that smile. He felt it was a bad omen, the deputy director knowing something he didn't. Dalton was too confident.

As they continued east toward the parking lot, Derek said, "Let's say I'm interested. How do I get in touch with Coffee?"

"Through me. C'mon, man. Blow off the helicopter and tell them you're going to take me in. Then we'll just . . . disappear, man. I'll take you to Fallen and we'll be on our way."

"Maybe I want to negotiate my own deal with Coffee," Derek said. "Why should I split with you?"

Dalton laughed. "I knew you were right for the deal. You split with me because I have access to Fallen. Without me, you're out of luck."

Derek was starting to get flares in the night scope. The parking lot and its lights were not far away.

"Where's Coffee?"

"You mean the Fallen. Richard Coffee's dead. He died in Iraq."

"Semantics," Derek said. "You're playing word games, and your own head's on the block. You're going in. If you cooperate, tell us where *Fallen* is, where *Coffee* is, well, things might go easier on you."

Dalton laughed. Derek didn't like the laugh. He liked it even less than Dalton's secretive smile. It was filled with contempt and irony, as if Dalton knew things that Derek did not. And Derek was afraid he was right, that he was seeing barely the tip of this particularly deadly iceberg.

"You are full of shit," Dalton said. "Full of shit and uninformed, pal. There isn't a plea deal in the whole universe for me."

Above them Derek heard the roar of the incoming Mako helicopter, circling in over the parking lot. The plan was to turn Dalton over to them and rush him to FBI headquarters. In his ear Cynthia Black said, "Derek, we've got something, we're not sure—"

Breaking out into the open, Derek heard a whooshing sound. Over the radio: "Shit!" Followed by an explosion. The sky lit up as the rocket-propelled grenade struck the Coast Guard helicopter. The night-vision goggles flared, and for a moment Derek was blind. Clawing at the goggles, he was too late. Dalton spun, his fist slamming into Derek's jaw.

Rolling away, still blind, the Colt rifle was ripped from his grasp. He knocked off the goggles, struggling to his knees.

There was a second explosion as the helicopter crashed to the pavement in a harsh, earth-shattering roar.

Dalton now stood with the rifle aimed at Derek. "So long—"

Derek never heard the bullet that killed Dalton. One moment he was on his knees waiting to die, the next Dalton's body jerked and fell forward onto the grass, blood soaking his camouflage fatigues. Dalton's last words were a barely audible, "That bastard . . ."

Derek lunged for the XM-177, but a bullet whined past him and he turned for the cover of the trees instead. In his ear he heard a familiar voice: Richard Coffee had tapped into his Coast Guard frequency.

"Hello, Derek."

Derek didn't reply. He moved deeper into the woods, staying close enough to view the parking lot but stay out of sight.

"Nice SUV," Coffee said. "Hope you've got insurance."

There was another whoosh, followed by an explosion that Derek was certain was the sound of an RPG hitting a Ford Explorer.

"I could use a man of your talents," Coffee said. "But you're going to have to come out with your hands up, or we're coming in after you."

Derek didn't wait. He turned and plunged deeper into the woods, racing north. Behind him he heard the rattle of gunfire as Coffee and more of his terrorists came on in pursuit.

31

FBI Headquarters

Agent Spigotta closed his eyes for a moment when the Russian woman announced that she was Irina Khournikova. He craned his neck back, as if to relieve tension, then pressed his fingers against his eyelids. Aaron Pilcher wondered if Spigotta was going to have a stroke right there in SIOC.

Pilcher recovered quickest. He said, "Not that identification seems to matter, but do you have any?"

The woman, Irina Khournikova, removed a wallet from her purse and handed Pilcher her passport. He gazed at it, then passed it to Spigotta, who glared at it, then handed it to Agent Unrau, who had escorted the Russians in. "Let's get this verified," he told her.

"Yes, sir," Unrau said, heading out of SIOC with Khournikova's passport.

Spigotta seemed unusually off-balance, so Pilcher took control. It surprised him that Spigotta and Deputy Director McIlvoy seemed so uncertain. "Mr. Tetchin, Ms. Khournikova, let's go to a room where we can talk."

"I want you over at the White House," Spigotta said.

Pilcher stared at his superior. "I think I need to be here for this, sir. There are plenty of agents at the White House. I'll go after I get some information here."

Spigotta again looked surprised, but McIlvoy nodded. "Sure. Good idea."

They led the Russians out of SIOC and down the hallway to an interrogation room, but unexpectedly, Ivan Tetchin stopped outside the room and turned. "I will be returning to my embassy," he said slowly.

"We need to talk to you now," McIlvoy said.

Tetchin cocked his massive shaved head, a stubby fat finger tapping at his cheek for a moment. "I know nothing of this dead impostor you have spoken of and even less about this attack on your president. Any information I may have about the Fallen Angels can be more directly handled by Ms. Khournikova. They are, I believe, her area of speciality."

Spigotta's voice was a low rasp. "I don't give a good goddamn what you say right now. You'll—"

Tetchin raised a hand. His voice was soft. "Agent Spigotta, Director McIlvoy. I have diplomatic immunity. I am returning to my embassy. What has happened at the White House and how or if it connects to the Fallen Angels and this attack on your research facility may or may not have repercussions for my government. I must brief Ambassador Romanovitch immediately. I will request that he assign somebody to cooperate with you fully in this matter if we are able."

"If you have information about the attack on President—"

Khournikova's voice cut Spigotta off. "If the attack on President Langston was made by the Fallen Angels, it is not a Russian matter, it is an American matter. The head of this organization is an American CIA agent named Richard Coffee."

"And you know an awful lot about him, Ms. Khournikova," Pilcher said. "Maybe you could enlighten us."

"Ivan, I will contact you later."

Tetchin met Irina Khournikova's gaze. Something passed between the two of them, something strange. Pilcher wasn't exactly sure what they were saying to each other, but he got the peculiar feeling that Tetchin was not upset to get away from Irina Khournikova.

With reluctance, McIlvoy and Spigotta had an agent usher Tetchin out of the building, then Spigotta and Pilcher directed her into a sparsely decorated interrogation room. It was not sweat-stained and didn't have battered furniture. It just looked like an empty office with a couple chairs. There was no two-way mirror, because the Bureau had a tiny camera embedded in the wall that could not be seen. Khournikova and Pilcher sat in two chairs on either side of a small Formica-topped table. Spigotta remained standing, leaning against the far wall.

Spigotta looked at the ceiling for a moment, then gestured for Pilcher to handle the questioning.

"Who are you?" Pilcher asked.

"Who are you?" she countered.

"Special Agent Aaron Pilcher, Federal Bureau of Investigation. This is Special Agent Frederick Spigotta."

"I'm Irina Khournikova. I am a Russian citizen in the employ of the Russian government. I am currently on assignment in Washington, D.C. I assume you are taping all of this."

"Yes," Pilcher nodded.

Pilcher thought he heard Spigotta grunt, but nothing followed. He paused for a moment, trying to get his bearings. Spigotta wasn't giving him much to work with. Spigotta's preferred persona for interrogations was Raging Bastard or Seriously Bad Cop. But Spigotta was just watching, which wasn't his style at all. Pilcher knew that the woman had already interacted with him, with both of them, in SIOC. Officious Prick was out, and so was Icy Bastard and Surfer Buddy. He was afraid he was going to have to play it straight, his least successful persona, Old Pro.

"Fine, Agent Pilcher," Khournikova said. "As you have no doubt determined, my area of expertise is Russian counterterrorism. Your country is not the only country to have to endure terrorist attacks. For several years I have been pursuing a man who for a long time we believed was a Chechen named Surkho Andarbek. We did not know much about this man. He appeared to be a loyal Chechen, a restaurateur, a man with very little background. Then he became part of the separatists, then a leader of the separatists. Then he was reported dead.

"At some point after he 'died,' a group operating on the Russian-Georgian border began smuggling weapons in and out of Russia. What little we could determine about them was that they were multinational and called themselves the Fallen Angels. They appeared to move in and out of any number of countries with impertinence. Rumors were that they were highly skilled intelligence agents, rogue agents who had fallen out of favor from their countries. They were more like a cult than a group of terrorists, in that they seemed to have undying loyalty to their leader, a charismatic man who called himself the Fallen, or Fallen. The few members of

226

the Fallen Angels who we . . . captured . . . provided no information that was significant. We did, however, acquire a photograph of their leader, this Fallen, and we determined that he was Surkho Andarbek. However, we received some information only recently that Surkho Andarbek was an American, a rogue CIA agent named Richard Coffee."

"How did you find this information?" Pilcher asked. "What's your source?"

"It is not important." She gazed steadily at him, her dark eyes unflinching.

Pilcher paused, glanced at Spigotta, who seemed lost in thought. He turned back to Khournikova. "It might be important."

She said nothing, but continued to meet his eyes.

He continued. "Where is Richard Coffee now?"

"Here," she said.

"Here? As in, the United States?"

"Yes. Here in the Washington area."

"Where?"

"I do not know."

"How do you know he's here?"

She shrugged. "I have contacts."

"Who?"

"It's not important."

"Yes," Pilcher said, leaning forward, "it is. We need to find out where Coffee and his people are. You can help us."

Her expression gave nothing away. "I have given you all the information I have. I would like to see this woman you claim is Irina Khournikova. If she is a Russian citizen, as you suspect, we will fully cooperate in identifying her if we can."

"You can," Spigotta said from the rear of the room.

Khournikova looked at the senior agent. "It speaks," she said.

Spigotta moved toward her, his large bulk menacing. "Why do you think Fallen is here, Ms. Khournikova?"

"My sources—"

"Who are?"

"It's not important."

Spigotta scowled at her. "I will decide what is and what isn't important."

She didn't respond.

Pilcher was going to open his mouth to speak when Spigotta said, "Agent Pilcher, I want you to continue with your line of investigation at the White House."

"But—"

"Now!" Spigotta snapped.

Doubtfully, Pilcher got to his feet. "You're sure?"

Spigotta's face turned beet red. His voice was low and guttural as he bit off the words. "I am sure, Aaron. Now. And one more thing." He paused.

Pilcher waited.

Spigotta said, "I want you to go next door, turn off the recorder, and destroy the tape of this interrogation."

Pilcher flinched. *This is an act, right? It's got to be.* "Sure," he said. He glanced at Khournikova, whose face was expressionless. "Yes, sir."

He left the room. Spigotta came after him, closing the door behind him. "Destroy the tape, Aaron."

Pilcher cocked his head. It hadn't been an act. "What're you going to do?"

"Whatever I have to do. It's none of your concern. Just do it."

Pilcher set his jaw. "Rick, if this blows up, you could lose your career."

Spigotta slammed the palm of his hand against Pilcher's chest, knocking him back against the wall. Up and down the corridor, heads turned. Spigotta's voice was a low rasp filled with anger. "Listen to me, Aaron. We are at war. Most of the heads of our government have been killed in a terrorist attack. The joint chiefs are dead. So are the directors of FEMA, HHS, the FAA, the FBI, and the CIA, and the national security advisor, just to name a few. If these Fallen Angels are behind it, we can't sit around worrying about anybody's fucking civil liberties because there's been less than nine hours between attacks. What's next? We need to know *now*. The rest of the government's going to be running around like a herd of frightened sheep trying to figure out who's in charge, not to mention the inevitable political infighting as the politicians jockey for position. So you do what you have to do and I'll do what I have to do."

Pilcher stared at Spigotta and slowly nodded. "Yes, sir."

"Understand?"

"Yes, sir."

"Go."

Pilcher turned his back on Spigotta and went next door to the room containing the taping equipment. On the monitor he watched as Spigotta walked back in the room. Khournikova looked up at him. In her accented voice she said, "So, the Bad Cop is back. Where's your rubber hose, Agent Spigotta?"

Spigotta reached out and slapped her so hard her head snapped back against the wall. "We'll get to that if we have to, Ms. Khournikova. We'll get to it if we have to. It's up to you."

Pilcher's finger hovered over the off button.

32

Rock Creek Park

DEREK CRASHED THROUGH THE trees, hands held above his face to protect his eyes from the clawing fingers of tree branches. Still, they whipped his face and snagged his hair and tore at his arms. Stumbling through a creek, up to his knees in water muck, he staggered away from the sounds of his pursuers.

The night-vision goggles were gone. The Colt assault rifle was gone. His phone was gone. He realized, swatting at his hip, that his Colt .45 was gone as well, lost in one of his struggles with Dalton.

He was caught in the trees, unarmed except his wits, his juju beads, and his four-leaf clover, being hunted by what he thought were four well-armed, highly trained, and utterly ruthless killers. And he didn't believe that Sam Dalton had been telling the truth. He did not believe that Richard Coffee, a madman from his past, wanted to take him alive. Maybe once. Maybe earlier. But not now.

And even if he was wrong . . . why risk your life on the desperate bargaining of a traitor?

He heard footfalls off to his right and veered left. Occasionally, a sliver moon peeped through the trees, but otherwise the woods were dense and dark, a wild place in the heart of Washington, D.C.

He broke unexpectedly into the open, crossing onto one of the many hiking paths in the park. This one was about six feet wide, a footpath of packed dirt created by the hard rubber soles of a thousand hikers.

Derek froze, considering. As best he could tell, the path ran roughly north and south. His pursuers were to the east. Should he cut back into the woods, or should he take the path, striving for a faster pace?

He strained to hear above the thunderous pounding of his own heart. There were the small sounds of scuttling nocturnal animals: raccoons, opossums, squirrels, chipmunks, and their hunters, hawks and owls, maybe foxes or feral cats. Small branches creaked and groaned in the light breeze. Farther off was the sound of D.C., the rumble of cars, a distant siren . . . many sirens, he realized, too many.

Behind him a dark figure appeared on the path.

Startled, Derek leapt into the cover of the trees, the decision made for him. There was the sharp rattle of gunfire, and something plucked at his leg. He staggered, fell, clambered to his feet, the sting in his leg growing into a hot blade of pain.

He pushed on, tree to tree, boulder to boulder, slowing.

Another rattle of gunfire. Bark splintered near his head. He turned, breath burning in his chest. He fingered the juju beads around his neck, wondering . . .

Two figures materialized around him, rifles raised.

Slowly, reluctantly, Derek raised his hands in surrender, hoping that Coffee—Fallen—still wanted him alive.

One of the men spoke into a throat mic with a thick Slavic accent. "Omega 3 and 4 have secured subject."

Derek didn't hear a response. All he could hear was the rushing of blood in his ears and the hard thud of his heart in his chest, his breath burning in his throat.

"Let's go," one of the men said, and shoved Derek toward the trees. Stumbling in the dark, he moved in the direction they told him to go, wondering bitterly just how long he had to live.

●

33

The White House

Aaron Pilcher felt overwhelmed by events. Donning a protective biohazard suit, he was being primed by an FBI agent on the Hazardous Materials Response Unit. She was an aggressive forty-something with thick glasses, mouse brown hair that looked cut with a kitchen knife, and all the tact of a four-year-old.

"Don't touch anything. Look and get out. Are you claustrophobic?"

"A little," Pilcher said, already starting to sweat in the heavy rubber suit lined with activated charcoal. Chem suits didn't breathe—that was the point.

"Don't panic. Keep calm. Take deep breaths. If you start to panic, leave, get out of the building. Do not open the suit." She brandished a finger in his face. "Do *not* open the suit. If you open the suit, you die. Period. Understand me?"

"Yes. Open the suit. Die. Got it." His stomach churned, but he ignored it.

"Once you're outside, either way, whether because you're panicking or because it's time to go, wait to be washed down. Can you handle this?"

Pilcher wasn't sure he could, but he said he was fine. Then he said, "How long will it take to decontaminate the White House?"

Agent Brettano fixed her hazel eyes on him. "It's VX gas," she said.

"Yeah?"

"You're looking at the former residence of presidents, Agent Pilcher. We'll probably never be able to decontaminate it."

He blinked, imagining it. What would they have to do? Incinerate it, one piece at a time? Block it off? Burn it to the ground and bury it in concrete, like Chernobyl? Involuntarily, he felt a wave of rage wash over him. Dalton, that bastard. They were going to get him for this.

Brettano snapped her fingers in his face. "Are you paying attention?"

He was now. "Yes," he said.

"Good. Listen closely. Your life isn't the only one you risk if you panic in there, understand? You put my teams at risk and all the other people in there if you freak out. So I'm going to ask you again. Can you handle this?"

Pilcher looked her in the eye. "Yes. I can handle it."

"Okay. Finish suiting up."

The suit was hot and awkward. The air from the tank smelled and tasted stale and metallic. He could smell his own sweat, bitter and acidic, the stench of fear.

The West Wing was well lit . . . for a graveyard. Pilcher had been told the body count was over one hundred. The VX gas had been released directly into the White House ventilation system through a cold-air intake. Brettano had said in an ominous voice pinched with anger, "In DHS Deputy Director Samuel Dalton's office." The missing man. Hundreds of agents hunted him now, but so far, nothing.

The VX gas canister had been described to Pilcher as being a Coke can on the outside, but there had been a timed release mechanism on the inside. Dalton had been able to flick a switch on the bottom of the can, screw the brass grate back over the hole in the wall, then leave the White House on business. When the White House had been full of cabinet members, White House staff, the joint chiefs, and various experts on dealing with biological and chemical emergencies, it had gone off, spraying a fine mist of one of the most dangerous substances on the planet through the ventilation system of the venerable old building.

An armed soldier in a chem suit, M4 carbine at the ready, met Pilcher. Pilcher pointed to the FBI stencil on his own suit. "I want to see Dalton's office. Ground zero."

The soldier nodded, waved over another similarly clad soldier, and led Pilcher up a flight of stairs and down a hallway lined with offices. Farther on he saw a larger area with glass-walled cubicles. Apparently in this administration the secretary and deputy director of the Department of Homeland Security warranted their own offices close to the Oval Office.

Two corpses remained in the hallway, one a young redheaded woman in a tan pantsuit, a sheaf of scattered paperwork dealt like cards around her body. Farther down the hallway was the body of a crew-cut man in a navy blue three-piece suit. In his ear was a piece of molded plastic. His suit coat was crumpled beneath him to reveal a gun and holster. *Secret Service,* Pilcher thought.

The half-dozen figures in chem suits and spacesuits moved about. This terrorist attack brought out every hazardous-site team in the United States—military, FBI, CIA, CDC.

The soldier stood at a door and gestured for Pilcher to enter. Sweat rolling down his forehead and into his eyes, he blinked, eyes burning. He wanted to wipe the sweat away but couldn't. Sweat rolled down his back. The urge to scratch his back, to try to get at the itch between his shoulder blades, was almost unbearable. For a moment panic dug its sharp claws in and he struggled to control the urge to pull off the mask, to rub his face, to take a deep breath of uncanned air.

Get it together, he thought. He thought of his wife. Of his daughters. He thought of the first lady and their two children, dead. He took a deep breath, then another. His heart calmed.

He went in.

There were three spacesuited figures in Dalton's office, and Pilcher's fourth was at least two too many for the space. He stood at the doorway and took in the office.

There was a large oak desk, the centerpiece being a PC with a large flat-screen monitor. There were filing cabinets. On the wall above the desk was a large cork board with dozens of notes affixed to it. Along one wall were photographs: Dalton shaking hands with the president; Dalton in full dress uniform; Dalton and a team of soldiers standing on a tank, a desert backdrop behind them. Pilcher squeezed in and took a closer look. He saw that one of the other soldiers, looking much younger, but much the same, was Derek Stillwater. He wondered if one of the two others was Richard Coffee.

A spacesuited agent worked at the desk, his gloved fingers slow and clumsy on the keyboard. The monitor screen was blank except for the words RECOVER ACTIVE blinking in the top left corner.

Another figure methodically emptied files from Dalton's filing cabinets. He laid them a page at a time on a credenza, and the other agent took a photograph of the page using a digital camera. Then the first agent placed the page into a plastic biohazard bag and sealed it with duct tape. The world's slowest, most dangerous crime scene, Pilcher thought.

His voice muffled in the suit, Pilcher ID'ed himself and asked what the computer tech was doing.

"Bastard wiped his hard drive on his way out the door," the agent said, voice equally muffled, but not enough to hide the nasal twang of New Jersey. "I'm doing a quick forensic recovery with some special software, then I'm going to dump the whole thing to my system so we won't have to mess with transporting this thing out of here. Okay, baby, lookin' good."

The screen was coming to life.

The computer agent muttered, "You're not as smart as you thought you were, motherfucker."

Inside his suit Pilcher raised an eyebrow. Dalton had damn near decapitated the U.S. government. He had no desire to underestimate this psychopath.

"Let's check his e-mail before I upload this . . . huh."

"What?"

"His last e-mail." The agent pointed with a rubber-gloved hand.

Pilcher shuffled forward and peered over the agent's shoulder. The message said:

THE ASCENT HAS BEGUN.

But his gaze locked in on who he had sent the messages to. The e-mail addresses were stillwater.derek@dhscom.gov and irinak@webmail.com. Derek Stillwater and Irina Khournikova!

"When were those sent?" he demanded.

The agent checked. "Looks like eleven this morning."

Before the assault on U.S. Immuno, Pilcher thought. *Dear God, they're in on it!*

34

Sharon Jaxon, in her spacesuit, wheeled a cart carrying a laptop computer and mounted digital camera into the Slammer. Liz Vargas lay propped against two foam pillows on the bed, writing notes on a yellow legal pad.

"We've got Dr. Hingemann waiting for a hookup," Jaxon said. "How are you feeling?"

"Okay," Liz said, though in truth she was exhausted. A headache was starting to pound behind her eyes. There could be perfectly good reasons besides Chimera for her to be tired and to be developing a headache. Stress was right at the top of the list. She didn't think it was stress.

"We're wireless, so let's get booted up, then I'm going to check your vitals."

Liz nodded. Much of her energy—her will to fight—of only a short while ago had waned. She knew this disease. She could try to ignore that she would probably die—and soon—but it was hard.

In some ways she wanted Sharon to give her a strong shot of Valium and just go to sleep and . . .

No! She had to fight. For future victims, if not for herself.

She sat upright and watched as Sharon plugged in the computer and pulled it close to her bed. As Sharon took her temperature, Liz turned on the computer and made the connections Sharon directed her to. After a few minutes, the image of her old college advisor—her mentor—appeared on the screen. He was older and bald, his beard as scruffy and unkempt as she remembered, more salt now than pepper. He peered through miles of cyberspace and said, "Liz! They've only told me a little bit about this, but I understand it has to do with this terrorist attack we're hearing so much about."

Her eyes filled with tears and she fought them back. "Les," she said. "Oh God! What did they tell you?"

"That you're working on a vaccine for this Chimera."

She sighed. "Yes. We hope so. I'm going to send you our records. This is vitally important."

Les nodded gravely. "Of course. I'll get right to reading. . . ."

Sharon, not visible to the computer screen, said, "Tell him."

Liz turned away from the camera to study Jaxon. "I—"

"Tell him."

"What, Liz?" Dr. Hingemann asked. "What's going on?"

"Are you familiar with USAMRIID, Lester?"

"I've heard of it, of course. Yes."

"I'm there. Lester . . . I was accidently infected with Chimera M13."

Hingemann looked startled, but only for a minute. "You need to tell me as much as you can. How long do you have?"

"Anywhere from six hours to twelve hours."

Hingemann paled. "That's so fast. Dear God. What is this thing?"

She told him, her voice clipped and urgent, cramming a tremendous amount of information into a very small time frame.

"It's a virus? Liz, I'm not a virologist. You know that. My work was on immunological reactions to bubonic plague."

"Yes! That's why I thought of you. We incorporated part of *Yersinia*'s DNA into the virus! It helped with immunosuppression."

Hingemann's bushy eyebrows raised. "What part did you incorporate into the DNA? Is it possible you incorporated . . . are some of *Yersinia*'s antigens incorporated into the viral capsule?"

"Maybe," Liz said. "Maybe." She felt a tickle behind her nose and said, "Excuse me," the sneeze building up fast. She quickly plucked a Kleenex from the night table and sneezed into it. She took the tissue away to see it was filled with spatters of blood and mucous. She felt liquid begin to run from her nose and pressed the Kleenex to her face. It came away soaked with blood.

"Liz!" Hingemann said, voice alarmed. "Liz, are you all right?"

Liz felt the world spinning around her, eyes filling with tears. The subject monkeys' first clear symptom of infection had been bloody noses.

"Liz! Talk to me! Are you all right? What's going on?"

Liz didn't hear him. She was thinking, *It's starting too fast. I should have had two to four more hours before the internal bleeding began. Oh God, oh God, ohgodohgodohgod . . .*

35

Rock Creek Park

AFTER WHAT SEEMED LIKE an endless march through the dark, Derek stumbled out of the trees and onto a grassy berm leading down to a road. He was nowhere near the parking lot, with its burning helicopter and cars and dead bodies. He wasn't sure where he was. He suspected that he had been marched east, away from the parking lot, but he had become totally disoriented in the darkness, his body aching, his wounded leg screaming with every step, staggering over tree roots and rocks and uneven patches of ground.

Two vans were parked by the side of the road. The passenger side door of the front van opened, and a tall, broad-shouldered figure stepped out wearing camouflage fatigues. Derek nodded to himself. Richard Coffee. Older, bearded, his face more lined, his hair more gray. Coffee strode toward him until he was arm's length away.

"Derek! Good to see you!"

Pure hatred exploded in Derek's chest. Without warning he launched himself at Coffee. Coffee easily knocked him aside. Staggering, one of his guardians slammed the butt of his rifle into the back of Derek's skull. Derek fell to the ground, fireworks exploding in his head. He tried to pull air into his lungs, but couldn't.

"Well, enough of that," Coffee said. "Bind his hands. Damn, Derek. Why can't you just play nice?"

"Fuck you."

A booted foot lifted him off the ground. Derek curled into a protective ball, retching and gasping for breath. Coffee said, "Enough, already. I need to talk to him later. Don't I, Derek?"

Coffee crouched down so he was on Derek's level. Derek looked up at him, feeling ill, wanting to kill the man who had once been his friend. Coffee said, "Or maybe we can talk right now? I really only have one question for you. Where's Irina Khournikova?"

Oh shit, Derek thought through his fog of pain. From bad to worse. "Who?" he croaked out.

Coffee backhanded him. Derek collapsed into a pile on the grass.

"Wrong answer. Get him into the van."

The two minders pulled Derek's arms tightly behind him and what felt like plastic flexi-cuffs snapped around his wrists. They lifted him bodily off the ground and dragged him to the front van. He fell unceremoniously onto the hard floor of the vehicle, and the two men climbed in after, bracketing him. Coffee held a canvas bag in his hands. In a soft, menacing voice, he said, "Irina is very important to me, Derek. I want to know where she is. When we get you to headquarters, you're going to tell me where she is."

"I don't—"

Coffee yanked the bag over Derek's head, cutting him off.

Lying on the floor of the van, feeling the vehicle move and turn, Derek thought about the woman who had told him her name was Irina Khournikova. He needed to buy time. When they got to wherever headquarters was, Coffee was going to insist he tell him where she was. Were they lovers? *Irina is very important to me, Derek.*

He tried to focus on a story. He could not tell Coffee she was dead. He could especially not tell her he had killed her while interrogating her. Not if he wanted to live very long afterward. Derek focused his mind and tried to think. He thought as if his life depended upon it—because it did.

It was only a short time before the van came to a stop. Derek guessed they were either still in D.C. or in one of the nearby suburbs.

Coffee said, "Get him out. Take him over to Trailer C."

Derek was lifted roughly by his arms. Once he was on his feet, the bag was ripped off his face. Blinking in the sudden illumination, Derek studied his surroundings. He stood in a large warehouse. Behind him were a series of metal doors, one of which the vans had driven through. A few dozen vehicles were parked near the doors: white vans, sport utility vehicles, a couple motorcycles, Army Humvees. It was a huge space, large enough to accommodate a dozen motor homes and trailers. A group of people moving around, loading luggage into vehicles, attending to tasks that to Derek looked like early preparation for departure. Everyone he saw was armed with a handgun or assault rifle.

Something odd caught his attention. It was a large trailer in one corner. It appeared to be a doublewide. It was painted a flat putty color and there were no windows, everything having been boarded up, painted with the putty and further sealed with what looked like plastic sheeting and duct tape. From the roof of the far end of the doublewide rose a number of metal tubes that extended upward and back to the rear wall of the warehouse. The tubes also appeared to be covered with putty and plastic sheeting.

A generator and fan roared next to the trailer. Next to the generator were stacked barrels of gasoline. It was the only trailer in the warehouse that had its own power supply and circulatory system.

He puzzled over what he was seeing, but only for a moment, because the two guards shoved him in the back with their guns and shunted him toward a different trailer. Coffee said, "I'll be around in a few minutes."

The two guards marched Derek across an open expanse of concrete to a motor home. One of the guards opened the door and went in; the other shoved Derek after. "Trailer C?" he asked, and was rewarded with a jab of pain in his left kidney. He climbed the two metal steps into the motor home and found himself in what must have been the Fallen Angels' infirmary.

No thank you, he thought. *It's not time for my yearly medical checkup. Besides, I don't think you accept my insurance.*

"Sit," one of his minders said, a muscular steroid-juicer with a shock of white-blond hair. Derek dubbed him Sven. Sven pointed to an examining table.

Derek sat, though getting up there with his hands behind his back wasn't the easiest thing he'd done all day.

Once on the examining table, he didn't have long to wait. An Asian man dressed in what looked like either black scrubs or pajamas entered the motor home, Richard Coffee behind him. Derek couldn't pinpoint the nationality. Probably not Japanese. Possibly Chinese or Filipino. Not Korean, he didn't think, though it was hard to tell. Something about his features suggested Chinese. Not Malaysian or Indonesian . . .

"Dr. Ling is going to take a look at you," Coffee said.

"No thanks. I'm fine," Derek said.

"You're limping and favoring your side."

"Yeah, it's been a rough day, but . . ."

Ling was tall and thin, long black hair swept off a narrow forehead. Derek looked into his eyes and saw nothing. Black orbs with no life in them. The man's lack of emotion chilled him and he flinched away from Ling's long fingers as the doctor touched his cheek and moved his head back and forth slowly, examining him. Derek jerked away. "Leave me alone," he snarled.

Ling didn't say anything, but cocked his head. In lightly accented English, he said, "Lie down, please."

"No."

Ling nodded to the two guards, who roughly shoved him down on the examining table. Ling opened a cabinet to reveal a tray of sterilized surgical instruments. "Cut off the cuffs and secure his arms and legs to the table, please. I need to take a closer look at his wounds."

"I'm—"

Ling gave a quiet, "Sshhhh, Dr. Stillwater. Please cooperate."

Derek didn't have much choice. The two men, Sven and his partner, a stringy, wiry guy with Slavic features that Derek had started thinking of as Ivan, cut off his cuffs and forced him back on the table. He knew he could take them if they got careless. The two guys were dangerous, but he could kill them. But then he would have to get past Ling and Coffee and out of this place with a dozen armed men all too willing to gun him down. And escaping wasn't why he was here. Although he had absolutely zero idea how to do it and the rock-solid knowledge that his odds of accomplishing it were probably less than zero, his mission was to locate Chimera M13. His mission was to retrieve or destroy it, and at the very least determine what Coffee and his Fallen Angels intended to do with it.

Derek's wrists and ankles were placed in padded cuffs and secured. Their presence didn't bode well, Derek thought. This was not exactly a medical clinic if they were prepared to restrain their patients. They could act like he was a patient, but he knew better. Dread crept up on him like a rising tide, but he forced it away, concentrating on the cover story he had created on the trip here. Ling walked over to him, a pair of scissors in his hands. He stood over Derek a moment, the shiny metal scissors held in front of Derek's face, as if the man was debating exactly what to do with them. To trim his hair, to cut his nails, to plunge the sharp shiny points into his eye socket. Derek stared past them into Ling's face, into his lifeless eyes, looking for signs of humanity and not finding any.

Carefully, Ling began to cut off Derek's clothing. The only sound was the snip and snick of the scissors and the soft plop of his tattered clothing falling to the floor of the trailer.

The scissors were cold against his flesh, and Derek found he had to control himself from trembling. He knew, rationally, that there was more than medicine going on here. He knew that forcing a prisoner to be naked gave the captors both a physical and psychological advantage.

Knowing did not necessarily help in dealing with the vulnerability.

After a few minutes he was totally naked on the table, arms and legs immobile. "Gee, you could have asked me to disrobe," he said, grateful they had left his beads and four-leaf clover.

Ling gently peeled away the dressing the coastguardsman had placed over the gouge in his ribs caused by the D.C. cop's gunshot. Ling pulled over a lamp on a tensile steel arm and shined the harsh light on the wound. "You are showing some early signs of infection. But it is not deep. It needs to be cleaned again."

Ling pulled on latex gloves and retrieved a bottle of saline. Skillfully, he began to wash out the wound, blotting it carefully with sterile gauze. Derek was not calmed by this. Instead, he was worried. Ling had skills. Ling . . . knew things.

Ling nodded his head and said, "It will require a few stitches and antibiotics. This wound in your leg, however, is another matter. It is deeper than the wound in your ribs. Hmmm . . ." He nodded thoughtfully to himself, picked up a metal probe, and looked over at Richard Coffee, who had been watching silently from next to the doorway. Ling nodded.

Coffee walked over to the examining table and looked down at Derek. "Where's Irina Khournikova?"

Derek said, "When I was with her I got a phone call from my FBI contact. He had found out that Halloran, the head guy at U.S. Immuno, had been having an affair with a Russian national named Irina Khournikova. Her cover was blown. I overpowered her and turned her over to the FBI. She should be at FBI headquarters now, under interrogation."

Coffee said, "Interesting," and nodded to Ling.

Ling took his stainless steel probe and deliberately, almost delicately, forced it into the wound in Derek's ribs. It felt as if a lance had ripped right through him. His body screamed as if every nerve had been dipped in acid. Lights exploded in his head and he shrieked, the sound seeming to come from outside him, from someone else.

Ling withdrew the probe, a slight smile crossing his lean face. "Yes, that worked rather well, didn't it? Nerve induction. It is a science. And you conveniently left me two openings in your body to probe the nerve directly. Saved me the time and trouble of doing so myself. Now, I believe the Fallen had a question. Where is the woman you know as Irina Khournikova?"

Derek stared at the man, sweat beading off his forehead and burning into his eyes. He couldn't seem to catch his breath. He could feel his heart thundering in his ears, taste blood in his mouth. "I . . . told . . ."

Ling inserted the probe once again, and this time the pain exploded along his body like an electric charge, and Derek let himself chase the exploding lights behind his eyes into darkness.

36

Walter Reed Army Medical Center

GENERAL JOHNSTON WAS SHRUGGING back into street clothing when Colonel Zataki appeared at the door of the examining room. Zataki now wore Army fatigues, his face pale, expression worried.

"*He* wants to see us," Zataki said.

Johnston cocked his head as he buttoned his shirt. "Have you talked to him?"

"No. I just got in contact with my people at the institute. I've got to get back there."

"Anything new?"

Zataki scowled. "Halloran committed suicide. Scully's dead. Vargas, the only remaining expert on Chimera, accidentally infected herself with it and is starting to show early signs of the infection. For all I know that's the *good* news. God only knows what the *bad* news is going to be. How about you?"

"Well, my hand-picked second-in-command managed to assassinate most of the heads of the U.S. government, and the FBI thinks my hand-picked troubleshooter is involved with it as well."

Zataki's face grew even paler, if that was possible. Slowly, he said, "The Bureau thinks Stillwater's involved in this?"

Johnston buttoned the top button of his shirt and began working on his tie. "Dalton e-mailed Stillwater around eleven today with some cryptic message: '*The Ascent has begun.*' The Bureau thinks it's a reference to the operation at U.S. Immuno."

"Huh." Zataki looked at his hands a moment. "This thing has all the feel of a full-blown act of war, Jim. We're fighting on multiple fronts, all of then unconventional. Biological, chemical, psychological. It's terrorism, but organized."

"Yeah, like two fucking jets into skyscrapers and one into the fucking Pentagon. I know."

Zataki shook his head. "I've known Derek Stillwater a long time. I can't see him involved in this."

"Well, I've known Sam Dalton for a long time, too, and he wouldn't have been my first candidate to decapitate the U.S. government with VX gas."

"But Derek . . ."

"I know." Johnston pulled his tie tight as if trying to strangle himself. "Over the years I've worked with Dalton, he was always a by-the-book guy. Always did what was needed, followed orders, followed the chain of command."

"Derek," Zataki said, "isn't like that."

"No." Johnston pulled on his jacket. All the clothing they had been wearing in the White House had been taken by the FBI HMRU to be incinerated. He had called his wife and asked her to bring a suit to the hospital ASAP. He sighed, thinking of her, now back at home, watching the news on TV. Waiting for the next wave of the attack. Because Johnston was sure that Dalton and whoever was at

251

the head of all this—and maybe it was Dalton who was at the top—had more planned. He said, "Derek thinks outside the box. That can actually be a problem in the Army, as you know. But I thought it was exactly what Homeland Security needed in a troubleshooter. I wanted creative thinking, not bureaucratic thinking."

Zataki nodded. "I went into a hot zone with Derek about six years ago. There was an Ebola outbreak in Congo. We were part of a UN team sent in to evaluate. On the trip in he was a mess. He was physically ill, throwing up, had the shakes, everything. I thought he'd never make it. Then we set down in Kinshaasa and he was in total control." He paused, thinking. "I don't for a minute believe Derek Stillwater would purposefully risk letting this bug loose on the world."

"I agree with you."

"Then you'll need to convince the president of that. You need to leave Stillwater out in the field to do his job."

Johnston shook his head. "Ben . . . I'll be lucky if I can convince them to take him *alive*."

President Langston breathed oxygen through a green plastic mask. His skin had a gray, parchment-like quality to it, and his eyes were red and swollen. He was surrounded by Secret Service and a small cadre of advisors. The few who were left, Johnston thought.

"Gentlemen," President Langston said, pulling the oxygen mask away from his face to talk. "I want to thank you both for saving my life."

"I'm glad I did, sir," Johnston said.

"I only wish we had saved more," Zataki added.

"Yes." Langston seemed to lose focus for a moment, thinking of his dead family and staff, no doubt. Marshaling his strength, he said, "I'll be leaving the hospital soon, heading to an undisclosed location. Colonel Zataki, a helicopter will take you to Fort Detrick. It is waiting at the hospital helicopter pad as we speak. Frida will take you there now."

A female agent with blond hair and freckles separated from the pack and nodded to Zataki. "Colonel . . ."

Zataki nodded, expressed condolences to the president, and followed the agent out of the hospital room, the door closing behind him. Another agent moved into position in front of it.

"Now, General," President Langston said, gaze focusing on Johnston. "We have a problem."

"Yes, sir. I think we do, as well."

Langston said, "Your deputy director is a terrorist, and so is one of your troubleshooters."

"Mr. President," Johnston said, "I have little doubt that Sam Dalton is behind this. I do not, however, feel that Derek Stillwater is involved. Everything about this, from the misinformation to the booby-trapped vans at the airport, have indicated a sort of . . . smoke-and-mirrors approach—"

"General," President Langston said, harsh voicing cutting off the secretary's words, "evidence points to an astonishing level of betrayal and corruption in your office. Perhaps it was unavoidable. Perhaps Dalton was the perfect chameleon in our midst. Perhaps. But, General, you were in charge. And your failure to see this . . . this devil amongst us, has cost this country many fine leaders and has personally cost me my family. I am asking for your immediate resignation."

Johnston nodded, having known that this was coming. He was no longer trusted. He had failed, and failed in a way that would go down in the history books. "Yes, sir," he said.

One of the advisors, a man Johnston did not know, stepped forward with a written document. He read it over. It was a letter of resignation awaiting his signature. He took the proffered pen.

"Mr. President," he said, pen in hand, "I am devastated by your loss, and by my failure in this matter. But . . . sir . . . I do not believe that Derek Stillwater was involved in this. In my heart I'm convinced that he has a better chance of getting to the bottom of this than anyone does."

"Your convictions are not shared by me," Langston snapped. "As far as I am concerned, Derek Stillwater is a conspirator in the murder of my family, and the full strength of this country's law enforcement structure is going to be focused on catching him and Dalton and prosecuting them to the fullest extent of the law. And if they die resisting, well that's just too damned bad."

Johnston met the gaze of the president. "With all due respect, Mr. President, I think you're wrong. I hereby tender my resignation." He signed the letter and put down the pen.

"You're dismissed," Langston said.

Without a word General Johnston turned and left the room.

PART III

Dance with the Devil

37

SPIGOTTA SLAMMED INTO THE interrogation room, towering over Irina. Five minutes earlier he had taken a call from Pilcher. "I just got a phone call from one of my agents saying you received an e-mail from Dalton at eleven today."

Khournikova frowned. This was not going well. Spigotta had spent the last hour asking the same questions over and over: *Where was Richard Coffee?* She wished she knew. If they would just cooperate with her, let her track down this impostor using the Russian government's resources, maybe, just maybe, they would have a chance. She looked up at the angry bear of a man and said, "Agent Spigotta, I am not your enemy here. The enemy here is Surkho Andarbek. You know him as Richard Coffee."

"Bullshit," Spigotta growled. "The enemy we have positively identified is Samuel Dalton. The deputy director of Homeland Security. He e-mailed you today. Richard Coffee is some phantom a suspected partner of Dalton's been talking about. In fact, the only people talking about Richard Coffee are you and Stillwater and Dalton. What we know is Dalton e-mailed you and Stillwater before this thing went down today."

"Perhaps he did," Khournikova said coolly, "but I have no connection to the man. I remember no e-mail communication with this man. I have no idea who Derek Stillwater is. What did the e-mail say?"

"Why don't you tell me?"

She shrugged. "Agent Spigotta, this is . . . a diversion. Has it not been a day of . . . red herrings? Richard Coffee, when he worked for your Central Intelligence Agency, successfully convinced Chechen rebels that he was one of them—and convinced us, as well. He has successfully faked his death twice. Now he has your Bureau chasing ghosts, convinced that I am a terrorist. He has convinced you that this man, Derek Stillwater, is a traitor. I know of no one by this name. I have spent over a decade trying to track down the man we know as Surkho Andarbek. And when I finally do determine that Surkho Andarbek is actually an American spy, the man dies again, only to reappear a year later working on the borders."

Spigotta chewed on his cigar, staring at her. "You know what, Ms. Khournikova? I think you're blowing smoke. I think Samuel Dalton, who nearly assassinated the president today, is in cahoots with you and your people."

"My people?"

"Russia."

"There is no advantage to Russia for the catastrophe that has occurred today."

"You are enemies of the United States. Have been—"

Khournikova cut him off. "Agent, the cold war is over. I freely admit that we lost. We wish to trade with the United States. We wish to have a strong economy, to be able to compete in the world marketplace. To have peace and prosperity."

"You're run by a bunch of mafiosos—what d'ya call 'em, oligarchs."

Khournikova dipped her head. "Yes, this is true. But it does not mean that decapitating the U.S. government is in our best interests."

"Who knows what you folks think is in your best interests? Maybe you think you can get away with this. What I want to know is, where's Sam Dalton?"

"I don't even know who he is. I have been hunting Richard Coffee."

Spigotta looked sour. "Richard Coffee died in 1991 during the Gulf War. That's what our records say."

"Perhaps you can explain to me why Derek Stillwater—a man you claim I must be working with—killed a woman claiming to be Irina Khournikova. She is not. I am—"

"We're working on an ID of the woman, don't you worry. We've got that handled, Ms. Khournikova." Spigotta leaned forward, getting very close to the Russian woman. In a soft, menacing voice, he said, "But you gotta tell me, lady . . . where's Sam Dalton?"

"I do not know who he is or where he is."

Spigotta's hand swept out. It did not connect as planned. The Russian agent rolled her head back and caught Spigotta's wrist in her hands. In a flash she was inside his grasp, leveraging him to the hard floor in a Judo shoulder-throw. She was at the door, realizing too late it was locked. She spun, thinking, *I will have to immobilize him or kill him to get out of here.*

Spigotta was on his feet, his gun in his hand, eyes hooded. "Fool me once, shame on you," he growled, and pointed the gun at the chair. "You *don't* want to take another shot at me, though. Trust me on that."

A drop of sweat beaded on her forehead as she sat back down in the chair.

38

The Fallen Angels' Headquarters

RICHARD COFFEE LOOKED DOWN at the unconscious form of Derek Stillwater. He tapped his chin with his index finger for a moment before turning to Ling, who was removing a sterilized tray of acupuncture needles from a cabinet, momentarily flooding the room with UV light.

"Well, Ling? Is your patient telling the truth?"

In an even voice Ling said, "His answers are consistent."

Coffee burst into a deep bellow of laughter. "Ling, that's not what I asked." He moved across the room in what was almost a lunge. Ling tensed, nearly a flinch, but Coffee stopped next to the examining table. He leaned down close to Derek. He patted Derek's cheek and in a soft voice, as if speaking to Derek alone, said, "Hey, buddy. I asked Ling here if you were telling the truth. It's a simple question. There are really only three answers. They are yes ... and no ... and *I don't know,*" he finished, his voice filled with quiet menace.

Ling's left eye twitched. Just once. In a barely audible mutter, Ling said, "I don't know, Fallen."

"Ah," Coffee said. "But you have hurt him."

"Yes, Fallen. I have hurt him."

"Perhaps you have not hurt him enough."

"Perhaps," Ling said, a touch of enthusiasm creeping into his voice.

"You can do this."

"With pleasure."

"Yes, I understand that about you, Ling." Coffee looked up and met Ling's gaze, judging him. Ling was the first to look away. "All men have a breaking point. Don't they, Ling?"

"In my experience, yes."

"And are you anywhere near Derek's breaking point, Ling?"

"He is very strong. He has . . ." Ling licked his lips, searching for the right words. "Derek Stillwater appears to have great mental flexibility. He is perhaps able to compartmentalize his response to the pain I am presenting him."

Coffee frowned. "Meaning what?"

"Meaning his answers appear to be too consistent. He is either telling us the truth, that he turned Irina Khournikova over to the FBI . . ."

Coffee took a step closer to Ling. The two terrorists, Sven and Ivan, who had observed Derek's torture with little or no emotion, now watched closely for any sign that Coffee would want them to act. "Or?"

"Or," Ling said, "he has created a story to cling to. As he faces the pain, he knows that his story is the only thing that will keep him alive or end the pain."

"So," Coffee said, considering. "What you're saying is, he's lying or he's telling the truth."

Ling's face fell just enough to suggest that Coffee had missed some of the nuance he was trying to provide. "I am saying that it is possible that Stillwater may fear the repercussions of the truth more than he fears the pain."

Coffee turned to look at Derek. "Will he tell me the truth?"

"With enough time . . . and pain . . . all men tell the truth."

"And when do you know?"

Ling shrugged.

"Can you wake him up?" Coffee said.

Ling sighed. "He is already conscious, Fallen."

Coffee turned suddenly toward Derek. "Playing possum, Derek?"

Derek opened his eyes but said nothing.

Coffee looked down at him. "Ling here can increase the pain. Would you like that?"

"No," Derek said.

"So tell me the truth. Where is Irina?"

"I told you. I turned her over to the FBI. Unless they released her, they've got her at the Hoover Building."

Coffee studied him. He nodded. "Okay. Right, Derek. Okay. I believe you. Or I believe you enough. I have someone inside the Bureau. I'll check. In the meantime . . ." Coffee gestured at Ling. "Ling will see if he can get you to change your story. He will see if he can determine whether you're more afraid of the truth than the pain. He's good at it." Coffee left the trailer, letting the door slam behind him.

Ling approached Derek. "It probably no longer matters," Ling said. He began to insert acupuncture needles into a number of points along Derek's body: in his temple, behind his left ear, by his collarbone, in his hips, and several in his feet and legs. Ling held up a needle. "I trust you will find this to be a very interesting experience. You see, pain is in your mind. Your brain can take only so much pain. It will then dampen the pain, creating its own opiates to numb it. The nerves become tired, your serotonin levels between nerve endings become depleted. But I can open you to an entire new level of experience. . . ."

Ling inserted the needle into the palm of Derek's right hand. It was as if a cool breeze was suddenly blowing over his fevered body. The previous aches and pains vanished. He felt an odd sense of well-being, almost euphoria. Every sense became acute. He could smell the sweat of the two terrorists, smell the gun oil and the gunpowder that clung to their clothing. He could hear Ling's breathing, vague sounds from outside the trailer, the hum of electricity, the air conditioning. The air around him caressed his body like a gentle lover's touch; it had weight, texture.

"Lovely, isn't it?" Ling said, and inserted another needle, this one into Derek's shoulder.

Derek bit back a scream as his body suddenly exploded as if on fire. Every neuron fired, telling his brain that he was on fire, that he had fallen into lava, that his skin was red, scorched, turning black, sloughing off his body.

Ling withdrew the needle. Convulsing, Derek gasped for air, his brain incapable of letting go of the agony of the flames. Ling said, "Now, perhaps I should ask you . . . where is Irina Khournikova?" He held up the needle. "Or we'll burn again? So tell me, old friend of Fallen's, where is Irina Khournikova?"

Derek stared at the Asian and thought, *Kill me. Kill me now. If I tell him, they'll kill me now. Why protect myself? I'm dead. Tell him that I killed Irina Khournikova in that apartment. Tell him. Anything. Anything but that burning . . . anything.*

Spangled fish danced before his eyes, and he was suddenly on his kayak, racing cross the quicksilver waves of Chesapeake Bay, feeling so light and nimble that it was like walking on water. In his mind he dipped his hand into the water, took a handful, thinking, *This is the shape of water*, and splashed it on his forehead, soaking his shirt.

Derek said, "I turned her over to the FBI."

Ling inserted the needle once again. Again, Derek felt the flames engulf him, but somewhere deep, deep in his brain, there was water.

39

RICHARD COFFEE LEFT LING's trailer, his mind in turmoil. He felt as if his brain were segmenting, fragmenting into shards of memory. The past had doubled back on him, a past he had spent years trying to forget. *Where is Nadia?*

The thought was a whisper, a chorus of voices in his head. *Where is Nadia?* For Nadia Kosov was Irina Khournikova. Yes. Nadia was Irina.

He stood in the expanse of pavement between trailers and felt a wave of confusion nearly overwhelm him. Irina Khournikova. The Russian woman from Directorate T who had been hunting him for so many years. With an effort he tried to control the explosion of memories spinning in his head.

He blinked, back in Chechnya. What year was it? It was '94? Maybe? Surkho Andarbek had been high in the Chechen rebellion, a tactician and leader. His particular skill had been in stalking Russian military units and assassinating high-ranking officers. Even then, his name was known—Strong Warrior.

There had been a visitor touring their sector, a lieutenant colonel from the Russian army. His name was Sergei Dobrovnik. He was evaluating the Russian mission in Chechnya, which was not going well at all. It was never-ending, Russia's second Vietnam. As if the Afghanistan war hadn't been bad enough, now this mess.

Coffee's intelligence network was prized by the Chechens and feared by the Russians, who only knew that their intelligence leaked like a broken water main. Their routes for the tour of the city were kept highly secret, known to only a few. Yet Coffee—Surkho Andarbek—had killed Dobrovnik with a rocket-propelled grenade as his convoy passed through the streets. The boldness of his attack had made his name known throughout the country.

And two years later, now the head of the rebels, Surkho Andarbek heard that he was being hunted by a woman, Irina Khournikova. This woman was more than just a top antiterrorist agent. Her lover had been Sergei Dobrovnik. Khournikova had sworn an oath to hunt the man who had killed her lover.

Coffee, then close to his fall, began to study this hunter. Indirectly, Irina Khournikova was responsible for the depth and breadth of Surkho Andarbek's intelligence network in Russia and the rest of the world. It was because of her that he began even more recruiting of spies from within and without, developing contacts, spinning a web.

Coffee blinked, back in contact with reality. He glanced at his wristwatch, puzzled, wondering if he had actually been standing in the one spot for ten minutes. He looked around at his followers, busy preparing for the rest of the operation. Coffee knew they believed his trances brought visions.

And maybe they did, he thought. Because you cannot escape the past. The past has a way of unfolding and folding back in on itself. History does repeat itself, even if you remember it.

Like Derek. Derek had appeared like a phantom from his past.

Grimly, Coffee strode across the pavement to the doublewide trailer Derek had noticed, the one with the elaborate ventilation system. At the front of the trailer was an intercom. He punched the button and waited. After a moment a metallic voice said, "Yes?"

Coffee switched to Korean. "What's the status of your tests?"

"Fallen. They are progressing."

"Are you comfortable with the results so far? I want to proceed with the next stage."

More silence. Finally, the speaker said, "I do not have 100 percent confidence in the vaccine. It has not been thoroughly tested."

"It works on the animals?"

"Yes, Fallen. So far they seem effective, though not enough time has passed."

"Yes. Yes. Do you need to test it on a human being?"

There was a longer silence. Finally, "Yes."

Coffee smiled, thinking of Derek Stillwater. "I will bring you your test subject, then. Your guinea pig."

"One . . . one of the Fallen?"

"No. A guest."

"Ah. Soon?

"He's with Ling. When Ling is done."

"We need him alive."

"Ling knows what to do."

"Very well. We will make preparations."

Coffee walked away, toward another trailer at the far end. As people passed, they nodded their heads in respect. His people. His Fallen Angels. He pushed his way into Trailer F. Three people were working at computer workstations. They were tapped into various news organizations and government agencies. The room was stacked with computers and TVs tuned to CNN and Fox and the other news networks.

"I need you to determine if the FBI has custody of Irina Khournikova."

The man he spoke to was a slim Malaysian, who nodded. He moved into the FBI logs and computer system, tapping at keys. He nodded. "Yes. It indicates that she is in an interrogation room on the fifth floor, in the Strategic Information and Operations Center."

Coffee nodded, thinking. Then he said, "I need e-mail. I need a direct e-mail, nontraceable, to our source in the Bureau."

The Malaysian tapped keys. "O'Hara?"

Coffee nodded, thinking of sacrifices. He was going to sacrifice Derek Stillwater. Blood for blood.

40

FBI Headquarters

JUDE O'HARA SAT IN his cubicle in the antiterrorism division of the FBI, sifting through computer files. He wore the typical FBI uniform of dark suit and white shirt, though his was as wrinkled and sweat-stained as the rest of the staff's. Hell, everyone was saying, had broken loose. They were mobilizing, but slowly, with so many cabinet members dead. He brushed a hand through his short sandy hair and closed his eyes, ignoring the pressure behind his ears and the pounding behind his eyes. His mind was a blank, frozen. Everyone was mobilized, the antiterrorism division was going absolutely apeshit, and he was sitting there trying to come up with a game plan.

Because he knew more about the Fallen Angels than anyone in the entire division. It had been his job over the years to make sure that the FBI knew nothing about the group. Whenever hints came across other agents' desks, it had been his job to question the veracity of the intelligence. Whenever he heard hints about the Fallen Angels, he had made the intelligence vanish.

He had been doing this for seven years, ever since a lengthy trip through the former Soviet republics in search of terrorists and thieves who were wholesaling stolen Russian military hardware to the highest bidders. He had been approached in a Moscow casino by a woman named Ekatarina, a voluptuous blond in a shimmery silver dress that could not contain her exuberant body. It had not been a difficult seduction . . . and by the end of it he had found himself with a Swiss bank account and a connection to the very group he was looking for. By the time Osama bin Laden's boys had changed the tenor of the war on terrorism, he was stuck. It was either continue or face a life in prison with a possible execution order.

He considered disappearing numerous times. Over the years he diversified the money, created a number of false identities, set up the pathways for a disappearance.

The Fallen Angels confused him. Originally, they appeared to be about money. Over time, the closer he found himself to the group, the more they seemed like some sort of whacked-out ideologues, an odd doomsday cult that believed themselves to be the eventual instigators of a new world order.

He had met the Fallen, the head guy, by the fountain in front of the Schlöss Charlottenburg in Berlin, just another old man feeding pigeons. Except up close, the guy wasn't that old. He said to call him Fallen. He spoke in the harsh, hard accent of a native East Berliner, which had confused O'Hara because all the intel he had gleaned on the guy suggested he was Chechen or maybe Russian.

He took the money and he took the sex and he convinced himself that this Chechen guy or this Russian was strictly a Russian or Eastern European problem. But now Fallen had come home, and O'Hara was starting to feel like his nuts were being roasted over an open fire. He was thinking about escape plans.

He had twenty grand in take-a-powder money in his safe at home, along with three different passports. He had a bag packed.

He could catch a train out of Washington, D.C., and fly from a smaller airport, maybe Frederick, to Atlanta. From Atlanta, almost anywhere. Atlanta to L.A. to Hawaii to the Philippines. From the Philippines he could lose anybody, hopscotch through Asia, backpack, slip back into Europe, the Mediterranean maybe, under a new identity. This might be the time for it.

His phone rang. He stared at it, transfixed. After three rings he picked up, saying, "O'Hara, FBI."

"Do you remember Schlöss Charlottenburg?" The same voice, accented. He had Fallen on the phone. O'Hara brushed a suddenly clammy hand over his jaw, his heart thudding in his chest.

"Yes," he said.

"We have a problem."

O'Hara felt like he was choking. He tucked a thumb under his collar and pulled it away from his neck. "What . . . sort of problem?"

"No," said Fallen. "That's not the correct answer. The correct response is, 'What can I do for you?'"

"Okay," O'Hara said, suddenly visualizing his escape route.

"Good. I need confirmation. Your people have a Russian woman in for questioning."

"Yes," O'Hara said.

"Her name is Irina Khournikova."

"Yes."

"I have weighed our risks. This woman, though she is personally very important to me, has now become a major liability. She must be eliminated."

"Um . . . I don't . . . understand."

"Yes, you do."

O'Hara leaned back in his chair and looked around. The division was a mob of activity. Here it was, four-thirty in the morning, and everybody was on duty. All the agents were on their computers, on their phones, or flying around the city or the world backing their informants into corners, demanding if anybody knew about this attack at U.S. Immuno—more importantly, if anybody knew about Sam Dalton and his attack on the White House. Nobody was looking at him. Brady Gallagher, the agent whose cubicle was to his back, had left an hour earlier to "have a friendly chat with a Serbian pal of mine who works at the U."

"What you're asking," O'Hara said, "is impossible."

"Is your computer on?"

"Yes."

"Good. *You've got mail.*"

O'Hara turned to his computer screen, looked around to see if anyone was watching, then clicked on his e-mail. Sure enough, he had just received a file with an attachment. The message said, *We're not negotiating. F.*

Stomach churning, O'Hara clicked on the attachment. There were three files. One was the entire transactions list of his numerous offshore numbered bank accounts, starting with the Swiss account the Fallen Angels had created for him. He quickly deleted it, swallowing hard.

The second was a video file. He clicked on it and saw a video of him and Ekatarina having sex in a Moscow hotel. He deleted that before it could last ten seconds. Bile filled his throat.

The third file contained what appeared to be the contents of a Russian dossier on the arrest of a woman believed to have been involved in the theft and sale of Russian stinger missiles to al-Qaeda cells in Tunisia, Iran, and Afghanistan. It was a large file, and it held interrogation records thoughtfully provided in Russian and in English, lists of known contacts—his name was on it—and photographs before and after her death by lethal injection. The woman was the blond, Ekatarina. There it was, a nice trail tying him to known terrorists.

There was not, he noticed, any record of a jury trial. Ah, the Russian way. Something the U.S. had somewhat adopted post–9/11: call them enemy combatants and lock them away for an extended interrogation session, isolated from family, friends, and legal counsel.

He deleted the file.

In his ear Fallen said, "Still there?"

"Yes."

"I have the e-mail addresses of quite a number of people who would find those materials interesting."

"I'll . . . take care of your problem."

"See that you do. Soon."

O'Hara flinched away from the buzzing in his ear and slowly hung up the phone. The agent opened his desk drawer, withdrew his handgun, checked that it was loaded, and left the division, heading for the restroom. He knew where the Russian woman was being held. But could he do the job and get out of the building? He had to have a plan.

As he splashed cold water on his face, he thought of one.

41

The Fallen Angels' Headquarters

LING REMOVED THE FINAL needle from Derek Stillwater's sweat-drenched body and placed it carefully on the tray. Stillwater appeared to be unconscious, yet Ling did not think he was. He was impressed, despite himself. Stillwater had stuck to his story about Irina Khournikova being turned over to the FBI. Ling did not actually believe the story. He knew from years of experience extracting information from political prisoners in China that Stillwater had been in tremendous pain. Also, when his patients were under that intensity of feeling, they would change their story. If they were telling the truth and the pain persisted, they would make up things, anything that they thought their torturer wanted to hear, hoping that something would satisfy them and end the pain.

Stillwater had never changed his story.

And Ling did not believe the story. He believed Derek Stillwater was physically strong. But he had broken physically strong men. They always gave in eventually. Clearly this man had a certain type of intellect, a psychological flexibility and strength that allowed him to deal with the pain in some fashion.

Ling believed all human beings could be broken. He had dedicated his life to it. He had harnessed his talents to the man who called himself Fallen, who had a vision and plan for the world. Ling believed he could, with time, break Derek Stillwater. But time was not a luxury he had today.

Ling believed from experience that the thing that was keeping Derek Stillwater in control was a sense of mission. He had tortured many, many people. The most difficult to break, he had found, were the believers. Religious people, in many cases; or people who had a profound belief in something: God, social justice, perhaps family. They believed they must hold on to some slim reed of belief while the world became pain, and it was this reed that Ling began to pick away at when he had time.

"You may open your eyes, Dr. Stillwater," Ling said. "I know you are conscious, so you can stop playing me for a fool. Open your eyes."

Derek opened his eyes.

Ling said, "I am done with you, I believe. Perhaps this is a lucky thing for you. To all eyes you appear to be telling the truth. Fallen shall return shortly with knowledge of your honesty or your deception. If he has proof that you speak true, very well. But I, Dr. Stillwater, know you to be lying. What do you believe in, Doctor? In God? In life everlasting? In your government? Your country?"

Derek didn't reply.

Ling began to clean Derek's wounds, suturing them, covering them gently with dressings. He injected Derek with ampicillin, explaining to him what he was doing.

"Eh, Doctor? Do you believe in America? Is that why you resist me? Fighting me for God and country? You understand that America is dying tonight. We almost got your president. We nearly decapitated your government. We took out very many of your generals and your bureaucratic directors. We have Dalton to thank for that, even if his prime target managed to escape."

Ling looked closely at Derek, at the tightening around his patient's eyes, at the sudden interest and glitter in his eyes. "You did not know?" he asked softly.

Derek said, "You're lying." His brain was in turmoil. It was a psychological ploy. Ling was telling him stories to confuse him, to make him give up hope.

"Ah," said Ling. "You do not know." He finished with his medical handiwork and looked down at Derek Stillwater. "Samuel Dalton released a canister of VX gas into the White House last evening. It was timed to coincide with a high-level emergency cabinet meeting. It killed the director of the FBI, the CIA, the director of Health and Human Services, the director of the Center for Disease Control and Prevention. It killed the national security advisor and your military joint chiefs of staff. It decimated a large majority of the administrative branch of the United States government, Dr. Stillwater. It is only through luck and quick reflexes that the president survived. Your president survived, along with a James Johnston and a Benjamin Zataki. Johnston, I believe, was the secretary of Homeland Security."

"Was?" Derek croaked in disbelief.

What might have passed for a smile crossed Ling's face. "It is my understanding that your president demanded Johnston's resignation. He could not be trusted when his deputy director turned out to be a terrorist. This Zataki I do not know. A military man, I believe? In your Army?"

Derek said nothing.

"Of course, Doctor," Ling continued, "they also believe that you are working for the Fallen Angels." He gazed at Stillwater. "Perhaps you will. Perhaps Fallen will recruit you, bring you in with us. Especially now that your own government believes you are a traitor. Hmm? What do you think, Doctor Stillwater?"

Derek's brain raced. Was this true? Had Dalton set off VX in the White House? He thought of all the helicopters, all the military and police traffic in the city. He initially thought it was because of the attack on U.S. Immuno, the heightened alert. But . . . had he somehow known that things had gotten worse?

What had Dalton said?

In Rock Creek Park, Derek had said, *"Semantics. You're playing word games, and your own head's on the block. You're going in. If you cooperate, tell us where Fallen is, where Coffee is, things might go easier on you."*

Dalton laughed as if he knew something Derek did not. He said, *"You are full of shit. Full of shit and uninformed, pal. There isn't a plea deal in the whole universe for me."*

With a chill he realized that Ling was probably telling the truth. Derek said, "When you throw in with madmen like Coffee—"

"Fallen!"

"Yeah, right. Fallen. When you team up with him, you have to realize how expendable you are. Look at what he did to Dalton. See how he repays loyalty? I'd watch your back."

Ling looked amused. "If you were lying about the woman you call Irina, Dr. Stillwater, and Fallen finds out, then it is you who must watch out. But I do not see you becoming one of us. I think you will die here tonight or die out in the greater world later, when we release Chimera."

"So you *are* going to release."

Ling fastidiously rearranged his instruments of torture. "Yes, Doctor. We most certainly are going to release it."

Derek stared at his torturer. Such madness. Didn't they realize? Of course they did. "And the White House attack was the first part of your plan."

"Almost completely successful, but alas, not completely."

"You're declaring war on America," Derek said, trying to hide the sound of desperation that entered his voice.

"No, Doctor," Ling said. "We are declaring war on the world."

The door to the trailer opened, and Richard Coffee stepped in, his face a mask of conflicting emotions. "Are we done here, Ling?"

"Yes, I have done all that can be done in the short time available."

"And he told you . . ."

"He remained consistent with his story. He subdued Irina and turned her over to the FBI for questioning."

Coffee nodded. "Release him, please."

Ling nodded and unbound Derek's hands and feet. Derek slowly sat up, massaging his wrists.

Coffee said, "Give him scrubs. I think that will do."

Ling nodded and removed a pair of green surgical scrubs from a cabinet and handed them to Derek, who slowly pulled them on. As he stood he staggered against Ling's tray, knocking the surgical instruments and acupuncture needles to the floor with a loud clatter. The two guards jumped back, as did Ling.

Coffee, in a move as swift as lightning, had his semiautomatic up in both hands, aimed directly at Derek's face. His voice rough with emotion, he said, "Don't try anything, Derek. You don't want to get cute with me right now. Yes, Nadia was at FBI headquarters, as you said. But I planned to have children with her. She is my wife. You have forced me to have her eliminated by our mole at the Bureau. She knows too much. She would have willingly sacrificed for our cause, but it's because of you that I have to sacrifice her. And for this you'll pay."

Derek didn't move. *Nadia? Nadia is Irina? Is that why Ling kept referring to her as "the one you call Irina"?* A sense of horror crept over him as he stared into the barrel of Coffee's gun, realizing what a knife edge he had been blindly walking. If Coffee confirmed it, then someone named Irina Khournikova—the real Irina Khournikova?—was being held at FBI headquarters. They weren't holding the woman he referred to as Nadia, because Nadia, who had been posing as Irina Khournikova, was dead. Derek had tortured her to death. But who was the real Irina Khournikova?

Derek expected Coffee to gun him down right here. He saw the mad light in his eyes, the way his finger pressed on the trigger.

Then Coffee laughed, a wild, joyous burst of laughter. He put the gun down, spinning it on his finger like a gunslinger and slipping it into his holster. "C'mon, man. Get dressed. Time to give you a tour of the facility. You're gonna love it."

Derek carefully got dressed. Very carefully, because the acupuncture needle he had palmed from the table was inserted in the waist of the scrub pants.

42

Rock Creek Park

Aaron Pilcher showed his ID badge to the cops who had cordoned off the parking lot near the park. The cop directed him to park his car to one side. Pilcher did so, climbing slowly out of the car, his energy nearly gone. His body was once again soaked in sweat from his nightmarish trip through the White House, fear and stress leaching from his pores. He would have to take a break soon, get a couple hours of sleep, but first Spigotta had told him to run over here, check on things. There were reports of shootings and then an explosion. . . .

What he saw was the burning wreckage of two vehicles and a helicopter. The area was lit up in flashing red and blue and white. The stench of burning fuel permeated the air. Heat baked off the wreckage. Half a dozen police cars, two fire trucks, a swarm of firefighters and cops. He gaped at the helicopter. Was it . . . ?

He looked around for the person in charge and located a bulky man shouting through a bullhorn at rescue workers. Pilcher strode over, ID ready. He introduced himself. The man's jacket indicated he was with the fire department. He glanced at the ID and said, "Probably need NTSB, too. Looks like somebody shot down a Coast Guard helicopter. Blew up a couple trucks. There's two dead guys, too. One over there and one over . . ."

Pilcher didn't wait around. He jogged over to the first body, which was being guarded by a uniformed cop, waiting for detectives or ME people to arrive. Pilcher flashed his badge again and took a look. The guy looked military. Maybe it was just the haircut, short on the sides, the old whitewalls. And not familiar.

"Any ID?"

"Waiting for the detectives. I'm not touching the body."

Pilcher frowned, glanced tiredly at his borrowed watch, then hurried over to the other body, lying near the woods. The female cop guarding this body placed her hand on her weapon as he approached. He slowed down, keeping his badge up.

He took one look at the body. "Shit," he said.

"Do you recognize him, sir? He looks familiar to me."

"He should. Shit."

Pilcher flipped out his cell phone and punched in Spigotta's direct number. On one ring Spigotta snarled, "What is it now?"

"It's Aaron. This accident site? There're two dead bodies in the area. One's unknown. The other's Dalton."

There was silence on the line, then, "Fucking dead, you said?"

"Yes."

"Well kick the motherfucking corpse for me, Aaron. Who killed him? I'll pin a medal on his goddamned chest."

"I don't know. We've got two burning SUVs and, uh, a downed Coast Guard helicopter. It looks like the one that was shuttling Stillwater around."

"Survivors?"

"I don't know." He looked over at the crumpled and blackened helicopter. A fire truck was pouring foam on the wreckage. "I don't think so, though."

There was uncharacteristic silence on the line. Finally, Spigotta said, "Is there anything you can do there, Aaron?"

Pilcher hesitated. He wasn't at all sure he wanted anything to do with the interrogation of Irina Khournikova. "I need to spend a little more time here."

"Fine. But get back here ASAP."

"Sure."

Pilcher nodded, took a moment to absorb the scene. As he did, somebody shouted, "I found someone!"

He spun on his heels toward the voice. A number of EMTs and firemen rushed toward the edge of the woods. He sprinted after them. Heat radiated off the burning helicopter, like standing at the gates of hell. He elbowed his way through the crowd to find two EMTs kneeling next to the crumpled figure of a woman in a Coast Guard flight suit.

"She's alive," one of them said. "Leg might be broken, shoulder . . . ribs . . . but she's breathing."

The crowd stepped back as someone brought in a stretcher. The EMTs deftly eased her onto the stretcher and attached a bag of saline. When the needle went in her arm, she opened her eyes. The EMTs placed an oxygen bottle over her mouth, but she said something.

"What did she say?" Pilcher shouted, barely heard over the sound of the trucks and the crowd and the fires. "What did she say?"

"Who're you?"

"FBI. This has to do with the attack at the White House. What did she say?" He pushed his way to the side of the gurney and looked at the woman. The scorched nametag on her flight suit said C. Black. He said, "What did you say?"

She looked confused, blinked, closed her eyes. Then: "Crew?"

Pilcher said, "How many were in your crew?"

"Two," she said, barely audible.

Pilcher looked up at one of the firemen, who shook his head, gesturing toward the helicopter. "Was there anyone else?" Pilcher asked.

"We've really got to get her to a hospital," the EMT said.

"Was there anyone else?" Pilcher asked again.

Cynthia Black opened her eyes for a moment and said, "Stillwater . . ."

"Derek Stillwater?"

"They . . . they caught him." Then she was silent. The EMTs rushed her out of the crowd toward a waiting ambulance.

They caught him, he thought. *They?*

He looked around the parking lot. At the two trucks that looked like they'd been hit by rockets. At the two dead men, including Sam Dalton. At the crashed helicopter with its two dead crewmen and the pilot who had miraculously survived the crash and resulting explosion.

They caught him, he thought.

Deep in thought, he walked slowly away from the flaming chopper toward his car. He stood at his car for a minute, looking around, wondering who *they* were. Wondering who had killed Sam Dalton. He shook himself, thinking it through. Thinking about his gut reaction to Derek Stillwater.

He climbed in his car and followed the ambulance to Walter Reed. He wanted to be there when—and if—the pilot of the Coast Guard helicopter woke up.

43

The Fallen Angels' Headquarters

DEREK STAGGERED DOWN THE two metal steps of the medical trailer after Richard Coffee, sinking to his knees on the hard pavement. Coffee turned to look at him, a speculative look on his face. "Bad day, huh?"

Derek struggled to his feet. "You might say that."

"Sorry," Coffee said. "I never thought you'd be the one coming after me. Dalton told me it would be a possibility, but he'd try to keep you off it."

Derek stood and tried to catch his breath. The world was gray around the edges, and he felt weak. His stomach roiled and churned, his wounds ached, and his head pounded. "You thought you could trust Dalton?" he panted. "You're dumber than I thought you were."

Coffee's backhand to Derek's face lifted him off his feet and slammed him to the pavement. Derek looked up again into the black maw of Coffee's handgun. "I have very little reason to keep you alive, Derek. Don't give me more reasons to kill you now."

Derek held his hands out to his side. Blood trickled down his chin. He waited.

Coffee put his gun away and held out a hand. Derek stared at the extended hand for a moment, then took it and let Coffee assist him to his feet. Coffee patted him on the shoulder. "Sorry about that. Been under a lot of stress. Had to give a death order for my wife, you know." The way he said it was jovial. "Hey, that reminds me," he said. "Whatever happened to that woman you were dating, that doctor. What was her name? Simona, right? Whatever happened to her?"

Coffee led him toward the doublewide trailer with the complicated ventilation system. Derek was pretty sure he knew what was there and pretty sure he didn't want to go in. And equally sure that he didn't have much choice in the matter.

"I married her," he said. "Then we got divorced."

"Didn't have to have her killed though, huh?"

Derek couldn't read Coffee's expression. Bipolar didn't quite cover the mood swings. Bipolar with delusions of grandeur and psychotic breaks might *start* to describe Richard Coffee.

"No," Derek said, "I didn't. And neither did you. You could have trusted her to keep her mouth shut if she was so loyal to you."

"Did you tell the truth, Derek? Did Ling get to you?"

Derek didn't reply. Because in truth, he had not told the truth. Would he have if Ling had a few more hours or another day or two? You bet.

"Dalton. Irina. I'm not sure it's safe being on your team, Richard."

"Sacrifices sometimes have to be made. Nadia would understand."

"Who's Nadia?"

Surprise and confusion, mixed with a considering expression, flashed across Coffee's face. "Her real name is Nadia," he finally said. "Nadia Kosov."

"Then who is Irina Khournikova?"

"The real Irina Khournikova?"

Derek nodded.

"A huntress," Coffee said. "A nemesis. A stalker. A vigilante. Someone who wants me dead."

"President of your fan club, right?"

"You might say that," Coffee said.

Derek didn't know who was being held at FBI HQ. It was, like about a million other things, out of his range of understanding. What he did understand was that Richard Coffee was nuts and that he had stolen Chimera M13 and that he and his band of merry men intended to use it. He also understood that while he was still alive, it was his responsibility to try to stop that from happening. Even if he died doing it. And of course, if he lived and the Fallen Angels succeeded in releasing the bug, he'd probably die anyway.

He didn't know if he could kill Coffee right here. Coffee had not been tortured for the last hour or two, been shot twice, or in general had a shitty day. If Derek jumped him, it was likely that he, Derek, would end up dead and Coffee and his Fallen Angels would go about their business as planned. Even if he did manage to kill Coffee, he didn't know if that would stop the plan from going into effect.

He was inside the circle. He was alive. That was probably more than anybody at DHS could ask for.

"What are you planning on doing?" Derek asked.

"I'll show you."

"I'd just as soon skip the show part of show-and-tell. Why don't you just tell me?"

Coffee turned, and for a moment Derek thought he was going to get a fist in the face again. Instead, Coffee laughed and said, "You're not calling the shots today, Derek. I don't owe you. I'm not glad you're here, but who knows? Maybe you'll be useful. Lee might be able to use your expertise . . . or something."

"Kim Pak Lee?" Derek said.

Coffee turned again. "You know him?"

"Irina—I mean, Nadia—showed me his dossier. Is he growing Chimera?"

"Indeed he is."

"Are you going to sell it?"

Coffee snorted and stopped in front of the entrance to the doublewide. "Money is going to be a thing of the past, Derek. Get used to the idea."

"Why? Why release the bug?"

Coffee smiled. "Because somebody's going to eventually, Derek. Why not now? Why not me?"

"This isn't Mount Everest. You don't have to do it just because it's there."

In a conspiratorial whisper Coffee said, "I'm doing it because I can, Derek. Simply because I can. Haven't you ever wanted to dance on the grave of the world?"

"Not literally."

"Well, I'm going to." He pointed to the entrance of the doublewide. "Time to see how Lee's doing."

Derek felt his heart rate accelerate. He didn't want to go into the doublewide trailer. It was a laboratory. Probably some sort of jury-rigged Level 4 containment facility. Dr. Kim Pak Lee was inside in some sort of spacesuit, growing Chimera. There was only death inside the trailer.

Derek walked through the doors, swallowing back bile.

It was an airlock, of sorts. A small anteroom with a double-sealed door and a keypad. Coffee punched four digits into the pad and said, "Steel reinforced." The lock clicked, and he opened the door, ushering Derek inside.

The next room, also small, was a locker room. Coffee said, "You're dressed fine. I'm stripping down. Don't try anything funny, Derek. I'm still armed."

"Where would I go?"

"You and I both know that if you killed me, a major part of your mission would be accomplished."

Keeping the gun aimed, Coffee kicked off his boots, slid off his jacket, and stripped down to his underwear, removing a pair of scrubs from one of four metal lockers. Awkwardly, but still keeping the gun ready, he pulled on the clothes. Derek did nothing, just waited.

They passed through another sealed door, having to push against a suction of air. This room was flooded with purple UV light. The spacesuits hung on hooks. Derek frowned. He wondered if the suits hung in the light 24/7. UV broke down most synthetic materials. It was okay to expose the spacesuits to UV for a limited amount of time to kill microorganisms, but around-the-clock exposure would cause the spacesuits to deteriorate prematurely. Small holes and tears, shredding—it was a good way to end up dead in a hot zone.

Coffee began to awkwardly slip into a spacesuit.

"Do I get one?" Derek asked.

"Sorry. Why bother?"

Derek felt lightheaded. His worst nightmare. Naked in a hot zone. He clenched his fists, trying to stop them from trembling.

From inside the spacesuit Coffee said, "In we go, buddy." He waved the gun at Derek.

For a wild moment Derek considered refusing. He felt panicky, butterflies spinning in his veins, the fear a tactile entity living inside his skin. He stared at Coffee. Coffee would be clumsy in the suit. He could end this now. Kill Coffee, put on a suit, enter the lab and kill Dr. Lee, and destroy everything inside the lab.

Coffee stepped backward, as if sensing his thoughts, and held the gun in two hands. His muffled voice could be heard clearly. "You're expendable, Derek. If you don't head for that door right this second, you're dead."

Derek headed for the door, which led through a makeshift decontamination area, a shower room. From there, they were into the laboratory.

Inside the cramped trailer two people were working in spacesuits. Derek couldn't identify them. Coffee shouted, "Lee, this is Dr. Derek Stillwater."

One of the spacesuited figures turned to nod at him. The other figure was working in glass-fronted hoods, transferring cloudy liquid from a flask to yellowish clear liquid in another. He or she did not turn and acknowledge Derek. He was thankful for that, sure the tech was working directly with Chimera.

Derek took in the room, his brain automatically slipping into observer mode, his mind doing the desperate calculus it had been trained for in Escape & Evasion school. It was a laboratory. Black-topped chemical-resistant counters. Two stacked incubators that looked like steel cupboards, attached to a number of gas tanks—

typically carbon dioxide. Most cultures required temperatures of about 98.6 degrees with a percentage of carbon dioxide pumped in to supply carbon for growth. The humidity in the incubators had to be kept high to allow for cell growth.

There was another room—at least another—beyond a sealed door. The walls on the inside had also been sealed with some sort of putty or rubber cement.

Coffee said, "About a year ago Dalton got us a copy of the black patent on Chimera M13. Lee has been working from them ever since to develop a vaccine."

"Any luck?" Derek asked, heart racing just a little bit. If the Korean scientist had developed a vaccine, then it might be enough to get his hands on it and escape. Not an easy task, but far simpler than destroying Chimera and stopping Coffee.

In a heavily accented voice, Kim Pak Lee said, "We are making progress now that we have the actual virus. It is showing signs of being effective on our test animals, but we have not tested it yet on a human being."

"Well," Coffee said. "Dr. Stillwater here has volunteered."

Derek turned to stare at Coffee through his faceplate. "The fuck I have."

Coffee raised the gun and pointed it at Derek's heart. "I could kill you now."

"I know what that shit does to a human being," Derek said, standing his ground. "I'd rather you shot me than—"

Derek felt something bite into his arm and lashed out. He spun and saw that Lee had injected him with a syringe. For a horrifying moment he thought the Korean had injected him with Chimera, but as the scientist stepped back, holding the hypodermic in one gloved hand, Derek felt the darkness close in around him. Staggering, he turned and tried to punch Coffee, get in one good solid hit, but as he slowly sank to the floor of the trailer, everything went dark.

When he came to, he was once again lying on a cot, but this time he wasn't strapped down. He got to his feet and glared around. It was small, the walls and floors bare. There was a thick glass mirror on one wall, which he imagined was two-way. Next to it was a mesh speaker with a button. He could be observed from the other side.

Coffee's voice came over the speaker. "Well, Derek. I just want to thank you. You will turn out to be very helpful in our enterprise after all. Dr. Lee injected you with our vaccine, then just a few minutes ago injected you with Chimera. We should know in a few hours whether the vaccine works. In the meantime, I've got a lot of preparations to make. It was nice seeing you, buddy. If you're lucky, this stuff will work."

"If it works," Derek snarled, "I'll hunt you to the ends of the earth, you bastard."

"Yeah, yeah, sure. Look, something to keep in mind, friend. You break out of here somehow, you're infected. You don't want to be the cause of the end of the world, do you? Why don't you just lie down and take it easy. Make peace with yourself in case Lee's potion doesn't work."

Derek slammed his fist against the glass, but it did not break. "It's not over," he screamed. "It's not over, Coffee! I'm coming after you! I'll stop you!"

"Goodbye, Derek. See you later."

"I'll see you in hell, Richard! In hell!" And with a moan Derek collapsed to the cot and buried his head in his hands.

44

FBI Headquarters

THE FBI MOLE, JUDE O'HARA, took in a deep breath. Standing in the men's room, staring at himself in the mirror, he steeled himself. This was it, he thought. He had to trust Fallen, this freak, this nutcase, that if he did what this guy wanted, he wouldn't turn his escape plan over to the authorities, wouldn't make his escape impossible.

What choice did he have?

He took his Sig Sauer 9mm out of its holster, double-checked that the magazine was full, that there was a round in the chamber, that the safety was off. From his coat pocket he took an excellent and highly illegal silencer and screwed it onto the barrel.

In his mind's eye, he rehearsed it. What he would have to do, the steps he would have to take. What he would have to do once it was over to make his escape.

He put the gun back in its holster, then filled the wastepaper basket with toilet paper and paper towels. He took paper towels and crumpled them into tight balls and stuffed them into his jacket pockets.

Now?

He thought it through. He knew he would require some luck. Maybe more than a little luck.

What choice did he have?

He could run. He could walk out the door, get into his car and drive home, grab his stash and his passports, and drive. He could be in New York, Baltimore, Philadelphia, Atlanta in a very short period of time. Catch a flight out using fake ID. Disappear.

No, wait.

He could transfer the money first. That way he'd be out of it, one step ahead of Fallen.

Sweat broke out on his forehead, and his stomach churned.

He could feel the weight of time pressing down on him.

The door opened and Bill Stallings walked through, one of the older agents, a guy who had been working antiterror for twenty-some years. Stallings had spent half his career in Peru talking to Shining Path psychos, advising the government. His pink scalp peeked through straggling strands of gray hair, and he had a scruffy gray beard. He looked a little like Santa Claus after a few too many drinks.

"Hey," Stallings muttered. "Fuckin' nightmare tonight, eh?"

"Yeah."

Stallings shoved into one of the stalls. There was the zwick of a zipper followed by the thud of gun and handcuffs hitting the floor with his pants, followed by a moan of relief.

O'Hara stared at the shoes beneath the stall, brain frozen. What the hell was he supposed to do now? Could he wait for Stallings to finish up?

"You heard?" Stallings said from the stall.

"What?"

"Big fuckin' mess out at Rock Creek Park. Coast Guard helicopter went down, couple trucks on fire. Pilcher, Spigotta's golden boy, called in to say the chopper pilot survived, it looks like that Homeland troubleshooter was out there, there was some sort of motherfuckin' firefight. And get this: they found the body of Sam Dalton out there."

O'Hara's blood went cold. "Dalton's . . . dead?"

"Yeah. Shot to pieces. Good riddance. The question is, was he working with these Fallen Angels or what? Or is this a coincidence? Taking advantage of another terror attack. MacNeil pulled me off, has me going back over every single file we've got, looking for any kind of reference to the Fallen Angels we can find. I'm talking to the Russians, that Stasi prick, Eberhardt, remember him? Back when East Germany was East Germany? He said he'd get back to me. And get this, you know what he said to me?"

"Uh-uh," O'Hara said, stomach cramping.

"Goddammed kraut goes, *'Ah, ze Falling Angels. Ja. I haf heard of zhem, natürlich. But we never wanted to discuss zhem wit you because we always suspected zhey had a mole in your CIA or your FBI. Zhey sold a lot of American ordinance.'* Can you fuckin' believe it?"

"Maybe he meant Dalton," O'Hara said, head feeling light.

"Maybe. But MacNeil's putting together a task force to make sure there isn't somebody else."

Taking a deep breath, O'Hara walked over, kicked the door in, and shot the FBI agent twice in the head.

"You and Elvis, dead on the toilet."

He closed the door, took out a lighter, and set the wastebasket on fire.

Now. Move it, move it, move it.

He walked from the men's room. Every time he saw an empty office, if the door was unlocked he stepped in, lit up one of the crumpled balls of paper towel, and dropped it in a wastebasket or recycling bin.

The hall was empty . . . for now. He sprinted to the stairwell and dropped ball after ball of flaming paper towel as he climbed the steps to the fourth floor. Soon the smoke alarm would go off. Sprinkler systems would kick in. And he'd better not be standing in the hallway lighting up paper towel when it—

The klaxon sounded, shrill, harsh, and insistent. Headquarters was more active than usual at five in the morning, but most agents were still out in the field; most support personnel were home in bed, preparing for the commute into work, perking coffee. He emptied his pockets and lit up the remaining paper, standing at the doorway, watching the stairwell fill with smoke.

He shoved through the doorway and raced toward the interrogation room where Irina Khournikova was being questioned. Half a dozen people were in the hallway, heading for the exit. O'Hara shouted, "This one's filled with smoke! Go the other way!"

They hesitated, then ran toward the opposite hallway. He saw Spigotta, big and burly, an ugly old bear on the first morning of spring, waking from hibernation. "Where's the fire?" he growled as O'Hara rushed toward him.

"Stairwell. Third floor," he gasped out. "Evacuate."

Spigotta glanced over his shoulder, and O'Hara had his hand in his coat, reaching for the Sig, was pulling it out and up when Spigotta turned, his own gun in his hand, already on the move. *Damn,* O'Hara thought. *How did he know?* O'Hara tried to get a bead on the older agent, tried to keep in motion, but Spigotta had his own gun aimed directly at him, his finger squeezing . . . and O'Hara felt the pain in his chest a fraction of a second before he heard the sound, thought, *That wasn't too bad,* and kept moving, bringing his gun around on Spigotta, squeezed—

And missed. Spigotta fired again, calmly, no expression on his face, the report loud over the sound of the fire alarm. People heading for the exits turned . . . everything seemed to slow . . .

O'Hara dropped to his knees, still clutching the gun. Blood dripped onto the tile floor, and a part of his mind thought, *Blood Spatter Patterns 101. I hated that subject.*

The floor rose up to meet him, and he was still.

45

Ben Zataki stood next to Sharon Jaxon in the animal room of the Level 4 facility and felt his heart sink. For a long, hopeless moment, he leaned against the far wall and just stared at the cages. Sharon clumped over to him, pushed her faceplate next to his, and pinched shut her air hose to decrease the roar. "Any ideas?"

Zataki was close to her, eyes only inches away. He felt something that was probably despair. Nineteen of the twenty monkeys had died. The twentieth monkey would soon be dead. Their plan for a possible vaccine had failed, and failed miserably. As far as they could tell, none of the weaker versions of the virus had even slowed down the contagion.

And what an ugly, evil disease, he thought. There were similarities to Ebola, severe hemorrhagic fevers, internal bleeding. But the animals seemed in so much pain. . . . His horrified gaze took in the slack, bloody corpses of all the monkeys. Even more troublesome was the astonishing speed of the infection. Ebola took four days before symptoms started to show. Chimera symptoms began within hours. They had engineered this bug to target vascular-tissue systems and made it so energy-efficient it was frightening. He'd never seen anything like it. From a purely technical point of view, he was impressed. It had been a technical tour de force to create this monster.

"Anyone working on a weakened virus?" he asked, knowing that they were.

"Yes. It's slow work." She hesitated. "Too late to help Liz."

Zataki nodded. He had checked on Dr. Vargas before he entered Level 4. She was showing signs of mild internal bleeding. They were providing her with clotting factor and saline and three types of antivirals. They had put her on a Valium drip. She was sleeping. It had occurred to Zataki that the most humane thing to do might be to overdose her. But he was a physician, and he couldn't do that. She was still alive and there was still hope. Not much, he had to admit, but some.

"What did Hingemann say?" he asked, wondering what Liz had been thinking when she asked the immunologist from Michigan State University to consult. It had been several hours since the talk, and Liz had gotten much worse. At first Liz had resisted the tranquilizer, but then it became obvious she wasn't thinking clearly and was, in fact, becoming hysterical.

"He said he would read the papers and see if he had any ideas. I hope he calls back soon."

"Let's ring him."

"We e-mailed him all the information on Chimera. It's a ton of material. He won't have been able to get through it all."

"We don't have time for him to get through it all. We'll call him."

"Okay," she said.

He and Jaxon moved out of the Level 4 containment area into the disinfectant shower—seven minutes under a stream of Lysol.

They called Hingemann from Zataki's small, spartan office. They had a high-speed Internet hookup, and the university professor looked tired on the screen of the computer.

"How is Liz doing?" Hingemann asked.

"She's hanging in there, but her condition is deteriorating rapidly. Do you have any ideas, Doctor?"

Hingemann hesitated. "I don't know if it will work."

Jaxon said, "We're grasping at straws here, Doctor. Nothing we've tried has worked. What's your idea?"

"Well," Hingemann said, frowning. He scratched at his beard. "I understand we were pressed for time, so I couldn't read as carefully as I had hoped to. . . ."

"None of us have," Zataki said.

"Yes, of course. This is a very interesting organism, Chimera. You understand that they grafted a number of odd things into its genome, taking sections of various viral and bacterial genomes and merging them into a viral genome. It's the possible antigens that caught my attention."

Zataki knew where Hingemann was going. All living cells had molecules on their surfaces called antigens. Antigens did a number of things, but what their primary purpose seemed to be was to act as keys. Those keys were designed to fit in locks in other cells—a way for cells to interact. The human immune system responded to antigens by producing antibodies specific to the antigen's key. Those antibodies were designed to kill the cells with the specific

300

keys that fit their lock. It was how vaccines worked. The immune system was alerted to the specific key, then churned out more antibodies to kill those specific cells if they should show up again. It was like a flu shot. The flu vaccine had specific antigens. If those cells appeared, the body's immune system recognized the bug and mounted an immune attack. Zataki thought, *Is he thinking what I think he's thinking?*

"Are they in the files?" Zataki asked.

"Well . . . some of them. But, as you may know, your own institution has done work on *Yersinia pestis* and vaccines using recombinant V antigen. I don't know for a fact that the V antigen is present on Chimera M13, but they used quite a large section of the *Yersinia* genome in piecing together their virus. I think it's possible."

Yersinia pestis was the bacterium that caused bubonic plague. Slowly, Zataki said, "You think we should inject Liz with the plague vaccine?"

"No," Hingemann said, leaning earnestly toward the camera. "I think you should inject her with *Yersinia*. With the plague itself."

46

Walter Reed Army Medical Center

Aaron Pilcher parked his car and raced into the Walter Reed emergency room, chastising himself for not having ridden in the ambulance. They were just wheeling the pilot out of the ambulance when he approached.

"Has she said anything?" he asked, flashing his badge.

The paramedic, a woman with thick black hair she wore tied back in a bun, looked up from where she was double-checking an IV line. "No. She's been out the whole ride."

"Will she make it?"

The paramedic shrugged. "Pretty messed up."

"I need her awake."

As they rolled the gurney in, they were met by a pair of doctors in green scrubs, who took one look and began to roll Cynthia Black deeper into the bowels of the ER. One of the doctors, a woman with red hair and purple-framed glasses, said, "Prep the OR, call Jamieson." The other doctor nodded and scribbled notes.

Pilcher said, "I need to talk to her."

"She's not talking to anybody," the female doctor said, not paying him much attention.

"I'm with the FBI, and she's a witness in this terrorist event—"

The doctor glanced up. "You'll have to wait. She's not talking. She's unconscious."

"Can you wake her?"

"No, and if I could I wouldn't. You'll have to wait."

"She may have information about this attack on the White House."

The doctor steeled herself. She pointed to a waiting area. "The answer is still no. You can wait. I'll talk to you when I can."

"But—"

She turned and walked away, leaving Pilcher to stew in his own juices. Staring at a sign that warned not to use cellular phones inside the hospital, he scowled and walked outside, pulled out his phone, and punched in the number for Spigotta. Nobody answered, and he was shunted to voice mail. Dammit! What was going on? He left a message saying where he was and what he was doing and that he would check in every fifteen minutes or so.

Feeling helpless, he clicked off his cell phone and went back inside to wait on news about the Coast Guard pilot.

47

Washington, D.C.

SECRETARY JAMES JOHNSTON—*CORRECTION,* he thought wryly, *ex-secretary*—hailed a cab outside Walter Reed only minutes before Aaron Pilcher entered the ER. The cab driver was, to his surprise, a young white guy who spoke English. He looked like a college student, with shaggy brown hair and an equally shaggy beard, and he couldn't have been any older than twenty-five.

"Where to?"

Johnston was about to give the driver his address in Fall's Church and have him take him home to his wife. He was now a disgraced bureaucrat during one of the worst days in American history, if not *the* worst day. What was there to do now? Go home, lick his wounds, and contact a literary agent to see if some publisher would be interested in his memoir?

Did he spend a career in the Army learning to throw in the towel in the face of defeat? Is that what all those years were about? Including his tours in Panama, Iraq, Haiti, and Serbia? Is that what he had learned as a Ranger, in the Army's Special Forces?

He thought of Derek Stillwater, still out there somewhere.

"Hey, pal, you awake?"

"Leave nobody behind," Johnston said.

The cab driver turned to look at him. "Maybe you'd better get out."

Johnston shook his head. "Sorry. Just thinking." It was the code of the Army Rangers—leave nobody behind. Derek was still out there, fighting the battle, even the war. *I won't leave him behind.*

He supplied an address in Georgetown. As they drove, he noted that the state of emergency hadn't shut down the city. On the contrary, even though there was an unusually high level of police and military activity on the roads, it looked like Washington was waking up and getting ready to go to work. He wondered, now that somebody else was in charge, if they would lock down the city— close the trains, subways, airports. What would the FBI and Secret Service do? Maybe the people with that authority were dead.

It didn't look like they were putting a ring around the city, trying to hold their enemies inside. Maybe because it was too late. Maybe the Fallen Angels—and Sam Dalton—were already out of the city, maybe even out of the country.

The cab pulled up in front of a red brick townhouse, and Johnston noted with satisfaction that lights were burning. He paid the driver and gave him a generous tip. He buzzed the front door.

After a moment the door opened, and an elderly man who looked almost eighty years old stood in the threshold. With a strong accent he said, "So, James . . . I wondered if I would hear from you."

"I need your help," Johnston said.

"Ah," he said. "Come in, come in."

Johnston followed him into the main floor, an elegantly decorated living room done in Early American.

"So, James . . ."

Johnston faced Ernst Vogel. "You're up, so you know."

"*Ja*. I know. Hell in a handbasket. Are you still working?"

"The president asked for my resignation."

"Foolish. A political decision, I would think?"

"Yes."

"A massive terrorist crisis and he thinks like a politician," Vogel said with a sad shake of his head. "Not a man for a crisis, I don't think."

"Just the ways of Washington. But . . . I think I can still do something." Johnston looked in the old man's faded blue eyes. "I think *we* can still do something."

"*Ja*," Vogel said. "Perhaps. Perhaps. Come upstairs, then. Tell me what you are thinking."

Vogel's office was upstairs. It was crammed with computers, large-screen monitors, and cable lines. Vogel sat down in front of one of the keyboards and turned his chair to face another, which he gestured for Johnston to sit in. Vogel, in the 1960s and '70s, had been at the leading edge of East Germany's cryptography efforts. In 1976 he defected, slipping out of East Berlin in a secret container built into the gas tank of a delivery truck. By 1979 he was consulting to the Pentagon and the National Security Agency. Johnston had gotten to know the old man in the '80s during a lengthy tour of duty in the Pentagon. An odd friendship had grown out of their working together on computerized simulations of military and terrorist attacks.

Johnston said, "You've been following the day's news? The terrorist attack on U.S. Immuno and the attack on the White House?"

"*Ja. Natürlich.* Are they related, these two?"

That question gave Johnston pause. *Were* they related? He hesitated. "What is the media saying?"

"Well, at the press conference, the new FBI director, let us see, Director McIvoy, said they had not found any proof that they were connected."

Johnston frowned, wondering if that was how the FBI was proceeding. Perhaps it was true. Maybe Dalton had been uninvolved with the Fallen Angels but had merely taken advantage of the chaos of the attack and the nine o'clock staff meeting to make his own mark on history.

But he didn't believe it. He thought they were related.

Thinking aloud, Johnston said, "The Bureau will be taking Dalton's background apart. That's old ground. Nothing for us there, I don't think. Stillwater—"

"Who is Stillwater?"

"My agent, a specialist in biological and chemical warfare. He was tracking the U.S. Immuno attack and went off chasing a theory of his that someone from his past, a Richard Coffee, was the head of the group. I've lost touch with him, but he may have been on to something."

"Let us assume for a moment," Vogel said softly, "that they are two prongs of a lengthy attack, *nicht wahr?* What would that mean?"

"Mean?"

"This biological agent they stole . . . the media is not saying what it is, exactly. Only that it is very dangerous, an experimental biological warfare agent."

"It is a virus that is highly infectious and completely fatal."

"So they steal this virus. To do what with it?"

"Use it? Sell it? Bargain with it?"

Vogel peered at Johnston with his clear blue eyes and shook his head. "If these incidents are separate—this germ and this attack on the president—then perhaps they will sell it or blackmail someone with it. But if the incidents are connected . . ." He shook his head even more vigorously. "My friend, if the incidents are *connected*, killing the president and throwing the government into turmoil, then they will plan to *use* this . . . germ. How will they do that? How much did they steal?"

"About a dozen test tubes of the stuff . . . not even that much. They were cryovials, about the size of your little finger. Jammed full of viruses, but nonetheless . . ."

"So they must grow more."

"Well . . ." Johnston wished Derek was here to answer these questions—or anyone who was a microbiologist. "I think so," he said. "I mean, they could do a lot of damage with twelve little vials, but yes, I would think if they wanted to do something big and . . . world-stopping, they would need more of it than a dozen small vials. Ultimately, anyway."

"So," Vogel smiled, "they would need a laboratory. A high-level laboratory, perhaps?"

"Yes," Johnston said. "If they had any sense—not a given—they would need something approximating a Level 4 containment facility."

Vogel turned to his computer and ran a search. Most of the listings he found were published by the CDC and provided definitions of the differences between the four biological containment levels.

Each level—1, 2, 3, and 4—built on the previous level. Vogel read while Johnston looked over his shoulder. "What are we looking for?" Johnston said.

"Something unique to Level 4," Vogel said. "Of course, my question would be, if the Fallen Angels were kind of sloppy or suicidal, would they stop short at Level 3?"

Johnston thought of the deft attack on U.S. Immuno, of the biosafety suits the terrorists had worn, of the speculative Korean exchange that Derek Stillwater had offered: "*Hurry up.*" "*You can't hurry this kind of thing.*" The Fallen Angels were many things, but sloppy was not one of them. "No," Johnston said. "They wouldn't stop short at Level 3."

"Well, then, the things that stand out for me are the biological level safety suits. Are there many manufacturers?"

"No, I don't think so. In the United States it's Chemturion. I actually know something about them. They're manufactured exclusively by ILC Dover in Delaware. Same company that makes spacesuits for NASA. I'm pretty sure there are others in other parts of the world, though."

"Yes," Vogel said. "Yes, I think so. I'll find them."

"What else comes to mind?" Johnston said, leaning forward to peer at the screen.

Vogel tapped the computer screen showing an article about a Level 4 facility in San Antonio, Texas, the Southwest Foundation for Biomedical Research, that used them for SARS research. "The type of safety hoods they use. They recirculate the air from inside the facility. Unusual, apparently."

"Okay. Can you—"

Vogel held up a finger. "I will need time, but I can track these down, see who has ordered these in the last, hmm . . ."

"Eighteen months," he said.

"You're assuming they're here? Local?"

"If they're out of the country, there's no hope for us."

Vogel nodded. "Give me time . . . and privacy, please."

"Can I use your telephone?"

"Certainly. Who are you going to call?"

General Johnston got to his feet and adjusted his suit. "An old friend of mine. General Stuart English."

"Still active?" Vogel asked shrewdly.

"No," Johnston said. "He runs a company called International Security Provisions, Incorporated. Better known as ISPI."

Vogel blinked. "They're—"

"Mercenaries," Johnston said. "Let's get to work."

48

FBI Headquarters

AGENTS RUSHED TOWARD THE sound of gunshots, finding Agent Spigotta kneeling over the still body of Agent O'Hara. Spigotta knelt coatless on the floor next to O'Hara, his suit coat wadded into a ball and pressed against the chest wounds he had inflicted. He knew it didn't matter. This guy, whoever he was, was dead. But what the hell had he been doing?

Someone shouted over the braying of the fire alarm, "What in God's name is going on?"

"Guy came out of nowhere, drew down on me," Spigotta said. "Anybody know him?"

"O'Hara," a woman agent said. "Antiterror. Is that his gun there?"

Spigotta looked to where she was pointing. It had a silencer on the end. "Yes."

She met his gaze. "He was coming after you?"

"Seemed to be. Didn't you think the fire alarm was . . . fishy?"

She swallowed. An older woman with graying hair and a fine crinkle of age lines around her eyes and mouth, she nodded. "But everything today—"

Acting Director McIlvoy appeared, jaw tense. "What's going on here? Is there a fire?"

Someone said, "Bathroom one floor down. We've got a dead agent in the john, wastebasket's on fire, burning paper towel in the stairwell. . . ."

McIlvoy stared at O'Hara's lifeless body. "What division? Is he one of ours?"

"Antiterror," someone said. "He's one of ours."

McIlvoy stared, then shifted his gaze to Spigotta. "What were you doing?"

"Interrogating the Russian. I heard the alarm and ran out in the hallway. I saw the smoke, turned to look down the hallway, and saw this guy running in my direction. I noticed he was reaching in his coat, and I didn't like the feel of things. I thought the fire alarm was the wrong thing at the wrong time. Too much weird shit's been happening today, and I just got a feeling something wasn't right. A fire alarm on top of everything? So I was drawing my gun and I turned around and he had his gun up and ready to shoot."

"You think he was going after you?"

Spigotta frowned. He struggled to his feet, adrenaline still pumping. "Maybe after me. Maybe after the Russian. She knows something about these Fallen Angels. She's the only person who seems to know anything about them. Pilcher thought there was a connection between her and Dalton. Maybe he wanted to eliminate a witness. Christ, I don't know."

"Where is she? Where's the Russian woman?" asked McIlvoy.

"Still in the interrogation room."

"She'd better be."

Spigotta turned and lumbered to the interrogation room, blasting through the door to find the room empty. His heart thudded in his chest and he spun, nearly knocking Director McIlvoy down in his rush out the door. "Search the damned building!" he shouted. "Find her!"

49

DEREK LAY ON HIS back on the cot and stared at the ceiling. He didn't know how much time had passed. He could have been out for minutes or hours. No one had come in to check on him. He had spent easily forty-five minutes studying his cell and trying to determine if there was a way to escape. The door locked from the other side, so even if he were capable of picking a lock with an acupuncture needle he couldn't have, because he didn't have access. The cot was lightweight plastic snapped together with a thin padded mattress on top. He could break it apart and maybe have a splintered chunk of plastic to use as a weapon, but it wouldn't be strong enough to get him out of the room. The walls appeared to be rubber sealant painted over thick plywood or something similar.

And time was running out. Coffee had told him he had been injected with Chimera and the vaccine. A human guinea pig.

He didn't know if it was true. His body was a mass of aches and pains—two bullet wounds, bruises, scrapes, and dozens of acupuncture needle pricks, none of which actually ached, and a sort of residual body memory of severe pain. Pain was in the mind, so everyone said, but his mind could remember the feeling of his body on fire.

They believed their vaccine worked—if it was the truth. Had they already injected themselves? Was he really a real-world test? A guinea pig?

And could he use that knowledge?

Derek cocked an eyebrow, thinking. A plan?

He thought about Chimera, about what he knew about it. The first symptoms were bleeding—nosebleeds, ears, eyes, gums. And the last symptoms, too, he reflected.

Blood.

Suppose he was their guinea pig? Suppose they had tested their vaccine on lab animals—guinea pigs, mice, rats, maybe monkeys. Maybe it had worked. And now they had him.

He smiled. The problem with a human guinea pig . . .

He knew the results they would want.

He fingered the acupuncture needle he had secreted into his waistband.

And he knew the results they would fear.

Derek rolled onto his side so his back would be to the two-way mirror. He slipped the needle from where he had hidden it and fingered the flimsy metal. He sighed. So thin it wouldn't cause bleeding if he poked it into his skin. But . . .

Taking a deep breath, Derek started scratching along the palm of his left hand, gouging through the skin. A thin line of scarlet appeared. Biting his lip, he dug deeper, ignoring the lance of pain that shot through his hand. Harder.

The scarlet line began to ooze, then drip.

Derek wiped his palm on his face, smearing the blood beneath his nose and on his chin.

The cut continued to bleed. He clenched his fist, clenched again, opened his palm. He wiped it again on his face, a line of blood by his ear.

Clenched his fist again, smearing the blood all over his hand.

Showtime.

He slapped his bloody palm against the mirror, once, twice, leaving bloody hand prints on the glass.

Then he slumped onto the cot, hand palm down, faking semi-consciousness.

And waited.

50

IN HIS TRAILER, RICHARD Coffee packed a bag. He looked around the interior of what had been his home for the last year, a place he had shared with Nadia.

Nadia.

His eyes misted momentarily, but he shook his head, pushing the thoughts away. Next to the Samsonite was his passport. It was an American passport made out to William Richard Black. It was flawless.

Next to the passport was a can of Coke. He looked at the soda can, mesmerized by the potential.

Because the Coke can was not really a Coke can. It was an aerosol bomb loaded with Chimera.

He was the point man for the new world order. Each of his angels had been inoculated against Chimera.

Each of his angels was given a Coke can loaded with Chimera. Today, they would begin to spread out around the world. They would fly to various points around the globe: France, Spain, England, Russia, Australia, South Africa, Israel, India, Argentina. On their flights, they would open their aerosol bombs and infect hundreds of people on every continent.

Chimera would spread around the world in days.

When it was done doing his work, he and his Fallen Angels would start over again to create a paradise on earth.

He pulled out his gun, debating whether to bring it with him. It could be a liability at the airport. But he believed he could get rid of it easily before he had to go through security, and before that point, he might need the weapon.

Coffee picked up a framed photograph of Nadia and himself. It had been taken by one of his angels when they were in Spain. For a moment his hands shook. He flung the frame against the wall, the glass shattering.

Coffee stared at it, then picked his way through the shards and drew the photograph of his beloved from the frame and slipped it into his shirt pocket.

It was time to say goodbye to his comrades. To his Fallen Angels.

51

Georgetown

SECRETARY JOHNSTON SETTLED UNCOMFORTABLY onto one of
Ernst Vogel's Early American–style chairs and picked up the phone.
He wished he had his Rolodex, but he was sure that everything in
his West Wing office was now fodder for a hazardous-waste incinerator, along with his cell phone, which had been destroyed with
his clothing. First he called information asking for International
Security Provisions, Incorporated, and wrote the number down on
a notepad that Vogel kept next to the phone. His gaze wandered
around the room, taking in the shelf full of books and the stacks
of albums, not CDs. Vogel was a fan of classical music, especially
piano music. You might go so far as to say he was a classical pia-
nist junkie, collecting autographed concert posters and albums of
people like Vladimir Ashkenazy and Peter Serkin and Gary Graff.
Johnston himself was more of a rock fan, and although he had
caught the Rolling Stones six or seven times, it had been years since
he bothered with live concerts. Too many crowds, too much money,
too little time. Which, he realized, he was wasting now.

With a deep breath, Johnston dialed information and asked for the home number of Stuart English in Manassass, then directed the operator to place the call.

It only rang twice before the smooth voice of retired General Stuart English answered with, "English here."

"Stuart, it's Jim Johnston."

"Jim, I'm glad to hear your voice. Hell, I'm glad you're alive. Is this official?"

"Yes."

"I'll call you back."

"You need my—"

"No. Give me a couple minutes."

Johnston nodded as the line went dead. English was undoubtedly moving to a secure line in a secure room of his house. Apparently caller ID or something more sophisticated was part of his home phone package.

He waited, thinking, trying to anticipate the problems this conversation was going to create and how he could address them. It was only about two minutes until the phone rang. He picked up. "Johnston."

"Jim, Stuart. What can I do for you?" Right to the point. That was the Stuart English who Johnston had served with.

"I may need about twenty men in a very short period of time."

"Tell me."

Johnston hesitated. "You understand my position."

"CNN claims you resigned over your connection to Dalton. I assume you were asked to resign."

"Correct."

"And?" English said.

"And that means that I am no longer in the employ of the United States government."

"Tell me anyway."

"I'm working to track the group that broke into U.S. Immuno today."

"What makes you think you're going to have more luck than the FBI?"

"I've got Ernst Vogel."

"Ah. Yes. Well, that might help. And if you do locate them . . ."

"I want twenty very experienced people to lead a raid on their facility."

"Why not just call the FBI and turn it over to them?"

"So far they seem to be running around with their heads up their collective asses. And if what my troubleshooter told me about Chimera and this group is accurate, we really can't wait for the Bureau to get their act together."

"I see. Will twenty be enough?"

"I hope so."

"But you have no idea of the Fallen Angels' numbers."

"No. Of course, I don't have any idea of their location, either. I'm making preparations."

"Yes, of course," English said. There was silence on the line. "Yes," he said. "Twenty local men with the kind of experience you need. Should be possible. As you are no longer the director of DHS, how will you pay for them?"

"There is an offshore account that I should still have access to," he said. The account was, in fact, very secret and would be known to only a few high-level people in the government. The president might know about it—the national security advisor did, or had, since she was now dead. In fact, the majority of the people familiar with this particular account were now dead.

"I see," English said. "Yes. That should do. Will there be repercussions later?"

Johnston could envision congressional hearings for the next thirty years if anybody in Congress was alive to hold them.

"Hard to say. This is a matter of national security, Stuart."

"They attacked the White House yesterday?"

"Yes."

"The press don't think the two incidents are related. Or so says the Bureau."

"I think they are."

Stuart was silent a moment. Then he quoted an amount of money and the numbered account in a Bahamian bank. It was a very large sum of money, but Johnston said, "That sounds a little low."

"As you know, I am a patriot. I still have to pay these men, and they are expensive . . . but you're getting a discount."

"Thanks, Stuart. Get them together and I'll set up a staging area."

"Here's my cell," English said, and recited a number. "I'll be on the move. Call me as soon as you can. And Jim . . ."

"Yes?"

"Be careful."

Ernst Vogel was working at three separate computers simultaneously. Johnston had seen him do this before, but it always amazed him to watch the man shift from keyboard to keyboard, from screen to screen, entering data from one into another, searching databases and corporate and governmental archives and computer systems. The data was like a symphony, and Vogel was like a concert master, directing it.

"I have not limited my search to Chemturion biosuits," the man said, bringing up a window that showed the records from the company's sales. "There are a number of companies and governments that produce similar items, but I think we will be dealing with Chemturion. They sold a number of biosuits this year, and not all of them make sense. There is an order of ten to a biotech company called Biosynthetica, Incorporated, in Maryland."

"Biosynthetica," Johnston said.

"*Ja*. However, although they are registered, they do not seem to exist."

Johnston raised his eyebrows. "Really?"

"*Ja*. Very suspicious. There is an address, but it is a suite in Essex. This"—he tapped at another keyboard and brought up a search engine and reverse phone directory—"is actually a UPS Store, formerly a Mailboxes, Etc."

"It's a letter box," Johnston said.

"Yes. They call their mailboxes suites so it might give the owner the appearance of having an office suite."

"Do they have a computer on site you can hack?"

"Not that I have found yet, but wait a moment."

Johnston knew better than to rush Vogel. The man understood the urgency, but he needed to lead Johnston through things step by step.

"We are also looking for biological cabinets—hoods, they call them—that can be used in Biosafety Level 3 or 4. The manufacturers of these are very few, and in the United States, even fewer."

"Is it possible they bought them from outside the country?"

"Possible, but unlikely if they are doing what you think they are doing. Why bring such a device through customs and immigration

323

controls? Why risk a possible red flag and the amount of paperwork necessary? Understand my reasoning?"

"Yes. Go on."

"This company, Beckman"—another window on a second computer screen—"manufactures a limited number of these types of biological cabinets. They recirculate the air within the facility only, not outside the facility. They have sold five of them in the last eighteen months. One to Fort Detrick. Two to the CDC. One to the University of Arizona. And one to . . ."

He tapped a key. Johnston read the invoice. "Biosynthetica. Damn. Same address?"

"Oh, no," Vogel said. "This was shipped to the Frederick Municipal Airport, where it was picked up personally by representatives of Biosynthetica." Vogel cut again to another screen, this one indicating a pickup of a large freight container delivered from the Beckman manufacturing facility in Houston.

"Jesus." Johnston's heart sank.

"Ah," Vogel said. "We are on the trail, my"—he smiled—"*comrade*. We are on their trail. You see, though we do not have access to the UPS Store computer, they did not pay for this biological cabinet with cash. They used a credit card. A corporate credit card with Citibank Visa."

"It has a mailing address," Johnston said, heart racing.

"Ah. UPS Store in Essex. The same drop box. However . . ."

Johnston looked at him, waiting.

"However," Vogel repeated, "this credit card has some very interesting activity on it."

"It's being paid."

Vogel brought up the Citibank Visa computer system. Johnston didn't want to think about the security they must have and how easily Vogel had gotten through it. "From an account in Geneva, Switzerland, Banque Diamantaire Anversoise (Suisse) S.A. That would take some time, I'm afraid. No, back to Citibank Visa. You see, they have been buying vehicles—Humvees and motorcycles and panel vans. These are interesting, but I'm afraid they are a dead end. No, what really interests me is this." The man's finger pointed to a line in the Citibank Visa listing. It was a reference to another credit card.

"What's that?"

"A second line of credit. For another company related to Biosynthetica. It is for a company called TFA Holdings, Incorporated. They have a corporate headquarters in Sioux Falls, Iowa."

"Address?" Johnston demanded, starting to lose his patience.

"Another UPS Store. It does not matter. I believe it's a mail drop for a shell corporation. TFA Holdings owns four companies."

He brought them up on the computer: Angelika Research, Incorporated; JavaJones Materials, Incorporated; RAC, Incorporated; Andarbek Industries, Incorporated. "They are all incorporated as offshore accounts, they all have credit, and, as far as I have been able to tell, they do not actually exist except as these corporations. However . . ."

Johnston waited. There was something in Vogel's manner that indicated that this might be worth waiting for.

"However," Vogel said, "Andarbek Industries, Incorporated, claims to be involved in warehousing nonperishable food products to be distributed to small stores—your so-called mom-and-pop fast-food stores."

Johnston looked confused.

"Andarbek Industries appears to have leased a large warehouse in Alexandria, Virginia, from TGLM Properties," Vogel said.

"A large warehouse," Johnston repeated.

Vogel brought up an address and a map of Alexandria. "*Ja*. I would check this out, James. But very, very carefully."

52

The Fallen Angels' Headquarters

DEREK, LYING WITH HIS own blood smeared on his face, didn't have long to wait. Only a few minutes after slumping to the cot, he heard a noise at the door. It swung open and a blue spacesuited figure stepped in and crouched over him. In one quick motion Derek hooked his arm behind the figure's legs and swept them out from under him. With a cry the figure crashed to the floor, thrashing awkwardly in the clumsy spacesuit.

Derek leapt over him, sprinting into the main part of the laboratory. A second spacesuited figure stood momentarily paralyzed before racing toward the door. But no one can run fast in a spacesuit, and Derek was on him in a second, catching the figure from behind, bringing his arm around the neck of the spacesuit and spinning around and hauling the figure over his shoulder with a spine-cracking thrust. The figure crashed to the laboratory floor and lay motionless, the helmet of the spacesuit at an odd angle.

Derek returned to the first spacesuited figure, who was climbing to his feet. He recognized the features of Dr. Kim Pak Lee through the visor of the helmet, eyes wide in panic. Derek rushed him as the Korean desperately tried to reach a laboratory bench. Derek intercepted him, grabbing the spacesuit material in both hands and slamming the scientist to the floor. It was no contest, really. With nimble fingers Derek detached the helmet and yanked it off Lee's head.

"Not in here!" Lee hissed. "This is Level 4."

"Life's a bitch," Derek said, pressing his forearm into the Korean's neck. "Now you're going to tell me what your plan is."

"I will not!"

"You will!" he said, applying more pressure to the scientist's neck, mindful of how this had gone horribly wrong with Irina Khournikova . . . or Nadia Kosov.

"No! It is too late. The Fallen has already begun. You cannot stop it!"

"Where is he?"

Lee clamped his mouth shut. Furiously, Derek tried to think of something he could say or do that would make the man talk. His gaze roved over the laboratory equipment on the counters and on the open shelves. He locked in on a glass bottle. It said H_2SO_4 on the label.

He hauled Lee to his feet and dragged him over to the counter. With one hand holding Lee, he picked up the bottle of sulfuric acid in the other. He uncapped the glass stopper.

"I'll start with your eyes," he said.

Lee blinked.

"And I'll burn off your face. And make you drink it. But believe me, you're going to tell me what you're doing with Chimera. Where's Coffee? Where's the Fallen?"

The scientist couldn't take his gaze off the bottle. Already the fumes were making his eyes water. "Fallen . . . is gone."

"He has Chimera?"

Lee did not answer. Derek spilled a drop of the concentrated acid on the Korean's forehead. It smoked.

Lee grimaced and writhed in agony.

"I tell you, I tell you. . . . It's too late for you to stop it."

Derek put the bottle aside.

"It's burning! Make it stop! Please, make it stop!"

Derek snatched a bottle of water off the counter and rinsed the acid off Lee's face. There was a red burned mark on the man's forehead.

"Talk."

Lee took a deep breath. "We are going to start over. We are going to start what you call Armageddon."

"How?

"Chimera."

"Where is Fallen? How many have been sent out? Where?"

"Fallen first. Just a little while ago. Then one at a time over the next day. Each with an aerosol canister that looks like a Coke can."

Derek waited. Lee looked triumphant, smug at being able to talk of their plan. He continued. "International flights. Different countries. We are to release the virus in the airplanes just before we land in the new countries. Then we catch a flight to our . . . meeting place."

"Which is where?"

Lee shook his head. "You cannot stop our plan. But you have been vaccinated. You can join us. But only if we trust you. And we don't trust you. *I* don't trust you."

Derek considered forcing the issue, but didn't want to get side-tracked. "Which airport? Where is Coffee—Fallen—flying to?"

Lee smiled, a dreamy look in his eyes. "It will start in France."

"Which airport?"

Lee smiled again, the expression in his face unsettling.

"Which airport?" Derek repeated.

Lee shoved him away with all his strength. Before Derek could stop him, the Korean seized the bottle of sulfuric acid and poured it down his throat. With a shriek the bottle dropped to the floor and splintered into a million pieces. Lee thrashed on the floor, spewed blood, and held still.

53

Washington, D.C.

Irina Khournikova slipped into the back of a diner only five blocks from the Hoover Building. She didn't completely understand what had happened back there, but she was thankful. It had been a mistake to agree to come with the FBI agent, Unrau. Unrau had told them that their expertise on this Russian national was required, a woman called Irina Khournikova of Directorate T. Of course she had come, but it should have set off alarm bells. Somehow Coffee—Andarbek is how she still thought of him—had set her up. A house of mirrors. Andarbek had set up traps for everyone. For her, for this man Stillwater, whoever he was. But Andarbek must have feared him, because so much of this operation seemed designed to ensnare Stillwater. She wondered who he was . . . and where he was.

There was a pay phone at the back of the diner. The diner was filling up with breakfast eaters, what seemed to mostly be midnight workers coming off their shift, grabbing breakfast before they went home to bed. She liked this place. It reminded her of Moscow. Good, solid people working, going about their lives.

She didn't have money, but it didn't matter. She had phone card numbers memorized. She dialed a number and waited for someone to answer. It was answered by a seven-digit series of numbers spoken in Russian.

"*Vosem. Devyat. Shest. Pyat. Tree. Dva. Odeen.*" (8965321.)

She recited a series of numbers in response: "*Tree. Dva. Dva. Shest. Vosem. Shest. Vosem.*" (3226868.)

"What do you need?"

"I need a pickup." She gave the current code word for an emergency—"*v pizdu*"—and recited her address. Then, "I need information on the leasing information for an apartment." She explained about the safe house where the false Irina Khournikova had been staying. "The FBI is probably looking into it as well, so be careful."

"Anything else?"

"No . . . yes. A weapon."

She hung up and slipped into the women's room. She had no identification, no gun, and, she realized, precious little time. Andarbek had gone crazy. He wanted to destroy the world. And he had the means to do it.

Her stomach churned. She turned the tap on cold and splashed water on her face, thinking of all the years she had spent trying to track down this man, the terrorist who had assassinated her lover. Each time she got close, he slipped away. Each round of investigations turned up more information, often conflicting. First he was a Chechen leader. Then he was an American CIA operative. Then he was dead. Then he was alive, running arms. Then he was a cult figure, his followers fanatically devoted to him. Each turn of the crank wound this mysterious terrorist tighter. His actions became more unpredictable, his attacks more vicious. It was no longer clear who his allegiances were to.

Well, now you know, she thought. *To himself.*

To his own brand of madness.

She left the women's room and slipped into a booth, the seats done in red vinyl. When the waitress came she ordered coffee and bacon and scrambled eggs and toast, hoping that the food would get delivered before her pickup arrived. The coffee came almost instantly, and she sipped it, welcoming the revivifying effects. There was a TV above the counter tuned to CNN. She watched it out of the corner of her eye. Talk about the attack on the White House, how the president was on Air Force One, how the alleged assassin, Samuel Dalton, had been found killed near Rock Creek Park. The anchor speculated that Dalton had been working for someone. They did not make a connection to the Fallen Angels. No mention was made of the shootings at the J. Edgar Hoover Building, though she thought it was only a matter of time before there was.

Just as the waitress brought her breakfast, an ice-blond man in a navy blue suit came in carrying a calfskin briefcase. He surveyed the crowd, then sidled toward her and slipped into the booth. He first placed the briefcase next to her and slid a set of car keys across the Formica tabletop.

"White Ford Taurus. D.C. plate, ED47LF. Parked just up the street on this side." He pointed. "Everything you asked for is in the briefcase, including a cell phone. Is there anything else?"

"Money and ID?"

"Taken care of."

"Good," she said.

The man, whose English was perfect, said, "There is a message I'm supposed to give you personally. From Directorate T."

She eyed him. "Yes?"

"They would very much like this matter with Andarbek to end. For good."

"Fine. I'll see what I can do."

"Good." He nodded, got up, and left. She finished her breakfast, took the briefcase to the women's room, and emptied it. A wallet with appropriate identification: driver's license, credit cards, and cash. Everything was made out to Irene Kramer, a resident of Washington, D.C., with an address at the Watergate Hotel. There was a 9mm Glock in a belt holster with an extra magazine and a silencer. There was a passport, U.S., which she hoped she wouldn't need, given tightened security during the crisis. There was a sheaf of papers backgrounding the safe house where Derek Stillwater had tortured the fake Irina Khournikova to death.

Included was the ME's preliminary report on the fake Khournikova and the Russian embassy's analysis of the woman's background. While Irina had been a guest of the Federal Bureau of Investigation, her people had gotten somebody over to the morgue to take fingerprints. They had faxed the prints back to Moscow to the Directorate to run on their own database.

Nadia Kosov. A Russian citizen, a former government computer programmer in Moscow. She had died in what had been called a Chechen terrorist bombing in Moscow that had killed eleven people in a bus station. At the time nobody had suspected that she was either involved or had been targeted. Her remains had been identified by a driver's license.

Apparently the woman had been involved in the bombing and the Fallen Angels had planted her identification there to convince the authorities that she was dead.

The Fallen Angels seemed very adept at this, Irina reflected. She found the report concerning Nadia Kosov's former job to be vague. Computer programmer for the government. She wondered which branch of the government she had worked for—if she had worked in computer espionage or cryptography. The very vagueness of the report pointed to a high level of interest.

She tucked the report away and glanced through the notes on the safe house. She saw that the management company that owned the building and presumably accepted rent checks from Irina Khournikova/Nadia Kosov had not been open during the night and that they had no known open computer access.

Irina checked the address, realizing the office was a place to start, though she worried that the FBI would be all over it as well. She left the diner, glancing at her watch to see that it was only eight o'clock in the morning. She found the Taurus, studied a map of the city, and drove to the three-story brown brick building that housed the offices of Delecourt Facilities Management.

For the second time in twenty-four hours, she found luck swinging her way. They weren't open. Their hours didn't start until nine, the sign on their frosted glass door said.

She didn't think she would have much time. Using the butt of the Glock, she broke the glass of the door, shoved her arm through, and unlocked it, rushing in.

The receptionist's office was crammed with filing cabinets. A quick search verified what she had suspected—DFM was a dump. A steel desk, a Dell computer system, filing cabinets. She began to quickly go through the filing cabinets, looking for anything under the name Irina Khournikova, Nadia Kosov, Richard Coffee, Surkho Andarbek . . . and then found it under the address of the building, a file of each tenant.

She took the one for Irina Khournikova, leafing through it quickly to see that the fake Irina had paid by check on an account with the Fifth Third Bank.

The real Irina was inside the DFM offices for less than ten minutes, and by the time she was back in the white Taurus, she was on the phone to her contacts asking them to do a financial-records search on the account number she gave them.

She could smell it, she thought. The trail.

54

The Fallen Angels' Headquarters

DEREK ROLLED AWAY FROM the body of Kim Pak Lee, now lying in a pool of blood, vomit, and sulfuric acid. His eyes watered from the acrid fumes, and he gagged, barely able to avoid vomiting. Staggering over to the second scientist, he removed his spacesuit helmet, then decided to go the whole way. He awkwardly removed the suit, donning it himself and hooking himself to the air hose system, which the scientists had momentarily disconnected themselves from when they'd come to check on him.

With relief his suit flooded with air and he took in deep breaths, fighting not to think about the madness that would cause a man to kill himself by drinking concentrated sulfuric acid.

He took in the lab for the first time, *really* took it in. Was there contact with the outside world? He knew that outside this double-wide trailer were terrorists who would kill him without a second thought. But if there was an Internet connection or a telephone or a cellular phone . . .

A search of the laboratory revealed the computer to be disconnected from the Internet and there to be no cell phone. There was a one-button telephone, and Derek was sure that it only connected somewhere within the warehouse.

He perched on a stool in front of the computer and read the files there. Mercifully written in English, they detailed the work Kim Pak Lee had done based on the "blueprints"—the black patent records they had stolen—and the further work he had done in the last day. Their vaccine worked well on animals. So well that they had gone ahead and injected it into all their members.

Madness, Derek thought. *Lee was nuts to make that leap.*

And then the Fallen had given him permission to inject Derek Stillwater, a human subject, with Chimera M13 and the vaccine. A real live human test.

Derek skimmed through the vaccine information, knowing he had to get this to USAMRIID. If Kim Pak Lee was to be believed, Richard Coffee, armed with Chimera, was at an airport heading for France with a Coke can filled with an aerosolized version of Chimera. Soon the rest of the Fallen Angels would be heading to other points around the world. Could they be stopped?

Time was racing away from him.

But he couldn't leave this information here.

He couldn't leave this laboratory stocked with live Chimera.

And if he was infected with Chimera and the vaccine didn't work, he couldn't leave the lab without potentially spreading the disease. He searched the lab and to his relief found the equipment needed to run an ELISA antibody titer to test for the vaccine's effectiveness. Locating a tourniquet and syringe, he partially stripped off the suit, the air still thick with acid fumes. He drew a tube of his own blood and spent precious time getting the test going.

It basically exposed his blood to antigens present on the virus's surface and measured the types and amount of his body's immune reaction. He made a prayer to St. Sebastian or anyone else who might listen and turned back to the lab bench while he let the test cook.

He scrounged through the drawers until he found computer disks and transferred Lee's records to disk. Opening the spacesuit, he slipped them into the pocket of the scrubs he wore.

Searching the lab, he found a cabinet filled with Clorox bleach. Perfect. Opening each incubator, he removed everything in them and moved all the flasks and test tubes to the hoods. Systematically, carefully, he sterilized the cultures by filling them with bleach, then transferred the now-dead containers to what he recognized was an autoclave in one corner. It was taking way too damned long, but he couldn't leave viable cultures of Chimera here.

It was in a locked cabinet that he found the real weapons—a case of Coke cans that had been labeled:

PRESSURIZED AEROSOLIZED CHIMERA
HANDLE WITH CARE

He removed the cans to the hoods and began the sterilization procedure again, opening each can with a hiss and fizz that was not releasing carbon dioxide like real Coke, but was spraying virus particles into the hoods.

He sterilized every single one of them with bleach, then cleaned the hood.

In a refrigerator he hit pay dirt—a dozen glass vials labeled *Vaccine*.

He turned back to the antibody titer test, heart pounding in his chest, blood rushing in his ears. The panic rat had full rein now, galloping through his intestines. Was he infected with Chimera? Did the vaccine work?

Derek performed the procedures with shaking hands, nearly holding his breath as he counted off the minutes. The microtiter plate was made of clear plastic, about four inches by three inches, with dozens of eraser-sized dimples or wells on its surface. Each contained different concentrations of his blood serum, individual antibody-antigen biochemical reactions.

Will I live or will I die?

He waited. Sweat beaded on his forehead, his armpits, rolled down his ribs. His breathing was loud in the spacesuit. His stomach churned.

Slowly the wells turned from clear to blue.

He breathed a sigh of relief. It worked! The vaccine worked!

Now, he thought, *I've got to get the hell out of here. But how?*

His gaze landed on several large cylinders of compressed gas— nitrogen and carbon dioxide—that were used in the incubators. Growing cells needed heat, usually close to 98.6 degrees Fahrenheit, high humidity, and sources of nitrogen and carbon and oxygen. All were supplied by the gases, which were pumped into the incubators to create an atmosphere of about 5 percent gas.

The cylinders stood almost five feet tall and were about ten inches in diameter. Each container held thousands of pounds per square inch of pressurized gas.

Which, Derek knew, if released all at once, acted very much like a torpedo. With a small smile, he went to work.

55

USAMRIID

Liz Vargas was unconscious. In her spacesuit Sharon Jaxon sat by Liz's bed for a moment, watching her. They had tried what the Michigan State University professor, Leslie Hingemann, had suggested. Because the original Chimera M13 had been constructed of bits and pieces of other infectious agents, a mix consisting mostly of viral genetic material and a bit of bacterial genome, Hingemann had quickly analyzed the possibility that Chimera's outer surface might hold antigens similar to *Yersinia pestis*, the bacterium that caused bubonic plague. His theory was that if they then infected Liz with *Yersinia*, essentially infecting her with plague, her immune system would start to create a defense against the plague.

Of course, the vast majority of people infected with plague over the last nine hundred years had died of it.

What had changed in the last century was the advent of antibiotics. Although resistant to many antibiotics, plague was susceptible to a narrow spectrum of antibiotics like tetracycline. So Hingemann had suggested that by introducing a bacteria like *Yersinia* into Liz's immune system to trigger an immune response, then shortly afterward treating her with antibiotics to kill the *Yersinia*, it just might be possible to kick-start her immune system into fighting Chimera M13.

Sharon Jaxon shifted her attention from Liz's pale face to the monitors reading out her vital signs. The last lab specimens she had taken indicated that Liz's immune system was going berzerk, cranking out a wide variety of white blood cells to fight the infection, and that her platelet clotting factors were dropping off the chart. Her temperature had been hovering around 103 degrees for the last hour. They were giving her antivirals and antibiotics and anti-inflammatories, steroids, clotting factor, infusions of whole blood . . .

But she was dying anyway. Hingemann's strategy had seemed to work, but only briefly. For a short period of time after the introduction of *Yersinia*, the amount of Chimera M13 present in her blood had fallen. For about an hour Liz had seemed lucid, her temperature had dropped to 99 degrees, her WBC counts, especially her T cell counts, had risen . . . and then all hell had broken loose.

She had suffered more bleeding, this time her gums and vagina and ears.

Sharon reached out and took Liz's hand in her own gloved hand, feeling an overarching sadness for this woman, who she had decided she liked very much. Liz was alone. Her husband had died, her parents had passed away years before, she had no children. There had been nobody except Hingemann to tell. Afterward, when Liz passed away, there would be only a short list of friends to be contacted. Most of her friends had worked at U.S. Immuno, now dead as well.

Sharon thought it would be only a matter of hours. They had run out of ideas. She thought it would take a miracle to save Liz Vargas.

56

Alexandria, Virginia

JAMES JOHNSTON WAS IMPRESSED with Stuart English's people. Twenty combat-ready men vouched for by the retired general. They were all in their twenties and thirties, the oldest appearing to be in his early forties. All were businesslike and came prepared. English had a conference room set up at a hotel on the outskirts of Alexandria, and when Johnston arrived, all the men were ready, wearing jeans, T-shirts, and lightweight windbreakers.

Ideally they would have wanted to do this as a commando unit, to suit them up in cammies and full gear and go ahead as an assault. But they were operating in a major U.S. city during a time of crisis, and there was no getting around the fact that twenty men fully armed in camouflage gear would get too much attention.

They didn't want to alert the Fallen Angels, and they didn't want to alert the FBI until it was necessary.

Stuart English was a wiry redhead, though most of his hair had faded to gray. He wore khakis and a white dress shirt, and everybody was listening intently as he started his debriefing based on the information that Johnston had supplied and, somewhat to Johnston's surprise, that he had acquired in the hour since their last telephone call.

On the computer screen English put up an aerial photograph of the section of Alexandria near the Potomac River where the warehouse was located. It was in a warren of similar warehouses, with a railroad line running very close by.

"Each of you will be given a palm computer with a detailed map of the area and this photograph. Still, it will be easy to get lost and confused in the area, so stay sharp. In addition, you'll get print maps. As you can see, there are multiple routes in and out. Our job is to provide surveillance and intelligence. We wish to determine the exact number of individuals inside the warehouse and get an idea of their defenses. General Johnston, what do you have to add?"

Johnston stood up. Twenty pairs of hawk eyes followed him. "We believe this to be the headquarters of a terrorist organization calling itself the Fallen Angels. It is multi-ethnic in makeup and led by a man named Richard Coffee, a former Army Special Forces captain turned CIA rogue. We believe the Fallen Angels to be highly armed, disciplined, and well trained. They are believed to have access to alternative weapons of mass destruction, like VX gas. They are believed to have in their control a biological organism called Chimera M13. It is a genetically engineered virus, gentlemen, and it is the purpose of this mission. Inside this warehouse we believe they will have set up a laboratory in which to grow this virus. Once inside this warehouse, it is our top priority to isolate and control this laboratory, to allow no one inside or out."

Johnston paused. "The Fallen Angels are ruthless, people. They will shoot to kill. They will show no mercy. And if threatened, they will use whatever weapons, traditional or non, in order to complete their mission. They are, in short, fanatics intent on destroying not only the United States of America, but the world. You must be just as ruthless. It is of the utmost importance that this laboratory be controlled, that if any of this group should head toward this facility, they must be stopped at all costs." He paused. "*At all costs*, gentlemen. Those are your terms of engagement. Is everyone clear on that?"

A sharp-featured man with a shaved ebony scalp raised a hand. His body looked like it had been carved from granite, even though he was wearing casual clothes. "Biocontainment gear?"

Stuart English stepped forward, giving the impression he was wearing a uniform and still held official rank, despite the fact that he was wearing slacks and a dress shirt. "You will be given a bio suit, but use them only if necessary. They will be too conspicuous. Is everyone here familiar with how to get them on and use them?"

All nods.

"General Johnston? Anything further?"

Johnston nodded, hesitant. He took a deep breath. "This is a very dangerous mission, gentlemen. The United States government does not sanction this action. If your mission is completed satisfactorily, I do not believe there will be negative repercussions to you, though I cannot guarantee this. If your mission does not end satisfactorily, then it will not matter. The Fallen Angels will release this virus on the population, and millions will die. Millions. This is your opportunity to back out. I understand your positions as professionals." He carefully did not use the word *mercenaries*. "This is a job. It is possible that this job's scope is beyond what you expected. If you are not up to it, or do not wish to risk the possible repercussions, say so, and you may leave."

He waited. None of the men stepped forward. Johnston nodded to Stuart English. "Back to you, General English."

English stepped forward. "Here is how we start. Each of you will be provided with a radio set. . . ."

57

The Fallen Angels' Headquarters

DEREK WAS FAMILIAR WITH laboratories. More than familiar. He'd spent most of his undergraduate years in laboratories. As a soldier, he found he missed the peculiar order and atmosphere of the laboratory. His brother, now a physician with Doctors Without Borders working in Congo, told him to go back to graduate school and combine the two, his love of science and his adrenaline addiction, and work in the field. It had been good advice, but not without its perils. He studied biological and chemical warfare. When he went back to school to pursue his doctorate, his life had once again returned to laboratories. But now he found a particularly vicious and determined form of evil in these laboratories hidden in dark corners of the world.

Laboratories were dangerous places. They were filled with hazardous, flammable, and often explosive chemicals. Many laboratories had butane pumped in via Bunsen burner gas lines, though this one did not seem to have that kind of equipment. It did have compressed air tanks. And many bottles of ethyl alcohol.

First, Derek stepped out of the spacesuit. He'd destroyed all the Chimera, and now he needed agility and dexterity. Moving quickly, he twisted off the steel safety caps on the gas tanks and examined the regulators. Yes, this would do nicely. He placed the five gas tanks—one oxygen, two nitrogen, and two carbon dioxide—together, then surrounded them with as many bottles of chemicals as he could find, preferably chemicals that when exposed to flame—or each other—would go up in a large and dangerous explosion. Derek tried to remember if he had seen a stack of gasoline containers along one side of this trailer. He was pretty sure there had been, but which side? He didn't know for sure, but there wasn't much he could do about it. He moved on.

He needed some sort of fuse. Some laboratories kept lengths of cotton-fiber rope to use as the wicks for alcohol burners, which could, among other things, be used to sterilize coverslips. But he found no rope in the lab. He turned back to the little room where he had been held captive. On the plastic cot was a thin mattress. He dragged it out into the main part of the laboratory and, using a pair of scissors, cut it into long strips and tied them together until he had a length of cloth rope nearly thirty feet long.

Using a large two-liter beaker, he filled the glass container with ethanol and dropped the cloth rope into it.

He carefully took the glass bottles of vaccine, wrapped them in padding from the mattress, and placed them in a small cardboard box that had once contained felt-tipped laboratory marker pens. He sealed the box with tape and tucked it under his arm.

Derek took a deep breath. If he wasn't careful how he did this, he would be at ground zero when all hell broke loose. He took a moment to think things through. Finding a piece of paper and a pencil, he drew a rough sketch of the warehouse as he remembered it. Thinking where the doors were, where the vehicles were kept, where the other trailers and various people were within the large rectangular space. Plotting his escape, he did what he had been trained by the U.S. Army to do: work out multiple escape routes.

When he thought he was ready, he opened the various doors to the trailer, leaving them open until he was just inside the final door to the rest of the warehouse. Heart hammering, he retraced his steps, took the alcohol-soaked cloth and wrapped it around the regulator's outtake manifolds, and then unreeled the sopping cloth through the trailer until it was just by the exit. The ventilation system was already working on the alcohol fumes, and he was concerned that the alcohol would evaporate too quickly.

He hurried back to the compressed-gas containers and turned the valves on full to release the gas. Carrying the bucket of alcohol, he poured it along the length of the cloth, emptying it by the final exit door.

With steady hands, he picked up a box of matches he had found in a drawer and lit one. The flame danced at the end of the matchstick. *One,* he thought.

He touched the match to the cloth. *Two.*

It ignited with a blue flame and fast, faster than he could have thought possible, the alcohol-soaked cloth caught flame.

His eyes grew wide, because it wasn't the cloth that ignited, it was the alcohol. The blue flame raced toward the gas canisters within the laboratory.

Slamming himself against the door, Derek rushed out into the main warehouse, sprinting toward the exit.

58

Alexandria, Virginia

STUART ENGLISH AND JAMES Johnston sat in a Ford Explorer four blocks from the warehouse they had identified as the probable headquarters of the Fallen Angels. English had a portable radio and was in contact with all of his men. The two men had agreed that English would be the tactical command and Johnston would oversee the operation.

English directed his men to slowly converge on the warehouse from all points of the compass. Because they were in a warehouse district—row after row of steel, concrete, and brick buildings—they entered the area in four trucks, as if to make deliveries. One man drove, one rode in the passenger seat, and three men were in the back. Once they were close to the warehouse, they would fan out and begin their mission.

Each truck was given a radio designation of A, B, C, or D. Each man in each truck was given a number, one through five. They were reporting in now.

"Alpha-three in, I have the target in sight. There are no signs of human guards."

"Delta-one here. I see video cameras. Confirm."

"Beta-five, I confirm three video cameras on north side of target."

Into his radio Stuart English said, "Confirm cameras on all areas."

In a matter of minutes it was confirmed. There were twelve cameras identified, two at each corner and one in the middle. It was not an unexpected problem. The problem was exactly how to deal with them. The cameras were mounted high on the sides of the building, and English's crew were not equipped to climb and reach them in a fast, effective way. Also, timing was an issue. Although they had enough sharpshooters to take out the surveillance cameras, the element of surprise would be eliminated if they did so—they would have to make a full-out assault on the building simultaneously. This would be problematic, because they had no idea what they were getting into. No idea how many people were inside, how they were armed, or what the layout of the facility was like on the interior. As far as anybody could tell, there were no blind spots.

English said to Johnston, "Any ideas?"

"Are there ventilation ducts?"

English passed on the question to his team. A moment later the Alpha leader, Alpha-one, responded. "Affirmative. On south side of building and on the roof. Suggestion, sir."

English raised an eyebrow at Johnston. "Go ahead."

"One of the trucks can drive by close on one side as if on their way by," Johnston said. "We can have someone flash one of the spotlights as we go by to cause a problem with one of the cameras. The passenger side, using a rope and grapple, will take that opportunity to get onto the roof. From there they should be able to—"

Alpha-one's report was interrupted by the crumping sound of an explosion coming from inside the building. There were shouts and confusion. Even inside their Ford Explorer, the two generals could hear the sound of the explosion from four blocks away.

"What's going on? Report!" English shouted into the radio.

"We don't know. Something from inside the warehouse. Some sort of explosion. We don't know what's going on."

Johnston gripped English's arm. "Tell them to go in. It's their diversion."

English paled. He could be sending twenty men into a deadly situation. Then he nodded. "Code Pellinor. I repeat: Code Pellinor. Go in."

59

The Fallen Angels' Headquarters

DEREK, BARE FEET SLAPPING on the cold pavement, did not get more than twenty steps from the trailer before he heard the loud *ker-whump* sound. He saw four or five of Coffee's terrorists turn from what they were doing to see the noise and spot him racing toward the nearest door.

Then there was a much louder sound. Derek felt a percussion wave slam into him like the hand of God, and he found himself flying through the air and slamming hard to the pavement. A rain of debris—glass, wood, shards of aluminum—fell around him. With a desperate lunge he threw himself under another trailer, clutching the precious box of Chimera vaccine against his chest. From beneath the trailer he watched the destruction of the laboratory. It looked as if it had been sitting on a volcano. The plywood that had layered the inside of the trailer burned with a huge cloud of black smoke. He didn't think his bomb had caused so much destruction; it must have been the stacks of fuel presumably used for the generators running the complicated ventilation system of the laboratory.

Sound came to him as if he had stuffed his fingers in his ears. Shouts. A few screams.

Gunfire.

Suddenly, explosions ripped the air as doors on opposite sides of the warehouse blew inward, followed by armed men.

Automatic gunfire chattered in return.

From his hiding spot Derek saw the tall, thin figure of Dr. Ling creeping toward a doorway, about to make his escape during the chaos.

With a flare of rage, Derek dropped the vaccine, lunged from beneath the trailer, and sprinted toward the torturous Asian. Ling must have sensed something, because he spun just as Derek reached him. His eyes widened in recognition. His hand darted inside his jacket and withdrew a stiletto. "So, Dr. Stillwater. You live."

Derek slowed, hands up, dropping into a defensive martial-arts stance.

Ling shifted the blade from hand to hand, moving in a circle. Around them was chaos, flames and gunfire. "I assume you are responsible for this."

Derek didn't comment. Ling's hands were very fast. It was difficult keeping his eyes on the blade. He needed to keep his concentration on Ling's center of gravity, on his hips and stomach, because that was where he would get a clue as to the man's intentions. Not the hands, the shoulders, the thighs. But he also needed to know where the blade was.

Ling lunged with his left hand. His empty left hand.

Derek spun, slamming his arm down to block the right hand, which held the blade. He caught Ling's wrist. With his left hand Ling jabbed his stiffened fingers into Derek's shoulder. Derek's free arm lost feeling.

Derek twisted Ling's right wrist, grinding the bones, and snapped his bare foot into Ling's knee. Ling grunted and lunged with the knife blade, up, toward Derek's wrist.

Derek kicked Ling's knee again. Ling dropped to the ground, bringing Derek with him, the knife point close to his wrist.

Derek tried to use his right arm, but it was numb. Ling jabbed his free hand at Derek's eyes. Derek flinched back, still clutching Ling's knife hand.

Ling's free hand curved into what Derek recognized as a shape called "the rooster's head." Fingers joined and curved downward, wrist up. It could be used to block and could be used to strike with the joined fingertips or the blunt edge of the wrist.

Derek fell forward toward Ling, using gravity, and swung his numb arm upward, slamming his elbow into Ling's face.

Ling stumbled backward, thrashing out of Derek's grasp, rolling smoothly and coming up on his feet. The stiletto was back in his hands. The Asian's eyes narrowed, and he moved cautiously, the blade moving back and forth, back and forth.

Derek lunged right, as if to go for the knife, then dropped to the floor and swept Ling's feet out from under him, spinning as he did, bringing his fist down on Ling's wrist with an audible crack. The knife dropped to the pavement. Ling snatched it up in his other hand and drove with a scream at Derek, who shuffled backward before the attack. Ling kept coming, backing Derek against the hard surface of a trailer.

A familiar voice shouted, "Freeze," but neither man paid any attention.

Ling thrust the blade at Derek's throat. At the last instant Derek shifted. Just a couple of inches. The knife plunged past him and into the thin aluminum skin of the trailer.

For just a fraction of a second, the knife stuck as Ling struggled to pull the blade out of the plywood and metal wall.

Derek struck Ling in the throat with a closed fist. There was the nauseating sound of cartilage crushing. Ling, eyes wide, let go of the stiletto and staggered backward, fingers scrabbling at his ruined throat. He tried to speak, but the only sound was a harsh gurgle, followed by blood spewing from his mouth.

Before Derek could take another step, James Johnston moved forward, placed a gun to Ling's head, and pulled the trigger. Ling collapsed to the floor, most of his head gone, very much dead.

Johnston walked over to Derek. "Are you okay?"

Derek held out his hand. "Can I borrow your gun?"

Johnston, with a baffled expression, handed over the Glock. Derek took it, stepped over to the corpse of Ling, and emptied every round in the magazine into the Asian's body. Each round made the body jump, and Derek felt something surge inside him at each twitch. After he had spent each round, he felt the anger seep away, leaving scar tissue like a burn on his soul.

With an angry jerk Derek dropped the empty magazine from the weapon and held out his hand. "Got more?"

"Not to do that."

"I need a weapon."

"You need to go home and sleep it off. You need some R and R. We've got it under control here."

"Coffee's gone. Headed for France. That probably means Dulles. He's got the virus and plans to let it loose on a plane. Even with instructions on how to make the vaccine, it might be too late if we don't stop him. This virus acts too fast, and getting it distributed will take too long. Millions might still die. I'm going after him. I need a gun. You need to start shutting down the airports in case he's headed somewhere besides Dulles, if you've got the authority." The expression on Johnston's face suggested he didn't.

Derek reached under his scrub shirt and retrieved the computer disks and leaned down to pick up the box containing the vaccine. "Get these to USAMRIID." He quickly explained what they were.

Johnston took the disks and the vials. "I'll get this over there right away. But don't go after Coffee alone—"

"Spare magazine. Now." Derek raised the gun in his hand and held out his other for the spare magazine. Reluctantly, Johnston dropped it into his hand.

Derek said, "I need clothes." His eyes darted. He forced his way into the nearest trailer, the one he had hidden beneath. There was broken glass on the floor. Furniture. A TV. It was almost homey. In the living area he found a closet with men's and women's clothing. He quickly drew on jeans, a denim shirt, socks, and a pair of running shoes. They were all a little big on him, but they would do. "Where are we?" he asked Johnston, who had silently followed him in.

"You don't know?"

"No."

"Arlington. By the river. Derek, I'll alert the Bureau. Don't go after him—"

But his words fell on thin air as Derek rushed from the trailer and sprinted across the warehouse toward a rank of cars, Jeeps, and motorcycles. Derek jumped on a cycle, kicked it into life, and roared out of the headquarters of the Fallen Angels.

60

DEREK RACED ACROSS TOWN on the motorcycle, in and out among cars, shifting onto the shoulder when the morning traffic clogged. Dulles was a long way from the warehouse in Alexandria, more than twenty miles west. He sped down Braddock to King Street through Sleepy Hollow and Falls Church, charging onto 66 to 267, the Dulles Airport Access Road. Cars, buildings, trees, parks, businesses were all a blur out of the corners of his eyes. All he felt was an urgency, adrenaline coursing through his veins like an electrical wire in his blood.

As he approached Dulles, his mind registered the signs indicating different airlines. Dulles was huge. Probably about a million square feet.

The Air France sign was the most obvious clue. If Richard Coffee was actually heading toward France, that was the way to go, Concourse B.

He parked the bike and stopped to take a deep breath. Security was going to be tight. He didn't have ID, and he looked like a wreck. What the hell had he been thinking?

He went in, browsing the computer screens behind the ticket counters. Dulles was a babble of voices in all languages. Flights to Paris . . .

There was one leaving in an hour.

His gaze scanned the crowd. Hundreds of people, men, women, children. All on the move. Waiting in line, in and out of bathrooms, in and out of the bars and lounges and restaurants. People brushed past him carrying laptop computers and carry-on luggage, hauling wheeled suitcases like reluctant overweight dogs.

If Coffee was here, what would he be doing? Would he have headed for his gate? If he had, Derek thought he might as well forget it. The thought made him feel desperate, panicky. Once again, he felt the panic rat gnawing at his guts. After all this, to be too late. Without his passport or a ticket, he didn't stand a chance of picking up Coffee here.

What would Coffee do?

If Derek were in Coffee's shoes, he would head for his gate at the last minute, staying in crowded areas with exits. Would Coffee be so cocky as to assume nobody was pursuing him?

Somebody bumped him and he stepped aside, eyes seeking through the crowd.

Something sharp pressed against his spine. Coffee's low voice said, "You are unbelievable. Come with me."

Derek tensed. "I'm perfectly happy right here, Richard."

The blade pressed harder into his back. "It would be seriously inconvenient for me to kill you right here, Derek, but I could. I could push this blade right into your spinal column, leave the knife there, and walk away and be gone. Move it!"

Derek walked the way Coffee directed him, toward an escalator.

"Where are we going?"

"Somewhere else."

"I've told the authorities you're here. They'll be here soon. We've caught the rest of your people."

"I'll find more."

They rode down the escalator, and Coffee directed him toward the revolving turnstiles of the baggage claim areas.

"Picking up your luggage?"

Coffee moved him close to where the conveyor belt slipped inside the luggage area. Suitcases rode on their endless journey.

"It's the end for you, Derek. I'm not—"

A tall, striking woman appeared from the crowd. She wore tan slacks, a white oxford shirt, and a maroon blazer. One hand was deep in the blazer pocket. "Don't move, Surkho."

Derek had never seen the woman before. Behind him Coffee said, "Irina. Well, well, well. Traveling today?"

"Let him go."

"I'd really like to know how you followed me here."

She seemed calm. "You think this is the time for it, Surkho?"

"I learn from my mistakes."

A small smile played across her lips. "Nadia had to pay for that apartment somehow. I backtracked the financials. Probably just a step ahead of the FBI. Now let him go."

Coffee shrugged and stepped away. Derek moved aside, his gun heavy in his own pocket. He looked around for security guards. He couldn't believe there were none to be seen. Where the hell were they all? One shout would bring them running, he was sure.

Coffee pulled a can of Coke from his pocket.

"It's not ideal," Coffee said, "but this will do."

Derek lunged at Coffee, grabbing onto his old friend's wrist. Coffee slammed his other hand into Derek's skull. His head felt like a gong, but he held on with one hand, hammering at Coffee's wrist with the other, wanting him to drop the can. He mustn't release Chimera here.

They tumbled onto the moving treadmill, bumped and banged by moving luggage. Somebody screamed. Somebody else yelled for security.

Derek slammed Coffee's arm down onto the stainless steel rim of the luggage carousel. The can slipped from his grip and went rolling and skittering across the moving treadmill. They both dived after it. Derek got his fingers on it, but it shot away.

Coffee spun after it, but Derek caught him by the belt and knocked him down. Coffee kicked out, connecting solidly with Derek's knee. Derek felt something snap, and a burst of pain exploded through his leg. He tried to stand, but his left leg collapsed beneath him.

He watched helplessly as Coffee chased after the Coke can.

Only to see it picked up by the woman with the blazer. Coffee stopped, eyes narrowed. "Give it to me, Irina."

Irina had a gun in her other hand. "Not a chance."

Derek finally got his own gun out, shouting, "Freeze! You're both under—"

Irina fired her weapon at Coffee, who simultaneously dived through the opening into the luggage carousel warehouse.

Derek shouted again. "Put the can down! Do it now!"

She stared at him, surprised. "He's getting away."

"Put the can down."

She stared at him, uncomprehending.

"Now!" He was on the floor, but his gun was steady. "I *will* shoot."

Their gazes locked. She carefully set the Coke can down on the rim of the carousel and, without a moment's hesitation, dived through the hatchway after Richard Coffee.

Derek crawled, dragging his useless leg after him, pain shooting through him until he reached the can of Coke. He leaned back against the carousel, the can clutched to his chest, the Glock in his other hand, ready to shoot anyone who tried to take it from him. When the first security guards arrived, guns drawn, he said, "My name is Derek Stillwater. I'm with the Department of Homeland Security. You need to contact James Johnston immediately."

The security cop was a broad-shouldered man with more than a little bit of worry in his dark brown eyes. "Put the gun down."

Derek shook his head. "National security matter. A terrorist just went through there into the luggage area. His name is Richard Coffee. He's very dangerous. Get your people after him. He's responsible for yesterday's White House attack."

"Drop your gun!"

Derek closed his eyes. His breathing was harsh and raspy. "I said . . ." He trailed off. He would not let down the gun until the Chimera was someplace safe. He had the canister of Chimera. He had stopped Coffee. He had retrieved the devil's pitchfork.

For now.

EPILOGUE

Ascent

EPILOGUE

Bayman's Marina, Baltimore, Maryland—Three Weeks Later
DEREK SPRAWLED IN A lounge chair on the deck of the *Salacious Sally*, his left leg in a walking cast. Richard Coffee's kick to his knee had caused enough damage to require arthroscopic surgery, and Derek would have the cast on his leg for at least another week. The sun was high in the sky, beating down on him. He lay with his eyes closed, listening to Dave Brubeck on the stereo system, a cold Corona at his fingertips and three more on ice in a cooler within easy reach.

A pleasant voice said, "Knock, knock."

Derek opened his eyes. Liz Vargas stood on the dock next to the *Sally*, smiling at him. She looked paler and thinner than he remembered, but otherwise seemed healthy.

"Well," he said. "Come aboard, Doctor. How are you feeling?"

"Still a little weak," she said, stepping aboard.

"The recovery time isn't bad. Three weeks."

She shrugged. "I was on my feet in one week, a little bit slow for recovery from internal-bleeding injuries, but not bad."

"Have a seat," he said, gesturing to another lounge chair. "Beer?"

"That would be good," she said.

He pointed to the cooler. "Sorry for not being polite, but the leg's still pretty sore."

He knew she had narrowly avoided death. Johnston had hand-delivered the vaccine to USAMRIID, and Ben Zataki had rushed it into the Slammer to administer a dose to her. The vaccine had not been designed for use after the disease set in, and it hadn't looked like it would work. In most cases, once a disease kicked in, the only thing a vaccine did was overload the immune system. There were exceptions—like smallpox, if caught early enough in the infection—and luckily for Liz, Chimera had been one of the exceptions. Slowly, the vaccine worked, and after a week of spiked fevers, anemia, and various other problems, she had started to recover.

"Anybody told you your recovery seems rather quick?" Derek asked.

She smiled hesitantly. "It's about average, considering I'm the only human being who's ever been infected with Chimera. Compared to recovery from Ebola—for those lucky enough to recover—I'm about average."

Liz took a swallow of beer, then set it down. "How's your knee? Are you on pain medication?"

"You're drinking it," he said.

"Oh. Well . . . I wanted to know . . . I mean, I know some of what happened, but not all of it."

He took a long swallow of beer, thought for a moment, then told her. He left out a few details that needed to be kept secret for national security reasons, but otherwise he told her as much as he could.

They had not found Richard Coffee. He disappeared. Irina Khournikova—the real Irina Khournikova—disappeared as well, though everyone knew she had disappeared back into Directorate T in Moscow.

The Coke can had been analyzed at USAMRIID and had been found to contain aerosolized Chimera.

"What are you going to do now?" she asked when he finished his recitation.

He looked at her. "Did Johnston send you over here?"

Her face flushed pink. "Well, Sharon Jaxon asked me to come, and so did Cindy Black."

Cynthia Black, the helicopter pilot, was still in the hospital. Her testimony to Aaron Pilcher cleared Derek of any connection to Sam Dalton. Derek felt he owed her for that—and owed Pilcher for keeping an open mind and for staying by her bedside until she became conscious.

Derek visited her every day. She had a broken back, fractured pelvis, and assorted other injuries. She would be able to walk someday, but her career in the Coast Guard was probably over.

"I haven't changed my mind," he said.

Johnston had been reinstated as secretary of the Department of Homeland Security, a national hero. He wanted Derek to come aboard as his deputy director. Derek told him no. What he actually said was, "You're fucking crazy. No fucking way." Then he turned in his resignation as a troubleshooter. Johnston said he'd keep the resignation in mind.

Derek hadn't changed his mind. But he did have a plan.

"So what will you do?" she asked again.

He shrugged. "I've got a couple ideas. How about you?"

"They've invited me to work at USAMRIID. I'm thinking about it. But I might just look for a job in academia."

He smiled. "I might, too. Or I might just retire. Or, I'm thinking some travel might be in order."

There was something about the way he said it. She looked at him closely, wondering. They sat in silence, enjoying the sun. She said, "What do you think happened to Richard Coffee?"

He looked at her for a long moment. Then he reached over to the paperback novel he had been reading off and on, pulled out a postcard, and handed it to her. "Got this in the mail yesterday," he said. "I haven't shown it to Johnston yet. You know, the Department of Homeland Security only has jurisdiction here in the United States."

She studied the postcard. On the front was a picture of a devil holding a pitchfork. Turning it over, she saw it said: "See you soon, Derek. Count on it." The postmark was from Mexico City.

She looked at him. "You're thinking of travel?"

"Haven't been to Mexico in a while," Derek said, tipping his beer at her. "Maybe I'll start there."

ACKNOWLEDGMENTS

I would like to acknowledge the various people who assisted me in this novel. My wife, Leanne, and my sons, Ian and Sean. My agent, Irene Kraas. My team at Midnight Ink, including Barbara Moore, Wade Ostrowski, Brian Farrey, and Kevin Brown. Various unnamed folks involved with the field of microbiology, and the staff at USAMRIID, as well as Richard Preston, author of *The Hot Zone* and *Demons in the Freezer*, both books that might be of interest to readers of *The Devil's Pitchfork* who wish to know more about the amazing and important work done by the CDC and USAMRIID in the fight against bioterrorism and emerging infections, as well as the long and never-ending battle against pandemics.

ABOUT THE AUTHOR

Mark Terry is a full-time freelance writer and editor. The author of a collection of mystery novellas and a crime novel, he currently reviews books for the *Oakland Press*. Terry also has a degree in microbiology and experience with infectious disease research and genetics. He lives in Michigan.